HARDSCRUB

LIONEL G. GARCIA

Arte Publico Press
Houston, Texas

This volume is made possible through a grant from the National
Endowment for the Arts, a federal agency.

PS 3557 .A71115 H37 1990

Garcia, Lionel G.

Hardscrub

Arte Publico Press
University of Houston
Houston, Texas 77204-2090

García, Lionel G.
    Hardscrub / Lionel García.
        p.   cm.
    ISBN 1-55885-005-8 : $9.00
    I. Title.
PS3557.A71115H37 1990   89-35417
813'.54—dc20   CIP

Cover photo by Evangelina Vigil-Piñón.

HARDSCRUB

BOOK ONE

CHAPTER 1

My father was not like most other fathers I knew. Well, he was short and thin like a lot of other men, but what I really mean is he was different in the way he was. I guess he never wanted to be married and on top of that my mother gave him three children that he never wanted.

I never saw him show any love or good feelings toward my sister Sylvia or my brother Richard or me. He treated my mother about the same way. But of the three of us, he treated Richard the worst. I mean, he could whip my brother Richard until Richard couldn't scream.

And you couldn't ask him for anything. He'd get mad. He had money for his friends though. I can't remember how many times Richard and me had to wait in the old pick-up outside the beerjoints while he treated his friends to a round of beer. "Your dad is a fine man," they would say to Richard and me as we walked the streets. "Hell, he'd give you the shirt off his back if you asked 'im for it. One time me and him got into a fight in Fort Worth and he beat up on this poor ol' man until I thought he had kilt him. Hell, he's a fighter and a woman lover. None better than him."

I never knew why these men told us things about our father. Like we wanted to hear that. They talked like they had a good feeling about knowing my dad, like we ought to have the same feeling. But we didn't. I could feel my brother Richard get angry when he heard the stories. I got angry too. I was glad my sister Sylvia wasn't with us when these men started talking about our father. She usually stayed to herself, reading. It was like that most of the time. Richard and me together and Sylvia stayed at home to read or help mother.

My father served what you call hardscrub time for killing a man in Oklahoma when we were babies. He killed a man in a fight over an Indian woman he was living with in Lawton. My mother moved us to Corpus Christi,

Texas, while he was in prison. My grandmother lived in Corpus and she helped take care of us while my mother worked as a waitress.

My mother stayed at home most of the time. My father thought that she should stay home and take in ironing and sewing. So she did this for years in all the many little towns we lived in. My father didn't want her out on the streets during the day and night being picked on by other men. No waitress jobs, he told her. Never again, he said. He had heard rumors about her. "If you take a waitress job, I'll beat the living shit out of you in front of the children," he said. And he said it in front of us, just in case she didn't think he was serious.

In November of 1952 we lost him for two days and then he showed up and made us quit school. Sylvia was in the sixth grade. Richard was in the fifth. I was in the fourth. He didn't talk to anyone about it. He took it on himself to go to school one day and he grabbed Richard and me by the hair and dragged us out of school. He didn't do it to Sylvia though. He just told her that same night that she wasn't going back. It was hard on Sylvia. But not on Richard and me. We really didn't want to be in school, anyway. My brother Richard and me had decided that school was not for us. Not that Richard agreed with me. He wanted me to go to school, but not him. He was too dumb, he said. Sylvia, she thought she would be a teacher someday. Or she was going to be a doctor or a nurse.

Sylvia took it hard. School was all she had. My mother begged him to let us stay in school but there was no changing his mind. He had another one of his ideas, another one of his wild plans that never amounted to anything.

My father was a bust at everything he ever did. Just about the time when we felt that he was back on his feet he would go down again. My mother never mentioned his problems to us, only to Aunt Betty. She just tagged along wherever he went, taking us along with her.

This time when he disappeared we knew he was in trouble.

"Why must we come along?" my mother cried that night. "Why do you drag us into these things? Why don't you go by yourself?"

But there was no talking to him. He kept telling her to shut up.

The oilfield had closed by then and there wasn't any more drilling going on. My dad had been a roustabout and now had nothing to do. Besides, we found out why we had to leave. He had been able to finagle his way and be one of the last to be let go, and this didn't sit very well with the other guys in his crew. Especially the ones that knew more than he did.

So they had a fight and my dad had grabbed a four by four and hit one of the men with it while the man wasn't looking and he almost killed him.

This is where he had been, in jail. He had stayed in jail two days while they waited to see if the man was going to live or not and, angry as he was, he came in from jail bitching and complaining that he needed to leave this dusty mother fucking West Texas town.

My brother and me found out the sheriff had told him to leave. We heard the talk at the barber-shop and one man said that the sheriff told my father to leave or get thrown out of town. The man in the hospital, the one he hit, had promised to kill him. Someone at the barbershop laughed and said the man would have to stand in line to get his chance. They all started to laugh and Richard and me got up and left without getting a hair-cut. I could tell Richard was angry again. He grabbed a rock and threw it at the barbershop wall and we both had to run. I looked back and the men hadn't even noticed, they were laughing so hard.

I didn't know why my brother Richard did some of the things he did. He had taken to stealing a lot. Just about every day I could see different things in his pockets. He would pull things out of his shirt that I knew he hadn't bought. He wasn't stealing big things, just small things that didn't cost much. I could swear on a stack of Bibles that I never knew when he did it.

He said I was crazy, that I was making up things about him. One thing about it, though, he shares everything he steals or comes up with with me.

After the sheriff cleared dad and he was sure that no charges were going to be pressed against him we were told to leave. It hadn't been too pleasant for my mother, Richard, Sylvia, or myself. The word had gotten out in this little town that my father had hurt a hometown man and that he had hit him when he wasn't looking.

So that was when he took us out of school and my brother Richard and me were glad to get out. After a while my mother said yes, knowing that she had to leave, but she made my father promise that we'd get into a school the first chance we got. He said it wouldn't matter to him, as long as we didn't bother him. He was drinking and my mother didn't want to bother him very much for fear of making the thing worse but she told us she could make him stick to his word later on. We knew well that she couldn't. Sylvia was crying and my father acted like he didn't hear her.

He knew Sylvia could not be hit. My mother would turn into an animal if Sylvia was hurt. With Richard he knew that he could hit him as much as he wanted. For some reason he didn't bother me as much as he did Richard. But still I was afraid of him.

He wouldn't let Richard and me get away with anything. One time Richard said he didn't like what we were eating and without saying a word my father reared back and hit him in the mouth. Richard flew backwards in a crazy way and he landed on the floor and he didn't move for a couple of minutes. When he came to, my father just looked at him and Richard got up and staggered back to the room.

"First thing I'll do when I get big is beat the livin' shit out of 'im. Then I'll kill 'im, but first I'll make 'im cry on his knees one day." Those were the exact words Richard said to me one night as we laid in bed. It scared me to hear my brother talk like that because I knew Richard and I knew that if my father didn't kill him Richard would make good on his word.

We packed all that night in the cold, running back and forth from the house to the small pick-up we owned and we piled up everything on top of the old truck and by early morning we were on our way. My mother and Sylvia rode up front and Richard and me rode in the back on top of all that junk that my dad had gathered after so many little jobs. We loaded the old welding machine, although God knows it hadn't worked in many years. His old carpenter's tools he could always use, so we were sure to load those. He had a fifty-five gallon drum that we carried around from job to job and he had it almost half-full with hard-ware: a lot of nail boxes, screws, washers, bolts, nuts... plus other things: old welder's gloves, hand tools, mechanic's tools, shop rags; and that was only what you could see at the top. Richard and me loaded up the drum some more with anything that wasn't nailed down and then we couldn't pick it up. We had to partly unload it before my father saw what we had done and then load it up in the back of the truck and then fill it up. We took mom's old bed and mattress, her favorite pillow and quilt, Sylvia's books, her teddy-bear and the dishes and the clothes. We had thrown the old tarp over the whole load and we rode under it to keep away from the cold wind. We had our coats on and buttoned to the top. The November wind was bad that morning and if it was bad in the morning, it was going to get worse by the end of the day. A norther was coming through. If you've ever lived in West Texas you'll know what I mean. There were days when you didn't even have school, the winds and the dust were so bad.

We were on our way to Artesia, New Mexico. My father was going to team up with my uncle Robert. Richard kept telling me that nothing good would come of this but I already knew. My uncle Robert was my dad's older brother. He wasn't as bad as my father. He managed to make a pretty good living. Aunt Betty, his wife, and Dolly and Junior, his children, all had whatever they wanted every time we saw them. "I already feel sorry for uncle Robert. Whatever it is, we're goin' to be in a lot of trouble," Richard whispered, shivering, from under the tarp.

I was worried that the over-loaded drum would fall on us, but Richard was keeping his foot against it to make sure it wouldn't fall. He said he had everything under control. We were making faces, laughing, although we were cold, and I started to act like I was playing a mouth harp, holding my nose closed with one hand and making a funny sound. I had always wanted to have a mouth harp ever since I saw an old man play one in a school assembly—Mr. Music Man they called him. Not only could he play the mouth harp, he played the harmonica, the guitar, the clarinet and the tuba, while his wife played the piano. I remember getting excused to help Mr. and Mrs. Music Man load and unload. They always smiled. That was the first time I ever saw someone smile all the time. That made them hard to forget.

We took highway Texas 380 straight from Graham through Haskell who we had already beaten in football that year. We went through Aspermont and then we turned south to Clairemont. At Clairemont we stopped to get some gas and water for the truck and to stretch out. We stopped at a grocery store with a gas pump in front. It seemed that the man at the service station knew someone my dad knew. They were talking about someone as my dad followed the man around while he checked and gassed up the truck and the service-station man kept shaking his head and grinning like he could imagine exactly what my dad was telling him. "Well, you tell the ol' sonofagun when you see 'im that ol' bad-boy Jim came by and got gas and peed and he watered his family in this ass-hole town, but he didn't have a chance to look 'im up. Tell 'im that I was tied down this time, but next time 'round ol' Jim's goin' to come here a free man and we're goin' to raise us some hell."

"Sure will," the man replied, chuckling at what my father had told him.

"I see 'im pretty near every day 'round town, 'specially now that he's got that new eye of his. He's real proud of that. He'd been goin' 'round with a patch over his socket for a lot of years."

My dad laughed and we all laughed with him. "I was with 'im when he lost that eye," my father said. "Shithead tried to do somethin' he couldn't handle. That's all."

"You're the one that was with 'im?" the man asked, as if he had finally caught up with my dad.

"That's me," my dad said. He seemed proud but I couldn't tell about what.

Richard and me were sticking our heads out of the tarp. Sylvia and my mother had gone to the girl's bathroom inside and my mother had bought some bread and baloney in the grocery store. Richard and me had already gone to the boy's bathroom outside in the cold. We were ready to go but my dad needed to keep on talking to this man now that he had him impressed.

If only he wasn't the way he was, maybe we could all get along. It was times like these when you saw him in a pretty good mood that you felt good about him. You could even say that there was some love in us for him at those times. You could even see pride in mother's face when he acted that way.

We were going to try to make it to the border by night- fall but shortly after Clairemont, after we had eaten the bread and baloney sandwiches my mother had made, the truck started to make a noise and Sylvia started feeling bad. She was sick and vomiting. My dad was cursing at what was happening and my sister Sylvia was trying to vomit and cry at the same time and my mother was trying to keep my father from getting angry with Sylvia. We stopped at Post and while my dad checked the truck my mother took Sylvia to the back of the service-station and got her to vomit everything she had in her. We could hear her tell Sylvia to stick her finger all the way to the back of her mouth. We could hear her gagging. The truck was over-heating and my dad was cursing. He was getting angry with the truck, with us, with the man at the service-station.

I stuck my face out and the cold wind was gusting and picking up a lot of dust.

"You need a new belt!" the man yelled to my father, trying to be heard above the howling wind. The man was under the hood checking things out. Richard and me got up on the truck bed. We were looking over the cab at the man. We had our coats pulled up over our heads and the tarp wrapped around our waist. The man was trying to pull on the belt and twist it to see how worn it was. "Maybe a new water pump. Can't tell yet. Maybe if I was you, I'd try the belt first and if that don't do 'er, then I'd go to the pump." He came out from under the hood and wiped his hands on a shop rag and then put his gloves on. He thought a few seconds and then he yelled, "You're burning oil too! Did you know that?"

My dad kicked the side of the truck as if he were kicking his own self. He was screaming at the man, cursing.

"Listen Buddy," the man yelled back, "it ain't my fault this shit happened. I'm just tellin' you for your own good. Take it or leave it. No one's payin' me enough to argue with you and they sure as hell ain't payin' me enough to get cursed at."

My dad bought the belt and outside of Post in the middle of a windy cold norther in the shelter of a ditch, after the engine had cooled enough for him to touch it, he changed the belt and tightened it a lot to see if he could get by without buying a water pump. Richard and me tried to help him, holding onto something or getting something from the barrel but after a while things went wrong and he started to curse at us and he threw Richard to the ground. Richard picked up a big rock and I thought for sure he was going to throw it at him behind his back but my mother got hold of him and my father didn't see what Richard had done. My mother got us out of the way and back on the truck. If he had seen what Richard had done he would've killed him right there. There was no doubt in my mind.

Sylvia had a fever, my mother said. She felt like vomiting again. "It's your goddam baloney sandwiches!" my father screamed at my mother as he started the truck. Richard and me by then were under the tarp. Sylvia was crying like she hurt a lot.

By the time my dad got through, the sun had gone down and it was getting dark. The wind had started to die down but it was getting colder. We slowly made our way into Tahoka and by that time the truck was smoking. "The oil pressure is way down," my dad was screaming. We were burning oil, but we knew that. Richard and me could smell the smoke from the burning oil creeping up from behind the engine and getting under the tarp. If the truck hadn't been moving, we probably couldn't have breathed at all. But moving as she was at least we were getting cold fresh air mixed with the smoke. Just looking out from the tarp Richard and me could see the trail of black smoke we were leaving behind, like a cork-screw of a black cloud. We could see we were the only ones on the road.

When we got to Tahoka, Sylvia was feeling sicker than before. Her fever was up, mother was saying to dad, but dad was too ticked off to listen and, besides, he was more worried about the truck than Sylvia.

We had to stop at the edge of town. My dad had the hood up and was trying to figure out where the smoke was coming from. "Oil coming out of every fuckin' place 'round the head," he said. He lost control and he started kicking the side of the truck until his foot hurt him so much that he had to stop. He sat on the bumper and rubbed his foot and cursed. Richard and me were looking over the cab watching him. He said, "Why does this shit have to happen to me all the time? Why can't I have something good happen to me once in a fuckin' while?"

After some time he said, "Shit, fuck it," and he got up and started walking off just like we weren't even there. My mother called him but he acted like he didn't hear. He walked off until we couldn't see him in the headlights.

My mother, Sylvia, Richard and me toughed it out in the cab of the truck that night. It's a good thing that the wind had died down. We took the tarp and brought it inside and we all covered up with it making sure Sylvia was in between my mother and Richard, the biggest and warmest bodies. My mother kept worrying over my sister. Through most of the night the high fever made my sister moan and talk like you couldn't understand what she was saying. Her talk made no sense to us and when she said something real silly, my brother Richard would punch me in the ribs and we would giggle. When Sylvia started having diarrhea we stopped giggling. We really didn't know how serious she was. If my mother had known she would have started walking to a hospital right that moment.

Early in the dark of the cold morning Richard and me woke up to the sound of a car creeping up behind us. We wiped the frost from the rear window and we looked through it and we could see the police light on top of the car. My father was inside the car. A large man dressed in khakis with a heavy leather jacket and gloves and a pistol had gotten out of the car. He was blowing steam through his nose. He went around the car and opened the door for my father. My father came out hand-cuffed. We looked at each other, my brother and me, and we wondered what trouble he could have gotten himself into. My mother was still asleep, thank God for that. She didn't see him cuffed. Sylvia was hardly moving. She was smelling bad.

"Is this man your father?" he asked.

We told him he was and he said, "I don't see how you could claim the sonofabitch."

My father said nothing. He had a large swelling under his left eye and you could see where someone had also hit him on the jaw. His face was lop-sided, reminding me of one time when he had been brought home all beat up and drunk and a whole bunch of us had been playing baseball and we had all stopped to see our father being dragged out of a funny-looking car. My mother had called Richard and me in the house. She gave us some nickels to give our friends to make them leave.

"Who else do you have in the truck?" he asked. He was having to shine a light into the cab through the frosted window.

"It's my mom and sister," Richard said.

"Why won't they come out?"

"Because," Richard answered, "my mom just now went to sleep. She's been up with my sister Sylvia who's been sick. My sister Sylvia's real sick and she can hardly move."

The deputy took a look inside through the window and he opened the door to talk to my mother. He asked, "You all right, ma'am?"

He scared my mother, but she figured out what was happening real fast and she apologized for the way she looked and for her family. She didn't know my father had been arrested. The deputy had uncuffed him.

"No need to, ma'am," the deputy told her about apologizing, "you're surely not the worst thing I'll see today. It's already started pretty bad. Your husband here," he pointed to my dad, "got 'imself into some trouble last night and he don't have any money for bail. So the sheriff made 'im a deal. He's got to be out of town right away or we'll throw 'im in jail and throw away the key."

My mother looked at Sylvia and she felt of her forehead and she told him, "My daughter is sick, very sick. That's what's worryin' me. We need to get her to a doctor. If we don't I don't think she's goin' to make it."

My dad went over and reached in the truck and shook Sylvia, trying to wake her up. He shook her real hard when she wouldn't answer him. "She's only tryin' to worry you," he said to my mother. "You know how spoilt she is. You got her so spoilt she likes to get attention."

My mother grabbed him by the neck. She was choking him. "Get your filthy hands off her! Don't you touch her! Don't shake her! You leave her alone. You know damn well you don't mess with Sylvia...If you do...I'll kill you!"

"You ain't killing no one, you whore," my father yelled as he tried to fight off my mother. He was about to swing at her when the deputy grabbed him. He held him in a hammer-lock and whirled him around and threw him against the police car. "Don't you touch that woman," he yelled trying to catch his breath, "cause if you do, you're goin' back to jail...and by golly sheriff or no sheriff I'll lock you up and shove the key down your throat." He grabbed my dad again like a rag doll and threw him to the ground and it scared my brother Richard and me. When my dad tried to get up, the deputy kicked him in the butt and sent him falling and twisting over to the front of the truck. "Now, you stay put," he said, pointing a finger at my dad just like he would be pointing at his dog.

"Now ma'am," the deputy said fixing his jacket, "what's this about your daughter?"

"She's sick," my mother told him. "She looks very sick."

The deputy thought a while. We were hoping he could help.

"I'll tell you what," he said, "if that husband of yours promises to stay by this truck, I'll take you and your family to the hospital."

He went over to the car and radioed in. My mother made my father promise that he would stay. I had never seen her so angry with my father.

We bundled my sister Sylvia up and we put her in the back along with my mother. My brother Richard and me rode up front with the deputy. As we slowly passed the truck, we saw my father sitting on the bumper as he had done the night before. The deputy had taken no chances. He had hand-cuffed him to the bumper. He looked beat, all dusty and his long hair over his face like he needed a bath and a hair-cut. I couldn't help but feel sorry for him no matter what he did to me or my brother Richard or my sister Sylvia or my mother; I still felt sorry for him.

When we arrived at the hospital, my sister Sylvia couldn't talk or move. The deputy had gone fast through the small downtown. The early morning people stared at us wondering who we were, riding in the police car.

The hospital was a one story building made of cinder block. The deputy took the emergency way to the back of the building. Richard and me were feeling bad. We were scared for Sylvia. My mother was scared too. We could tell. Her mouth was tight and shut and she wouldn't talk. She kept looking down at Sylvia in her arms and she stroked Sylvia's forehead with the palm of her hand. "You're goin' to be okay. We're almost there," she kept saying.

Just as soon as we pulled up, the deputy jumped out through his door and opened the rear door for my mother and he took Sylvia in his arms and my mother followed him as he ran inside the emergency room.

My brother Richard and me got out and we didn't know what to do. So we stayed outside and sat on the wooden bench next to the door.

"What do you think?" I asked Richard.

"I don't know," he said. "She looks bad to me but I don't know anythin' about these things."

"Do you think she's goin' to die?"

Richard turned red. He couldn't help it. He started to cry. "She better not," he kept on saying.

I was crying too, but not as much as Richard. I loved Sylvia. I loved her a lot, although I had never told her.

"If only we had stayed home," Richard said to himself. He was banging his fist on his thigh. "I bet this would've never happened. Sylvia's never been sick before."

"Well," I remembered as I cried, "she had the flu last year." And that was true. To me she had been awfully sick then.

"But that's the flu. The flu is nothin'. Everybody gets the flu and no one dies from the flu. This is serious."

"Do you think this would've happened if we had stayed?"

"I bet it wouldn't have," he said. He thought for a while, then he said, "I'll tell you one thing, if anythin' happens to Sylvia, that sonofabitch will pay for it."

And that scared me, listening to my brother Richard talking like that. It scared me because he was so young. Twelve.

It was cold out there and we were crying and trying to keep warm. At least it was not windy.

The deputy came out running through the emergency door and he got in the car and took off. He looked worried to me but Richard said that was the way he looked when he brought my father in this morning. My mother came out after him and told us not to cry. She said Sylvia was being looked at and we wouldn't know for a while what the problem was. She dug into her small purse and she looked around at the bottom and she found two nickels with her trembling hand and she told us to go get a candy bar for breakfast. My brother Richard said he needed to go to the bathroom and so did I, so my mother took us inside. We could see my sister Sylvia on a table at the end of the hall and some people were around her trying to put needles in her arms. She wasn't moving or crying.

When we got out of there Richard and me went down the street and we found a little grocery store where we bought our candy and we ate it on the way back. Then I noticed that Richard was reaching inside his coat pocket and pulling out something and putting it in his mouth. Later, he shared with me. I didn't ask him how he got the cookies but I just knew he had stolen them.

We got back to the hospital just at the same time the deputy drove up and we saw that he jumped out of the car in a hurry and ran to the emergency door. Then is when he saw us walking up to the wooden bench. He turned to us and he asked, "Where's your mother?"

"She's inside," we said.

"Well," he growled, "I need to tell her. Tell her that the sonofabitch is gone. Flew the coop. Your dad escaped."

CHAPTER 2

My brother Richard and me didn't know what to think. Our father had gone. Like the deputy was saying, my father had deserted us. But that wasn't too much on our mind. The important thing was that Sylvia was very sick and we didn't know what she had or if she was going to live.

The deputy had run inside to talk to my mother to tell her about what my father had done and then he came out, slower this time and he walked to the car, got in and slammed the door real hard and drove off in a hurry, spinning the wheels and creating a great cloud of dust. He hardly looked at us as we sat on the bench but when he did he shook his head like he couldn't believe it. Richard and me were sitting still side by side, the sun warming us up.

There were no winds to speak of this morning. The front that had attacked us last night was half-way through Texas by now. It had left the whole town covered with a thin layer of dust.

A short while later my mother came out and said that the tests on Sylvia were going to take a while. They were going to do X-rays and they had already taken blood from her and that she was hooked up to the tubes to feed her in the veins.

She sat with us and asked us if we had heard the deputy. We told her that the deputy told us that our dad was gone. She said the deputy was right. "Your father somehow slipped out of the handcuffs. You know how small his hands are. Then he started the truck somehow and he's gone. He's now probably crossed the county line and might even be close to the border. Who knows. I'm so worried about Sylvia that I don't care. But I do worry about 'im. I'm really scared for all of us."

"That don't bother me," my brother said, looking down at his feet. "He can keep movin', for all I care. We don't need 'im, do we Mom?"

My mother looked out over the low building in front of the hospital like she was looking for a sign or something and she didn't say anything for a while. I could tell my brother felt bad after he said it, like a traitor to the family.

"Don't judge your father. Don't judge him. He's all we got and we need 'im a lot. He may not be first class, but I believe that deep down he loves us. He just doesn't know it."

"Well," I asked her, "when's he supposed to find out how much he loves us?"

"He'll find out one of these days," she said. "Soon, I hope. Right now it's Sylvia we're worried about."

"He'll never find out," Richard said. "He'll die before he does. He may even kill us before he finds out how much he loves us."

"Don't you be talkin' like that, Richard," my mother cried. "You're too young to be sayin' things like that. You make me cry when you children talk like that."

My mother was crying and she was wiping her nose with a small handkerchief from her purse. She was crying because of Sylvia and not because of what Richard had said. She stayed with us for a while longer, fixing us up to where we looked a little better and then she came up with another two nickels and she told us to go get ourselves another candy bar. Richard and me, we looked at each other and could hardly keep from smiling. We were liking all this attention.

My mother left us and gave us all these instructions, like she always did: Don't get into any trouble; don't do anything that you even suspect might get you into any trouble; watch before you cross the street; all I need is for one of you to get run over, with Sylvia as serious as she is; don't go anywhere away from the hospital except to the grocery store; don't smoke (We hadn't smoked in a long time.); don't steal anything in any place. (This was meant for Richard even though my mother had never caught him stealing. Richard was very hard to catch.)

My mother went back inside and left us sitting at the bench and we didn't know whether we ought to go get our candy now or wait a while. Richard went over and asked an old man that was sweeping the dust from the sidewalk across the street what time it was and he came back and told me we ought to go.

"What time did he say it was?" I asked Richard.

"Let's go. It's time to eat," he said.

We walked over to the little store and the same old man was there sitting at the cash-register and he said hello to us and asked us what brought us both back, like he was interested in us. Were we new in town? "We're new," Richard told him.

"I didn't recognize you boys this morning...just wondered who you were. You're staying with someone?"

"No," Richard said. "We're having to stay at the hospital where our sister is being taken care of. She's sick."

"I hope she's not too sick," the old man said. He had put the newspaper down to talk to us.

"We don't know how sick she is," Richard told him.

"Well, you never know about those things. My wife died a couple of years ago at that hospital. She died after they operated on her for her female parts. She had a problem. Just came up one day...but you children don't care...you've got your own problems. What doctor has she got?"

"We don't know nothin' yet," Richard said.

"I guess your momma and your pappa are taking care of the situation, aren't they?"

"Our mom is with her," Richard said.

The old man came from behind his little counter. He was tall and very thin. "How much money you kids have?" he asked us and we showed him our nickels. "Well," he said, "you kids need to eat more than a nickels worth," and he went over behind the meat counter and he opened it up and took a slab of pressed ham out and laid it on the butcher block and he cut four thick slices off the slab and he placed them on butcher paper and folded the paper neatly around the ham and gave it to us. Then he went over to the bread and reached to the back of the stack of bread and gave us a small loaf. He gave us one candy each and sent us on our way. "Be sure you kids share this with your mother and your father," he said.

We hurried back to the hospital to tell our mother what had happened to us. Sitting outside we divided up the pressed ham and made sandwiches and my brother Richard got my mother to come outside. My mother started to make fold-over sandwiches and it must have been our first meal since the baloney that made Sylvia throw up and made her sick.

My mother was surprised at how nice the man was to give us food. She wanted to make sure that we had thanked him. "Did you thank him?" We didn't remember. "You should have thanked him not once but many times. You've got to show your gratitude at times like these. We don't have nothin'," she said, but we knew that. "And when someone that has more than you shares, you've got to thank them." She needed to comb her hair and wash her face. She was chewing slowly and she said, "I don't know what I'm doin' tellin' you all things like that at a time like this." She put her fold-over sandwich on the bench. "I'm not even hungry," she whispered.

"You didn't steal anythin', did you?" she asked Richard.

"No ma'am," Richard said. He fidgeted and sat up straight.

"Don't you do it," she scolded him. "Not from somebody whose helpin' us out."

"I didn't," Richard said.

"Well, don't even think about doin' it."

"I didn't even think about it," he answered.

"You've got to help me. I need both of you now more than ever," my mother said and she walked inside.

We stayed around the hospital all day long and at night- fall the three of us got together again and we ate the rest of the ham. Mother could not eat very much. Her stomach was upset. She went inside to be with Sylvia.

We sat on the dusty wooden bench and watched the clear West Texas sky turn red with dust from a storm somewhere on the edge of the horizon and then it cleared up all of a sudden, the dust having gone somewhere away from us and the sky turning a deep black and shining with millions of stars. The wind was picking up and it was getting very cold and Richard and me huddled up close and after he was sure my mother had gone inside the hospital, Richard pulled out a pack of Bugler tobacco that he had stolen and me and him rolled us each a cigarette and we lit them and with our legs stretched out side by side and warmed up and satisfied from having eaten a good meal, we leaned back and smoked and enjoyed the night.

CHAPTER 3

We were trying to get warm but couldn't, even though Richard had his arm around me. We couldn't go to sleep. I could feel Richard's body shivering. The wind gusted from time to time. The bench was hard and there was always some commotion in the Emergency Room, people coming and going all night long. Finally we went to sleep sometime during the night without knowing it. In the morning my brother Richard and me woke up early and sore. We were up even before most of the people at the hospital had showed up for work and we went inside to go to the restroom. Inside we used the toilet and washed our faces and Richard picked up extra toilet paper and rolled it around his hand and stuck it in his back pocket just in case, he said, we had to go in the woods. I went over and got some for me too. We also took a little soap just in case. I didn't consider this to be stealing.

As we walked out of the restroom we could see my mother at the end of the hall talking to some nurse. She saw us and came over. She looked very tired. Her hair looked dirty.

"Well, did you all sleep all right?" she asked us.

"We sure did," I said, knowing that if we told her the truth she would worry about us too. "We slept good, real good, didn't we Richard?"

"We sure did, mom," Richard said.

"It's just that Sylvia was worse off last night," my mother said. We could see that she hadn't slept. She was beginning to look sick herself.

"What did the doctor say?" Richard asked her.

"They'll know by this afternoon," she said. "I'm so scared I don't know what to do. I was worried all night long about you two. It wasn't too cold for you?"

"Richard and me huddled all night," I said. "We were warm."

My mother's hands were trembling as she looked for another pair of nickels inside her purse. "I need to find some money for you children to eat this morning. Are you all hungry?"

"Naw," Richard answered her. "Jim and I are fine. Aren't we, Jim?"

"We sure are, Mom. We're not hungry."

"Thank God for that. I can't find any money in this purse. Look at my hands how they're shakin'. I'm a bundle of nerves."

She sent Richard and me out to sit on the bench until she could find some money for us to eat with. But we didn't see her until around noon when they let us in to see Sylvia. First Richard went in and stayed a while and he came back looking very worried. He didn't think Sylvia was going to live. He was scared. "You're not goin' to like it," he told me. "She's got tubes goin' into her in every arm and leg and in her nose and in her mouth just like she's ready to die."

I didn't know whether I ought to go in or not. Richard had scared me. I didn't know if I could stand seeing Sylvia like that.

"You'd better go," my mother told me very calmly, as if she were already expecting Sylvia to die and she had accepted it. "If you don't go you'll regret it for the rest of your life. Now go on in and be a little man. And for Christ sake don't ask her if she's going to die! She can't talk or move, but she may be able to hear you. Just tell her you love her and that she's going to get well." I still didn't want to go. "Go in," she demanded, "go in and act like a man."

I was so nervous that I was shaking as I walked into the room. At first I couldn't see her. All I saw were the tubes and bottles hanging over-head inside this curtain where Sylvia was. I went around looking for a place where the curtain opened up and finally, after feeling stupid, I sneaked underneath the curtain and there was my sister Sylvia. My brother Richard was right. They had a tube going from a bottle into each arm and in her nose was a tube and in her mouth was another tube with spit inside it. They had tied her ankles to the bed so she wouldn't be moving around and I knew why. When Sylvia got it in her mind she was going to turn in bed there wasn't anything you could do about it. She was going to turn. If Sylvia would have been healthy she would have knocked down all those bottles and tubes.

I got up close to her to see if she was breathing. It scared me at first. I thought she wasn't and I thought then for a second that Sylvia was the first dead person I had been alone with. I wanted to run. Then she took a long breath and held it for the longest time before she let it out.

Looking at her I couldn't help but start crying, even though I had been told not to cry in front of her. I could see that I was making her worse. She started to fight, trying to turn and she moaned. "How're you doin', Sylvia?" I whispered in her little ear. "Do you hurt?" I don't know why I asked her that. She barely moved her head to say yes. And I thought how funny it would have been for her if she could have seen me crawl under the curtain when I couldn't find my way in. I felt like telling her about it but I thought I ought to keep my mouth shut. I could see tears coming up in her eyes and it made me feel good and then it made me feel very sad. I felt good that I had seen Sylvia. And I thought that if she lived I would never make fun of her again. She could cry and whine as much as she wanted. She could have anything she wanted. Richard and me wouldn't mind. I felt sad, though, very sad, to see her like she was. The more I looked at her with all the tubes going into her the worse it got for me. I tried to talk to her again, to ask her something even though my mother would think it was silly but I asked her how she felt again and her eyes started to roll back to the top of her head. I had never seen anyone that sick in my life. Of course I was only ten at the time.

I ran out. I couldn't take it anymore. I found the way out where the curtains parted and out in the hall my mother was standing next to Richard.

"How's she doin'?" Richard asked me even before I got there.

There wasn't much I could say. What could I say? I didn't know. I guess I panicked. I started to run.

"What happened?" they were both asking me as I ran past them. I didn't know. I thought I was going to faint. I could feel the coldness in my skin. Having seen Sylvia like that had made me feel sick.

My mother ran after me and caught me at the nurse's desk. She panicked when she saw me up close. I was about to faint. She grabbed me and shook me and looked into my eyes like she was seeing a ghost. I couldn't understand what she was screaming to me. She thought I couldn't talk because Sylvia had died, that she had died while I was in the room with her. She was screaming at Richard and me. She ran down the hall screaming for a nurse or a doctor, anyone that could help her. I couldn't believe what was happening. People were coming from all over the hospital running to my mother to see what the problem was. Richard grabbed me by the neck in a hammer-lock and he was shouting for me to answer him. "Is my sister Sylvia dead?" he kept shouting but he wouldn't give me a chance to answer. I couldn't talk, not with his arm around my neck. Finally when he saw I was passing out he let go of me and I fell to the floor when the nurse and a doctor ran past me to take care of Sylvia.

She wasn't dead! They just hadn't given me time to say something. It was just that after seeing Sylvia I was all choked up and I was trying to keep from crying and I felt bad and couldn't talk. I was ready to pass out. From the way I was acting, my mother thought that Sylvia was dead. Well, she wasn't. And when the nurse and the doctor came out of Sylvia's room they were angry with us, especially with my mother who had been screaming and running up and down the hall.

From now on, we were told, only our mother would be able to see my sister Sylvia, which was okay with Richard and me. We didn't like seeing her like she was anyway. We were happy to get out of there. People were standing out in the hall trying to figure out what had happened. They were asking who had died? Did the young girl die? She was so young, they said. They felt sorry for my mother and for us.

We were told to go outside until they could settle every one down. It didn't feel cold anymore. After we had been outside for a while sitting on the bench, Richard and me asked my mother if we could walk around town or maybe go to the grocery store. We were tired of sitting and waiting. My mother said we could go as soon as things quieted down and were back to normal.

We waited a few minutes and then Richard and me started walking.

From the hospital we took a left up the street, opposite from the direction to the grocery store. A few blocks up and we could see the downtown stores and the courthouse that we had passed when we rode the deputy's car. We kept on walking not caring really where we were going, except we knew we were going to the center of town. Richard was walking real fast and had unbuttoned his coat and I did too. Walking like that made us hot.

The courthouse was a big three-story building made of large pink stone. The windows were very big with wooden frames and the window panes were so thick that they made everything inside look weird. Around the courthouse were some small trees and bushes that had been whipped and beaten by the West Texas winds. They were bent and missing a lot of leaves. They looked like they were not going to grow anymore. But I remember Richard saying that it was November and they would put on leaves again in the spring. Richard knew about plants because he had helped my father one summer when my father had worked for a nursery but my father had gotten fired from there for selling plants that didn't belong to him.

There were four palm trees, one at each corner planted between the sidewalk and the curb. Wooden benches like the one at the hospital were set by the sidewalk all around the square. I guess the town had bought the benches because they were all the same, the ones here and the ones at the hospital. There were a few old men all bundled up against the cold wind, sitting and talking, their thin legs crossed. It looked like all of them were smoking and wearing khakis. We could hear them talking as we passed and one of them asked another if he recognized us.

"Who are they?" he asked his old companion about us.

"Don't know," the companion said. "I don't think I've ever seen them around here before."

Across the courthouse at the corner was a small diner. Richard and me went in when we saw that it was empty. We looked around a while until a waitress came over and asked us if we were ever going to sit down. She was a heavy-set older lady. Richard said we didn't have any money. We were just looking for our father, which was a lie. The waitress asked us what he looked like and Richard told her what our dad looked like, even down to the boots he was wearing. The waitress said she hadn't seen him.

"Well," Richard said, "we were supposed to meet 'im here this afternoon. Looks like he didn't make it again." He looked at me acting worried. "I guess we've got to go," he said to me. "Another day of not eating."

We were leaving when the waitress stopped us. "You kids haven't eaten?" she asked.

"No ma'am," Richard told her. "We've been waiting for our dad for two days now and he ain't showed up. Something must've happened to 'im. Our mom's looking for 'im but she can't leave my sister's side."

"Is she the little girl at the hospital?"

"Yes ma'am," I said.

"I heard someone talk about her this morning. She's real sick isn't she?"

"Yes, ma'am," Richard answered.

"You boys sit down," she said. "I'll cook you both a hamburger each and some french fries. How'd you like that?"

Richard looked at me and asked, "What do you think, Jim?"

Of course, I thought it was fine. I was starving. She cooked the best hamburger and french fries I ever ate. On top of that she gave us a each a glass of milk.

We couldn't thank the lady enough. She wanted us to have pie. So we ate the apple pie and she gave us another glass of milk. Then we could tell she was beginning to get worried, like she had thought of something she hadn't thought of before. "You kids better not say a word about this to anybody. If the boss ever finds out I did this he'll fire me and take all this food out of my pay-check."

We weren't about to say anything about her to anybody, but now that she had brought it up it made us feel bad that we had eaten so much and taken so much of her time. We should have just taken the hamburgers to go. So just as fast the whole thing changed. She was pacing around behind the counter acting very worried. "Hurry up and eat," she said, "so you all can get out of here before the boss shows up."

We got up to leave and she said, "Don't come back telling me sad stories again. I'm good for one meal. That's all."

And we left as quietly as we had arrived.

As luck would have it and as unlucky as my dad was, some of it had to rub off on us. We were walking through the small downtown looking at the shop windows, killing time before we went back to the hospital. We noticed that we were being watched by three boys from across the street. One of them was a big guy, like he was very big for his age and he didn't need to go to school and the other two were smaller, but still a lot bigger than us. Richard noticed them when he saw their reflection on the window where we were looking at some shoes. He told me slowly and quietly about them so they couldn't hear. "Don't look across the street," he said, "but there're some guys lookin' at us and it looks like they mean trouble." We started easing our way back to the hospital, trying to be cool about it but my heart was pounding and my brother Richard was redder in the face than I had ever seen him. I would have run for it but my brother said we couldn't make it. So we slowly tried to get back to our mother but they caught us.

They trapped us in the alley behind the theater. By this time we had panicked and we were running as fast as we could but Richard was right. They caught us in no time. They pushed us down on the ground and wouldn't let us up. They asked us who were we? They had never seen us around town before. Where did we come from? They wouldn't let us answer. They had a wild imagination. The smaller two boys kept telling the big one that we were there to make out with the home town girls. That was crazy. My brother Richard and me were twelve and ten years old. I was going to be eleven this month. We didn't even like girls yet. But they kept egging the big boy on, saying we were going to get into some girl's pants, maybe even his girl friend and we kept saying, no way. We were not there for the girls.

The big one ordered the other two to kick us while we were down. They had to do what he said but I'm sure they wanted to kick us anyway. They didn't hurt us very much but they scared us. They were kicking dust on us more than anything else. When they had covered us with dust, he called them off. He said he'd let us go if we were out of Tahoka by sundown. We tried to explain about our sister Sylvia but once he said it and the other two agreed with it there was no changing his mind, except that as he stood over us Richard put his hand inside his coat pocket and brought out some squashed doughnuts that he had stolen at the diner and they were glad to take them and leave us alone. "But," the big one said, stuffing the whole doughnut in his mouth, "this don't change things. Be out of town by sundown. No one comes here and gets into my girlfriend's pants without gettin' a beatin' from me."

We were in a terrible fix. We couldn't hide inside the hospital on account of what had happened this morning. And we couldn't be seen after the sun went down.

CHAPTER 4

I was glad that Richard was able to get their mind off us by giving them the doughnut. I didn't see Richard steal the doughnut. He was like a master of illusion. Later on I found out that he operated by causing some distraction. When no one was looking, he took what he wanted.

The big guy and his friends left us there on the ground. We were told not to move until they had walked through the alley and had reached the street. "Don't think the doughnuts count for shit," the big guy said, still chewing a mouthful of dough. "You all ought to be honored that we accepted your goddam doughnuts all crunched up and stale. What'd you do...sit on 'em? We shouldn't have eaten 'em. Right gang?" The other two agreed. "And another thing," the big guy said, acting like he was going to kick us, "if you tell anyone that we whipped up on you, you'll pay for it. We'll cut your balls off. Won't we, guys?" His friends were laughing at us. "That way we'll be sure you ain't thinking of screwing no one in this town. Stay put till you don't see us anymore."

Richard and me waited until they were gone and we got up and ran as fast as we could through the alley. Finally we came out to the street between two buildings and ran across the street to the court-house square. We ran down the side walk by the old men sitting on the benches and we didn't stop until we got to the hospital.

When our mother saw us she couldn't believe it. "Where in the world have you two been?" she asked. She couldn't under stand what had happened to us to get so dirty. "And look at your hair," she said, running her fingers through our hair. "What happened to both of you? Did you roll on the ground? What were you doin' rollin' on the ground? I just don't understand. Will one of you answer me? What happened to you all?"

I was trying to look hurt, with a faraway stare, hoping that if I held this pose long enough our mother would give up and go back inside. Richard, on the other hand, loved to make up things when we got in trouble. He didn't surprise me at all when he started talking. "Well, Maw," he started, "we almost got killed but we didn't want you to know."

"What happened?" my mother wanted to know.

"Jim and me, we went downtown and as we were crossing the street this car came as fast as it could and it almost hit us. We had to jump to get out of the way and Jim and me rolled over to the curb where all this dust was. Jim was the one that almost got it. I was a little bit farther away from the car and I screamed at Jim when I saw the car. Jim barely got out of the way. He almost got killed. And the car didn't even stop to see if we got out of it all right."

Our mother was shaking her head giving thanks, grateful that we were both alive and well. "Oh, my God," she kept saying as Richard spoke. "What else can go wrong? I don't know what I would do if somethin' happened to either one of you at this time. How much else am I supposed to endure?"

Richard took off his coat and began shaking the dust off it. I took mine off too and our mother started to help us wipe the dust off with her hands. By now she had changed her tune and was angry with us. "Didn't I tell you boys not to get into any trouble? Didn't I? What was the first thing I said?"

I said, "For us not to get into any trouble."

"That's the first thing I said. Do you remember?

"Yes, ma'am," we answered.

"And the first thing you two do is get in trouble. Now is when I wish your father was here so he could whip the both of you. I ain't got the time. But from now on both of you are stayin' close to the hospital. Do you understand? I can't let you two out of my sight. How many times have I told you not to be walking in the streets? The streets are for cars, not people. You two were walking in the streets, weren't you? Don't answer. I don't want no damn lies from you Richard. You were walking in the streets. I know it! You Richard, as old as you are. At least you should take care of your little brother. What kind of brother are you, anyway? Don't you love anybody? If your daddy was here he'd take care of you."

I felt sorry for Richard but he had made up the story. After the nurse came out to tell my mother that the doctor wanted to talk to her, I told Richard that he should not have worried our mother like that. Richard called me a shit-head. He was so angry that he was crying. In a way I knew how he felt.

I didn't think it was right for our mother to talk to him that way. But that's the way they were, Richard and our mother. Whenever she got angry with us, it was always Richard's fault.

The nurse came back out for us and asked us to come in. She took us down the hall to a lab and she told us to please sit down. She kept looking at how dusty we were, like she was wondering what in the world had happened to us. She smiled and said, "Looks like you two boys have been rolling in the dirt. Was it fun?" She walked over to another woman who was working in the lab and both of them began preparing shots. We were hoping that they weren't for us. They were talking about things, not paying any attention at how scared we were. When they were ready, they brought the shots in a metal tray along with some cotton balls dipped in alcohol. We were hoping, again, that they were going out of the room, taking the shots somewhere else but it didn't happen. The older lady that worked there placed the tray on the little table in front of us and she said, "Take off your coats and roll up your sleeves boys. This is goin' to hurt." And I could feel my heart skip a beat. I could feel the hurt already.

Sylvia had polio, they said.

We were allowed to sleep inside because we had just been vaccinated. We had been told that we might get sick with a fever from the shot. So Richard and me slept on the chairs in the small waiting room, slept as well as we could with all the people and children going in and out all night long, and with the pain in our arm from the shot. We got up several times and felt each other's head. We were both all right.

So far we had not seen our mother.

CHAPTER 5

Early in the morning our mother and the nurse, Nurse Wilma, woke us up. My mother had good news. Sylvia had gone through the crisis and had survived. Mother was so happy and excited that she hugged Richard and me and then she hugged the nurse.

Nurse Wilma said, "I've told you, Mrs. Johnson, that this was only one crisis. She's looking good, but the doctor wants us to be cautious. Of course, every day that she improves is one good day for her. We've got to play it one day at a time. So don't expect her to be all well in a short time."

"I understand," my mother replied. "I'm sorry if I'm acting like a fool. It's just that I thought that she might not make it through the night. And there she is breathing better than ever. Better than anytime since she's been here in the hospital. She's a fighter, though. Sylvia is a fighter." She was sitting in between my brother and me and she grabbed us and hugged us again and laughed. She told the nurse, "All...all my children are fighters."

The nurse grinned at us and walked away.

Later that morning my brother and me washed our faces and ran water over our hair in the men's room. We dried off with paper towels. Our mother gave us each a nickel and told us to go get something from the grocery store.

"Just eat what the nickel will get you. Don't beg for more. Don't come back with lunch meat and bread and all that. Don't accept it. The man was nice enough to give you something one time. Don't wear out your welcome. Richard? Richard?"

Richard didn't answer. He was angry from last night.

"You'd better not ..," and she was going to say something and then she changed her mind when she realized that Richard would not talk to her. "Richard, don't get into any trouble."

On the way over to the store Richard asked me if I was hungry and I told him all I wanted to eat was the candy we could buy with our money. In other words I was telling him in an indirect way that I didn't want him stealing for me. I was tired of feeling guilty over something I hadn't done. And, besides, the old man was nice and he didn't have a big store. There were some things that he only had one of.

The man at the store was sitting by the cash register on his stool. He was eating soda crackers and drinking coffee. He looked happy to see us. He offered us crackers and we ate some. He asked us how our sister was doing and we told him all about Sylvia. He was glad to hear that Sylvia was doing better. He had heard some people that had come in the store talk about her.

"They were sayin' that she was in serious trouble. But now it looks like she's goin' to be all right. Thank God."

"The nurse says that it's too early to say just yet," Richard told him. "But she is doin' better. Our Mom's got her hopes up, that's for sure."

"Well, children, only God knows about these things. God only knows...How'd you like the pressed ham and bread?"

"We ate it all in no time," I told him. "We shared with our mom."

"That's what I was goin' to tell you boys...that you had to share with your mother if she hadn't eaten. I'm glad you did. It shows me you have a good heart. I hope your mother didn't think I did it out of pity, either. I was just tryin' to help you children out. If my children had been through somethin' like that, I'd want someone to give 'em a helping hand."

The old man was nice to talk to, nice to be around, like a grandfather, so we stayed with him for a while. We talked about the store and how long he had been there. He told us he lived next door and that he had had the store for over thirty years. He wasn't making money anymore, but he was happy. The larger stores had taken over.

"They opened up a big grocery store on the other side of Main Street and now most people like to go there. My wife even goes there. Makes some people laugh when they see her. I don't blame her or the other people. This is a neighborhood store, like in the old times. There used to be ten, fifteen of these little stores all over town. Times change. Now people have refrigerators. It used to be they had to go grocery shoppin' every day to keep everything fresh. Now you see people go to the grocery store once or twice a week at the most." He looked at us and winked. "I'm just here out of habit, I guess. Doin' it for my health. I'd go crazy if I didn't have anything to do."

As much as we enjoyed the old man, we had to leave. We didn't want to worry our mother again. We ate our candy on the way back to the hospital. Richard wanted to play some marbles, so we drew our circles on the ground behind the hospital but in a while we found out it was too cold to play, so we went in. (Don't ask me where Richard got the marbles.) Our mother was sitting by herself in the waiting room. The excitement had worn off and she looked tired and worried again. She looked like she was thinking of what to do now that Sylvia was doing better, like she had traded that worry for another one.

We went and sat by her and it hadn't been ten seconds when the deputy walked in. He had news of our father. Someone had spotted him crossing the Texas-New Mexico border. He remembered seeing him because it looked like the truck was on fire. It was burning that much oil.

"The man was travelin' with his family, stopped at the state line to take pictures and he said he could see your husband comin' for miles. He left a trail of black smoke a hundred yards long. He was really pushin' it. He had his boot to the floor board. He whizzed on by and made it into New Mexico. He's out of our jurisdiction, anyway. But I just thought you'd like to know."

"Well," Mom said, "in a way it's a relief to know where he is."

"That leaves you with a problem, Mrs. Johnson," the deputy said. "You ain't got no money, unless you've got some and ain't usin' it. And you ain't got no place to stay. Now I've been talkin' to the sheriff and he says for me to try to fix you and the boys up with something permanent. I've just talked to Nurse Wilma. She's willin' to help, maybe not permanent but until you all can find a place. Wilma says that you might be here for a long time."

"That's what the doctor says," my mother told him.

"You can't have these two boys sleepin' out in the cold." He pointed at us. "I've been going by here at night seein' 'em huddled up on the bench asleep like bums. It ain't good for 'em."

That night we stayed with Nurse Wilma at her house. She offered to take us in until we could find a more permanent place. I know we all felt bad leaving Sylvia all alone in the hospital for the night but we had to get something to eat and we had to clean up and sleep.

Nurse Wilma lived only a block from the hospital in an old small house painted in white with a red roof, the house she had lived in all her life. Her parents were dead, I heard her tell my mother as we walked through the wind in the cold dark night. She had never married. Her mother never thought anyone was good enough for her and as she got older and her job became more and more important to her, she thought less and less of marrying.

"You mean you don't regret not having gotten married?" my mom asked her.

"No," she said and that was all.

"I would have felt bad not gettin' married," Mom said.

Nurse Wilma looked at her from head to toe and said, "Well, you're you and I'm me."

For supper she and Mom fixed some meat and potatoes with beans. Richard and me had eaten so fast that we had to wait a long time for Nurse Wilma and mom to finish. After supper Richard and me helped with cleaning the kitchen. Nurse Wilma apologized for not keeping us for a longer time. She was used to living alone and the house was too small. Having people around the small house disturbed her. She couldn't even take her relatives. My mother said she understood. She was just grateful to have a roof over our heads tonight. Richard and me were happy to get out of the cold wind. That night we took a bath and slept in a clean bed. I never remembered being clean felt so good before.

In the morning we woke up and our clothes had been washed and it felt good to have clean pants and shirt and underwear and socks. The coats were dirty but you couldn't wash a coat. Richard and me were going to beat them clean with a stick. Our mom had slept good and she was in a good mood. She had needed the sleep, Nurse Wilma said. After breakfast we all put on our coats and we walked back to the hospital. The first news we had was that Sylvia was not doing any better, maybe a little bit worse. Nurse Wilma said that it was too early to start worrying. It was too soon for Sylvia to really improve. We could tell that my mother was worried again. Nurse Wilma said she needed to talk to the doctor before she could say anymore.

"Oh, well," Mom sighed a long time, "it was too good to be true," like she had given up.

Nurse Wilma walked on past the other nurse and went to Sylvia's room. Richard and me went outside. We were feeling a little sad. We had hoped that Sylvia would have been better.

My brother and I spent the rest of the morning playing around the hospital. We were just running after each other. At around noon Richard said he was tired so we sat on the bench. Then he complained that he was tired of the bench. He wanted to walk to the tree in back of the hospital and sit and rest. I thought it was too cold but he kept saying we needed to go.

When we got there he reached inside a hole in the trunk of the tree and he pulled out two candy bars. We ate those and then he pulled out a new package of Bugler tobacco and we rolled us a cigarette and smoked. I asked him where he got the money to buy all this stuff and he said he had had some money left over from a long time ago. He was lying. We both knew where the stuff came from. It was a little warmer and, Richard and me, we talked and smoked and played marbles.

"Who do you trust?" Richard asked me.

"I don't know," I answered.

"Do you trust Dad?"

"Yeah."

"Do you trust Mom?"

"Yeah."

"Do you trust God?"

"Yeah."

"Do you trust everybody?"

"Yeah, I guess I do. And you?"

Richard was on his knees on the ground cocking his eye to shoot his marble. "I trust you and Sylvia," he said, knocking my marble out of the ring.

In the afternoon just before sunset we were running races around the hospital when the deputy drove in. He asked us where our mother was and he went inside the hospital when we told him. He had come to tell my mother that they had found a place for all of us to stay.

My mother wanted us to go without her. She didn't want to leave Sylvia alone but Nurse Wilma talked her into going with us for a while at least so she could get away and then she could come back later that night and she could sleep in the room with Sylvia. My mother gave that some thought and agreed. Maybe she could at least take another bath like the one last night, she said. I didn't think my brother Richard and me needed another bath. We were pretty clean from last night.

We were to stay with the Allens.

We got in the car with the deputy and he drove toward where Nurse Wilma lived and we passed her house and kept going for about three or four blocks and then he turned left and went another three or four blocks and he stopped the car in front of this nice looking house. "Here we are," he said and he got out. "Come on," he waved, telling us to get out. The deputy knocked on the door and the Allens must have been waiting because they opened the door right away. Mr. Allen was an average-sized man, maybe a little fatter than my dad but softer looking, especially in the face. He looked old to me but later Richard said I was dumb and that he wasn't that old. Mrs. Allen was a short squatty lady with a small pink face and swollen joints in her hands. Her fingers were twisted and at night after her chores were done, when she read the Bible, she rubbed alcohol and camphor on them and smelled up the whole house. Richard and me agreed that Mr. Allen looked younger than her and he dressed better and neater. He looked like he never got dirty.

They seemed to know the deputy real well. They greeted him by his first name, Arlan. Mr. Allen introduced himself and Mrs. Allen and he asked us to kneel down on the living room floor and Richard and me saw him take a large Bible from the little table and he read out loud from it for a long time, until our knees hurt. The deputy stood at the door watching us pray. Afterwards he said he had to leave and said goodbye. He'd be back and check on us once in a while. My mother thanked him and he shook the Allens' hands and thanked them for taking us in.

My brother Richard and me were to stay in one bedroom, a small room at the back of the house. The Allens had fixed up a room for my mother right next to ours.

We were surprised to find a change of clothes on top of each bed. Somebody, Nurse Wilma I guess, had told them about what size we were.

Mr. Allen was a retired railroad worker living on a pension and it looked like he was doing okay. They didn't seem to hurt for money. The house wasn't big but it wasn't small either. It was very clean, like Nurse Wilma's. We would find out that Mrs. Allen cleaned the house almost top to bottom every day. It was bigger and cleaner than any house we had lived in. As you entered there was a living room and then the dining room and then the kitchen, all very small rooms and then the house went on back from the kitchen like a railroad car. The hall was on one side and three rooms came off of it and at the end of the hall was the door to our room. Our room had been added later so it made the shape of the back of the house like an L. The Allens lived in the first room. The second room was the bathroom. The third room was my mother's room, a room that had a pleasant smell, like candy.

Mr. Allen's job at the railroad had been as a clerk. He had done mostly paper stuff, keeping trains running in the right direction, he told us. He was almost bald and had only white hair like a thin rim around his head.

He was good with his hands, and he showed us how to do some things when he worked on his car or in his garden or with his chickens.

You couldn't say anything bad about Mr. Allen, except something I'll tell you about later on about him and a woman and I'll let you be the judge of that, and when he started up on religion. Like one day he got so excited talking about Jehovah that he started swinging his arms around with a wrench in his hand and he accidentally hit himself in the eye. Richard and me had to help him into the house because he couldn't see. Never once did he curse, which amazed us.

Mrs. Allen was really nice too. She tried to be like a grandmother to us. "Do you all have a grandmother?" she asked.

"Yes," we replied, "she lives in Corpus Christi."

"Do you only have one?"

"Yes ma'am," we replied. "All the other ones are dead."

"Oh my!" she said, like we had scared her. She stopped darning her socks and she looked down at the floor like she couldn't believe what she had heard.

Even though she was pink faced and a little scaly you could tell she had been real small as a young girl. Now she had gotten squatty. She was into religion but she didn't seem to enjoy it as much as Mr. Allen. I mean, she practiced whatever it was they believed in, but Mr. Allen seemed to get carried away with it more than Mrs. Allen. Mr. Allen would stand at the door of the Post Office and give out "The Watchtower" leaflets to people coming by and later on, after we had been there about a week, he used to take us with him in his little car and Richard and me would give out "The Watchtower" along with Mr. Allen and it would make him angry for Richard and me to yell out "Watch—-Tower! Get your Watch—Toweeeer," to the people that passed by, but we thought it was funny. We wouldn't laugh then because we knew Mr. Allen wouldn't like it but the minute we were by ourselves we'd break out laughing until we cried.

When we didn't work the Post Office we would go out in the cold wind northers of West Texas to the courthouse or to Main Street to pass out "The

Watchtower" to the old people sitting out on the benches by the sidewalks, old people who would look at "The Watchtower" and then throw it on the ground and spit on it. We'd go inside the courthouse too. We were like an army for Jehovah, he preached to us, and Richard and me were the foot soldiers. There was no place on earth that we wouldn't go to, was what he told us.

We really didn't mind listening to Mr. Allen talk about religion. Richard and me had never had any religious training and it was sort of interesting. We enjoyed listening to Mr. Allen talk about the Bible and Jehovah and Richard and me always thought Jehovah was a funny name. We didn't mean any disrespect by it, but Jehovah was funny to us. Jehovah was the God that the Allens believed in and he must have been pretty good to the Allens, seeing that they had just about everything a person could want. But Mr. Allen said that he loved Jehovah because Jehovah was God and not because he had given them all they had. Even if they didn't have anything, he'd still love Jehovah, just like you'd love your father just because he's your father. Well, Richard and me thought that it wouldn't work for us since we didn't love our father.

Their two kids were all grown and gone. The Allens showed us their pictures. They had one daughter who they said never wore make-up and still she got married to a fine man. In the picture she looked like a man with a moustache. Her husband was thin and little, like our father. The daughter and her husband had two children, two boys that looked like their mother and Mr. Allen. She lived somewhere in California. They worked for the church. The Allens had one son who was married to a real beautiful lady and he lived in central Texas north of Austin in Georgetown and he usually came to see them once or twice a year. In his picture he looked like Mrs. Allen and his wife looked like a movie star. Now she was really wearing make-up. They had no children.

So, all in all, the Allens were pretty content with their lives and they said they had no one to thank except Jehovah. They sounded to me like they were all through and were just waiting to die, and in the meantime they would help people like us.

Living with the Allens was kind of an awkward time for Richard and me and our mother. It's the same everywhere when you don't belong, when the house isn't yours. We never knew what was expected of us or what to do or when to do it. It made it hard especially when we were trying very hard to please. Just as an example, we didn't know when to get up. If we got up too early, Mrs. Allen had to get up with us because she wanted us to have breakfast. We were growing children. If we got up late then she'd be standing by the stove tapping her foot, like she was angry with us for holding her up. So in the mornings, at first anyway, we'd be awake real early listening for the sounds of Mrs. Allen walking the hallway on her way to the toilet.

You couldn't take your shoes off and run around barefooted. We felt uneasy, didn't know what to do next. And I didn't think the Allens thought too much about it. They had cared for other people before and they knew what to expect. They knew that we weren't going to be there forever. Also, my brother and me thought that they thought that we were all a little on the dumb side.

In the mornings, Richard would wake up first and stretch out and give out one of his long sighs. If I didn't move he'd fart once. If I didn't say anything about that he'd fart over and over again until I would start laughing. Then he'd come over to my side of the bed, get on top of me and try to choke me with his pillow. I'd kick and hit him until I'd knock him off. We'd wrestle for a while and we'd put our clothes on and then we'd sneak around the hall to see if the Allens were up. If they were, then we'd make a little noise, just to let them know we were around. Mrs. Allen would be waiting on us for breakfast so we'd act like we were in a big hurry and eat.

If they weren't awake, my brother Richard and me would sneak out through the window by the bed and we'd go out and play, marbles mostly, until Mrs. Allen would call us in for breakfast. My mother would come in from the hospital around the middle of the day, around noon time, and she'd tell us about Sylvia and how she was doing and how Sylvia was sitting up and taking food and crying because she didn't have her doll with her. She'd help Mrs. Allen for two or three hours, bathe, change clothes and then she'd leave.

Sometimes she didn't have to walk because the deputy would give her a ride.

After breakfast my brother Richard and me would help Mr. Allen around the yard or with the house or with the car. Richard was good at working with the car. He and Mr. Allen could read the repair manual and fix anything. Mr. Allen had some chickens and a hog he was raising and we helped him at that too. The vegetable garden was gone for the winter but we turned over the dirt and cleaned it out real good.

What interested my brother Richard and me the most were the chickens. The hog was no fun. He just laid there like a whale or something, just grunting and not doing much of anything all day long. The chickens were different. They were always excited. They didn't do anything without running around clucking and making a lot of noise. They were mean to each other. If one of them looked sick, if it didn't move very much and its eyes were half-way shut, then the rest of them would jump on that chicken and start pecking on it until they'd kill it. We used to find dead chickens almost every day and Mr. Allen said it was all part of raising chickens. You had to expect them to do it to each other, like people, he said.

I don't know if I should tell you this but one day, when Mr. Allen was not around, Richard stuck his finger inside a chicken's butt and he said it was so hot it almost burned his fingernail off. I didn't know whether to believe him or not. But he walked around all day long blowing on his finger acting like it hurt him.

In the afternoon was when we'd go hand out "The Watchtower." I never saw anyone take so much abuse as Mr. Allen over "The Watchtower" magazine. And it wasn't even a magazine like Life or The Saturday Evening Post. It was a thin little paper maybe four pages thick. But he enjoyed doing it and the insults didn't seem to bother him one bit.

One time one man grabbed all of "The Watchtowers" out of Mr. Allen's hands, yanked them away, and tore them up and threw them in his face. But Mr. Allen always had a supply of these things. We used to go to the train depot to pick them up, boxes of them.

At night we sat in the living room and listened to the Watchtower Bible as read by Mr. and Mrs. Allen, always something about Jehovah and how he was going to save us all from sin, and Richard and me would wish my mother would come and that my sister would get well soon and that we could be on our way to New Mexico. Even being in New Mexico was better than this, we thought, but then again, we didn't know what trouble he was in.

One day my brother Richard and me were tired of "The Watchtower" so we decided we'd sneak out early and go see my sister Sylvia. It wasn't hard to get away. We jumped through the window early in the morning, like we always did. The only one who saw us was the neighbor's dog and he let out a little bark and that was it. Richard acted like he was going to pick up a rock and throw it at the dog and the dog ran back to his yard and looked at us like he hadn't done anything wrong. Richard had this little prayer he said whenever we had a mean dog chase us. It was the only prayer he knew and we never got bit.

We walked the ten blocks to the hospital. We went to the side and peeked through the windows until we came to Sylvia's room. You could see her sitting up in bed. She was by herself acting silly, making faces at a mirror in her hand and Richard and me started laughing out loud. She couldn't hear us and she kept making faces. We were screaming. Richard fell on the ground, he was laughing so much and I had to sit down and hold my belly, it hurt so much.

When we couldn't laugh anymore, we looked through the window again and Sylvia was talking to herself and making funny signs with her hands and this time we banged on the window and she saw us. We were laughing like we always did at home when my father wasn't around and she started to laugh out loud.

I don't have to tell you that the Allens were not very happy when we got back. Mr. Allen said that that was why we were in the situation we were in, because we didn't accept responsibility. We didn't care for anyone but ourselves. We were selfish. Mrs. Allen said that this frame of mind was inherited and had something to do with a lack of Jehovah's blessings on our family.

When my mother showed up they didn't say anything to her about what we'd done. That was how nice they were. They didn't want to worry my mother, we figured.

From then on Mr. Allen nailed the window shut and we could hardly breathe. For punishment he followed us in the car for several days as we ran from house to house sticking "The Watchtower" to all the front door handles in town. And it was cold, real cold.

CHAPTER 6

Of all the instruments I had ever heard I liked the mouth harp the most. I enjoyed acting like I was playing the mouth harp for my brother Richard. At night when we lay in bed I would play songs for him, any song, softly so that no one would hear us. All he had to do was give me the name of the song and if I knew it, I could imitate it. Richard would lie still for as long as the song lasted. After I was through, he would sigh like the song had really affected him like he was thinking of some girl and then he would ask for another one. I could make a pretty good noise, almost like the real mouth harp we had heard in school. I'd close my mouth and make the sound come out of my nose like a twang.

"What you ought to do is learn to play the harmonica," Richard said to me one night. "Anyone can play the mouth harp. The harmonica sounds good." At first I thought he was pulling my leg, trying to make fun of me and the mouth harp. But he kept saying that I ought to play the harmonica.

So I began to learn how the harmonica sounded. I had to get that down before I could play the harmonica. The odd thing about it was that Mr. Allen had a little harmonica and he played it from time to time, religious songs, only things like that. Mrs. Allen would sing along with him, and we would sit still until they finished and looked at us to make sure we appreciated their music. There was a lesson for us in everything they did. Well, from this music I began to get the sound of the harmonica.

One day something happened to inspire me some more. Richard and me sneaked into the movies and we saw a little bit of My Darling Clementine with Henry Fonda and that was it. Every time I heard "My Darling Clement-ine" I wanted to learn to play the harmonica. Richard, and in a way Mr. Allen, had gotten me started but this was too much. Every time I heard the song I felt like playing it. I had really liked the way Henry Fonda had played the harmonica, like it was no effort at all. I liked the way Henry Fonda sat on a chair tilted back against the wall on the sidewalk in front of the hotel taking his harmonica out of his pocket and tapping it a few times against his thigh to clean it out.

I just knew I could learn to play the harmonica. It seemed easy enough for me after having played the mouth harp. I'd put my hands to my mouth as if I did have a harmonica and I'd make the noise sort of like the harmonica. After a while not only could I play "Clementine," I could play "Red River Valley," some parts of "How Great Thou Art," and "Bringing In the Sheaves," these last two learned from Mr. Allen. "Down In the Valley" was not good on the harmonica. It took too long to play. In other words, the notes lasted too long. It bored Richard. When I was in the middle of it I'd get bored myself and I'd quit and ask Richard what else he wanted to hear. Richard acted real serious and he would think real hard and he'd come up with one of his favorite tunes. Sometimes he would fall asleep on "Down In The Valley" and I would have to wake him up.

Once we went to the hospital with my mother and I play-acted with my harmonica for Sylvia and Richard sang and Sylvia laughed and laughed at us. This was about two weeks after she had gotten sick and it was the first time we had noticed that her legs were shrivelling up. She was laughing but I could tell she wasn't feeling good. She looked worried to me, like she knew she wasn't through with this sickness. She was real pale and skinny. She had trouble talking and as soon as she got through saying some thing she'd go back to day-dreaming like she was away from us all. She had her teddy bear in bed with her and she kept rubbing its head. Richard and me were happy that we'd made her laugh, especially when everyone said it was good for her, even the Allens.

The Allens began getting clothes for us from their church friends. And pretty soon we had a nice set of clothes. They weren't perfect fitting but they were better than we ever had, better than what my father escaped with to New Mexico.

In time, my mother made a deal with the Allens and she started ironing for pay to help out with our keep. She also needed to save enough money for us to go on our way once Sylvia was feeling good enough to travel.

The deputy and the sheriff helped my mother in getting people to bring their ironing to her. They gave her some of the county laundry to do—jail uniforms, sheets and pillow cases, uniforms. Nurse Wilma was also bringing her stuff over as were several of the people that worked at the hospital. Even several doctors' wives would bring clothes for my mother to do.

My birthday was on the Tuesday before Thanksgiving. On the Monday before my birthday Richard and me had been given a break by Mr. Allen, sort of pardoned or paroled from religion for the day and we had walked downtown to see what was going on. No, we hadn't forgotten the bullies but we were going crazy staying around the Allens all the time and, besides, all the kids should have been in school. We visited the diner and the waitress there, Madge, remembered us and asked us about our father and our mother and Sylvia. She had heard some people at the diner talking about us and that we were living with the Allens. She knew Mom was taking in ironing. She was careful not to ask too much, though, like she didn't ask about our father. She looked like she was afraid she'd break down if we told her a sad story like we had before and she'd wind up giving us some food. She remembered the food she gave us and she said that she could have lost her job doing what she did for us. She had been scared her boss would find out. She had added up what we ate and it had been quite a lot. She didn't say anything about the doughnuts, the ones Richard had stolen.

We said goodbye to Madge and we left. She seemed happy to see us go. Out on the sidewalk we looked around, trying to figure where to go next. I was waiting on Richard to make up his mind. We could see almost all of main street from there. The weather was doing good. We had had no bad winds for a couple of days. The cold norther that had passed through us on Friday was gone and the freezing rain that came with it had melted and now there was mud in the street. It was a bright sunny day and the courthouse benches were full of old men sunning themselves. You still needed a coat though.

As we were walking on the sidewalk right at the corner by the jewelry store we saw the bullies across the street. They must have gotten out of school early for Thanksgiving. They kept following us. Richard and me went into this little music store. Richard kept asking the man there a lot of questions about guitars and drums and harmonicas, like we were going to buy something, hoping the bullies would get tired and leave us alone.

"Well, what instrument do you really want?," the man asked us. He was getting cross.

"It's not for us," Richard lied. "It's for our dad."

"What instrument does he play?"

"He plays a lot of instruments. Bugle. Trumpet. Harmonica. Drums. You name it. But mainly harmonica."

The man reached under the glass case and brought out a harmonica. "Harmonica you say? Here's one. Not the best, but it'll do." He was holding the harmonica in its cardboard case showing it to us. "How much are you boys willing to spend? There's all kind of things here for different prices. Name your price."

"What about the guitar there on the wall?" Richard asked him. He was pointing at a used guitar hanging by a nail.

"That's a repair. Not for sale," he replied. "Unless the owner doesn't pick it up on time. Then I can sell it."

After a while the man got tired of showing us instruments and he figured we weren't going to buy anything and he asked us to leave. "You boys get on out of here. I don't know who you all are, but I ain't got no time to be fiddle-fartin' 'round with you." He showed us the door.

There was no escaping the bullies. We hadn't come close to them for a long time, about three weeks to be exact. That was the Saturday when they threw us on the ground and made us eat dirt, the same day Sylvia had been so sick, when Richard stole the doughnuts. We'd seen them once in a while when we ran around town delivering "The Watchtower" but we had been with Mr. Allen and they hadn't bothered us.

We should have known better than to come to town. All of a sudden being with Mr. Allen wasn't bad at all. "Are you scared?" Richard asked me. I could hear the trembling in his voice.

"I'm scared," I admitted. My knees were shaking. "And you?" I asked.

"Me too," he said. "I wish I was home right now and this was just a bad dream."

"Does your prayer for bad dogs work on them?" I said.

"I don't know," he said, "but I'm goin' to try."

Richard bowed his head in prayer. I was wishing that we were back at home but I knew that couldn't be. The bullies were walking toward us. Then I was trying to imagine how much it hurts when somebody hits you in the mouth with his fist, like my dad did to Richard one time, like Richard used to tell me that it hurt. I could taste the blood in my mouth already. We were in for it. Richard wouldn't look at me and I wouldn't look at him.

We were embarrassed to look at each other, to see the fear in each other's eyes.

They were almost across the street. They spread out enough in front of us to where we couldn't go in any direction. They sort of had us cornered. The big guy stopped right in front of us and we froze, wondering what was going to happen. He didn't say a word but he looked tough. He grabbed my brother Richard real hard by the elbows and another one grabbed me at the same time. They picked us up and carried us through the small alley between the music and the jewelry stores to the back alley where they started to work us over. The big guy threw Richard down in the mud and I heard Richard's body make a cracking sound, like he had broken something. Richard started to cry. Richard was hurting. He was on his back holding his arm like it was in pain. Seeing Richard in pain made me want to kill them. The one that had hold of me threw me on top of Richard. I fell on my brother and he accidentally kicked me on the head. It knocked me out for a second and then it started to hurt. I started to cry. I didn't know if I could taste blood or mud in my mouth. I had something inside my mouth. I had landed on top of Richard and then slid off face first into the mud. Richard had a lot of blood on his lip. He had bitten his lip when I hit him in the face with my knee when I fell on him. Our arms and legs were all tangled up. We didn't dare move. The big one finally spoke. He wanted to know exactly who we were and what the hell we were doing in his town, his territory.

"Quit your cryin', goddamit. We haven't even touched you yet. We've been watchin' you pecker-heads runnin' 'round town actin' like you owned it. You've been givin' out those shit papers them holy rollers read. Haven't we seen you doin' that? You pecker-heads know what we do with that paper of yours?"

Richard and me shook our heads. We weren't about to ask.

"We wipe our ass with it. That's what we do."

The three of them started to laugh. "Yeah," the other two said, "we all wipe our asses with it."

"Knock it off," the big one said to the other two. "These two pecker-heads have a lot of explainin' to do. Let's see what kind of story they give us. It better be good, cause you two have me pissed off."

One of them told us, "You don't piss off Clarence and get off easy."

"That's right. No one pisses me off and gets off easy. Now you shit heads ought to know from the start that there's something about you two that I don't like. You shit-heads piss me off. Just lookin' at you pisses me off. Like why don't you all wear clothes that fit ever? Who the shit are you? Goin' 'round town dressed like hobos. Where the shit did you all come from? You guys got imported here to grab all the pussy in town and go around acting like holy rollers?"

"We ain't holy rollers," Richard said. "We're just here waitin' for our sister to get well so we can be on our way to New Mexico."

"New Mexico!" Clarence shouted, "What the shit is there in New Mexico? Bunch of Indians and queers. You all queers?"

"No sir," we said and they started to laugh.

"Sir?" one of the other ones said. "Sir? They're callin' you sir, Clarence. What do you think of that?"

"They piss me off. Talkin' to me like I was their father. Hell, I ain't no father to no pecker woods." He put his hand on his crotch. "And what about pussy?" he said. We didn't know what he was talking about. "What about it? What about pussy? Answer me you pecker heads. Are you all after all the pussy in town?"

I was only ten years old. Richard was twelve. This guy didn't understand that we didn't know too much about those things. Richard, thinking he'd better speak up, said, "We ain't lookin' for no pussy. We don't want no pussy." And they started to laugh so hard that they were falling to their knees in the mud.

They had been pulling our leg.

They asked us about our sister because they were real horny and they were looking to get laid.

"Your sister pretty?" Clarence asked.

"Yes," Richard said.

"What about your brother here?" he asked pointing at me. "Don't the shit-head ever talk? Don't you ever let the shit-head talk?"

"He talks," Richard said about me. "But not much. Mostly he listens."

"Have you ever seen your sister's pussy?" one of the other ones asked us.

"No we haven't," Richard said.

Clarence said, "They're a bunch of queers."

"Can we get up?" Richard asked.

"How about it, gang? Can they get up from the mud?" Clarence said. The other two said it was all right with them if it was all right with Clarence. Clarence told us to get up. "You guys look like hogs in the mud. Why don't you guys get up? You guys all right? You aren't hurt, are you? You guys looked dangerous to us." He looked at his friends and winked and they all started to laugh again. "You guys understand we had to protect our territory. Now tell us about your sister."

Richard told them about Sylvia and what had happened to her. Clarence thought we were lying to protect her from him and his friends. He was going to take us to the hospital so we could show him Sylvia. If we were lying they were going to beat us up.

So all five of us walked over to the hospital. Richard and me felt like prisoners being marched off to work in muddy clothes. We sneaked over to the window at Sylvia's room and we peeked in and showed them our sister. "Shit," Clarence said, "she ain't nothin' but a little runt." They started laughing. They had seen my sister Sylvia making faces at the mirror on the wall and sticking her tongue out at herself.

We all started to laugh at Sylvia and we knocked on the window to get her attention. At first she looked surprised when she saw us. Then when she saw that there was someone with us, she looked embarrassed. She knew we had been there watching her make all those faces. She waved to us and she started smiling like she was glad that we were there. She lifted her teddy-bear and showed it to us. She acted like she approved of our new friends. She looked at all of us like she was real happy for us. She couldn't get out of bed, though. She was trying but she couldn't. Afterward she gave up and threw up her hands.

We never had any trouble after that. They became our best friends. Clarence, the big guy, was good to be around with because no one picked on you when he was there. The other two were Jim, like me, and Phil.

Thank God Mom was not home when we got there. Mrs. Allen made us take our clothes off out on the porch even though it was getting real cold and she made us take a bath and go to bed without supper. She and Mr. Allen were so angry that they didn't say a word. Mom got there too late to know what had happened but we could hear her washing our clothes into the night.

The next day on my birthday Richard sighed real loud early in the morning and he started smacking his tongue against his swollen lips. He stretched out until he hit me with his arm. He waited and waited in silence. He knew I was awake. He knew and I knew what was coming. But the more he waited the funnier it got until finally, finally, he let out a little tiny fart and we both cracked up.

He got up laughing and he reached under the mattress and brought out a little long cardboard box and he gave it to me. He told me happy birthday and I opened it and inside was a harmonica. The same one we had seen. He had stolen it yesterday at the music store.

CHAPTER 7

We were in bed looking at the harmonica, at how beautiful it was. I had never had anything so beautiful in my life. I was looking at how many holes it had. It had twenty-eight. It was an Echo Harmonica made in Germany by a person named M. Hohner. On the outside of the box it came in was the large letter G. Richard was proud that he had gotten it for me. There were times like he acted like my father and this was one of them. He wanted to tell me how to hold it, how to take care of it.

"It costs a lot of money," he said. "You need to read the little book to make sure you know how to take care of it. I don't have money to buy you all these things all the time."

"Where'd you get the money?" I asked, studying the harmonica.

"I still had money left over from Abilene," he said.

"You haven't had money from Abilene in years. Heck, we haven't lived in Abilene in years."

"Yes, I have money from Abilene. What do you know? You're a little fart that don't know nothin'. You never know where I get my money. I ain't stealin'. I'm buying my stuff. You just don't know how I do it. You don't believe me, do you?"

"No," I said.

"Well, today we'll go by the music store and we'll take the harmonica and you can ask the man if I stole it. Go ahead, we'll go." He jumped out of bed and started to dress. "You sonofabitch, you're always accusing me of stealin'. What do you take me for? I get tired of that shit. You're always thinkin' that I steal everythin'."

I knew when Richard had stolen the harmonica. It was when we were talking to the man and the man turned his back on us to check the price on something. I remembered that the man had been placing all different kinds of harmonicas on the counter. By that time he had lost track of how many he was showing us. That's when Richard struck and I never saw him.

I didn't know how to feel. "You really didn't have to buy me a harmonica," I told him. In a way I was glad to get the harmonica. I always wanted one. But on the other hand, it didn't feel good to have gotten it by stealing. I felt like giving it back to the owner of the store. But I knew that it would break Richard's heart if I did it. And besides, how was I going to explain to the man how the harmonica came into my hands? So I decided to keep it. It would be forever stolen and I had to be careful where or when I played it. No one except Richard and myself could ever know about the harmonica.

It's one thing to act like you're playing the harmonica and make music with your throat. It's another thing to really play the instrument, especially when the instrument has twenty eight holes. I was sure after looking at the real harmonica that instead of helping me out with my dreams Richard may have ruined them. I was happy at making believe and Richard didn't understand. Richard believed in trying to make dreams come true, not for himself—but for other people. He didn't have to steal, not for me anyway. But he just had to do it to please someone else. He just didn't understand about things like that. He didn't understand that I loved him, that he didn't need to steal. Truthfully, I loved him better when he didn't steal. We were more relaxed and happy when I knew he wasn't stealing. Not that I didn't appreciate the gift; I did. But what was I supposed to do with it? I put it back in the box and I could see that Richard was hurt.

"You don't like it?" he asked.

"It's not that," I said.

"You don't like it. I can tell. You don't want to play it."

"I don't know, Richard. I just can't play it right now. What if Mom and the Allens hear us? What are we going to do?"

"You sound like you're playing the harmonica anyway," Richard said. "What difference does it make?"

"It's different. The sound is different. They'll know the difference. You've given me something I can't use. I can't play it unless we're alone or we're out of the house."

"I'm sorry," Richard said. "I guess I should of thought about all of that. Maybe we can go return it. Get our money back."

I knew we couldn't and that he was putting on a show for me. "That's all right," I said. "We'll play it when no one is around."

In the meantime we hid the harmonica under the mattress and started to get dressed. I wasn't angry with Richard and he wasn't angry with me. That had all passed.

After we got dressed we went to the kitchen. Remember I said that you couldn't wash a coat? Well, Mrs. Allen had washed our coats and she had placed them on the oven door to dry. She didn't say a word about what she was doing.

Mom was gone. Mr. Allen was sitting at the table. He had finished his breakfast and was reading the newspaper. He looked over to one side to where we were. "Mrs. Allen tells me that you boys came in drenched in mud yesterday. Is that right?" He was asking the question from behind the newspaper.

"Yes sir," we answered together.

"What happened to you?"

Mrs. Allen was busy in the stove, looking over her shoulder at us like she was the one that had tattled and we were about to get it.

"We were beaten up," Richard said. I was glad that he had chosen to tell the truth and then I realized why. He was going to put the blame on Mr. Allen. "These boys beat us up because they don't like us handin' out 'The Watchtower'," Richard said. "They called us all kinds of names."

Mr. Allen looked at him firmly. "Like what did they call you?"

We fidgeted for a while.

"Now come boys. What did they call you?"

Richard said, "Holy rollers." And Mrs. Allen gasped like she had when we told her all our grandparents were dead, except the one in Corpus. Mr. Allen leaned forward toward us. Richard and me covered our heads. I thought we were going to get hit. But instead of getting angry Mr. Allen got more interested. He put his newspaper down and studied us for a while. We were standing by the table, frozen. I could not believe Richard had come out with the words "Holy Rollers." Mrs. Allen had quickly turned to face the stove so she would not see the blows raining on our heads.

"I'm proud of you," he smiled. "Let that be a great lesson to both of you. There is a lot to suffer for in your religion. This won't be the only time that you'll be called to suffer for your faith. I hope that you did not retaliate," he continued. "That would have played right into their hands. The heathens always enjoy proving us wrong. Like we're one of them. They want us to be one of them. Don't you understand? It's the Devil and no on else talkin' through them. Did you strike back? Did you fight back?" He seemed excited over what had happened.

"No, we didn't," Richard answered.

"And you?" he asked me. "Did you fight back?"

"No, sir," I replied, and lowered my head.

"Hallelujah!" he cried. "Sit down for breakfast," he said and we were glad. We were hungry. He seemed to be pleased that we had suffered for Jehovah.

Afterwards, when our coats were dry, we tried to put them on and they had shrunk. They barely fit but we needed them because it was cold outside even though the sun was shining.

Richard and me fed the chickens and the hog and then we were playing marbles in front of the house when the guys came over. We didn't dare introduce them to the Allens. We sneaked off and we went to see Sylvia at the hospital. We saw our mom in the hall-way and we saw Nurse Wilma. Mom asked us what had happened to our coats and we told her Mrs. Allen had washed them and dried them on the oven door. Richard and me got to see Sylvia up close in her room but she didn't recognize us this time. Nurse Wilma said she was just resting and the medicine was making her sick.

We got out of there and we went to Clarence's house and we played marbles some more. Clarence lived with his mother out toward the west end of town, like toward New Mexico. They lived in a little house surrounded by open fields about a hundred yards off the highway, one of those sad little houses that Richard and me used to see from the back of our truck, especially at night off in a distance from the highway, its small lantern light shining through the windows. I would always wonder who lived there and how they were doing, how had their lives turned out?

We played until Clarence's mom came out and ran us off because we were making too much noise. She was nice looking and tall, like Clarence, but you could tell she had been drinking. You could also tell that Clarence had not expected her to be there and he was ashamed for us to see her drunk.

"Come on, guys," he said, "let's get out of here. It stinks here anyway."

At night my Mom came home and she brought a cake mix with her and made a cake for my birthday and the Allens and us ate it all and they sang Happy Birthday to me. I was eleven years old that day.

CHAPTER 8

I'm going to tell you now about what happened with Mr. Allen and the woman.

We had heard Mrs. Allen say that every Wednesday night, no matter what the weather, Mr. Allen would go over to the church and work on something. He said that there was always something to fix at the church. Since they didn't have a regular preacher, he said it was up to him to go every Wednesday and clean up and fix things around so everything would be ready for weekend services. Mrs. Allen was usually busy at the house on Wednesdays, being the middle of the week, and he used that excuse for not inviting her.

We had been there two weeks and Mr. Allen wouldn't take us with him either and we couldn't figure out why. He normally took us with him when there was work to be done. This fired up our curiosity. Why was it we could go on weekend services and help him out but we couldn't go on Wednesdays?

My brother Richard and me decided we would follow him to see what it was he was doing. He acted awfully guilty every time he left on Wednesday. Richard said to me that Mr. Allen acted like he was doing something that Jehovah didn't like and then he laughed.

By that time we had unnailed the window and fixed it so we could open and close it without anyone knowing it. My brother Richard and me had taken the nails out and cut them at Clarence's house to where they were sticking into the frame only about an eighth of an inch. All you had to do to open the window was pull on the nails. The nails would come up with the window and when you slid the window down all you had to do was push the nails back in and no one could tell the window had been opened.

On this Wednesday we went to bed early but we kept our clothes on. We only took our shoes off. We could hear Mr. Allen from our darkened room down the hallway. He was arguing with Mrs. Allen that he had to go. She sounded like she was crying. He had to go every Wednesday, we could hear him yell, and by now she should understand. He sounded angry, like a person that's lying, like Richard gets when I accuse him of stealing. Somehow Mrs. Allen knew something was going on. She normally wouldn't mind him going anywhere but you have to admit that when a man starts going out on the same day at the same time every week, it gets pretty suspicious. Mrs. Allen was crying very quietly trying to keep us from hearing. It sounded like she had a pillow over her face.

We heard the front door slam and we waited for the sounds of the car. Right next to our window, we heard Mr. Allen clear his throat and spit. The car door opened and closed. He started the car and backed it out slowly. As soon as he left, my brother Richard and me got up, put on our shoes and our coats, and left through the window. We ran as fast as we could between the two houses and the dog didn't have time to bark, he was so surprised. We took a left and ran the next three blocks and then turned right. The night was clear but cold. We had already had our norther for the week. We ran right by Nurse Wilma's house. We could see her through the window doing her dishes. From here it was about half a mile to the church on that same street and Richard and me ran as fast as we could. We crossed Main Street, old highway 380, and kept on hoping we could get there in time.

We were really out of breath when we got to church. To tell the truth we started to slow down right after downtown and by the time we got there we were walking. We couldn't feel the cold anymore by then. We could have taken off our coats.

The church was a little building made of wood, nothing fancy in the way other churches were, nothing like the Baptist or the Methodist church or the Catholic church in Abilene. We went over to peek through the window in the dark and we could see Mr. Allen sweeping the floor and re-arranging some chairs. We stood at the edge of the light coming through the window and we couldn't see anyone else but we could hear Mr. Allen talking to someone.

In a short while we could see that there was another man in there with him that we had not been able to see before. It looked like he had been in the room behind the altar and he had just come out. Mr. Allen was sweeping and the other man was arranging the chairs. This couldn't be what Mr. Allen felt guilty about.

"He's got to be doin' somethin' wrong. Somethin' more'n this," Richard whispered.

I agreed. Why was he going to all that trouble with Mrs. Allen just to come to church to clean up?

We decided that we would stay. We didn't have anything else to do. We weren't in school yet.

At about nine or nine-thirty the two men stopped working like they knew that the church was clean. They were talking to each other about something across the room. They were pointing at something that we couldn't see. Mr. Allen went across to where they were pointing and he moved something around. Then they looked around and the other man went behind the altar and came out with a large cloth and he covered the altar with it all by himself. When he was through they started closing doors and turning off the lights.

Richard and me were going to start running to beat Mr. Allen back to the house but we grabbed each other like we were both saying that we shouldn't be in a hurry to leave. We were thinking the same thing. There was something suspicious about Mr. Allen. We couldn't explain what it was. It was just a feeling Richard and me had. For one thing, he didn't seem like he wanted to leave. He was sitting on the little porch at the steps talking to his friend who by now we recognized. He was a Mr. Henry or Hendricks, something like that. He went to church with us. Mr. Allen was acting like he didn't have a care in the world. He looked like he was trying to tire out his friend. It didn't look right. It was too cold for a man to be sitting down like he didn't have any place to go. He acted like my father acted when he was up to something no good.

Mr. Allen talked until the man said goodnight and got in his car and left. Mr. Allen watched the car drive off and then he started looking around and up and down the street, like he was watching out for someone. After waiting a while, two minutes or so, when it looked like he was satisfied, he stood up and turned off the porch light and locked the front door and he walked slowly to his car in the dark. He got in without banging the door and drove off very slowly without ever turning on his lights.

"What do you think?" Richard whispered to me in the dark.

We were right beside the church, right by the first window by the porch. We could see Mr. Allen plainly as he eased the car out to the street without making any noise.

"I don't know," I answered.

"We'd better do somethin' quick if we want to beat Mr. Allen home," he said.

We were both excited. We knew something was going on. But what? We didn't have to think about our decision too much. I already knew what Richard was thinking because I was thinking the same thing: Chances were that Mr. Allen wouldn't check our room anyway and we wouldn't get caught, and if we did get caught, we would only have to put up with an angry Mr. Allen for a day or two. Richard and me decided we were going to take the chance. We weren't leaving until we were sure he was going home.

He drove off in the right direction but he still had his lights off. We saw that he turned to the right at the middle of the block into an old abandoned driveway.

At that exact same time a figure turned the corner coming from downtown. It was a woman, tall and skinny. She was wearing a long overcoat and it looked like her head and face were covered with a heavy scarf to protect herself from the cold. She was walking fast and nervous. She looked back behind her, like she was being followed. One hand was in her pocket and the other was holding the scarf together around her neck. She crossed the street and walked on the side opposite from the church. Richard and me were pressed against the wall of the church so she couldn't see us. The woman was almost running, she was walking so fast. She made it a point not to look across the street at the church and she walked past it and right past us. We were afraid she could hear us breathing.

The woman walked just beyond the church and she stopped under a tree by the sidewalk. If we hadn't followed her, we couldn't have seen her. She was that well hidden from the moonlight. I guess she was staying there to make sure there were no cars coming. She crossed the street in a great hurry, holding on to her scarf and she was coming straight at us. Richard and me went down fast and scrambled under the church. She had not seen us. She was mostly worried of anyone walking down the street or a car turning onto the street. She went across the sidewalk and into the yard next to the church, right where we had been. She cut across through the dried weeds. We could hear her heavy breathing and her pounding foot steps from under the church as she walked to the back. At one point she was not more than three or four feet from us. She climbed the stairs in the back and she looked like she was looking for keys inside her coat pocket. By that time Richard and me had crawled to the back of the church to see if we could tell who the woman was. She unlocked the door and opened it slowly and walked in. We had not been able to see her face.

Here came Mr. Allen! We saw him first as a movement jumping through some bushes and then like a shadow across the street under the same tree. He raced across the street, jumped the sidewalk, and followed the same trail the woman had taken. He hugged the side of the church where it was the darkest and he came to the back, climbed the stairs quickly, opened the door and walked in and closed it and we could hear him lock it.

We could hear Mr. Allen's voice in a whisper asking the woman how she was and she said she was doing fine. We couldn't recognize her voice. How long had it been? Just two weeks. It seemed longer. They had missed each other last week. What happened? She had been there and waited and waited until she was afraid she would get caught. He had to take Mr. Hendricks home. He got sick. Thought he was having a heart attack. Did he miss her? Yes, very much. He had came by after seeing that Hendricks was all right and hadn't found her. She was sorry. She had waited but got real scared of being alone. His week had not been the same. Why did he look sad? His wife was very suspicious tonight. More than that. She probably knew. Would she follow him? No, she wouldn't. She wasn't the type to create an incident. Have you got your protection? Yes. Can we kiss? Yes, but we'd better hurry, it's so cold. Maybe we shouldn't undress too much, it's so cold. (She was shivering.) Just take your panties off, that's all we need. What are you going to take off? Whatever you want. Just pull your pants down; it's so cold. Do you want it on the floor on my back? Whatever. Standing? Fine. From the rear? Fine. Tell me how you want it. I'll give it to you anyway you want. I don't care, just give it to me. Like this? Yes. A little more? Yes. Are you ready? Yes. Do you need for me to play with it? No. Am I wet enough? Yes. Are you in? Yes. It's so cold I can hardly feel. Can you feel that? Now I can. It's just that it's so cold, but now I'm warming up. Can you feel it better? Yes, I can feel everything now. It's warming up real fast. Do you like it like this? Yes. You like it standing up, don't you? Yes. And on the floor on my back. Am I getting it all? Can you move a little bit more? Can you give me a little bit more? That's fine. Keep it up like that. How is it? I'm so warm I could take my dress off. Don't, we don't have too much time. I won't but I can move all this other goddam stuff out of the way. Can you give me more? Yes. Faster. Yes. Faster. Faster. Don't come out. No I won't. Faster. Can you give it to me faster. And faster. And faster, and faster, and faster...are you ready? Yes! Me too!

And then the woman let out a small cry.

After about five minutes the woman came out first. She took the steps slowly like she couldn't see very well. Mr. Allen was holding her hand to steady her. Once down, she walked to the corner of the church by herself and stood there in the shadows for a while looking in all directions to be sure she was not being watched. She was right by us and we saw her face for the first time. My heart stopped. It was Clarence's mom.

She bundled herself up again, covering her face and she took off in an awful hurry until she got to the sidewalk. She turned right and slowed down some. By the time she got to the corner the street light shone on her and she looked to be an innocent lady going home from visiting a sick friend.

Mr. Allen was standing right by us, watching the woman walk away. When she disappeared from view he went back up the stairs and locked the door, walked down the stairs, and walked past us as we held our breath. I swear we could have touched him. He looked around before he went out into the street. He ran across and disappeared into the bushes from where he came.

It was here that Richard and me ran back and beat him to the house.

The following day was Thanksgiving and Mr. Allen read from the Bible before we all sat down to eat.

After that, whenever we drove by the tree across from the church, Richard and me would start to cough real loud and Mr. Allen would look at us like we were crazy. And we'd start to laugh. Mr. Allen would tell Mrs. Allen that we were ungrateful.

CHAPTER 9

Now that she had more or less gotten used to Sylvia being sick, Mom started to worry about our school. We didn't know it but she had talked to the deputy about us and the deputy had taken her to the school and she had signed us up. She told us after Thanksgiving that we were starting school on Monday.

She took us into our room and sat us down on the bed. "You boys have been wastin' your time doin' nothin'. No tellin' what you two have been up to without any supervision. God knows, you two can get into trouble even when I'm around." We both looked away from each other. We didn't want Mom to even suspect what we'd found out about Mr. Allen. "The Allens have been good to all of us, so good that we'll never be able to repay 'em. You all can't be hangin' 'round here learnin' nothin'. You two need to go to school, 'specially you, Jim. You're the smart one. I would hate to see you not go to school. Maybe college some day."

I hated for Mom to say that about me because I knew that it hurt Richard. Him and me never talked about who was smarter. There were things that he was real smart with. I wasn't smarter all the time. Richard was smarter with people. He could do things and get me to do them but I had a hard time getting Richard to do things I wanted. I wished I could have been more like him in other ways. He made friends easier than me. Our friends liked him more than me. Our friends came to see Richard, not me. I just tagged along. The people that liked me the most were teachers and old people. Richard acted happy around other people but around me with both of us alone he was different. He cut up and all that and made me laugh but he was troubled and sad.

On Sunday we went to church and Richard and me couldn't sit still, thinking of what had happened on Wednesday night inside that same building. My brother Richard had ruined the whole thing for me before we even went.

"Do you think Clarence knows?" I asked.

"I don't know. If he does, he's doin' a good job of hidin' it."

"What do you mean?"

"I mean, little brother, that he's not showing it."

"Maybe that's why he's a bully?"

"Maybe. Maybe not. He's probably a bully because he's so big. He can get away with it. Like Dad. He knows who he can beat up. He ain't goin' to pick on a big guy who can give 'im trouble."

"So you don't think he knows?"

"I don't know, but I'm sure not goin' to ask 'im. One thing you and me have got to do and that's stay out of this. Don't mention this to anybody. Do you hear?" I nodded. I agreed. I was scared of the whole thing. I wished we had never seen what we saw. "If he ever finds out from you or me. Well, that's curtains for us. He's the kind you can't figure out. He may know and is keepin' it quiet, until someday he can come out with it. Or he may not know. And one day when he does, he may explode. I just don't want to be around when he explodes. Some day he's goin' to. I'll guarantee you that."

"Do you think he'll hurt Mr. Allen?"

"He'll hurt everybody."

"That's sad. I feel kinda sorry for 'im, don't you?"

"Yeah, in a way, but I feel sorry for us too," he said and then he began to imitate Mr. Allen and Clarence's mom. "Is it good? Yes. Do you like it like this? Yes. Like that? Yes. On the chair? Yes. On the floor? Yes. On the side? Yes. Faster! Faster! Faster......!" Richard had me laughing so hard and it was so cold in the morning that I started to cough. The Allens came out and heard me coughing and Richard started to cough too, he was laughing so hard.

"My word," Mrs. Allen said, her cold dimply cheeks red as apples, "what in the world is so funny? You two sound like you're choking to death laughing."

Mr. Allen was angry over something and he looked at us and told us to get in the car right away and to stop this laughing and coughing, but the more he spoke the more it reminded us of what had happened. He grabbed us each by the ear. He led us to the car and put us in the back seat. Mrs. Allen was telling him not to hit us.

"Don't worry," he said trying not to raise his voice, "I won't. What they need is some good Jehovah's discipline and it's not my job to give it to 'em.

Let their father do that, whoever he is." And he got in the car and started it and we drove off to church, all of us in an angry mood.

In church, like I said, we kept looking around to see where they had done it. It had been the back room. We knew the room well. We had been there with Mr. Allen many times. It was where they had all the supplies and where the preacher changed.

After the service Richard and me went to the back room while the Allens talked to their friends and the preacher and we saw where they had done it. Richard went over by the closet where the preacher kept his uniforms on an old chair by the corner and he smelled the seat and held his nose like it smelled bad. Richard shoved me toward the chair so I went over and smelled it and it didn't smell any different to me. "That's ass," Richard said to me.

In the afternoon my mother came over and caught us before we could get away with the guys. We had to go see our sister and afterwards we had to come straight home. Tomorrow was a school day and she didn't want us out in the streets at night. My mom bathed while we waited outside sitting on the curb getting warmed by the sun. We were both disgusted that we had to go to school.

The guys came over while we were waiting. As they came nearer, Richard said, "Remember what I told you about Clarence. If you don't want to die young, keep your mouth shut. Forget the whole thing ever happened."

Clarence wanted to play football so we played football in the street. Clarence made a touchdown every time he got the ball. He was playing football in elementary. No one could tackle him there either. They were all excited about us going to school.

"It ain't no big deal," Clarence told us. "It's a little piss-ant school just like all the rest."

"What grade you in?" Phil asked Richard.

"Fifth," Richard said and he pointed at me resting on the curb and he said, "He's in fourth."

"Well, fifth," Phil said, scratching his head. "You better hope you don't get Mrs. Abercrombie. She'll work you to death. Ain't that right?"

Jim was throwing the old slick ball up in the air and catching it. "Yeah," he said, looking up at the ball, "old fart-face thinks everyone of us is a genius, Einstein or the guy that got hit on the head with an apple."

"Poor mother-fucker got hit on the head and he didn't do shit after that,"

Clarence said. "He walked around town goin' da da da all day long. It was one of those goddam apples that weighs a ton." He was trying to get the ball away from Jim. "Throw me the goddam ball," he said. He ran for a pass and Jim hit him right in the chest and he caught it. "Ol' Abercrombie's going to bore you a new ass-hole if you get her. Just you wait an' see. An' little guy here," he said as he ran toward me trying to scare me, "is going to get Mrs. Smith."

"Oh! No!" they yelled. "She's going to tape-measure your pecker to see what you're made of the very first day and your ass'll be hers from then on. You won't even think of having an ass of your own. She'll have your ass in her hip pocket. That's all I have to say. Poor little guy. Hell, she gave me a hard time. She'll beat your ass too. Right?"

The guys all agreed to everything that had been said about the two teachers. They had us worried.

My mother came out putting on her coat and she looked pretty, all washed up. Clarence and Jim and Phil said goodbye to us and left. They went down the street, Jim throwing the football to Phil and Clarence was in between trying to intercept.

At the hospital Sylvia was stretched out on a hard bed like a rubber doll that wouldn't move. She only moved her head and her eyes to look at us and she started crying when she saw Richard and me. She could talk, but barely. She wanted to go home, she said. I could tell what she was saying. But where was home? She didn't care. She liked it the last place we lived at and that was home to her. She wanted to get well. That was what she really wanted. She was tired of being sick. My mother was trying to calm her down. One more week, she told my sister. One more week. Just hold on for one week and she'd be out. She promised my sister that that was all it would take and Sylvia felt better.

"Tell your sister about school," Mom said, waving at us to get up closer to Sylvia.

We got up close, real close, close enough that I could smell clabber in her breath. What was there to tell?

"We're startin' school tomorrow," I said, "and it's supposed to be a lot of fun."

"We're goin' to have really, really good teachers," Richard said. He was hoping just like me that it would be true.

But Sylvia had fallen asleep. She had not heard a word we said. Our mother gave us each a nickel and we left.

Outside it was late afternoon. The sun had gone down early and the whole sky turned a dirty reddish brown. The wind picked up and blew dust into everything, even into your mouth and nose. It was getting colder. Richard and me buttoned up tightly and we headed for downtown with the wind at our backs. We weren't going home just yet.

We could see Clarence from way far as we walked. He was standing in front of the theater. Jim and Phil were over to one side, like they were leaving him alone. As we walked up the people started coming out of the building. The movie was over. Clarence said hello and then Jim and Phil said hello. Jim had the football. He had it tucked under his arm. Richard asked them what was going on. Clarence didn't have time to answer. He was staring at the door at all the people coming out. Just then a girl came out of the theater holding her hands over her eyes. She had a big dirty coat on. Clarence had been waiting for her. He said something to her as she walked out and he grabbed her by the waist and walked off with her. She was giggling. Clarence looked back at us and he waved for us to follow them.

So the four of us, my brother Richard and me, Phil and Jim, followed Clarence and his girl as they walked away.

We crossed the street toward the music store and then we turned left and walked to the end of the block to the diner. We all went inside. Clarence had money. He ordered a hamburger and fries with coke for the girl and him. We sat at another booth watching them eat. Richard and me ordered a coke and used up our nickels. Jim said he wasn't thirsty and Phil said he wanted water. They didn't have any money. Madge wasn't there. They had an older lady that I guess worked on Sundays. She gave Phil a hard time about the water and she said Jim shouldn't just come in to sit. After all, they weren't there for charity or to take in bums, she said. Jim shot her the finger when she turned around and Clarence's girl giggled.

Clarence was acting like a real big shot in front of his girl friend, like he knew exactly what he was doing all the time. He told the old lady to lay off. He ordered cokes for Jim and Phil and french fries just to shut her up. He asked Richard and me if we wanted anything. We were embarrassed because the girl giggled at us and we said no that we weren't hungry, which was a mistake. When the french fries came we stared at them. They looked and smelled so good but Jim and Phil didn't offer us any. They must really have believed us when we said we weren't hungry.

The waitress was getting impatient. We were taking too long. Clarence then got up, taking his time and went over and paid the bill. Richard and me went over and each of us gave her our nickel. She seemed to feel better that we were leaving.

Outside it was dark and cold. We buttoned up real tight and pulled up our collars. We followed Clarence as he walked with his arm around the girl's waist. They were so close to each other and Clarence was holding her so tight that they seemed to be falling with every step they took. She had her arm around his waist. Her name was Mitzi and she was old for elementary school. She had a pigeon-toed walk and a dirty face.

At the courthouse Clarence and Mitzi turned from the sidewalk to the walkway that led to the front entrance. Then slowly, without turning loose of each other, they walked up the steps to the porch that went around the courthouse. They stopped as they reached the porch and kissed. We had to stop half-way up the stairs to give them time to finish kissing. Clarence wanted more but she looked at us and said no. She wasn't giggling anymore. We were trying to look the other way.

They walked together over to the corner of the building under the fire-escape where they were protected from the cold wind and started to kiss some more. By this time we were standing on the porch by the top step. Clarence and Mitzi sat down on the floor at the corner. Clarence looked toward us. Mitzi was clinging to him. Her legs were wrapped around his. He looked like he was trying to get a cigarette out of his shirt pocket. He did get one and after he lit the cigarette he threw the pack and the matches at us and we all had a cigarette while we sat on the steps, acting like we weren't watching Clarence and Mitzi.

Clarence knew what he was doing. When we looked, he had undone Mitzi's coat and blouse and she didn't seem to mind or care about how cold it was. She did giggle and squirm the first time Clarence touched her breasts with his cold hand. Now that his hand had warmed up, he was squeezing her breast and she was enjoying it. Her eyes were closed, even as she took a drag from the cigarette.

The light from the street-corner lamp shined brightly on them. Only once in a while when the wind moved the trees by the lamp did the shadows prevent us from seeing. And when that happened, it seemed an eternity before Mitzi's large breast in Clarence's hand could be seen again.

In a little while she reached behind her and undid her bra and the other breast plopped out. Clarence tried to gather both of them together with one hand but he couldn't. He played with one and then the other. Back and forth, back and forth he went. Then he reached under Mitzi's dress and when he did, she acted like someone had put an electric shock through her and she told him to leave her alone. Clarence kept trying to get into her panties but she kept kicking and holding his hand away and saying no to him.

Clarence said okay. Okay! He wouldn't try it again and she got close to him. He wanted to suck on her breasts and she let him do that but she wouldn't let him touch her down there.

Richard told me afterwards that if Clarence had done it, gotten to touch it, she would have given in without a fight. Phil said too that all you had to do to a girl was touch her you-know-what and that's all. She would be yours forever. So be careful who you touch, my brother Richard had told me. If it's the wrong girl, well, you may have the wrong kind of girl following you around for the rest of your life.

Clarence reneged and tried touching her you-know-what again and she sat up, threw him off her and said: "I told you before, Clarence, don't touch me down there—that's special! No one touches me down there."

"Please," Clarence was begging her, "I'm goin' to have stone-aches if I don't do somethin'."

"Well, do somethin' by yourself!" she yelled and then that struck her as funny and she started laughing. She threw the cigarette in our direction.

It was getting even colder and Mitzi was not as willing as she had been. Clarence was boring her. While he was busy sucking at her breasts, she asked us for a cigarette and Jim lit one and walked over and gave it to her. Then she asked what time it was and we didn't know. She was smoking her cigarette and looking up at the sky like she was counting stars, except that there were no stars to count. She was starting to shiver in the cold. She started to complain, saying that Clarence was getting too rough and that her breasts were hurting. "Be gentle, dammit," she said. "You're too rough. You're hurtin' me."

Mitzi told him to stop and he wouldn't. She screamed at him to stop. "Goddamit you're hurtin' me, you dumb-ass." He stopped but he slapped her. The cigarette went flying into the shrubs below. She was crying, hiding her face in her hands, her large breasts hanging down in front of her between her arms, heaving forward with her every sob.

She saw that we were watching her and she very gently placed each tender breast into her bra and snapped the bra back in place. She got up, buttoned herself and left crying. We saw her run across the courthouse lawn.

CHAPTER 10

We left Clarence, Jim and Phil and we started walking home. The cold wind was in our face, our eyes were watering. Ahead of us we could see Mitzi walking toward home. She was a block ahead of us. She was walking fast but not as fast as we were. Her coat was wrapped around her tight and I could see her pigeon-toed legs. She looked back and saw us from that distance. She stopped and waited for us.

"Are you two followin' me?" she asked as we got nearer. She was angry. She was holding her old coat together at the throat with one hand and the other hand was in her pocket.

"No," we said.

"Then why are you here?" she cried. "Can't you leave me alone? Can't you guys leave me alone?"

"We're only goin' home," Richard tried to explain.

"We live with the Allens," I said.

She turned around when we almost got to her and she said: "Sonsuvbitches. All men are sonsuvbitches."

She walked away and since there were no more street lights in the part of town where we lived she disappeared real fast into the dark. We could hear her crying for a while and then every thing went real quiet and Richard and me stood there in the cold, shivering, wondering why she had called us sonsuvbitches.

That night I dreamed about her. And for a while afterwards I'd think about her before going to sleep as I played my harmonica under the covers very quietly so only Richard and me could hear. I would think of Mitzi and me locked together, kissing and holding each other tight. I mean, I wouldn't grab her breasts like Clarence, rough like an animal. I would first talk to her and kiss her, sort of build up to it. I would stroke her breasts gently. Then and only then when I had been real tender, she would let me touch her you-know-what. And like Richard had said, from then on she was mine! My own woman!

Richard would be watching me real close and when he figured I was at that part he would punch me in the ribs. I was at that part in my dream and yet I couldn't imagine what it felt like to touch a girl down there but Richard told me it's the same as touching steel wool. The hair is that tough. I didn't know where he got that.

When we got home we got a surprise; Mom was there. She was not happy with us. The Allens had called her at the hospital to tell her that we were not home and it was past ten. She had been so worried that something had happened to us. They had called the sheriff. Where had we been? Mr. Allen had driven around town looking for us. The deputy was out looking for us. I guess we had lost track of time because Mom said it was past eleven and we should have come straight home from the hospital. Richard was to blame for keeping us out so late. Mr. Allen was saying that we should be whipped for causing so much trouble. Mrs. Allen was looking at us like she didn't like us. She was wrinkling her nose. Mr. Allen said that didn't we know that with Sylvia as sick as she was our mom needed all the help she could get? We were just making her problems worse. He knew we were ungrateful, but were we really that ungrateful? Had we been smoking? Why did we smell so much like tobacco? Richard said we had not been smoking. Richard said we had been at the diner with our friends sitting next to a man that was blowing smoke in our faces. My mother spanked Richard in front of the Allens and sent us to bed. Richard cried in bed for a little while and called Mom a whore.

We could still hear the Allens complaining to Mom about us when the deputy knocked on the door. We could hear his voice and laughter and in a short while he left, taking Mom with him back to the hospital.

The Allens were beginning to get tired of us. This was the beginning of the end.

CHAPTER 11

We started school the next day, on Monday. Our mom had walked over from the hospital and gotten us up early to make sure we would not be late. Sylvia was doing a little better and that made Mom feel better too. She was also feeling good because we were going to school. She acted like she had forgotten last night. The Allens were in the kitchen and they looked like they had not forgotten. Mr. Allen was angry at all the trouble we had caused. "I never had to do this with my own children," he growled. "Never had to go looking for them in the middle of the night."

"Now, now, Mr. Allen," Mrs. Allen replied, "it was not the middle of the night. It was nine thirty. You called Mrs. Jones. You got everyone stirred up."

"What was I to believe? That these children were safe? Wouldn't you have worried?"

Mrs. Allen said, "We all worried."

Mom was trying to help with breakfast but Mrs. Allen kept telling her to sit down, that she was just in the way. When she sat down Mr. Allen said: "There are certain things in a man that are intolerable. Lying is one of them. So is untrustworthiness. So is alcohol and smoking. I will not permit anyone to drink or smoke in this house. I won't even mention drinking. You boys are much too young for that. But smoking is another thing. You have access to that. I won't permit it in my house! If I catch anyone of you smoking, why, I'll kick the whole lot of you out!"

Mom said, "We understand, Mr. Allen. We understand perfectly well what you're saying."

We didn't eat too much breakfast after that and Mom sent us to our room to put our coats on.

When we came out Mom was talking to the Allens. They sounded like they were on better terms. "Just remember," she was saying, "that you have my permission to whip 'em if you think they need it. Richard, specially. He's the one that gets the other one in trouble. All you need is to whip Richard and all your troubles are over. I know that's what their father says."

"We wouldn't dare spank 'em," Mrs. Allen said. "They're much too good for that."

Mrs. Peters was the elementary principal and you can imagine what fun the children had with her name. We learned the jokes fast, about ten the first day. They all had something to do with the boys you-know-what: Somebody (Name a person.) loves Peters. Peters is good for you. Peters is bad for you. She's got Peters on her mind. You look like you've been whipped by Peters. Have you ever had a Peters sandwich? Have you ever seen a girl with Peters? Peters is another name for prick, pecker, dong. They even got personal— Clarence is a Peters head, it said on the rest room wall!

There was so much writing on the rest room walls that I'm sure Mrs. Peters must have known what was going on but she didn't show it. She was a large lady that was easy to laugh at. We didn't know who she was when we walked into the office. My Mom said hello to her and she said she was the principal and was glad to have us in school. My mom had all the papers and she gave them to her and she went inside the office and asked us if we would please follow her. She studied the records and kept saying "hum."

After a while she leaned back in her chair and we could see how big her stomach really was. She looked down at Mom and then at us. She was wearing one of those dresses that look like tents. She had her arms folded over her head and we could see the many folds that her fat caused in the skin of her arms, not to mention the hair in her arm pits where she had tried to shave and missed.

She fixed Richard and me with her stare like she was telling us that she may appear to be a nice lady but that deep down if we messed with her she could be mean. She looked at Mom then. "Arlan has told me all about your problems, Mrs. Jones. I'm sorry to hear about you daughter... Sylvia is it?" My mother leaned forward to better understand. "Yes...Sylvia," she said.

"I hope she's doing better today. Has the doctor said anything?"

"No, nothin' definite. We just go day to day."

"I thought Arlan said she had...polio...was it? Am I right?"

"Yes, she has it right now. She has polio."

"Oh, I thought you said that the doctor hadn't said what she had. I misunderstood."

"I'm sorry. I thought you meant had the doctor told me anything today?"

"We're just nervous. For you and the children it's the first day of school. I realize how tough it is on you, Mrs. Jones, and we'll try to help in any way we can. Remember that we're here to help. Your two boys seem eager to start. How about it boys? I understand you're staying with the Allens?"

"Yes, they are."

"The Allens are fine people, Mrs. Jones."

"They sure are. Very fine to put up with us."

"Arlan, the deputy, really thinks a lot of you, Mrs. Jones. He admires your courage. He's very impressed with the whole family. He thinks it's too bad you're married."

"Oh, he's just kiddin' around. You know how he is. He can do a lot better'n me."

"Oh, I'm sure he was kidding too. But he admires you greatly. I just thought you would want to know that someone appreciates what you're going through. We here at our little school appreciate what you're going through also so don't hesitate to ask for help if you need it..." She stared at us again and then broke out in a smile. "Now, for the boys...We'll assign them teachers this morning, Mrs. Jones," she said, "and then they can start right away, this morning as a matter of fact. I think we can keep Richard in the fifth grade and Jim will go to fourth."

Just as Clarence, Jim and Phil had said, Richard got Mrs. Abercrombie and I got Mrs. Smith. We dropped Richard off at Mrs. Abercrombie's room and Mrs. Peters introduced Mom to her. I watched as Richard went in the classroom and found an empty seat at the back.

"No, no, no," Mrs. Abercrombie told Richard, "you musn't sit at the back of the room. You must sit up front where we can all see you and get to know you better."

Richard blushed and got up and found a desk on the front row. "Go ahead and take off your coat, Richard," Mrs. Abercrombie said and that was enough to start the whole class laughing at Richard's coat. I dreaded going into my class wearing my coat. "It's too hot for you to be wearing your coat." Richard took off his coat, but not before blushing again. The girls giggled and the boys started to fan themselves acting like the room was hot. "Oh, oh, it's hot," they said.

"Now children, let's be courteous to our new friend. His name is Richard Jones and we want to make him feel welcome."

All this time Mom and Mrs. Peters and me were standing at the door with Mrs. Abercrombie, watching Richard find his seat.

"And who's this one?" Mrs. Abercrombie asked, putting her hand on top of my head.

"This is Jim, Richard's younger brother. He goes in fourth grade with Mrs. Smith. We're on our way there," Mrs. Peters said.

"Well, I'm sure Richard will fit right in with us just fine." Then she turned to the class and asked them if it wasn't so. "Yes, Mrs. Abercrombie!" they all screamed and laughed. Richard had his head down writing his name on his tablet.

"Now, now, class. There's no need to be rambunctious."

We left her talking to the class, trying to settle them down. Fourth grade was next door and farther up the hall. Mrs. Smith was at the blackboard writing an assignment. She looked to me to be a kind lady. Mrs. Peters introduced Mom and me to her when she came over to the door. The children in this classroom had been taught to say hello to Mrs. Peters, so they all yelled "Hello, Mrs. Peters," all at the same time and this broke them up. No telling how many of them were thinking of the writing on the rest room walls.

"Hello class," Mrs. Peters replied and the children laughed even more.

"We don't know how advanced Jim is in his studies," Mrs. Peters said to Mrs. Smith, "but we have time to evaluate him. We'll see if he can catch up. I believe he's behind for the year, just as his older brother is. His brother, by the way, is next door with Mrs. Abercrombie. His name is Richard."

"Well, that's nice to know," Mrs. Smith said absentmindedly, looking at me. "And you, Jim, how are you doing?"

"Fine," I replied.

"Do you like school?"

"Yes," I lied.

"What is your favorite subject?"

"English," I said, "and sometimes math. Sometimes geography. The one that's the easiest."

She laughed a little laugh, like she was nervous about what I had said and the class laughed out loud with her. "Class, class. Let's be polite. Remember Jim is a new student and we must be polite to him."

Mrs. Peters smiled at me and Mom. I was blushing when Mrs. Smith took me by the hand and sat me down up front just like they had done with Richard. She helped me out of my coat and I could feel myself blushing and the whole class got the giggles. And the more they giggled, the more I blushed. Finally Mrs. Smith got serious and she said, "Class, class. If you don't stop this giggling we're not going out for recess." This quieted them down. "Now start on your assignment. Henry," she said, " get your dirty feet off Paul's desk." And the whole class started to laugh again.

At the first recess I found Richard but I also found Mitzi. Richard was happy the way things were going and he asked me about me and I said that I was happy too. Mrs. Smith had been nice. Mitzi was across the sidewalk where the girls played, separated from the boys. We were watching her. She was playing her favorite: Volley-ball. I couldn't help but admire the way she ran and jumped, pigeon-toed as she was.

It didn't take me long to figure out where Mitzi was most of the time. I had her schedule down pretty well. I knew right away where her room was and who her teacher was. She was in seventh grade. I knew who her girl friends were and who she came to school with, who she played in recess with. So the first week my brother Richard and me would hide from the guys and we'd wait for her by the side of the school building and we'd follow her and my brother wanted to know when I was going to say anything to her. I didn't know. He'd pester me to talk to her.

"Go on," he'd say, always great with advice, "go talk to 'er. You'll never get anywhere 'til you do."

He'd grab me by the arm and act like he was going to throw me to her, even though she was a block away. It was embarrassing the way he did it, but what could I do? He was the only one that knew that I was in love and I didn't want anyone else to know. Richard knew that he had me where he wanted me. I couldn't say much to offend him. I was afraid he'd tell Clarence and the guys, and then the word would get to Mitzi. He never threatened he would squeal on me but I could see it in his eyes when I did or said anything that he didn't like.

We both knew I didn't have the guts to talk to Mitzi so Richard started to build up my confidence. After a while he said that he thought I was ready.

The only thing left was to figure out when and where I was supposed to talk to her. At that time I was supposed to ask her to go steady. I was not supposed to go too fast. "Take it easy at first," Richard would coach me. "You don't want to scare 'er. Talk about school first. Then when it looks like you don't have anythin' else to say, go to somethin' else, like sports. Volley-ball'll be nice. She likes volley-ball. Go to the things she likes. Don't talk your ass off about yourself."

That was not the problem. I didn't have anything to tell about myself except how we came to live in this town.

"Sure you've got somethin' to say," Richard said. "Talk about how good you do in school."

But I was sure someone like Mitzi could care less how I did in school.

We'd talk about it as we lay in bed waiting to go to sleep, my harmonica silent in its box. I had traded it in for a girl.

"Just imagine," Richard would whisper to me, "how it would feel to kiss her like Clarence did."

I'd imagine it and I'd wish that Clarence had never been born.

CHAPTER 12

It was Saturday morning. We were through feeding the chickens and the hog and we were out front just hanging around waiting for something to happen. We had been talking about going to see Mitzi and we were trying to get enough courage to go. Richard was sitting on the curb breaking off pieces of a twig and throwing them out into the street. I was sitting on the porch steps cleaning my fingernails, trying to get out the little pieces of laying-mash we had fed the chickens. The sun was out and for the first time all week the winds had died down. The streets looked clean. But we had overheard Mr. Allen tell his wife that there was another norther coming in today.

Richard stood and stared off into the distance. "Here come Clarence and the guys," he said, looking to his left. I stood also and saw them coming. Clarence was in front. I couldn't help but think of his mother every time that I saw him. When they got there, Clarence acted like we had done something wrong. "I'm pissed off at you shit-heads. I've been tellin' everyone that you two piss me off," he was saying.

"What've we done?" Richard asked.

"What've we done? Is this shit-head askin' 'what've we done'? You know goddam well what you done."

"No we don't," Richard said. "We'd never do anythin' to get you angry. You know that."

"You shit-heads have been hidin' from us after school. You've been sneakin' around. What are you guys doin', jackin' off somewhere?"

I could tell Richard's mind was going a mile a minute. "We've been havin' to run back home to help print up some Jehovah's stuff for Mr. Allen," Richard lied to him. "It's kind of secret stuff that no one should know about but him. You know how he is."

"Yeah," Clarence said, "he's an odd fart."

"Religious shit-head," Jim volunteered.

"Stuff so secret we don't even know what it is. My brother Jim does one part and I do the other part just so we don't find out what it is, just like the G-Men. We have an oath to secrecy to each other. I can't tell 'im what I do and he can't tell me what he does."

He said, "Well I'm glad to hear that. We were beginnin' to think you two pecker-heads were off hidin' thinkin' you were better'n us, not wantin' anybody at school to know we hung around together. We were beginnin' to think you all were screwin' the pig every afternoon or jackin' off in the ole' chicken coop. You can go crazy doin' that."

"That's for sure," Phil said and he started to act crazy, walking funny with drool coming out of his mouth.

Richard and me were looking toward the house hoping the Allens were not watching what was going on, hoping Mr. Allen wouldn't come out and run them off. All we needed was a confrontation between Clarence and Mr. Allen.

"Knock it off," Clarence said. "We were only kiddin'. The real reason we're here is that we just found out the carnival got into town last night. We need to go over there and see what the fuck is goin' on. You guys comin'?"

"Sure," Richard said. "Jim and me can go. Right Jim?"

"Yeah," I said. "We ain't got nothin' to do."

"Are you sure, pretty boys," Phil said, talking like a girl, "you don't have little papers to hand out to people that don't want 'em? You don't have the fuckin' hog to feed? You don't have the garden to hoe? You don't have the chickens to fuck... Er... I mean to feed?"

"Goddamit," Clarence said, "are you piss-heads slave labor or what? What the fuck is goin' on in that house? You all take all that shit from that shit-head? If he tried to tell me what to do I'd cream his ass. If I lived with him I'd cream his ass. I wouldn't take no shit."

Richard said, "Man, we gotta. We've gotta eat and sleep somewhere. Unless you want us to move in with you, Phil."

Clarence laughed. "Shit. Phil's folks don't have no money to feed Phil, much less you all....But who brought up this shit about all this shit? Let's go to the carnival. But first, you guys, should we let 'em in on the secret now?"

"You might as well," Jim and Phil said. "Tell 'em our plan," they said to

Clarence. "They may not want to go along with it. They're kinda young for that kinda thing."

Before Clarence could tell us, Jim thought it would be a good idea if we got out of there, away from the Allens. Jim was afraid the Allens might hear and ruin the whole thing. So we started walking toward town with the tall Clarence in the middle of the circle we made around him.

Clarence told us this story: Some of the kids they knew had gone to the carnival last year and they had met a guy who worked there and he had become friendly with these kids. They would joke around and the kids went there almost every night. "You know how it is," Clarence said as we walked. "Pretty soon when an older man takes you in as a friend you start to feel real good about 'im. Like he's better'n your ole' man. He was real friendly to these guys. They got to know each other real well. One day he started talkin' about girls and he started askin' about girls. He come to find out that no one there knew anythin' about girls. Nothin'. He just shook his head. He couldn't believe it, specially with all the good lookin' girls in town. So, not only did he show 'em things about the carnival and all of that but he spoke to 'em about girls, always talkin' about girls and how they acted and what to do to 'em."

"Like what?" Richard asked, excited.

"Just wait, goddamit."

Jim said, "Wait for the fuckin' story, will you, shit-head?"

Richard said, "Sorry."

Clarence raised an eye-brow like he was offended and then he said, "Anyway, to continue, after I was so rudely interrupted. (We all laughed to hear Clarence talk like that, like an English teacher.) He told 'em things about girls that these guys had never dreamed of. Just to give you an example of how good this guy was, he told 'em that if you ever go out on a date and you want to really make your date hot, all you have to do is keep your fly open, like you accidentally left your fly open. I mean unzip your pants, and he showed them how he did it, and go pick up your date and believe you me before the evenin' is out, with you standin' and sittin', your fly openin' and closin', your date'll be ready to grab your pecker and play with it. Talk about hot! So there you are. Open up your fly and that's all there is to it. Ain't that easy?" he asked, shaking his head. "Ain't he smart?"

I thought about the question and I was hoping no one else had but Jim was pretty sharp. Jim asked, "If it works, why didn't you try it with Mitzi?"

Clarence replied, "She ain't worth fuckin' that's why. I ain't much for seconds."

His words caused me pain. I could feel it all the way to my stomach. I felt like going back home.

"Why hadn't you all told us this before?" Richard asked him.

"Goddamit, you're a dumb-ass. We just hadn't talked about it because the carnival wasn't in town. Now that they came in, it's goin' to be the talk of the kids. Everyone'll want to go."

We had stopped for a short while, while Clarence answered these questions. Now we were walking again. He said, "He told 'em that he was more or less an expert on women. One of his favorite tricks was to put a squirt of tabasco sauce on his middle finger before a date, not a whole lot, just a squirt, and when he'd touch the girl's pussy she'd go wild!" Clarence threw his head back and laughed like he was ready to try it on some girl. "Cigarettes would do the same thing. Just take a cigarette and roll it on your finger-tips until you get all the tobacco out of the paper and your fingers would be like magic to a girl. I guarantee you she'd never leave your side. She'd follow you across oceans."

We hooked a left at the courthouse and Clarence was still going strong. We went through downtown, by the diner, the bus station across the street and then a couple of blocks later we turned right, went one more block and there in the middle of the open fair-grounds was the little carnival. Everyone seemed to be working at something—putting up rides, putting down boards on the ground, hooking up strings of light bulbs to electricity poles, putting up tents, games. It was like a beehive. And as if we didn't have enough of it, they were kicking up their own dust.

We approached with caution, slowly, like we might be intruding. Several of the men looked at us for just a glance and then they went back to their work. We were attracted to an older lady in a long Gypsy dress that was standing in the middle of all the work going on. She was telling women and men what to do. We walked over her way and when she saw the five of us she smiled and asked us if we were coming to the carnival tonight?

We all answered that we were. She promised that we were going to have a lot of fun. Where had they been all year? "All over," she laughed. "All over these United States. Never stop movin'. Never stop goin'. Ah, that's the life! Maybe one of you'll take up the carnival life someday. Lots of fun, boys. Know what I mean? Lots of pretty young girls. Lots of pussy for some fortunate boy." She looked at us, all of us, one by one. She leaned toward me and she stared, eye to eye. She said, "You look like you'll grow into a carnival man. You've got the look. Yessir, you've got the look. You look like you've got a big pecker."

Everyone burst out laughing, including the Gypsy.

"No ma'am," I said and that made everyone laugh more.

"What's your name?" she asked.

"Jim," I barely said. My mouth was dry. Her look made me tremble. I had never heard a woman talk like that before.

"Jim," she repeated, looking at me with her head tilted to one side, like she was studying me. "Jim. What a name. It's a good carnival name. You can do a lot with a name like Jim in a carnival. One of my husband's name was Jim, but his pecker was little, like a little Vienna sausage. He tickled me to death, Jim," she said again and looked at me for a long time, which to me was embarrassing. Then she bent over and grabbed me and rubbed my head. "For the evil-eye," she said. "And for good luck."

"Jim won't go to carnivaling," Clarence said. "Hell, it's hard enough to get 'im away from his mama." And they all started to laugh, including me. Richard looked at me and he looked relieved, just like me, that the lady had turned loose of me.

"You all leave the boy alone," she said, backing off. "He's just a little child. So young. Come back tonight and have some fun," she told us and she started to leave. "I've got lots of work to do," we could hear her say.

Clarence ran to her and asked, "Could you tell us if Pete made it this year?"

"Sure," she said, "Pete made it back with us. He almost didn't, but he has a way of getting off light. What you boys want with Pete?"

"He's our friend from last year," Jim said.

"Yeah," Clarence said, "we want to say hello to 'im."

"Well," she replied, "there's his trailer yonder," and she pointed off to the corner of the fair-grounds to a small silver painted trailer still hitched to the old car.

We said goodbye to the Gypsy and she made a funny sign at us like she was blessing us and we started to giggle. She laughed with us and she turned around and said to the workers, "Come on, goddamit, we don't have all day. We got us a show tonight," and they all stopped looking at us and started to work real fast.

Clarence walked up to the trailer by himself. He had told us to stay behind. The trailer was resting at an odd angle, tilted forward, since it was still hitched to the car. Clarence knocked on the door. No one answered. He knocked again, this time harder. We were starting to giggle. Clarence looked back at us like he wanted to kill us. He knocked again. "You all cut out that bullshit," he said and, really, it made us want to laugh more. He got angry with the trailer. He beat on the side and it sounded like he was hitting a tin can. Then we heard the sleepy voice from inside. "Who the fuck is it?" it asked.

"It's Clarence."

"Who?"

"Clarence!"

"Clarence?"

"Clarence!"

"Clarence?"

"Clarence!"

This was just too much for us. We started to laugh as hard as we could. Even the name Clarence didn't sound real anymore. It sounded like Clarence was saying something else.

"Clarence who? Who the fuck is Clarence?"

"Clarence Johnson!" he shouted through the door.

"Are you with the law?"

"No."

"Then stop beatin' the shit out of the trailer, you bastard. Whatcha want?"

"We're just some guys came over to visit. That's all."

"Whatcha want to visit about?"

"We'd like to join the class like you had last year."

"We ain't havin' no fuckin' class this year. Beside I don't know what the shit you're talkin' about."

Clarence started to walk away when the voice came back, "Who told you about a class?"

Clarence had to go back to the door. "Friends," he said.

Pete opened the small trailer door, shielding his eyes from the sun. He was a middle-aged man, thin and small, something like my father, and he hadn't shaved in a while. He didn't have a shirt on and he didn't have shoes on. We could see his belly- button and the hair below it.

He wanted to know what we wanted and Clarence asked him if we could come in. He stepped aside and looked out into the fair- grounds like he was searching for something. Then he looked us over real careful like the Gypsy had done. He opened the door some more and jerked his head at us telling us to go in. I swear there wasn't room for all of us in there but we squeezed in and he asked us what it was we wanted and Clarence started to tell him about what he'd heard from his friends about the classes.

"What'd they tell you?" he asked.

Clarence told him, but Pete wasn't about to admit anything. Clarence kept talking and Pete kept listening, like he was checking us out. I figured he was being pretty smart. He may have thought the sheriff had sent us out just to get him in trouble. He was sly. He'd say something and then he'd say he hadn't said it.

It took him a while to size us up, to make sure we weren't with the sheriff.

We were all standing body to body on one side of the trailer across from Pete's bed. He was sitting on the bed rubbing his toes. He got relaxed with us after a while. He explained that the sheriff had it in for him, not only in this town but in any town he played at. "I'm smarter than those sonsofbitches and they hate me for it. I don't work one-tenth what those sonsofbitches work and I have a million times more fun and I make a hundred times more money than them. I irks 'em, the sonsofbitches." He giggled and shook his head. He was thinking of something. "Who's the little fart?" He was looking at me. "Ain't you kind of young to be chasin' pussy? You'd best be careful cause if you do catch up to it, it can turn 'round and pussy whip you." He was looking at me and I couldn't move one single inch. I was scared. He was looking at me only with one eye, his head cocked like the Gypsy woman. "You ever been pussy-whipped, you little fart?"

"No he ain't," Richard said for me.

"What's the matter? Cat got your tongue?"

My mouth was dry. I tried to talk and my voice came out like a squeal. "No sir," I said in that high voice and everyone started to laugh. I looked at Richard and he was trying to laugh but I could tell he was feeling sorry for me.

"Well," he said, "let's not forget everyone else. Who's been pussy-whipped here? Who knows what bein' pussy-whipped means? Exactly?"

No one knew. Clarence was trying hard to figure it out.

"Just like I thought. Bunch of pussy-strangers. You all are what I call pussy-strangers cause you're strangers to pussy. We ain't havin' a class this year," he said. "But we're goin' to have a viewin' and that's what you boys need. You need a viewin'. I thought about all this class stuff and it don't do you men any good. But in keepin' with my tradition of the great innovator in sex, let me tell you what my favorite is now. Ran across it by accident. Anyone got a cigarette?" My brother Richard got out a new pack from his sock. God only knows where he had stolen the cigarettes. Pete looked at the brand, opened the cellophane and the pack and took one. He lit it and inhaled and let the smoke come out real slow. He was going to let us wait for this one. "Well men," he said, getting smoke in his eye and rubbing it, "I was out in the good ole' state of Arkansas when I run into this good-lookin' gal and we started to drink whiskey and before you know it we was drunker'n a skunk. I had to have a seltzer pill. I really needed one. So I had some in the trailer just in case something like this ever happens to me and I mixed it in water and drank it, but then I got this idea. I took one of those pills and I put it up this girl's pussy and you've never seen anythin' like it in your life. It started foamin' like it had a life of its own. We screwed all night long and she kept saying that that was the best screwin' she ever did have. Now that time I was almost pussy-whipped. Almost, but not quite. You see, pussy-whipped is when you can't take it no more."

He flipped the long ash from the cigarette to the floor and took another drag. He grinned again his yellow-toothed grin. Clarence was looking at him without blinking, in a trance. Phil and Jim were grinning at the thought of it. It embarrassed me and Richard to hear a grown-up man talk like that to kids like us. I mean, my father was bad and all that but you'd never hear him talk to kids about things like that.

He slid open the window behind him and he threw out the cigarette stub. It was getting so stuffy and smokey that we could hardly breathe. And that was the biggest room in the trailer. At the rear, behind a curtain I could see a little room with a little commode on the floor and next to it a one-burner stove.

"How many of you ever seen a real live girl naked?"

No one answered. Then Clarence said he had peeked through a knot-hole at a girl taking a shower.

"Have you all ever seen pussy?"

It turned out that not one of us had ever seen that part of a girl, not even Clarence, although he said he had seen it when the girl turned toward him while she was taking a shower. "That don't count," Pete told him. "I mean up close. Have you all ever seen pussy up close?"

Well, that was what the viewing was going to be about. He was going to show us that part of the girl, the one we're always talking about and it would be live, a real live woman. He had women in the carnival that we could see. He was real good in his description of it. He was going to show us the outside, the middle, and the inside of the you-know-what and we would be experts by the time he was through with us.

When he got through he had us all leaning toward him and all excited. Clarence was ready to pay for the viewing ahead of time. There would be plenty of time for paying, Pete said, and besides he didn't know how much he was going to charge.

You'd have to say that the man had a good imagination and that he could paint a picture with words.

He showed us out of the little trailer. Outside the winds were starting to blow. The norther that Mr. Allen had talked about was here. We buttoned up real good. Pete said that he would tell Clarence when these viewings were going to take place. Clarence could then pass the word. He bummed a handful of cigarettes from Richard and he went back in and closed the door.

On our way home Richard told Clarence that we weren't interested in what Pete was going to do.

"What's the matter?" Clarence said. "You guys queers or somethin'?"

"No," Richard said, "it's just that my brother and me don't want to and besides we don't have the money."

"Suit yourself, shit-heads," Clarence said. "All that means is that we other guys get to see more."

We needed to get rid of the cigarette smoke on our clothes so Clarence said that we ought to find us a dirty dog and rub him up real good so we could get rid of the smell. We found two real dirty dogs on the way back and Clarence and Jim and Phil held them for us while we rubbed all over against them. We were laughing because the poor dogs looked confused, like no one had ever loved on them before.

When we got home the Allens said that we smelled like something they had never smelled before.

"It's dog," Richard said, like everyone should have known.

Mr. Allen shook his head.

CHAPTER 13

In the morning Mrs. Allen had washed our clothes, including our jackets. We dressed for church and went to breakfast but Mr. Allen said that he didn't want us to go to church with them, which was just as well because when they were gone, Mom came over from the hospital and told us that she had decided to forgive our father and she had just called him and he was doing real good in New Mexico. He wanted all of us to go with him. He and Uncle Robert were making a lot of money helping the Indians at a reservation.

Mom was still at the house when the Allens got back from church. She helped Mrs. Allen with dinner. After we ate, Mr. Allen went into his bedroom and brought back a large scrapbook. He placed it on top of the kitchen table. He sat down in front of the book and gave out a great sigh. He took out his reading glasses, the ones he used for the Bible, and wiped them. He stuck the glasses in his mouth and breathed on them, first on one side and then on the other to moisten them, and then he wiped them with his handkerchief. He opened the book and a large yellow-faded piece of newspaper fell to the floor. I picked it up and handed it to him. He thanked me. He adjusted his glasses. The newspaper that I had picked up was dated 1941 and was full of war pictures. Mr. Allen looked at the front page that I had just handed him and he seemed to be reading it to himself. I was sitting next to him and I noticed that he had trimmed his eyebrows. He looked different, like he was missing something at the top of his eyes. He kept looking at the newspaper. Mrs. Allen and Mom had come to sit with us.

"Today is a special day for me," he said, taking off his glasses as he spoke. He looked at his glasses like they were something alive in his hands that he was studying. He turned them one way and then another. "Today is December the seventh," he said. "Eleven years ago the Japanese attacked Pearl Harbor. I was there as a conscientious objector. You know what that means?" He was looking at Richard and me. "It means that I didn't believe in fighting in a war. They took me anyway as a medic, to help the doctors in the military. They took me in when I was forty-five years old." He shook his head. "That wasn't fair, don't you think?"

"Of course it wasn't," Mrs. Allen told him before we could answer. "Why, they weren't even taking younger men. The war hadn't even started then when you went. But it was religion. Pure and simple religion."

"That it was," he said. He looked at the newspaper some more. "They weren't taking men half my age that had any excuse at all. But what can you do now? That's what I try to teach you boys. Do the best you can with what you've got. Pick good friends. You know I had to run off your friends last night." He looked at us for a second and then he remembered his own family. He said, "I don't know why I should expect you two to pay any attention to me when my own children never did." He studied the newspaper some more. "This here's the headline in the newspaper in Hawaii on December the eighth, the day after the attack. Look at the pictures." He passed the newspaper around. He had the scrapbook opened and he started passing out pictures telling us all about that day.

"I always take out these pictures to show people the horrible thing war is. Now we're in another one in Korea. Thank God it looks like it's winding down. Who's to know? That part of the world is a mystery to us. They need the power of Jehovah to help them sort themselves out. Why are we fighting in Korea? I wish I knew."

He had taken out some more photographs and passed them around. One of them showed a dead soldier with his legs missing. "And that's not bad," he said. "I've got other ones I won't even show."

"That he does," Mrs. Allen said.

"Let me have them back," he said. He took up his pictures and his newspaper and put them back into the scrap-book.

Mrs. Allen said, "We really appreciated that, Mr. Allen. Right boys? We always are interested in what you have to say."

"The boys really appreciate seein' somethin' like that...history," Mom said. "They love things like that."

"We sure do," Richard said.

"Don't you, Jim?"

"Yes, Mom," I said.

Mr. Allen got up and took the scrapbook with him and he walked out.

"He always feels a little bad on this day," Mrs. Allen whispered behind her hand. "But it does him some good to take out his pictures. I don't mind," she said, "do you?"

"Oh, no," Mom said, surprised, "and neither do the boys."

Mom looked at us like she would kill us if we said anything. She got up from her seat, "I've got to keep on ironin'. I'm so far behind," she said.

"Mrs. Jackson called yesterday wantin' to know when her iron- in' would be ready. I forgot to tell you."

"I'm through with hers," Mom said. "Is she supposed to call or am I supposed to call her back when it's ready?"

"She said she'd call today. She's in no rush, she said. She was just wonderin'."

"Well, I think I can catch up today," Mom said.

"I think you can too. I was tellin' Mrs. Jackson I've never seen anyone iron as fast as you can. Mr. Allen and I were wondering, where did you learn to iron so fast?"

"When you need to do it you do it," Mom replied.

"Good for you," Mrs. Allen said, like she was proud of Mom.

"Well, I better get to ironin'. It ain't goin' to get done with me standin' and talkin'."

"I'll be in the livin' room," Mrs. Allen said, "that way you can have more room here to iron."

She went into the living room and took the Bible and started to read from it.

"You boys go out and play," Mom said. "Get out of our hair. But," she pointed at our clothes, "you need to get out of your Sunday clothes before you go out and play."

We looked at Mrs. Allen.

"I don't think Mr. Allen needs you all. Your mother's right. Go on out and play."

"Remember that tonight is a school night, boys," Mom said as we walked out after changing. Our jackets were hot from the oven and fit snug again. "I need you two in by seven. And remember I'm sleepin' here tonight so I'll be checkin'."

"Don't be wrasslin' dogs anymore," Mrs. Allen said and we ran out. We could hear Mom asking Mrs. Allen what she was talking about.

We didn't see anyone on the street so we decided to go look up Clarence and Jim and Phil. Richard said that they probably were at Clarence's house. The weather was nice for a change and only the cold remained. We walked toward downtown and at the courthouse we turned right. There was no one outside the courthouse. There was only one car parked at the back and that belonged to the sheriff. From here it was a straight shot up main street to Clarence's. We passed one block from the hospital.

Clarence, Jim and Phil were playing football out front. They stopped when they saw us.

"What are you dumbheads doin' over here?" Clarence asked us. Jim and Phil were laughing, throwing the football to each other.

"Nothin'," Richard said, "just wanted to play."

"We got run off last night by the high and mighty Allens," Clarence said. He looked angry. "Who the shit do they think they are? God almighty?" he answered himself. "They ran us off like you'da run off a pack of goddam dogs. Where were you shit-heads when all this was goin' on?"

"We were in bed," Richard said.

"In bed?" Jim said. He was smiling. He was holding on to the ball.

"Come on, Jim," Phil said, "forget about that and throw me the ball."

"The Allens put us to bed early. We screwed up. They just didn't let us go," Richard said to them.

"And you don't have any say so? They ain't your real mom and dad. How the shit can they tell you what to do. You mean your old lady let's 'em treat you like shit. What kind of shit is that?" Clarence said. He was up close to us. Jim and Phil were playing with the ball.

"Leave 'em alone," Phil said. "Let's forget the whole thing. It didn't amount to a hill of beans."

"It pissed me off royally," Clarence said. He wanted to keep on. "The fuckin' Allens ain't got no right to run my ass off or your ass or your ass," he said, pointing to Jim and Phil. "It just pisses me off, that's all."

"Phil's right," Jim said. "Forget it. Richard and Jimmy ain't big enough to speak up for themselves. And look at it this way. They're eatin' the Allen's food and usin' the Allen's home. What the shit kind of say-so do they have? It would be kind of ass-holey for 'em to demand things."

"Still I'd like to get some kind of apology for what happened last night," Clarence insisted.

"Shit, Clarence, what do you want?" Jim said. "Leave 'em alone."

"I want someone to apologize to me for treatin' me like a fuckin' dog with mange, that's all. Ain't I due some respect from my friends? Aren't we friends or are we?"

We both said yes right away. "Well, ain't you goin' to apologize for the goddam Allens?" Clarence asked.

"I apologize for the Allens," Richard said.

"Well it's about time," Clarence replied. "Those shit-head motherfuckers better not treat me like that anymore or they'll be sorry. I know about that sonofabitch and his holy-roller ways. He's got his pecker in his hand all the time, lookin' for pussy. That's what they say." He looked at us to see what we were thinking. "Can't forget that you all were in bed at seven o'clock at night and missing out on all the fun. And I can't forget that you all didn't even come out and say something about the shitty way we were bein' treated. Shit man it wasn't late. It was just seven. 'No they can't go out,' he said like he was God. 'Get out of here. Get out of my sight.' Like we was some kind of freak."

"All right," Jim said, "they've apologized already. Do you accept the apology?"

"What choice does a man have? When you run around with shit-heads you can expect to get shit on yourself," Clarence said.

"Well shake hands on it," Phil said, "so we can play us some football."

Clarence stuck his big hand out and first Richard and then me shook it. Richard started to walk away and I was following him.

"Where are you guys goin?" Clarence asked.

"We better go on home," Richard said. "My brother and me don't like it when someone is angry with us. We don't like to hang around when things get like this. And besides, we need to get in early. Mom is goin' to be home tonight."

"Goin' home? Don't you want to hear about the carnival?" Clarence said. "Listen guys, I'm sorry if I blew my top. I don't know why but I like you two little shit-heads. No sense in leavin' now. We just now started playin'."

Richard thought about it for a while and then he looked at me. I would do whatever he wanted. "Well, maybe we can stay a little while," he said for both of us.

Clarence and me beat Richard, Jim and Phil something like sixty to twelve, and afterward we sat down and heard about the carnival. The rides and stuff like that was for the birds. It had been a lot better last year and the years before that.

Pete had not set a time when he was going to start the viewings. He had five carnival women lined up to show their thing, including the old Gypsy. He promised that all five had different looking things. That would be enough to give anyone a complete education. He did know that he was going to charge five dollars for each viewing. That left Richard and me out and in a way I was relieved and I'm sure Richard was too. We were just too young to be seeing things like that.

They did tell us that Pete had asked all the boys to check their thumbs. Afterward, when they asked why, he told them that a man with a flat thumb has a short pecker. It may be big around but it's short.

We got back home before seven, ate supper, washed up a little bit and Mom put us to bed and it was a good thing that we had come home early because at around nine or so someone knocked on the door and we could hear that it was the deputy. We could hear my Mom crying and saying, "Oh no! Oh no! Please God, no!" We could hear the Allens asking questions and the deputy answering. Mom kept crying, "Please God, no!"

Our sister Sylvia had taken a turn for the worse, we could hear. She was in real bad shape. We could hear them say some thing about her having a hard time breathing. We heard them leave, the Allens taking mother in the car.

We lay in bed, Richard and me, not moving but looking at each other in the dark. We were lonely and afraid.

CHAPTER 14

I don't remember going to sleep that night. In the morning we couldn't hear a sound. We went into the kitchen and there was no one there, no one in the house. The clock on the wall told us we were late. We ran into the room and as fast as we could we put on our clothes and we ran to school. The streets were deserted. All the children were in school already.

Mrs. Smith just smiled when I ran in out of breath, even though I interrupted her. The girls started to giggle at me. I had forgotten to comb my hair.

I saw Richard at recess and he told me Mrs. Abercrombie hadn't said anything to him for being late. It was a real nervous time for Richard and me. We didn't feel like playing. We just went off to one side and we stood together by the building. We didn't feel like talking. We knew what was in each other's mind.

Right after recess Mrs. Peters came by my room. She looked worried. She called Mrs. Smith over to the door and Mrs. Smith excused herself to us and went to talk to her. They whispered and Mrs. Smith was shaking her head. Mrs. Smith looked at me from the door and said, "Jimmy, you've got to go with Mrs. Peters. Don't forget to take your jacket."

"Yes, ma'am," I replied.

The whole class had stopped what it was doing. I could feel their eyes on me as I gathered my books and put my jacket on. I felt numb and I tried not to look at anyone.

I heard Mrs. Peters say, "Don't take your books, Jimmy. Leave them here."

I stayed in the hall while Mrs. Peters went across to Mrs. Abercrombie's room. Mrs. Peters talked to Mrs. Abercrombie and they called Richard over. He looked at me to see if I knew what was going on. I shrugged my shoulders.

From here we walked back to the office. The deputy was waiting by the secretary's desk. He greeted us and told us we were to go with him to the hospital.

Mrs. Peters went with us and put us in the front seat of the car, the same front seat that my mother had carried Sylvia in. She closed the car door for us. The deputy got in and we drove off. Still no one had said anything. But I guess no one needed to say anything. We could sense it. There was something in the air that told you that something had happened. It was cold and windy and almost a dark day, like a drizzle was about to begin. My hands were cold, so cold. The wind moved the speeding car from side to side.

My sister Sylvia had died.

The deputy kept looking at us and he looked like he wanted to tell us something but didn't know how to begin.

"Is it Sylvia?" Richard finally asked him.

"Is she real sick?" I asked him.

"No," he replied softly, "she's dead. She just now died 'bout an hour ago."

We got out of the car slowly. We didn't want to be there. We were scared. My knees were shaking. We loved Sylvia but we were afraid of her now. Richard and me were afraid of the dead. We walked up the stairs behind the deputy. Inside we saw the Allens and Mom. Mom was sitting between the Allens and Mrs. Allen was hugging her.

"She's in heaven now with God," Mrs. Allen said as she held Mom close to her. "Just think. She'll never suffer again. She's in paradise and experiencing great joy."

Nurse Wilma was walking real fast from Sylvia's old room to the lobby. "Where's the doctor?" she was asking the other nurses.

"He's in the lab," they said and she stopped and went back to the end of the hall.

She came out as fast as she had gone in and she walked over to Mom and held Mom's hand.

Mother was crying real hard. Her face was buried in Mrs. Allen shoulder. She had not seen us yet. Everyone was trying to help her.

Nurse Wilma said, "There, there, Christie, you've got to stop crying. It's not good for you to carry on like this."

Mom looked up to see Nurse Wilma and she saw us. "She's dead!" she yelled at Richard and me. I don't know about Richard but I felt like running away. Even Mom scared me. She didn't look like Mom. She looked like an old woman.

"She's dead! She's dead!" she screamed over and over again. She was trying hard to make herself believe what had happened. "She died in my arms...in my arms." She looked at her arms like she couldn't believe it.

Like her, I was hoping that this was all a nightmare, that Richard would wake me up and it was all a lie and then I could tell him what a dream I had.

"My little angel died in my arms!" she cried. "She suffered so much. Why couldn't you have done somethin' to help her with the pain? She was in so much pain." She looked over to us and she started wailing again.

"We did all we could," Nurse Wilma replied.

"Come over here, Jimmy and Richard," she cried as she opened her arms. "Let me hold both of you. You're the only thing I have now. Come over here, please, please!"

Richard and me didn't want to go but Mr. Allen was waving at us telling us to go over to Mom. She held us tightly and she cried over us. "You're the only thing I have left. The only thing," she cried.

The doctor appeared. He had come out of the lab and was in the hall. This was the first time Richard and me had ever seen him. He came over to Mom and knelt down, putting his arm around her. "Mrs. Jones, I'm awfully sorry," he said. It looked like he had been crying too. He was fat and looked like he had a hard time breathing.

My mother cried softly on his shoulder. "My little angel is dead," she said.

"But she's in heaven," Mrs. Allen insisted.

"I don't want her in heaven," Mom yelled. "I want her here with me...What happened? I thought she was supposed to come home. I thought she was goin' to be all right. I can't understand it. I just can't believe it. Did everyone make a mistake? Doctor? Didn't you know this was goin' to happen?"

Mom was looking down at the floor, more or less quiet, giving out a sigh now and then. She was chewing on her handkerchief. She looked stunned. She wouldn't blink. We were all quiet letting Mom think about what had happened. Richard and me were sitting on each side of her. Mrs. Allen was sitting by Richard. Nurse Wilma was sitting next to me. She had her arm around me. The doctor was standing in front of Mom, embarrassed, trying to figure out how to get away. He hugged Mom one more time. He spoke into her ear. "All I can say, Christie, is that I tried as hard as I could." He backed off. "She took a turn for the worse suddenly. There was no way to predict that. I felt like she was making excellent progress. If we had known, we would have moved her to Lubbock where they have an iron lung. But even then...Who knows? I'll talk to you later. I've got to go." He went down the hall and into the lab.

"Dr. Morgan really took it hard. He's a good doctor. He loved Sylvia," Nurse Wilma said, like she was talking to herself, looking at the wall. She was rubbing my back as she spoke. "How are you boys doin'? Are you two feelin' all right?"

"Yeah," Richard said. "Just a little scared."

A young couple came in, the father carrying the sick child, a little girl with dark hair. Her eyes were rolled up into her head.

"Where does it hurt?" the nurse asked the child, but she couldn't answer. She couldn't hold her head up.

"She was awfully fretful all night long and this mornin' she woke up like this," the mother said.

Nurse Wilma had gotten up from where she was sitting next to me and went and placed her hand on the child's forehead. "She's awfully hot," she told the other nurses. "Go ahead and put her in Room One. I'll go get Dr. Morgan." She walked into the lab and we could hear her talking to the doctor.

The sick child had made my mother stop crying. She was staring at the young couple, shaking her head. "She reminds me of Sylvia when Sylvia was that age," Mom said. "I hope she's not too sick. Poor baby."

"She's goin' to be all right," Mrs. Allen replied.

Nurse Wilma and the doctor came out of the lab and the doctor went into the room where they had placed the child. Nurse Wilma walked over to where we were. She talked to Mr. Allen. "Why don't you go ahead and take Christie on home along with the boys? They're goin' to need a lot of rest before the funeral."

Mr. Allen got up and Mrs. Allen helped Mom. Once they were walking, Richard and me got up from our chairs and we followed behind. Just then Mom started to scream again about Sylvia and the Allens held her up as she tried to collapse. They dragged her out of the hospital and into the car. The nurses were shaking their heads. Mom was screaming that she wanted to go back to see Sylvia one more time. Richard and me were scared again when we realized Sylvia was still there in the hospital, dead. "She's dead," Mr. Allen said, getting in the car. "Can't you understand that?"

The wind had picked up a steady cold drizzle making it hard to see from inside the small car. The windshield wipers were mixing the drizzle with the old dust and they were churning the mud in streaks across the windshield. Mr. Allen stopped the car and got out and cleaned the windshield with a red shop-rag he always kept under the driver's seat. He got back in and threw the rag under the seat and we kept on, slowly covering the ground back to the house. Mom looked like she was going to be quiet. She was sitting in the back between Richard and me. She was staring at the floorboard, chewing on the handkerchief, like she had done at the hospital.

"Don't forget to remind me that that rag is dirty," Mr. Allen said to Mrs. Allen.

When we got home we all sat in the living room to talk because the Allens wanted to find out who needed to be called about Sylvia's death. Mom was sitting off to herself in the corner chair. Richard and me were sitting on the sofa with the Allens. We were still scared of Mom. No telling when she would start screaming again. Mom was thinking. She spoke softly. "You need to call my mother in Corpus, my husband in Artesia, New Mexico, or if you can't get 'im, talk to his brother Robert or his wife Betty. They're all living together in Artesia." She thought a moment and then she got up and went toward her room. "I'll get the names and phone numbers for you. I really appreciate this. I don't know if I could do any callin' right now in the shape I'm in."

Mrs. Allen got up and she said she was going to fix something to eat for all of us. That would make us feel better. She went into the kitchen.

Mr. Allen went into Mom's room and we could hear them talking. He came out with a paper with the names and phone numbers on it. "You boys take out the Bible and read it while Mrs. Allen cooks something and I do the callin'. Your Mom's goin' to bed for a little while. She hasn't slept all night long." He acted like he had thought of something. "Think I'll call the hospital and have Nurse Wilma get us some sleeping pills for your Mom." He picked up the little telephone book and looked up the number. He dialed and waited for it to ring. He asked for Wilma and he waited.

"Wilma?...Yes...Fine...Fine...Fine...Fine...I tell you fine. They're doin' fine...She's in bed but I don't think she can sleep...That's what I was callin' about...Sure...Sure...Oh, sure...I know about those things. Remember I was a medic in the army...Well, it's been a long time. People forget. I know about those things...I'll be careful...Yes...I can come...Okay...If... that's what you want...Well, call Dr. Morgan first...Yes...Send them over?...You sure?...That's fine with me. Keeps me from drivin' in this weather...Listen, thank you...Oh, it's the least I can do."

He put the phone down and looked at the piece of paper that Mom had given him. He studied it for a while and then he picked up the phone again and dialed. "I'm callin' your grandmother," he told us. Richard and me looked up from the Bible to watch what he was doing. He talked to the operator and she let the call go through. He let the phone ring for a while and then he set it down. "No answer," he said. He dialed again. "Now I'm callin' your father in Artesia." He spoke to the operator and she had to re-dial for him. He stood with the phone by his ear, tapping his foot.

"Yes," he said, "Operator, I'd like to speak with a Mr. Jim Jones...Well, where is he?...uh huh...Can I reach 'im there?... Well, how do you get hold of 'im when you have an emergency?... Well, we need to...That's not what I want. I need to talk to 'im right away...Yes...Yes..." Mr. Allen was looking at us and shaking his head. "It's your Aunt Betty," he whispered. Then his attention was directed to the telephone. "Yes...I know your name is Betty...They're staying here with us... Allen... No, that's my last name...They're here...They've been here for almost a month...Well it's bad news...Sylvia...Yes, she was very sick... No. It's her I'm callin' about...I'm afraid so. Yes...At about ten thirty this morning...Christie's all right. She's takin' it very hard. We're tryin' to see if we can get her some sleeping pills...Will you tell 'im?...The funeral? Probably Wednesday... Well I'm sure she'll understand."

He put the telephone down and sat on the sofa with us. "They can't get hold of your father. He's livin' with the Indians and he doesn't come home except on Friday. They're goin' to try but they don't think they'll be able to get hold of 'im before the funeral. Your Aunt Betty says he probably can't make it since he's had all the trouble with the law and all and your Aunt Betty says she can't make it on such short notice. Your Uncle Robert's livin' with your father. So I guess that's it. I can't get hold of your grandmother. But I'll try later on."

The deputy arrived with the sleeping pills. He came in like he was intruding, very slowly, with his hat in his hand and asked how Mom was doing. You could tell the weather was bad. He was wearing a rain-coat that was muddy and wet. His boots were sprinkled with snow. Mom was in her room crying but we could barely hear her. Mrs. Allen took the pills and went into the kitchen and got a glass of water. He went into Mother's room.

That night we cried for the first time, not much because then we got scared again, scared that Sylvia would appear to us as a ghost. We could hear Mom crying and even though we were scared we felt sorry for her. My brother Richard repeated what he had said many times before. He said that he would kill our father some day. He believed my sister's death was somehow connected with his bringing us to this place. He started thinking about it a lot and at night I could hear him cracking his knuckles, all five at the same time. He wouldn't go to sleep even though I told him I was going to tell my mother but he said that my mother had enough problems to think about without having to put up with us. And he was right. So I let him think about what he was going to do and after a few days he had a normal sleep and he sighed and stretched in the morning like he always did and he kept me in suspense until he let out some kind of fart, never the same one twice. I swear, he was good at that and he made me laugh, although I didn't feel like laughing for a long time.

But I knew Richard and I knew that he didn't forgive. I knew that no matter how normal he acted he still had a plan in back of his mind.

Mr. Allen tried calling our grandmother all the rest of the day but he could not get her. Finally on Tuesday morning he talked to her. She was in shock. But she said she was in no condition to travel by bus such a long distance on such short notice. There was no way she could make it for a funeral on Wednesday. Would she make it if the funeral was on Thursday? No. She was having lots of trouble with her health. She would write a letter to Mom. Then she got angry because she had not been told that Sylvia had been sick. She had had no warning. What were they doing in Tahoka, so far away from home? Where was Tahoka, really? What kind of daughter had she raised that wouldn't pick up a telephone and call to tell her mother that her grandchild was sick? Mr. Allen didn't argue with her. He just kept answering as best as he could.

Mom slept all day Tuesday but at night we could hear her throwing things in her room.

CHAPTER 15

On Tuesday Mr. Allen went to pick up a dress for Sylvia from one of the church members and when he came back from the funeral home after he had delivered it he said that there would not be a wake in his home. Sylvia was to stay at the funeral home. So that night Mr. Allen read from the Bible more to us than he normally read and he tried explaining to us the mystery of death and why it's got to be. Richard and me didn't understand. It was too complicated. I couldn't understand how Christ died for my sins when I wasn't even born yet. Once in a while he'd look up from the Bible and catch us day-dreaming and he would clear his throat and fix us with a great stare to get our attention and then he would keep on reading.

"This is for your benefit," he said. "To tide you over your days of grief."

Mr. Allen had also brought with him some clothes for us to wear to the funeral. There were two black suits, two raincoats, two caps, two white shirts, and two ties. Mrs. Allen had had us try the clothes on and she measured and she tried to fit them to us. She was not a good seamstress.

On the morning of the funeral she came into our room while we were still in bed and she placed the clothes on the chair. Everyone dressed quietly. Outside, we could hear the gentle noise of the wind and the drizzling rain as we sat at the kitchen table and drank coffee. No one was hungry so no breakfast was made. Mr. Allen slurped his coffee for the last time and pulled back from the table. "Well," he said looking at his watch, "it's time to go. You'd better go get your raincoats."

Waiting for everyone else, I looked out of the window in our room and I could see the sleeting rain, Mr. Allen's car, the neighbor's house across the fence, its four windows on the side covered with ice. Everything looked unreal, like I had never seen it before.

When we got to the funeral home Mr. Allen got out and opened the back

door of the car for us. I could tell that my mother did not want to go inside
to see my sister Sylvia. I could tell Richard didn't want to go. I didn't want
to go either but the Allens prodded us into the small building and there right
as we walked in, against the wall, was Sylvia in a little coffin that looked like
brushed cotton on the outside, like a play coffin. She looked like she was
asleep, looked a lot like her but the shock of seeing her dead was too much.
I kept shaking my head and Richard kept shaking his head and my mother
was shaking her head like all three of us just couldn't believe it. That was
what it was. It was impossible to believe.

The Allens were behind us looking over our shoulders at Sylvia.

They had dressed her in a light blue dress, the one that Mr. Allen had taken
over to the funeral home. It had a white lace collar and her hands were clasped
together just beneath her tiny breasts. She had a white celluloid belt with a
silver-plated buckle. Around her head the embalmer had placed a wreath of
small white buds, flowers that were about to bloom but never would, I
suppose, just like my sister Sylvia.

My mother started to cry after a short while and she stroked my sister
Sylvia's head and called her her little baby girl and she kept sobbing and
shaking her head. She wanted us to touch her and my brother Richard touched
her first and then I touched her and she felt so cold and very hard like she
was made of clay. We were scared. I was afraid she would jump up and grab
us.

Afterwards, my mother said we could go out if we wanted to. There was
no place to sit inside for all of us. We left Mom there with the Allens and we
sat on the porch to get away from the drizzle. Across the street a man was
trying to start his car until the battery gave out. He went back inside and
slammed the door. We could hear him screaming.

The deputy drove up slowly and stopped in front of the mortuary. He got
out and walked over to where we were sitting. "How you boys doin?" he
asked as he walked by, clumps of ice and mud falling off the side of his boots.
He stomped on the boards and cleaned off the boots on the mat just outside
the door.

"Fine," Richard said as the deputy opened the door and went inside.

We were at the grave standing in front of the wet coffin. Richard and me
were standing on each side of Mom. Mr. Allen was by Richard and Mrs.
Allen was standing next to me. Mrs. Allen was crying a little. Mr. Allen never

did cry. Across the coffin was Mrs. Smith, my teacher, and her husband and Mrs. Abercrombie and her husband. Mrs. Peters was there with them but alone. The deputy had led the way to the cemetery from the funeral home and he was standing behind us in a yellow raincoat leaning on his car, like he wanted no part of this. Just as the preacher was about to begin we heard a car drive up behind us and two doors slammed shut. We could hear two people running. It was Nurse Wilma and Doctor Morgan.

The preacher was Reverend Anderson, the Allen's regular minister who used to come over from Lubbock to preach, the same one we saw on Sundays when we went to church. He was pretty good at preaching. He was dressed in a black suit and a black raincoat and a black hat. He was a tall thin man with a very deep voice and a large Adam's apple. He scared us just to hear him talk. His eyes were almost black and he seemed to look right through you when he looked at you, like you couldn't lie to him without his knowing it. He had a real strange laugh, like a monster in the movies. He had large thick eyebrows and a small patch of dark hair growing on the edge of both ears.

He started the ceremony with a psalm from the Bible. After the psalm he closed the Bible and he spoke about my sister Sylvia and all he had been told about her, how she had suffered and he went on about her life on earth and how God chose to call her to Him. "As surely as He will call all of us here present," he reminded us. He spoke of the glory of God and how God had a plan for everyone, but I guess I never could understand the "ways of the Lord," as the Allens called it. It just didn't seem fair to me, not if God had all that power.

At the end he said the Lord's Prayer for Sylvia and he said one for the next one of us present who was to die.

My mother was crying softly. The words from the preacher were too much for her. Mrs. Allen got between Mom and me and stood next to her to help support her. The preacher bent down and grabbed a handful of fresh dirt that had been covered from the drizzle and spread it over the coffin and he said, "Ashes to ashes and dust to dust, says the Lord, Jehovah." The man from the funeral home came over and lowered the coffin. The sudden jolt that the coffin made as it began to go down startled my mother and she gave out a little scream. She tried to fall but Mrs. Allen was holding her up. Nurse Wilma came to help Mrs. Allen. I was trying not to cry. I couldn't see Richard. I looked across the coffin as it was lowering and everyone was crying.

The coffin disappeared from my view but the straps that were slowly lowering it kept unwinding with a squeaky noise. Finally the coffin stopped and the funeral man had us each, starting with Mom, reach under the cover and grab a handful of dirt to throw on the coffin. I could see the coffin deep down at the bottom of the hole as I passed by. This is where my sister Sylvia would stay forever, in a pauper's grave.

CHAPTER 16

(I built a dream about Mitzi where she and I ran through a field of bluebonnets. You could hear her laugh throughout the field. I could see her hardened legs with their powerful muscles, like plates of steel, as her skirt moved up higher and higher the harder she ran. She was like an animal pounding the flowers beneath her. She breathed to the rhythm of her legs. I was a big man in the dream, six feet, much larger than Clarence. I was able to keep up with her but knowing the view would be better from the rear I stayed behind her, acting like I couldn't catch her, adoring her body—her panty covered buttocks—as it sliced through the beautiful flowers. She laughed out loud and looked back to me, begging me to hurry up and run by her side, hand in hand. We got to a tree, breathless, and we sat down to rest. She kissed me and I kissed her. We held each other close and she asked to be kissed again. As we embraced I slowly placed my hand in the front of her neck and then I slid my hand downward. I brushed her left breast through her dress and she did not object. She let out a small sigh through our kiss. I touched her right breast lightly. Again no complaint. I gently let my hand slide inside her dress and I had all of her left breast in my hand. I squeezed it gently toward the nipple and the breast seemed to have a life of its own. It moved even after I had stopped stroking, like the fur on a cat. I unbuttoned the front of the dress with my free hand. I was not about to let go of the breast. The breast in my hand was exposed. As I looked down while holding our kiss I could see the other breast about to break out, free itself from the dress. For the first time I noticed that she did not have a brassiere!)

(As we lay in bed in the dark I must have let out a sigh or two without knowing it. Richard knew what I was doing. He needed to interrupt the dream, to destroy it. He farted, not the little one, the big one, the one he called the block-buster.)

It had been a week since Sylvia's funeral. My mother was working very hard. She was ironing from morning till night. The deputy had been coming over every day to check on Mom. And some times the sheriff had come over. The deputy especially had made it a point to let us know that if there was anything Mom needed that we should let him know. Mrs. Allen didn't like that. She felt that it was not proper for him to be calling all the time. He was married, she said. What would his wife think if she knew he was calling on Mom? What would Dad say? Mom brushed the whole thing off. "He's just trying to be nice," she said. "I think he loves the boys."

Mrs. Allen laughed at that. "You've got to be kidding," she said.

"When is school out, anyway?" Mom asked. She was ironing her way through a pile of clothes on the floor.

"Friday, the nineteenth," I said. "Then we're off till January the fifth."

"That's a long time if you ask me," Mr. Allen said. "When I was going to school we never had such foolishness. You went to school and that was it. Looks like to me that nowadays you go to school to see how many days you can get off. They're not educating the children anymore."

Mrs. Allen was in the kitchen fixing supper and every once in a while she would come to the door to ask Mr. Allen what he had said.

"I said that they're takin' too many days off from school nowadays. It's just not like it used to be when we were in school."

"I don't know," Mrs. Allen replied, "it seems to me that it's always been the same. It's just that you don't remember. It's been so long." She looked at Mr. Allen and her mouth tightened up into a straight line. "Are you goin' out tonight?" she asked him.

"Tonight?"

"Yes. Today is Wednesday."

Mr. Allen acted like it was a complete surprise to him. "I had forgotten all about it," he said. He got up and called his friend Mr. Hendricks and spoke to him. Yes, they decided by the end of the conversation, they would meet. Mr. Allen seemed excited. It was all a sham. He had planned to go out all along.

He put the phone down. "I've got to go tonight," he said to Mrs. Allen, who had been waiting by the door. "Hendricks says the church really needs to be cleaned up since I missed last Wednesday."

Mrs. Allen gave out a little cry and she put her apron to her scaly face and fled into the kitchen. Mom looked at us like she didn't understand what was going on. She laid the iron down and walked into the kitchen. Mr. Allen got up and went to his room. As she went by us sitting on the couch Mom said, "Don't you boys have somethin' to do? Play? Anythin'? Just get out of here. Get out of people's way."

Richard and me didn't think twice. We ran out as fast as we could and headed for Clarence's house.

I swear to God on a stack of Bibles that we did not tell Clarence or Jim or Phil anything about Mr. Allen, especially Clarence. But one time when Madge the waitress asked us if it was true that Mr. Allen was going out on his wife I came to understand that a lot of people in town knew about him or suspected him. The guys knew there was something going on. There had been talk for a long time, years, before we got to Tahoka. The guys were there when Madge asked. But they didn't know exactly what it was because they had not followed him like Richard and me had done. I only hoped that Clarence would never find out.

What brought all this up was that Clarence had started on the Allens again. He was still sore because the Allens had run them off that night when we were supposed to go to the carnival. But the real reason Clarence was angry all over again with the Allens was because Mr. Allen had told us not to pass out "The Watchtower" in the trashy part of town. He gave us the exact borders and he informed us that, "those people aren't worth saving." Well, that's where Clarence and Jim and Phil lived. And to Clarence that was like being called white trash. Richard had made the mistake of telling Clarence and the guys what Mr. Allen had said. Mr. Allen had branded them white trash. He'd never forget that, Clarence said. We were trying to calm him down.

"Leave 'em alone," Phil said. "They didn't do us no harm. Just ran us off, that's all. And called us white trash. Lots of people have called me white trash. No sense gettin' worked up about it."

"It may not piss any of you guys off but it sure does me." Clarence said. "That's the second time he farts me off. That ain't fair. First he runs us off and then he calls us trash. 'They ain't worth savin,' the sonofabitch says. Fuck, he ain't worth savin' as far as I'm concerned. Piss-head."

"Knock it off," Jim said. "Can't you see you're workin' yourself into a lather and it ain't doin' you any good. You're acting like a half-fucked goose in a hen house."

Clarence broke the stick he was playing with in half and threw one of the halves as far as he could. We were all sitting on the steps leading to the front door of his house. Clarence was thinking. "Quiet you guys," he said when Phil started to say something. "Can't you shitheads see I'm thinkin'." He broke the remaining stick in half and threw that half across the yard. He kept doing that until he wound up with a piece of stick about an inch long that he couldn't break anymore. Still he was thinking. Jim and Phil got up and Clarence didn't notice. Richard and me got up and he didn't even say a word either. We left him thinking.

That night after supper Richard and me went to bed. I played the harmonica real quietly under the quilts for him and we talked about things, mostly girls and then almost all about Mitzi. Richard gave me advice and I listened very carefully. We fell asleep after I put up my harmonica. At around ten or eleven we woke up with the sound of Mr. Allen's car coming into the drive way. There was something about the way he had driven in that made us wake up. It must have been that he drove in faster, in danger. The little car slid along the driveway as he braked it to a stop right before he hit the chicken coop. We heard him slam the car door shut and run from the car and into the house. If we had seen his face it would have been as white as a ghost. We could hear him rush about the house. He took a long time in the bathroom. When he came out he hurried to the kitchen and we could hear him running water for a long time. Mrs. Allen had gotten up. We could hear her shuffle her house-shoes on the hardwood floors as she walked around behind him asking questions.

"Shut up!" he yelled. "Can't you see I'm hurt?"

We heard Mrs. Allen's voice like a mumble.

"I told you to shut up!" he screamed. "It's none of your business! Nothing that I do is any of your business! Do you understand?"

We could hear Mrs. Allen crying and I was sure Mom could hear her too.

"Get away from me you old scaly hag," he screamed. "Can't you see you make me sick?"

She was really crying now, like a little baby. Maybe even the neighbors could hear her.

The Allens were not there for breakfast. Mom cooked for us. She looked worried. We ate fast and hurried on to school. At the corner the guys were waiting. They had a smile on their faces. This is the story they told us:

Last night Clarence, Jim and Phil followed Mr. Allen to the church. They were supposed to throw a pack of firecrackers inside the church and run. The only problem was that their matches wouldn't light. They messed around until they had to hide under the church and were listening to Mr. Allen and Mr. Hendricks talk. They waited until Mr. Hendricks left and were waiting for Mr. Allen to leave but he wouldn't. They figured that Mr. Allen was up to something, just like we had. They waited long enough and Mr. Allen did the same thing he had done before when we were there. He left the church and got in his car and drove to the side street and he parked behind the empty buildings. Then a woman showed up and went to the rear of the church and went in. Mr. Allen was hiding behind the tree across the street. He sneaked to the church from across the street and went in. They started to do it right above Clarence and Jim and Phil, right on the floor. Clarence took out his matches again. On the last match he was successful. He was able to make it light. Everybody got ready to run. He lit the pack of fire crackers and by that time Jim and Phil had gotten out and were running. He threw the firecrackers right under Mr. Allen and his own mother and he crawled out and ran as fast as he could. Jim and Phil yelled at him. They were waiting for him by the tree across from the church. The three watched as the firecrackers went off and they could hear the commotion inside the church as Mr. Allen and Clarence's mom ran and fumbled around looking for their clothes. Clarence's mom was the first to come out, dressing as she climbed down the stairs. She ran across the church yard. All they said they saw was a fast running shadow as she streaked toward town. She was dressed in black with a black overcoat that she held up over her head. She hadn't had time to put it on. God only knows if anyone recognized her. For sure Clarence had not. Mr. Allen ran out right after her and he ran across the street, jumped the hedges, ran across the empty lot, went behind the buildings where he had hidden his car and got in and sped off.

"He was really huffin' and puffin' when he went by," Jim said.

"He was pickin' 'em up and layin' 'em down. That's for sure," Phil said.

"That oughta teach the sonofabitch not to call us white trash," Clarence said as we walked to school.

Two days before Christmas, as sad as she was, my mother went out and bought us Christmas presents and hid them in her room. She was trying to do the things for Christmas that she always did before. That night we could hear her cutting wrapping paper to wrap our gifts.

The Allens were still angry at each other. But each day you could see that they talked more and more. By Christmas they would be all right. They were too old to stay angry. Mr. Allen was slowly getting over his bruises but his limp was still there. Mrs. Allen wanted to rub him down every night even though her heart was broken. Whether she did it to see where the bruises were or because she felt sorry for him I never could figure out. "How in the world did you get hurt there?" Richard and me heard her ask him as we sneaked by the door. The chickens were back to laying again and the pig was eating, both had settled down now and did not over-react when Mr. Allen drove in.

Richard and me had been trying hard to stay out of trouble during Christmas vacation so that Mom didn't have to worry.

One day we all went to the little grocery store and talked to the old man. He was happy to see us and he knew exactly who Clarence and Jim and Phil were. He knew their parents and all that. He had a memory like an elephant. He did not say too much about Clarence though. When he came to Clarence he kind of trailed off like he knew he had put his foot in his mouth. Clarence acted like he hadn't heard. The old man said that he knew about Sylvia and he was sorry. We bought our stuff with Clarence's money and when we got out we noticed that Richard had stolen candy from the old man. Clarence and Jim took it away from him and were fighting over it. Later that night Richard came up with a two-bladed pocket knife, a yellow-handled one, that he hid in the room. I didn't know at that time where it came from and I sure wasn't going to get involved by finding out. I was pretty sure it had been stolen. It couldn't have belonged to the groceryman. I was hoping so anyway. He said he had found it at the carnival. But I could tell he was lying. I think that he had had it hidden for a while.

Even though we tried not to get in trouble, temptation was there all the time, it seemed. If it wasn't Richard, it was in the form of Clarence, Jim, and Phil.

They had come over on Christmas Eve and invited us to go to the carnival with them. They insisted on going in with us to get permission from Mom, just to bug the Allens. So we all had to go inside the house to ask Mom. My mother said it was all right with her if we went as long as we behaved ourselves and didn't get into any trouble and didn't spend any money. Mr.

Allen looked at Clarence and Jim and Phil and then he looked away, back to his newspaper, like he had seen someone nasty. They grinned, walked over to him and shook his hand, very formal-like. They also shook Mrs. Allen's hand and then they went over to Mom and shook her hand too, grinning all the time.

"You sure have a nice house here," Clarence told Mrs. Allen and she was thrilled at how nice our friends really were.

"You're so dear for saying so," Mrs. Allen said. "All of you are so well behaved. I'm glad that Jim and Richard have you all for friends."

"Be sure and button your jackets and wear your caps," Mom said as we left.

Outside the sun had set and the wind was beginning to get very cold. It had not rained since the funeral and the wind had dried the land and it was getting dusty again. Even with this weather, the carnival would be full. There wasn't anything else to do in this town.

As we came closer and closer we could see a huge cloud of dust rising above the yellow carnival lights and a crowd of people running toward us. Clarence stopped us as he silently studied the mass of people running away from the carnival. He looked like a dog sniffing out danger. "There's some kind of trouble at the carnival," he said and pretty soon some men and women and children all bundled up against the cold were running by us and screaming something about a fight.

"Let's go!" Clarence shouted and Jim and Phil and Richard and me ran toward the carnival. Clarence was shouting at us as we passed the crowd running in the opposite direction. "There's a big fight goin' on," he whooped and I was scared. I could feel the hair on the back of my neck stand up. The other three, Jim and Phil and my brother Richard, seemed to be enjoying this but I wasn't, so I stayed behind, going slower and slower. Soon they had left me behind and as I walked slowly toward the carnival in the howling cold wind I could see them disappear as they turned right at the entrance to the carnival. By this time most of the crowd had disappeared and as I walked up to the entrance, just to the left and not ten feet away, I caught a glimpse of a man as he staggered toward me. His face was covered with blood and dust. And still the blood came. It was running from the top of his head down his forehead, over his eye-brows and down his face. I could not see his eyes. He was reaching his hand out for my help, making a gurgling sound. Once more

I could feel my hair stand on end. The skin on my back was crawling. My legs felt like giving out on me. He kept reaching for me, staggering as if he were about to fall on top of me. I was paralyzed. Then, when he lowered his head I saw something terrible, horrible. Someone had hit this man on the head with a claw-hammer and the claw was still embedded on the back of his head like a tomahawk. He began to fall over me. Finally, scared and screaming, I jumped backward and I knew that I could move. I ran! I ran as fast as I could without looking back. At times it felt like he was catching up to me. I imagined I could hear his foot-steps right behind me.

I caught up with Richard and the rest of the guys at the other end of the carnival and they asked me if I had seen a ghost. I looked bad, I guess. I felt bad too. I looked back and I couldn't see the injured man anymore. I had just imagined that he was after me. I told them what had happened to me and Clarence said that everyone seemed to be gone and that we better leave before the sheriff got there. So we ran as fast as we could and we took a short-cut through the darkened part of the carnival where the Gypsies had their trailers. I tripped on some kind of cable and fell on my face and I felt numb, like it hurt me so much it didn't hurt. Richard saw me fall and he stopped and came back to help. "Are you hurt?" he asked, whispering. The guys stopped running. They waited to see how seriously hurt I was. We were in the middle of the trailers. Gypsies were running in and out carrying stuff. They were trying to hide before the sheriff got there. I wanted to cry but with all the guys there I couldn't. With Richard's help I got up limping. I felt my face and I was okay. Clarence checked me over real quick and said I wasn't hurt. "I ain't ever seen a piss-ant get hurt yet," he said. We all started to giggle but we had to get out of there fast. No telling what the Gypsies would do to us if they found us there.

We were too late. Here came the law. The deputy and the sheriff were speeding toward the carnival. The red and white lights on the top of the car were spinning as fast as the deputy could make them go. The siren was blaring. They were coming right through the middle of the carnival. The deputy slammed on the brakes and the car skidded sideways toward Pete's trailer covering it with a cloud of dust. We hid in the dark to see what was happening.

The deputy and the sheriff jumped out of the car. They looked angry, like they meant business. They ran to the trailer and the deputy knocked on the door as the sheriff waited impatiently. He was tapping his revolver. The deputy had his holster strap undone and his hand on the butt of his pistol. When no one answered, the deputy began to curse. The sheriff, big and fat as he was, pushed him out of the way and he kicked the door hard and it flew open with a crash. The deputy shined his light inside. We could see Pete standing against the corner of the small trailer holding his hands up.

"Are you the sonuvabitch that started the fight?" the sheriff asked him. He didn't wait for an answer; he grabbed Pete by the neck and slapped him hard. We could hear the slap all the way outside, like a crack of a whip. "Are you the sonuvabitch that started the fight?" he asked him again. Again no answer and the sheriff slapped him again and knocked him down on the bed. Pete bounced a few times on the mattress. "Are you the sonuvabitch that started the fight?" the sheriff asked him again and slammed his fist at Pete as Pete curled up into a small ball on the bed. He grabbed Pete by the hair and threw him at the deputy and the deputy slapped him back to the sheriff. "Are you the sonuvabitch that started the fight?" the sheriff kept asking and Pete wouldn't talk. His face was becoming a bloody mess. They had cut his upper lip, his nose was bleeding, his right eyebrow was cut. His right eye was swelling shut. They were bouncing him around the trailer. Finally they handcuffed him and sat him down.

"It wasn't my fault," Pete cried and begged.

"What do you mean, it wasn't your fault?" the sheriff said. "Here you come into this nice, peaceful town and you take people's money by robbin' 'em with your crooked games and you say it ain't your fault? You'd better be prepared to tell the Judge another story. You're goin' to jail tonight for the time bein'. We ain't about to disturb the Judge on Christmas Eve."

Pete cried, "He was gamblin' without any money."

"That don't mean shit to me," the sheriff said.

"Tell it to the Judge one of these days," the deputy said.

They both grabbed him and picked him up like a little rag doll and they threw him out across the door. He fell on the ground. He was going round and round on his butt and could not get up with his hands cuffed behind his back. They helped him up and threw him into the deputy's car, the same one Richard and me had ridden in, and they took off. As they did, they shined the lights on us. The deputy stopped the car. The sheriff lowered the window and yelled at us on that cold windy December night for us to go home and stay there.

Clarence was the first to run and in a panic we all ran after him. I was left behind and as we ran in single file, Clarence about a block ahead of me and everyone else in between, we passed the injured man, the one with the claw-hammer embedded in his head as he staggered home, and when I saw him again he looked at me like he wanted me to help him again. I swear I felt like running so fast that no one in the world could have caught me.

On and on we ran into the teeth of the cold blowing wind. At main street I could see that Clarence and Jim and Phil took a left. They were running home. Richard kept on running straight. I was going with Richard. We were going home.

We burst into the house. My mother was up and she asked us what had happened and when we told her she said that we would be the death of her yet. She was glad the Allens were asleep and were not there to hear what had happened to us.

That night I noticed for the first time that I had lost my harmonica. I was trying to remember the last time I played it. Richard said he couldn't remember. Then I started thinking that I hadn't seen it in a while, at least two or three days. It wasn't under the mattress. It was nowhere to be found.

We bundled up finally after looking for the harmonica and not finding it and we got close to each other to stay warm. It had been a strange kind of Christmas Eve. Richard was jerking as he fell asleep. That night I dreamed of the man with the claw- hammer stuck to his skull and he kept running after me in a dark street. But instead of the hammer he had my harmonica sticking out of his head and every time he moved the harmonica would make a sound. The faster I ran, the faster he ran.

CHAPTER 17

In the morning Richard came back from the bathroom, yawning. His pajamas were old ones that used to belong to Mr. Allen and he had to hold them up at the waist when he stood up. He said that everyone was up already and Mom wanted us to get dressed.

Mom and the Allens were already at the table when we got there. Mrs. Allen got up and began to clean the turkey Mr. Allen had killed the day before. Mr. Allen was reading the newspaper still drinking his cup of coffee. It had been about a week and his bruises were almost gone but not his limp. Mrs. Allen looked to be in very good spirits. Mom finished eating quietly and started cooking breakfast for us.

"Isn't this a beautiful day?" Mrs. Allen said. She was washing the inside of the turkey with running water. "This is a special day for all of us that love Christ."

"Amen," Mr. Allen said, and he looked at us. Then he asked, "Were you two in trouble last night? I heard you all running into the house like someone was chasing you."

Mom answered for us. "They said that there was a big fight at the carnival last night. A man was hurt real bad. The carnival men ganged up on 'im and beat 'im up bad. They hit 'im on the head with a hammer and Jim and Richard were tellin' me last night that the man had the hammer still stuck inside his head and was running home like that."

"Is that right, boys?" he asked, eyeing us with suspicion. Lately he didn't want to believe what we said.

We stopped chewing and answered, "Yes sir."

"These are the people that will never enjoy heaven on earth. You know how I've told you about heaven on earth, don't you? And even though Judgment Day is one thousand years long these same people will never repent in time. At the end of the one thousand years, on that last day, when Jehovah shows himself to all of us and when his one-hundred-and-forty-four thousand faithful witnesses come to us, there will still be people like the ones you all saw last night. They will not be given another chance. They will be destroyed!" He stared at us for a long time. His voice failed him as he tried to talk. He swallowed and cleared his throat. "And you two are heading in the same direction. No purpose. No discipline. No religion, except what little I can force into the two of you. Mark my word," he said and he seemed to stare a hole into us, "one of you or both will end up in jail. Still, even now, there is a golden opportunity for heaven on earth if only you would take it."

Mrs. Allen shook the water out of the turkey and placed it on the counter and began to dry it off, inside and out, with a cloth. She was more gentle as she said, "I've told you children much the same thing time and time again." She was patting the turkey like she would powder her face.

"Goodness knows I've tried," Mom said, crying. "Goodness knows things have gone badly for me."

"They take after their father, that's why," Mrs. Allen said. "No amount of trying is going to change them. I don't think it's your fault, Christie. Remember that blood is thicker than water."

"Amen," said Mr. Allen.

"They need to be with their father," Mom said. "That's their problem here. They're afraid of their father and that's when they behave. I'll be so glad when we're back with their father."

Mr. Allen turned the page on his newspaper and shook it to straighten it out. He said: "If they make it that long."

After all that talk Richard and me didn't feel we deserved anything for Christmas but after breakfast we were sent to the living room to wait while Mom went to her room to get the presents.

The Allens believed in a simple Christmas. The Jehovah's Witnesses religion didn't allow for all the frills like Christmas trees and decorations—lights and all those other things. Neither did they believe in exchanging gifts. Mr. Allen had told us that Christmas celebrations were for pagans, people that did not believe in God and Jesus Christ, "like the hated Jews and other atheists. We believe in Jehovah and Christ but we don't believe that you have to go out and spend money in order to celebrate the birth of Christ," he said, sitting down with us in the living room to finish the paper. He was not going to take part. He was going to ignore our celebration.

Mom came into the living room barely holding all the gifts in her arms. Richard and me helped her set them down on the floor in the middle of the room. One by one Mom arranged them in the order to be opened. Mr. Allen took his eyes off the newspaper just long enough to watch what was going on. He looked sour. Mrs. Allen was enjoying it a lot. Mom passed out her gift to the Allens first. "Here," she said, on her knees, handing over a large box to Mrs. Allen, "this is for both of you from all three of us."

Mrs. Allen's face lit up. She opened up the gift. Mr. Allen put down his paper and reached for the Bible. He looked at Mrs. Allen like he did at us, like he didn't approve of what he was seeing. "You're showing too much excitement," he said. "It's almost like greed."

Mrs. Allen, with her swollen joints and her chubby hands, was quickly taking the wrapping paper off as fast as she could. She didn't bother answering him. She kept on tearing away at the paper.

When she finally opened the gift she was delighted. It was a ceramic dish in the shape of a turkey. It was painted turkey colors and the upper half was the lid. You could put a turkey in there and bake it with the lid on. Mrs. Allen was so excited when she saw the dish that she put both her hands to her mouth and she shook her head slowly. "Thank you," she said to my mother and she reached her small frame over toward my mother and she kissed her on the forehead. My mother blushed.

"I'll use it today for our turkey. But first I must wash it out real good. No telling what's been in it," she said, inspecting the inside of the dish. She read the label inside the lid. "Made in Yugoslavia. Those people are good with ceramics," she said, admiring the gift.

"Don't show too much greed," Mr. Allen cautioned her. "You know what the Bible says."

"I know. I know. But can't I feel good about something sometimes?"

"Yes, you can," he replied, "but be sure you're not feeling greed."

My mother then turned to Richard and me and she smiled. "These are for you guys," she said and she winked at us. Richard and me smiled. She handed the boxes to us. We opened our gift and inside each was a heavy jacket. We took them out of the box and put them on. They were a perfect fit. I was thinking that we were not going to have to wear our old shrunken jackets again, not to school anyway. I looked at Richard's jacket as he tried it on and it was exactly the same as mine. They were both dark blue and had black knitted collars and black knitted cuffs so they wouldn't show the dirt.

Mom was on her knees making us twirl around and around in front of her as she admired the way we looked. Richard and me were acting dizzy and running into each other. "You don't wear these to play. You understand? You can wear the old ones to play. These are for school and church and things like that."

"Don't they make a handsome pair," Mrs. Allen said. "Come over here and let me touch them...Christie, these are nice. I like the material." She held on to the hem on my coat and studied it. "It's like cotton with a sheen to it. That's fine."

"Thank you," Mom said.

"Oh, I almost forgot," Mrs. Allen said to me. "There's one more present here and it's for you. Someone left it on the table on the porch by the door either this morning before we got up or last night. Anyway I found it this morning when I went out to get the paper." She handed me a small long box with a card on the outside. It was from Mrs. Smith, my teacher, but it didn't look like her handwriting. I began to open it. Everyone, including Mr. Allen, was watching to see what it was that Mrs. Smith had given me. It was something hard wrapped in a lot of tissue paper. I peeled the paper off layer by layer, my mind wondering what this was all about. I finally scratched a hole in the last layer of tissue and I could see what it was. My mind couldn't believe it at first. It was like a trick. Inside the box was my own harmonica! Richard was giving it to me for Christmas, but he was using Mrs. Smith's name! I couldn't believe what he had done and without warning me.

My mother was thrilled that Mrs. Smith had thought enough of me to give me a harmonica. "You must be doing great in school," she said. "Still it's confusing. I wonder if she gave out presents to all the children?"

Mrs. Allen said, "That's hard to believe. That would be expensive."

"It sure would," Mom said, thinking. "I guess she's really taken a likin' to you, Jimmy. But teachers always have liked Jim."

Richard had really done it this time. Now we would have to lie about Mrs. Smith and God help us if she and my mother got together. I could see the look of confusion on both faces as they tried to talk their way through the harmonica conversation. I could have killed Richard. Anyway, my mother and the Allens thought that it was awfully nice of Mrs. Smith to go to all the trouble to buy me a harmonica for Christmas.

Mom was beaming with pride. "Is there a card?" she asked.

I looked inside and there was nothing. Richard hadn't enclosed a card.

"She must have forgotten," Mom said, in her innocence. "I've got to thank her next time I see her."

I don't need to tell you that from then on we did everything in our power to keep Mom from ever talking to Mrs. Smith again and to our credit we succeeded.

Mom thought for a while. "Maybe you acted out your harmonica playin' for her like you always like to do. Did you do that? Did she like it?"

"Oh, Jim's always doin' that in school," Richard said. "Even in class."

Mom said, "Well, I was sure it must have been somethin' like that for her to know how much you enjoy doin' things like that." She thought a while longer and she said, "But Jim, be sure you're not cuttin' up in class and not studyin' or not lettin' the other children study. But I'm sure Mrs. Smith wouldn't let you get away with that. Did you play for the class?"

"Yes, ma'am," I lied, getting deeper and deeper in it. What else could I do? I had to go along with my brother Richard.

"Well you play only when Mrs. Smith tells you to play. Don't be takin' advantage of 'er. She's so nice."

"I could tell she was a nice lady when I met her at the funeral," Mrs. Allen said. "She has kind eyes. You can tell she's nice."

"You'd be surprised at some of these teachers," Mr. Allen then continued in the same vein. He had taken his reading glasses off and placed the closed Bible on his lap. "They are actually good people. Some parents don't think so but I have had occasion to know some teachers and they have been honorable and Christ-fearing. Of course," he said, "I'm referring mostly to the Christian teachers. Although we Jehovah's Witnesses love everyone."

He reached for the Bible, opened it at a red bookmark and he started reading to us but my brother Richard and me were uncomfortable with the whole thing and besides we were getting hot with our heavy jackets on. He kept on and on reading his favorite, Jeremiah, and finally Mrs. Allen interrupted him and said that that was enough and we all got up and went to the kitchen to help with the turkey. We left him there reading silently from the Bible to himself.

Mrs. Allen began to wash the ceramic dish with plenty of soap while Mom started to stuff the turkey.

The phone rang in the living room and it had not rung in such a long time that it startled us. We could hear Mr. Allen answer it. "It's for you, Christie," Mr. Allen said from the other room. Mom cleaned her hands quickly and she went into the living room.

We could hear her say, "Hello?.....Well hi, Betty.......Yes. Merry Christmas to you all too. We've thought about you all. How is Jim?..... Yes.....Yes......Well does he ever come down from the reservation?.....Oh, I see.......No, we're all fine....Yes, she suffered so much. It was a tragedy and real sad, but we're fightin' it and we're feelin' better every day.....I understand........I understand.......(She was crying.) Listen, what is family for anyway? You and I go a long way. We know each other and what we married. You don't have to make anythin' up to me. What's done is done. You remember the pact we made?.......Enough said...........She couldn't make it to the funeral either. It's so far from Corpus. By bus it would take 'er two days and she wasn't feelin' well." Then she and Aunt Betty started talking about the families, happy talk, going over everyone, how each one was doing, how tall he or she was, how much weight they had put on, what grade they were in school. Finally, we could tell that the question had been asked: When were we leaving and moving to Artesia with our father where we belonged? "We'll be goin' soon," Mom replied. "Well, I don't have a definite day but it will be soon. Tell Jim we'll be there before he knows it.......Well, we miss him too........It's just that I've got to save up some money before we can travel.....If he wants to......Does he have any money?.........Don't bother 'im. I'd rather get the money myself. That way I won't put any pressure on 'im. I don't want 'im gettin' into any trouble because of me............Yes, we love you too. Goodbye."

We were all in our rooms getting ready for morning prayer meeting. I had jumped on Richard the minute he closed the door. I knocked him on the floor and had him pinned down with my body and left arm and I was trying to hit him with my right as hard as I could but he kept blocking my fist. He was laughing as he easily fought me off. And the more he laughed, the angrier I got. "What the shit's the matter with you?" I kept asking him and he kept laughing. "What are we goin' to do with Mrs. Smith?" He was laughing so hard that he couldn't fight back anymore and he rolled into a ball and went over on his side. I could hit him now all I wanted but I didn't have much strength left. I was about to hit Richard again when we heard the phone ring. We stopped fighting, listened, and we heard Mr. Allen answer the telephone. We were panting. I was so close to Richard that I could smell the egg on his breath. I had stopped in motion, my fist in the air, ready to hit him. Richard said for me to be quiet. We heard Mr. Allen's foot-steps in the hall. He knocked on Mom's door and he called her to the telephone. "It's your mother this time," he said.

Mom and grandmother talked for a while and then we could hear Mom yelling for us. Grandmother wanted to say "Merry Christmas." And did we miss Sylvia? We had gotten jackets, heavy ones for the cold wind and snow. We already had caps. We had gotten them for the funeral. We didn't tell her they were second-hand. She was not sending us anything except her love. She was too sick to go out and buy anything. She coughed throughout the conversation just to remind us how sick she was. She smoked three packs a day.

After the call Mom looked at our jackets and she shook her head. "Where have you two been?" she asked. "Your jackets are all covered with dirt and lint."

Richard and me were checking our jackets out like we didn't know what she was talking about.

"Have you all been rollin' on the floor or what?"

"We were wrestlin'," I said. "On the floor."

"Go to your room," she said, with tight lips and a strained voice, "and clean your new jackets and stay there and don't come out until I tell you to. Do you understand?"

"Yes, ma'am," we answered.

Later that morning, after we had been sitting on the edge of the bed waiting for Mom to tell us when to leave the room, Mom came over and knocked and said for us to go sit in the car and wait. Richard and me went and sat in the back seat. We were pushing around and Richard knocked me down. I landed so that I could see under the front seat. And there under the seat was what looked like a piece of white cloth next to Mr. Allen's red shop rag. I reached under the seat even as Richard was kneeing me in the back and I came out with the cloth and waved it over my body. Richard stopped kneeing me and yanked the cloth from my hand. We sat on the back seat and slowly unraveled the white cloth, little by little. It was a pair of panties, Clarence's mom's panties, worn and frayed at the crotch. Since the fire crackers incident he must have been taking her out in the car. Richard smelled the panties and made a face and held his nose. He dangled them in front of me. Then he had a thought. He dropped on all fours and got out Mr. Allen's red shop rag from under the front seat. He wrapped the panties inside the rag and then placed the rag back under the seat.

We were laughing when Mom and the Allens got in the car. "My, my," Mrs. Allen said looking back at us in our new jackets, "you boys are in a happy mood for Christmas."

My brother Richard was holding his nose.

CHAPTER 18

After dinner Clarence and Jim and Phil came over. Clarence wanted to go see Pete, so we all went. When we got to the carnival, a lot of the people had left and the rest were pulling up their tents and folding up their rides. Clarence ran to Pete's trailer and banged on the door. No one answered and he banged on it some more. He went over and peeped through the window and said he was seeing a girl inside asleep. "She's got on panties and that's all," he said, excited. "God almighty, look at her." He was wrapping his tongue around his lips. He tapped lightly again. "She's on her back now. Wow!" He tapped on the window again. "She's awake. Somebody knock on the door so she'll hear you." Phil went to the door and knocked. Clarence said, "She's puttin' her clothes on. I'm seein' everythin' guys." By the time she opened the door, we were all waiting. We had not seen her before. She was young and had long hair. She was wearing a thin house coat, holding it at the waist like Richard did with his pajamas.

"You woke me up. What do you all want?" She sounded angry.

Clarence stepped to the front and said, "We're Pete's friends. We're lookin' for Pete."

She yawned and covered her mouth. "Pete's not here right now. Can you all come some other day?"

"Like when?" Clarence asked her.

"Well, he's in jail and I don't know when he's gettin' out. Depends on a lot of things."

Clarence said, "You don't know anythin' about him showin' us guys somethin', do you?"

"No, I don't. But you know Pete. He's always got something up his sleeve. He'll be out soon. Why don't you kids come back then."

"He's got some of my money," Clarence told her.

She looked at Clarence and shook her head. "I'm sorry. You shouldn't have given him anything. But maybe he still has it with 'im and the sheriff took it. I don't know. I do know that he didn't leave any money here in the trailer."

"Is the whole carnival leaving?" Clarence asked.

She covered her eyes with her hand and looked out to where the people were working. "I guess so," she said. "I've been asleep all day long. I had a rough night. I was in jail too."

"That makes me angry," Clarence told her. "Real angry. He's got my money. And now you all are leavin'."

"They're leaving. I'm not. I'm staying until Pete gets out. I'm sure he's got your money. He's not the type to skip town. You all know Pete."

"That's what I'm afraid of," Clarence said.

That Christmas evening when we got back home and after we ate, Mom asked me if I would try playing the harmonica and I went and got it and started to play and everyone except my brother Richard was amazed at how well I did. As a matter of fact, Mr. Allen said that he had read where this man in Germany a long time ago had been born a musical genius and could play the harpsichord piano at the age of five, only a little bit younger than me. He could also write music at an early age. "There's something good in that boy," he said, pointing his finger at me. What was bad was that we could not tell them that I had had the harmonica and I had been playing it all this time. Mom was really thrilled. She said, "Maybe the way you used to imitate playin' was what helped you. It really is amazin'. I didn't know you would pick it up as fast as you did. In one day? My word. Wait until your father finds out about this."

But after a month of playing they were amazed at how little I improved after that first day. I could see that Mr. Allen had given up on me. I was not the musical genius he had described as being another Beethoven. Mom forgot about it. I was one more of the failures that had plagued her life. Little by little they asked me less and less to play for them until the requests stopped altogether. I did play for myself and for my brother Richard. Richard said that I played good anyway, good enough for him.

The other problem we still had with the harmonica was to keep Mom from seeing Mrs. Smith. We couldn't think of a plan that day. Richard and me stayed awake for a long time trying out ideas on each other but nothing seemed to work.

It took over a week of arguing before we came up with a very simple plan. We told Mom one day after school that Mrs. Smith had left town suddenly. Her husband had been moved to another state, which one we didn't know. We didn't want to make the lie too complicated. "Oh, poor her," Mom said to all of this, "I wish I could have thanked her before she left. She did a lot for you, Jimmy. And she was nice enough to give you the harmonica for Christmas."

We felt we were safe with this plan. Mom was ironing so much that she wasn't going out of the house and chances were that if I kept my nose clean she would never see Mrs. Smith again. On the other side of the lie we told Mrs. Smith when she asked about Mom that Mom was feeling so bad that she never wanted to talk to any one again as long as she lived.

Mom had been to visit Sylvia's grave almost every day for about the first month. She would go in the early morning before anyone was awake. She would bundle up to protect herself from the cold and she would walk head down pushing her frail body, fighting her way against the wind. On her way back when we were all awake we could see the wind gusts push her from behind with such force that it almost made her run. She would return with her face lined with tears. Often the deputy would give her a ride back.

"You have got to quit this grievin'," Mrs. Allen said one morning after Mom had returned from visiting Sylvia's grave. "It's gettin' you down. You're health is goin' to suffer. One of these days you're goin' to come down with some kind of pneumonia and you're really goin' to get seriously ill. You mark my words. Here, have some coffee," she said, placing a cup before her on the table.

Mr. Allen watched as Mom sipped from the hot cup. "She's right, you know," he said, straightening out his paper. "It's all right to grieve but I think you're carryin' this a bit too far. It's more a form of idolatry, as the Bible says and that's not good. As a matter of fact...it's a sin."

Mom looked at him like she didn't care what Mr. Allen thought. "I know this is your house and all but with all due respect, I'll stop when I'm done," Mom replied. "It doesn't affect my health. I'm in good health. I feel that I have to grieve right now instead of lettin' it come over me later on. I'll get over it. You all don't know what Sylvia meant to me. Not only was she my only daughter, she was my partner also. She and I were like mother and daughter and we were like friends. It's hard to explain. She was just that way. I loved 'er so very much. It's hard to lose someone like her. I still feel that a big part of my life is missin'. But I guess you wouldn't know," she said to Mrs. Allen.

Mrs. Allen glared at Mom. She came over and sat down with a cup of coffee. She took a sip and then she laid the cup on the saucer and started to slowly turn the cup around by its handle. "That's where you're wrong," she told Mom. "And that hurts me. You hurt me. You and I have been kind of close, Christie. But you don't seem to think I've been through much. You've got the idea that you're the only one that has ever suffered. Well, you're wrong."

Mr. Allen put his paper down and said, "Now, Mrs. Allen...do you really need to go into this?"

She took another sip of coffee and she acted like she had not heard what he had said. "When I was about your age," she started, "I got pregnant and had a baby. We were living in Amarillo then. Mr. Allen had been working for Southern Pacific for about five or six years in Amarillo. We'd been married only one year. We didn't have any children. This was the first one. I started to have it all by myself. Mr. Allen was at work. It was the middle of the day. There was no one to turn to. Being Jehovah's Witnesses in Amarillo didn't give me much in the way of friends. I was by myself. I could tell something was wrong with him. In the condition I was in I still ran next door and the neighbors tried to help me but they were Mexican and they couldn't understand too well what the problem was. Finally I was able to make them understand that the baby had been born and they carried me back home. They wouldn't let me walk, bless their souls. They were afraid that I would bleed to death. I had left a trail of blood, you see. At the same time they sent one of their sons to go fetch Mr. Allen. The baby was dead by the time we got back to the house. He was black and blue."

She took the hem of the apron and wiped the tears from her eyes.

Mom was crying with her. "I'm sorry," she said. Mr. Allen was nodding his head at what Mrs. Allen was saying. Richard and me had had enough of this sadness stuff. Why didn't we talk of something else?

"I love that baby to this day," she said, "so don't say that I don't know how it feels. I'll tell you something else, the bad part. When Mr. Allen came home with the doctor I told the doctor that I needed to hold my baby before they took him away. So I held him and tried to make him nurse. I squeezed my breast and then squeezed on the nipple until I could get a drop of milk for him and I placed his little cold mouth around the nipple and gave him my milk, forced it down his little throat. He would not go out of this world without his mother's milk. I held him for a long time and then they took him away from me. I didn't want to let go. They forced me to give him up. I was beginning to think that by nursing him I could bring him back to life. But I was wrong, you see. I should have never done what I did. Sure I loved the child but it was wrong for me to force milk down his throat even though he was dead. I was wrong not to let go. I'll never forget that and I hope that Jehovah has forgiven me. I was trying to be greater than God. Death is a temporary state that we all go through in wait for the resurrection. You'll see Sylvia someday."

"I'm sure he's forgiven you after all these years," Mr. Allen said. "You weren't in your right mind when it happened. You had lost a lot of blood. Even the doctor admitted he couldn't tell me if you were going to be all right or not. You weren't responsible. Jehovah understands that."

"To this day I still don't know what possessed me to do what I did."

Mr. Allen said, "The devil, that's who made you do it. He caught you in a moment of weakness, and I mean physical weakness. The loss of blood. You were probably delirious. Look at the tremendous strength the devil gave you. You weren't normally that strong. It took the doctor and me and the Mexican lady to get the baby away from you. You had animal strength, devil strength. Remember we saw a small monkey in the zoo in Dallas that had carried her dead baby around for days and no one could take it away from her? Remember how strong they told us she was, that little animal that hardly weighed a pound?"

"God have mercy on me," Mrs. Allen said, crying.

Mom had gotten up and she had her arm around Mrs. Allen's shoulder calming her down. "I'm sorry," Mom said to her. "I didn't mean to bring this up. I really am sorry. If only I had known."

"It's not your fault," Mr. Allen said. "She needs to talk about this once in a while. You know that they say confession is good for the soul. The Catholics have been doing it forever."

In time the visits to the cemetery became fewer and fewer. I don't think

Mrs. Allen's story affected Mom. I do believe that it is hard to keep that feeling of grief going for a long time. It's not human nature. It wears off after a while, regardless of how much one cared. And that wasn't necessarily bad. It was not an insult to Sylvia. It was just that she lived in our memory always and there was no need to be going to the grave every day.

It was now February. We had returned to school after the holidays. I was beginning to notice some of Mitzi's bad points. What I mean is that she was not the perfect girl for me. I was dreaming of her less and less. My brother Richard and me had been to her house several times during the holidays and all she did was complain about her mother and her father. Her father was a big man with breasts larger than a woman's and he cursed all the time at Mitzi and her mom. Mitzi would curse back at him and at her mom. Her mom was short and fat and her breasts lay parallel to the floor over her large stomach. She had problems seeing, having to cock her head sideways like a parrot Richard and me saw at a store one time in Abilene, the parrot that only knew part of a song. Anyway, Mitzi's mom cursed at Mitzi and at Mitzi's dad and every time we saw her she was holding a broom to hit someone with.

Women being what they are, as soon as I lost interest in Mitzi she started to notice me more, nothing serious but at least now she knew my name and yelled at me during recess. She would mess up my hair on the way to school. Richard thought I had really improved my way with girls. He said, as if he knew all about it, "You've got to act like you don't like 'em. Look at John Wayne. He never goes out and makes a big play for a girl. Girls don't like boys who go crazy over 'em. No one likes Clarence, do they?"

I had taken the harmonica to school once and Mitzi loved the way I played it. The coach told me not to bring the harmonica back to school or he would take it away from me and give it to Mrs. Peters and Mrs. Peters would keep it until the end of school. This was recess, he told me, not music period. Then he said, "Just in case you haven't noticed, dumbhead, we do not have a music period at Ross Elementary."

My brother Richard and me were doing pretty good in school. I was a good student. I did everything the teacher wanted me to do. Mrs. Smith liked me. I could tell. Things in school came easy for me. It was the things that went on after school that I wasn't very good at. That's where Richard and Clarence and Jim and Phil had it over me.

Just for your information I saw Richard's grades. He had a D in arithmetic, an F in language, a C in geography, an a D-minus in recess. The reason for his low grade in recess was that he was a suspect in a theft of a pocket knife. I was sure he hadn't done it but once you get a reputation you get blamed every time something is missing. They weren't talking about the yellow pocket knife that Richard had had. That one he stole from Pete and then gave it to Phil on Christmas day because Phil had not gotten anything for Christmas.

Clarence and Jim were on the basketball team so we didn't get to see them as often as we had before. My brother Richard and Phil and me would stay after school to watch them practice. Clarence played under the basket and Jim was the guy that brought the ball in. Richard wanted to play and he asked the coach, the same one that told me not to bring the harmonica to school, but the coach said he couldn't because Richard stole. He couldn't take the time to be watching over Richard all the time.

We went to one game before we left Tahoka. Clarence was so much taller than anyone else that all he had to do was stand in the middle and hold the ball above his head. Then he'd turn around slowly like Frankenstein and shoot but every time he'd do that the referee would blow his whistle and he'd say that Clarence was taking too many steps without dribbling. Clarence would get real frustrated with himself and he'd slap himself and the people in the stands would laugh out loud. The coach would jump out of his chair and yell at Clarence and Clarence would turn red. Next time he would get the ball from Jim he'd do the same thing all over again. Even the referee laughed.

CHAPTER 19

My father's name was coming up more often. My mother was talking to us a lot more about him than before. And even though I could tell Mom was hurt because he had not called or written, I could also tell she was looking forward to being with him again. Richard and me didn't want to go. I think that if the Allens had asked us we would have stayed. I don't know why she wanted to go. There would be nothing but trouble and bad treatment for all of us, especially Richard. I was scared but I knew Richard had to be more scared.

One week before we left Tahoka Mom walked over to the bus station and bought the tickets. That same day she wrote a letter to Aunt Betty telling her when we would be leaving and when we were supposed to arrive in Artesia. By the middle of the week she had finished all her ironing and all the clothes were out of the house by Friday.

On Saturday she left the house very early. She stayed gone for a long time. Richard and me had gotten up and washed and dressed and had eaten breakfast and still she had not returned.

"Did anyone see her leave?" Mrs. Allen asked.

As usual Mr. Allen was hiding behind the paper, drinking his coffee. "I didn't," he said. "She must have left before any of us got up."

Mrs. Allen was picking up the dishes from the table when the deputy arrived in the car with Mom. When Mom and the deputy walked in you could tell she had been crying. "You boys better get finished with your breakfast. You've got to get everythin' done today," she said, walking toward the table. The deputy stayed at the kitchen door.

Richard and me got up with our plates and put them in the sink. We were standing by the refrigerator looking at the deputy and listening.

"We were beginning to worry about you," Mr. Allen said.

"I was sayin' my last goodbyes to Sylvia," Mom replied, sitting down and straightening her hair. "And then Arlan drove by and he took me to see Wilma and I said goodbye to her and just by chance Dr. Morgan was there and we talked a little and I said my goodbyes to him too. Then there were the other nurses to talk to."

Mrs. Allen was washing dishes. Without turning around she asked, "Is everyone doing fine?"

"Yes. Everyone is doing fine. It's so cold outside," Mom said. "Do you think we should offer a cup of coffee to Arlan?"

Mrs. Allen realized that she had not offered the deputy a cup of coffee and she seemed embarrassed. "Oh! I'm sorry," she said. "What must I have been thinking about?" She dried her hands and opened the cupboard and got a large mug and poured coffee for the deputy.

"Maybe I better not," the deputy said. Now he was embarrassed because he had not been offered the coffee without Mom's coaxing. Either way he was not going to win. Finally Mom prevailed and he sat down to have his cup.

"It's the least we could do," Mrs. Allen told him, placing the mug on the table in front of him, "for being so conscientious about taking care of Christie all this time."

"It wasn't nothin'," the deputy said. "It was really a pleasure." He remembered for a moment and then he said, "You know, I was the first person in this town to meet this family. They were really in lots of trouble. That's when Sylvia was so sick and their father left 'em. Do you all remember?"

No one answered. Mom blushed.

"I didn't mean to embarrass anybody by bringing up bad memories. But that's just like me. Well, I've got to go," he said and he got up. Then he spoke to Mom. "Will you walk me to the door?" he asked her and Mom got up and went with him.

We heard them go outside. Mr. Allen looked at Mrs. Allen and then they both looked at us. Richard and me knew that they wanted us to leave so we went to our room. We had a lot to do. We needed to pack some more and we needed to say goodbye to Clarence and Jim and Phil.

Our last day of school had been Friday. Mom had wanted to go pick up our report cards but we lied to her and told her that our grades would not be posted for another week or so, that Mrs. Peters had said for us to tell Mom that she would mail us the report cards as soon as we wrote to her and gave her our new address. Then we told Mrs. Peters and Mrs. Smith and Mrs. Abercrombie that Mom couldn't come to school and that Mom said that she would write for all our school records.

At recess I saw Mitzi. She had crossed over to the boys side of the playground. I didn't know how to talk to her, how to say goodbye. She held my hand and shook it and said, "Is Clarence right? Is today your last day of school, scum bag? I thought it was next week," she said, laughing. "Well, see ya later, alligator." And she ran to her side of the playground before the teacher could see her and get her name. And the first love of my life was gone, just like that.

Clarence, Jim and Phil came over late Saturday morning after basketball practice while we were still packing. Mom had still been outside talking to the deputy and she had told them to go ahead and knock on the door and ask for us.

Mr. Allen came and got us and when we went out we noticed that Clarence had a black eye. No one made mention of the black eye so I figured that Clarence didn't want to talk about it. The deputy asked what had happened to the eye and Clarence said he had fallen down. The deputy laughed.

We had the idea of walking around town for the last time. We asked Mom if we could go and she said yes, as long as we came back early enough to finish packing.

"You better bundle up too," the deputy said, "because we're fixin' to have us a blue norther to end all northers."

"Really?" Mom said. "It's goin' to get colder than this?"

"It sure is. It's comin' in from Colorado and New Mexico this afternoon with winds and sleet and snow and God knows what. It's supposed to get down to ten degrees and with the wind it'll feel like minus one hundred. Lots of accidents too, so you all be careful." He turned to Mom and we could hear him say, "I was hopin' to convince you not to go tomorrow. The roads'll be bad. There's no cause to leave in such a hurry."

It felt colder already just to hear him talk. And you could see the darkness in the sky to the north. We buttoned up our jackets and we started walking to town.

The deputy was talking loud enough that we could still hear him. "The only reason I'm not in Korea right now killin' gooks is because I wear a badge and the state of Texas needs me," he said, making himself proud.

We went by the hospital and Richard ran up the front stairs and sat on the wooden bench for a few seconds. We went around to the side of the hospital to peek through the window and we saw Nurse Wilma walk past the door going down the hallway, a tray of medical supplies in her hands. We were looking into the room where my sister had died.

A great puff of wind that made us shudder came through the alley. The norther the deputy had talked about was coming in. We started to see snowflakes drifting in the air. We walked to Main Street and turned left and headed toward downtown. We were almost to the courthouse when Clarence decided that we should go to where the carnival had been and we all agreed that that was a good idea. So we crossed Main Street with the wind to our backs and we took the street between the diner and the bus station, the same street we took that Christmas Eve when we went to the carnival and we saw the man with the hammer stuck to the top of his head.

We stood in the middle of the field and we looked around. Clarence enjoyed just looking around at where the carnival had been, like he wanted us, before we left, to relive what had happened that night. We could hardly see his face. He had covered his head with the hood on his jacket and besides he had a cap pulled over his ears. He was rubbing his black eye, like it bothered him now that the wind was blowing harder. "That's where the fight started," he said, pointing at the place where one of the tents had been. "And I heard say that they went round and round tryin' to get to each other on the ground and wound up by the cotton candy machine. That's where Pete let him have it. Bam!" Clarence went, slamming the air in front of him.

"Over there was Pete's place," he said.

Pete's trailer was gone. Pete's girlfriend had finally given up on Pete. She had stayed for a while to see if he would get out but when Pete couldn't make bail she took off to join the rest of the carnival. Once in a while we had gone by the trailer with Clarence. Clarence was still trying to see her thing. But she never let on that she knew anything about what Pete was doing. She had passed her empty time by painting a rainbow on both sides of the trailer. Under each rainbow she had printed the words, "Pete DeLiro's Rainbow Circes", circus with an e instead of a u.

We were all looking at the empty spaces when Clarence yelled, "Let's go see Pete," and as soon as he said it he started to run back to town toward the jail.

I got left behind as usual but I saw Clarence up front go around to the back of the courthouse and the others follow him. As I turned that same corner a blast of cold air hit me and it felt like someone had thrown ice in my face. It had started sleeting and the wind was really howling on the north side. By the time I got there the guys were looking up at the jail cells, looking for Pete.

Pete had closed the window and we couldn't see him and I don't think he could see us. Clarence yelled at him and nothing happened. Then he yelled again and picked up a small stone and threw it at the window. Still no answer. Clarence picked up another stone, bigger this time, and threw it at the window again. It was a good thing he missed because I think that if he had hit the window it would have broken. Clarence yelled again, louder this time. Pete could not hear us but the sheriff could. He had stepped out of his office without us knowing and he was standing at the doorway. He yelled at us to come inside. We had no choice but to go in.

"What in the hell are you boys doin' out in this weather?"

Clarence spoke for us. "We came to see Pete," he said.

"What for?" he asked.

He had gone behind his desk and was sitting in a large wooden swivel chair. He leaned back and rocked back and forth. You could tell he was studying us, rubbing his chin.

We felt bad, I know I did anyway, that we had taken all that trouble to come and see Pete. We still had not answered him. He seemed disappointed in us. He got up slowly, grabbed his coffee cup with a hand as large as a small brisket, the same hand that had slapped and bloodied Pete's face. He drank the last of the cup. He called upstairs through the bars and Pete came down the stairs slowly. He was barefooted and his face was covered with a yellow beard. He was wrapped in an old dirty Indian blanket and was shivering. We could see his thin legs under the blanket. He was not wearing any pants.

"You cold up there, Pete?" the sheriff asked him.

"It sure as hell is," Pete said, his tongue slurring the words.

"It's colder in Huntsville," the sheriff said.

"It cain't be," Pete replied, shivering. "Everyone I know's been in Hunstville tells me it's nice and warm even in winter."

"Well, your ass is going to be cold and that's that," the sheriff said.

Pete looked at us and I could tell he was both embarrassed and desperate. He looked from one of us to the other like he wanted help. He sat down on one of the stairs behind the bars. It looked like it bothered him that he had lost so much weight. He kept trying to hide his body with the blanket. His finger nails were longer than anyone's I had ever seen and his fingers shook. His long teeth were yellower. He had black coarse hair coming out of his ear holes that I hadn't seen before.

"I guess the boys here want to say goodbye," the sheriff told him. He pointed at us with his coffee cup.

"Where are you all going?" Pete asked.

"Well only these two are going," the sheriff said and he pointed to Richard and me with the cup. "The other three are staying. Right, boys?"

We all said, "Yes, sir," right away.

"I don't know why they want to say goodbye, but they're here. Seems to me there'd be someone more important to say goodbye to than you. Say goodbye to Pete, boys."

He pointed his cup toward Pete telling us to go over and shake Pete's hand. "Don't know why these good kids want to say anythin' to you but you ought to be grateful. I'm sure the boys don't have anythin' else to say. Right boys?"

"Yes, sir," we said, and we didn't even go to shake Pete's hand.

When the sheriff saw that we were not going to say goodbye to Pete he told him to go upstairs and Pete got up slowly and waved at us, letting go of his blanket just long enough. He stopped and looked at the sheriff. "Can I have a cigarette?" he asked him. The sheriff shook his head. "Just one, please?" The sheriff shook his head again. "Well then can I have some heat upstairs?"

"I've told you a jillion times that the upstairs furnace is broken. And we can't get a part for it. In the spring, when we don't need it, the county is goin' to buy a whole new one. Now is that clear? Just hope some of the heat from downstairs gets up there. That's all. And quit beggin' for stuff. You're already gettin' on my nerves."

Pete walked up the stairs slowly, one at a time, like he didn't want to go. He looked beat, alone, like he knew that the others in the carnival had left him behind. He just didn't look like the Pete we had met before. But jail will do that to you. It'll calm you down.

I know, because one time when my father was working for a road fixing company he got caught stealing a large tractor. He was put in jail for six months. When he came out he was a changed man, looking like Pete, thin and meek. He talked in a low voice like he was afraid the person next to him would hear him. He hid his cigarettes so well that even my mother couldn't find them and at times he went into the bathroom to smoke. Those were good days for us. We could get away with lots of things and he acted like he didn't mind. But then one night, about a couple of months after getting out, he went and got drunk and he forgot all that he ever learned in jail. He tore through the house and he almost killed us all. He was back to being his old self again. And I'm sure Pete was the same way. Just because he acted whipped that day doesn't mean he stayed that way after he got out.

"You boys get over by the heater, warm up a bit," the sheriff said to us as he poured some more coffee into his large cup. Above the coffee pot was a piece of plywood with short wooden dowels to hold each cup. Besides the sheriff there were cups for three deputies and one dispatcher. Once he saw that we were around the heater he sat down in his chair again and leaned forward, his hands held together and said, "There ain't nothin' good that's goin' to come over your association with Pete. There ain't anythin' Pete has or Pete knows that's of any earthly benefit to any of you. Pete is a bad influence. He's a crook and a pimp. Now if you were lookin' for him for pimpin'..."

We all denied it. You could hear the "Oh, no's" go on forever, like echoes.

"Well, I'm glad to hear that," the sheriff said and smiled. "You had me worried. Pete's no good. Probably never was and never will be. These kind of people don't change. I've been in the law enforcement business a long time, children, and I've seen Petes all that time. If he's not in jail here he'll be in jail somewheres else. And for somethin' else too. He's got a record a mile long." He opened the desk drawer and brought out a file. He flipped it open with his large thick fingers and went through the stack of papers. He found what he wanted and looked at it a while. He turned over page after page. He read: "Assault with a deadly weapon, Houma, Louisiana. Attempted rape, San Antonio, Texas. Carrying a concealed weapon, Fort Worth, Texas. Assault and criminal trespass, Leesville, Louisiana. Statutory Rape, charges dropped, Enid, Oklahoma. Breaking and entering, Albuquerque, New Mexico. Narcotics possession, Lexington, Kentucky, sentence probated." And on he read. Finally he stopped. "So you see boys," he said, "I don't want to ever see any of you back here again. I don't want to have to be the one that locks you up some day for somethin' I encouraged you to do. Pete's a bum, not a friend. Go out and have a good time. Chase some pussy." He made us laugh. I hadn't expected him to say that. "You're young. Don't spend the best part of your life in jail. So go on now. Forget about Pete. Let 'im serve his time and let 'im get out of town. Forget about 'im." He had been looking at Clarence's eye while he talked. "Someone got you good in the eye, didn't they?" Clarence blushed. "You don't have to tell me who did it. I know that you had a fight with your momma. Some one called about you all and one of the deputies went out but you had gone by then. Did she hurt you bad?"

"No, just the eye."

He looked at Clarence and shook his head. "You people can never behave, can you? Got to be fightin' all the time. What was it this time? Never mind. Don't answer...I didn't mean to embarrass you...Go on. Get! Get outta here," he said and we ran outside and he acted like he was going to run after us but he was laughing and he stopped at the door and laughed some more and waved goodbye at us.

The wind and cold felt worse now since we had over-heated inside the jailhouse. I felt like my body moisture was turning to ice inside my pants. It was sleeting so bad that we could hardly see the street.

When we got home we stood shivering by the gate for a while, talking. Mom stuck her head through the door from inside and invited all of us in. "You boys are goin' to die of pneumonia if you don't get out of this weather," she shouted. We brushed each other off on the porch and Mom let us in.

Clarence and Jim and Phil said goodbye to Mom. They were very serious and shook her hand. Richard and me were laughing at them. Mom thanked them for being such good friends and for taking care of me and she went into the kitchen to be with the Allens. It was an awful time. No one knew what to say.

"What time does the bus leave?" Jim asked but we didn't know exactly.

"About the middle of the day," Richard said and Clarence and Phil and Jim laughed, very quietly, so that no one but us could hear. Then Clarence whispered, "You shit-head, how're you goin' to take the bus when you don't even know when you're leavin'?"

"I don't know," Richard said. "Mom takes care of that."

"Mom takes care of that," Clarence repeated, talking like a girl and we all laughed.

Then we were quiet, very quiet, like the time had come to part after so many days of being together. Clarence stuck out his hand and he placed it in the middle of the circle that we were making. "Everyone put out his hand," he said and we all put our hands together. "We all promise that we will always be faithful to each other and that some day we'll all meet again," Clarence said in a whisper and we all said, "I do," like we were getting married.

Afterwards Mom made us take a bath so that we wouldn't smell so much in the morning.

"No one'll be able to stand you in the bus," she said, "unless you do."

CHAPTER 20

My Mom had the tickets. The reason we knew she had the tickets was because Mr. Allen must have asked her a hundred times if she was sure she had the tickets. And when we were loading our bags in the car he asked her one more time. He asked if we had tagged our luggage. Then he made all of us get out of the house, Mrs. Allen too, and he went in to check the whole house to make sure we had not forgotten anything. Finally, he came out of the house, locked the front door and walked to us as we all waited, shivering, inside the little car.

It was sleeting worse than it was yesterday and our breath was turning to ice inside the car. Mr. Allen was having a hard time walking against the wind. We could see his figure bent against the wind, like a ghost in the sleet.

You should have seen us. My mother had made us dress in the best we had. She was wearing a wool outfit that she and Mrs. Allen had made the week before. For us, she had taken the trouble to lay out our clothes the night before. "We don't want to get to Artesia looking like bums," she said. My brother Richard and me were wearing corduroy pants Mrs. Allen had given us. Mom thought Mrs. Allen would appreciate it if we wore them when she saw us for the last time. Mom had given us flannel shirts and with the new jackets and our caps, we looked good. Anyway, we looked a lot better than when we first got to Tahoka.

We couldn't tell what was keeping Mr. Allen. "What in the world is he doing?" Mrs. Allen was asking. "Looks like it's taking him forever to get in. What's he checking now?" We could see him in front of the car by the pig pen and the chicken coop. Finally he opened the door and came in, at the same time letting in a gust of wind that almost blew Mrs. Allen's hat off. He slammed the door shut. "I don't think the chickens are going to survive the winter," he said as he put the car key in the hole.

"I'm not going to survive this winter," Mrs. Allen replied although she hadn't been asked.

"Yep, you will," Mr. Allen remarked and he didn't seem pleased.

"What do you mean by that?" she demanded to know.

"Oh, that the good Lord knows when he takes us all. That's all." He sighed like he knew that scaly Mrs. Allen was going to be around for a long time.

He got the car started and we backed out of the driveway and into the street. My mother was looking at the house all covered with ice as it stood like a frozen white rock with a green roof. Richard and me looked at it too until we had to almost look backward to keep seeing it. Slowly it disappeared as we turned the corner and headed towards town.

We passed by Nurse Wilma's house and we looked to it to see if we could see her through the kitchen window but she wasn't there. The house was dark. Mom wiped the tears from her eyes. She asked the Allens to forgive her.

We did see Nurse Wilma for the last time when we got to Main Street. She was walking toward the hospital, going to work. She was all bundled up against the sleet but we could see her white stockings and her white shoes. Her head was wrapped so that she could not hear us when Mr. Allen honked his horn. Mom lowered the window and yelled at her but she could not hear. She kept her head down.

The deputy's car was parked at the coffee shop. We saw him inside drinking coffee and eating a doughnut. He was laughing and talking to Madge.

Mr. Allen slowly turned the car toward the curb at the bus station and he parked. We were early for the bus, but the Allens had to go to church.

We all got out and Mr. Allen opened the trunk and we helped him unload the three suitcases. By then the deputy had seen us park and he came over and he took Mom's suitcase inside. Mom followed him in. Richard and me had our own suitcases and we went in after Mom. The Allens were right behind us.

Mom went over to the ticket counter to check on the bus and when she came back she said that the bus was running late. "I told you so," the deputy said to Mom. Mr. Allen wanted to know how late the bus was. "About thirty minutes," Mom said.

"That isn't bad," Mr. Allen declared. He looked around at all of us and he said, "Well it's time to say goodbye." He and Mrs. Allen grabbed my mother and hugged her real tight and then my brother Richard and then me.

They were going right to church from here and they would pray for us. "Just think," Mrs. Allen said, "by the time we get out of church you all will be gone."

"I only hope so," my mother said, rearranging the hair that Mrs. Allen had messed up. "But we won't be far along. I just hope the bus is only thirty minutes late. It's so bad outside."

Mom opened her purse and looked inside and brought out some money. She tried to give it to Mrs. Allen but Mrs. Allen would not take it. "Take it please," Mom insisted, but Mrs. Allen kept backing up and refusing. Mr. Allen was also saying that Mom did not owe them anything. "Well," Mom said, "will you take it so that you can buy Sylvia some flowers once in a while?"

"Why don't you wait till it's time for that," Mrs. Allen said, "and then you can send me the money."

"Will you go visit Sylvia once in a while?" Mom asked her.

"Yes, I will," Mrs. Allen replied. "Mr. Allen will take me or if he won't I can always walk over. After all it's not a long walk."

"Visit her as often as you can. Please. I beg you. She always hated to be alone. She always needed someone to talk to. Give her our love when you go there. Tell her that we had to leave but we will never forget her. She will always be in my mind and in my heart. Tell her that some day I will be back and if I have the money, I'll take her with me to Corpus. I know she knows all this, as many times as I've told her but tell it to her again. Maybe coming from you she'll be more likely to believe it. Put some flowers on her grave. Remember she died on December the eighth but I'll write to you to remind you beforehand and I'll send you money for the flowers."

Mrs. Allen was crying and Mom was crying and she hugged Mom one more time and she said, "Be sure and write. Let us know how you all are doing and how you all got there."

The deputy and Mr. Allen were having a hard time keeping from crying. The deputy walked away to talk to a man he knew that worked at the bus station. Mr. Allen started to cry and when Mom saw him she embraced him.

Mr. Allen took Mrs. Allen by the arm and they walked out, both of them stooped under the weight of their heavy clothes. We followed them in silence as they opened the door and went out. We could see them on the sidewalk. Richard and I ran to the window to see them off. Mrs. Allen got in the car. Mr. Allen opened his door and reached under the seat for his shop rag to clean the ice off the wind-shield. He was wiping the windshield when he noticed that inside the shop rag was another rag. He stopped to inspect the shop rag and he slowly pulled the inside white cloth away from it. Not realizing what it was, he started to separate the white garment from the shop rag. Mrs. Allen was looking at him intently through the windshield. Mr. Allen, in horror, not able to think, undid the panties that belonged to Clarence's mom and held them at arms length and stared at them. We could not hear Mrs. Allen but we saw her put her hand to her mouth to quiet down a scream. Mr. Allen let go of the panties like they were on fire, throwing them down on the gutter and ran inside the car and took off. Richard and me were laughing and Mom told us to get away from the window. She was sitting at a bench talking to the deputy. I could see that she finally had calmed down.

We had been sitting at another bench but my brother Richard got tired and he got up and walked to the window. He wanted to watch out for the bus. I felt for my harmonica in my pocket. It was in my jacket pocket but so far down inside that sometimes I would reach in and could not feel it.

As the time came close for the bus to get here some more people came in and bought their tickets and scattered throughout the station like no one wanted to be close to anyone.

My brother Richard ran from the window to where we were and yelled that the bus was coming. Suddenly we heard the brakes groaning to stop the big machine. We could see through the double doors leading to the garage as the bus turned in, the bus driver straining to turn the wheel so as not to hit the brick columns that divided the garage into bays. He could not come in straight. He stopped the bus, put it in reverse and straightened it out and then he drove the bus in and parked. He jumped out of the bus and helped everyone down. You could tell he'd been doing that for many years. I decided I wanted to be a bus driver right then and there. But I didn't tell anyone, especially not Richard. I would never hear the end of it if I did.

The bus driver was a tall red-skinned man with white hair and white eyebrows. He wore cowboy boots and a heavy wool coat over his blue uniform. He wore black gloves and a cap. He stayed behind until everyone that was supposed to get off got off and then he double checked to make sure no one had left anything behind. I could see him going up and down the aisle looking at the empty seats, talking to the passengers that had not gotten off. He was pointing at them and asking them questions that I couldn't hear. He got off the bus and stood by the door and everyone inside the station got up. He came over to the double doors and stopped us and said we couldn't get on.

"Hold your horses, podners," he said. "We cain't load just yet. Got to unload and get some things out of the way. We'll announce when we're ready to load. Just keep your seats. Stay inside. It's too cold to be out here waitin' on me. I'm liable to be a while."

He went behind the ticket counter and he joked with the lady and poured himself a cup of coffee. "Jesus Christ it's cold out there," he said, taking off his cap and his gloves and warming his hands on the cup. "It's really blowing from Decatur on to here. It never stopped once."

"What time did you leave Decatur?" the ticket lady asked. She looked bored, tired of the people she had to deal with.

"Left about seven this morning," he said.

"That's not bad time," she figured. "They say it's worse the farther west you go."

"And that's exactly where we're headed," he said, shaking his head.

Some men were working on the bus and it was taking longer than the bus driver had thought. The passengers were getting cold so he ordered everyone off the bus and into the lobby. The people going to the bathroom reminded my mother to ask us if we wanted to go but we didn't need to. She had to, so Richard and me and the deputy stayed and watched her purse while she went.

All the bags that were staying in Tahoka came through the doors in a wheelbarrow and the people that first got off the bus and were staying in Tahoka took their bags and left. This made the crowd a lot less and I didn't worry about finding a window seat.

The bus driver announced over the loudspeaker that the bus was ready to be loaded. "But please wait," he begged, "until I get the bus door open and I'm ready to receive passengers before you step out into the bays. Please have your ticket ready so we can load faster. Please be sure your name and destination is on your baggage. If you need to, before you get on the bus please be sure to give your baggage to the baggage man. Thank you." He put on his cap and tipped it to the ticket lady and hurried to the bus through the double doors putting on his coat and gloves. The deputy said goodbye to Mom and to us. "Be good boys," he said. "Treat your mom right. She's been through a lot. Bye-bye, Christie," he said and he kissed Mom and handed her her suitcase.

When we finally loaded into the bus Richard found his window seat and my mother sat by him and I found my window seat and next to me came and sat this fat man who squeezed me against the side of the bus until my mother noticed me and got up and found another seat for me. The bus driver looked back through his mirror at my mother and me walking around while the bus was warming up and he smiled as my mother smiled at him. She found a window seat for me and sat me down.

The bus pulled back slowly, the bus driver using the side-mirrors to guide it. He narrowly missed the brick column on the right, coming to within two or three inches of hitting it. Somehow he maneuvered the bus, checking from side to side, slowly getting us out of the garage bay.

Once out on the street, still going in reverse, he turned the bus with great effort. The bus stopped abruptly, jerking our heads backwards as he hit the curb. He slid the cold gear shift to first, low low, and started in a yanking motion, turning the bus as it went forward for the first time.

We were at the intersection right by the diner. The deputy was sitting down having another cup of coffee. When he heard the bus he came out and waved. The bus driver waited a while to make sure no one was coming in either direction on Main Street and he started the bus moving again, turning left into Main Street and going past the courthouse. The deputy was still waving at Mom when we left.

I was sitting by myself by the window but I wasn't really looking outside. I was thinking mainly about the things I forgot to do before I left. I forgot to go say goodbye to Mrs. Smith. The last period on Friday had been recess and she didn't go out with us that day so when the bell rang I just came home. Richard and me had our jackets and our caps on for recess so we ran home together. I thought maybe we wouldn't have recess that day what with the wind blowing so hard.

I was thinking that with the wind everyone was a good punter in Tahoka. All you had to do was kick the ball hard and the wind would carry it and make it roll forever. Kicking against the wind was a different story. One time at a football game Clarence kicked the ball into the wind and it went up high in the air and pretty soon it started to come back and it went past Clarence and he wound up having to catch the ball himself and run with it. We were all laughing in the stands and Clarence heard us and he yelled that he was going to get us if we didn't shut up. That was about the same time he said he was going to kill his stepfather if he ever showed up. We didn't even know he had a stepfather until then.

I forgot to say goodbye to Mrs. Abercrombie and there was no excuse for that. She was out on recess duty with us and I ran past her on the way home. It seemed that as bundled up as she was that she didn't have time for me. I felt I was wrong in not stopping to say goodbye but now it was too late.

I had seen Mrs. Peters in the morning in the hall and she had asked me if we were still leaving and I had told her we were. I said goodbye to her but I could have done it better.

The bus moved slowly through town. Mother was looking outside at the few people in the streets. Suddenly she shot up, like she had seen a ghost. She said to us, excited, "I'm sure I just saw Mrs. Smith and her husband walking by the jewelry store."

"It probably was them," Richard said, looking out of the window, without even looking at Mom, "they come over to visit Mrs. Peters. They only live about fifty miles away."

"I thought you all told me she had moved out of state?" Mom said.

"She did," Richard lied, "but they're back. Her husband got fired."

"Poor her," Mom said, "and I thought I was the only one with husband problems. That goes to show that even the educated have their problems."

"Oh, they've got more problems than we do," Richard said, like he knew what he was talking about.

Mom said wistfully, "I wish you all had told me about her. I never got a chance to thank her for giving Jim the harmonica."

CHAPTER 21

We were heading west to Brownfield, heading right into the sleet. A noisy heater was blowing hot air around the driver and against the windshield. The windshield wipers were pushing the ice off the warm windshield as fast as it fell and melted into slush. A man that was sitting behind the driver was trying to help keep the windshield clear by wiping the condensation off with a rag. He and the bus driver were carrying on a conversation among all the other small conversations in the bus. I couldn't understand what anyone was saying. The weather and the confusion in the bus were making me nervous.

We went past the last house in Tahoka, Clarence's house, the small lonely wooden house that sat far out from the road in an open field, the house where Clarence would kill his mama one day.

We settled down and the trip was starting to get boring. Richard kept looking back at me between the window and his seat and making faces to see if he could get me to laugh. My mother punched Richard in the ribs and he stopped, but the minute Mom started to talk to the other passengers he would make a face at me. Mom got impatient and tired of Richard so she got up and sat us both together and took my seat.

The wind was coming through the cracks in the windows. Some of us, the ones that didn't have heavy clothing, were feeling cold, especially in the feet. An old lady who had boarded the bus at Amarillo complained to the bus driver that she had been on the bus all day long and she was feeling bad. She suffered from poor circulation. She was shivering and rubbing her hands. Her face looked gray. Her eyes looked glazed and her lips looked blue and she kept wetting them with her tongue. She said that if she didn't keep busy she would fall asleep and freeze. Mom went and sat down with her and put her arm around her to get her warm.

Four men about my father's age were sitting together at the back on the long seat. They were playing a card game but they had to stop once in a while to cross their arms around their chest to keep warm. They were passing a bottle of whiskey around and laughing.

We arrived at Brownfield in about thirty minutes. We came in fast for having such bad roads, went right through town before we stopped at the bus station in an old two-story hotel built of petrified rock and logs. From where we sat, the hotel looked warm. Several people got off at Brownfield and two people, a couple, got on. They acted confused trying to decide where to sit. The old lady that was turning blue wanted to get off at Brownfield. She said she couldn't take it anymore. Her feet were frozen. Her children were just going to have to wait for her a few more days. She wasn't about to travel in this weather. She talked to the bus driver and he took her by the hand and led her slowly off the bus and into the hotel and as far as we could tell he got her a room. He came back without her. He took a form from the glove compartment and went back into the bus-station. It took a short while and he was back. He closed the door and released the hand-brake and the bus started rolling forward. "Next stop, Seminole," he yelled. Then, "Forty-five minutes."

"You've got to be careful with old people like that," the bus driver said to his friend sitting behind him. "You've got to account for everyone on the bus. Can't go 'round losin' passengers. That's a good way to get fired. I just had to get a passenger-release form filled out. That way everyone knows where the old lady is."

"Never thought about it like that. It sure would be easy to lose someone on a trip."

"You're damn right. Friend of mine lost a kid one time and it took days before they found 'im. The parents wanted to sue. I don't blame 'em."

"Me either," the friend agreed.

Pretty soon the story got back to us, each row passing on the conversation about the old lady and the friend that had lost a child.

The last we got was that the lady was supposed to go to Odessa, but she had signed a piece of paper saying that she was sick and wanted to stay at Brownfield.

The couple that had boarded at Brownfield decided to sit across from Richard and me. The lady leaned over across the aisle and poked Mom on the shoulder. "How has the trip been?" she asked. There was something funny about the way they talked. They sounded very excited and loud about everything, especially the lady. Anyway, it seemed funny to me and my brother Richard. I was trying to be real serious but Richard kept making faces at me and we started giggling and couldn't stop. Now every time the lady opened her mouth we started laughing until my mother excused herself and got up and beat us on the head with her purse. It really embarrassed us because the couple looked at us like we were crazy and couldn't control ourselves. Richard was red-faced looking out the window, tears running down his face. I cried a little too because the rap on the head hurt. The thin man with yellow fingers that had kept looking at us was laughing. The men at the back stopped their game and watched. The passengers that had not seen it were asking what had happened. Row after row we could hear the information being passed forward. When it reached the bus-driver he chortled in glee.

After Mom went back and sat down, the lady continued like nothing had happened. "My daughter says that when you boil an egg you always, always start off with tepid water and a tepid egg. Let them both, the water and the egg, reach a boiling temperature at the same time and you'll never get a cracked egg. Which is what I intend to do this Easter. She read it somewhere."

The lady looked at my mother suspiciously to see if my mother was going to follow her advise. She waited a little while for Mom to answer.

"That's good to know," my mother said, trying to sound interested. The truth was that Mom was not into cooking. She could cook the basics but that was all. We weren't into eating fancy food.

Richard was wiping the tears from his eyes with a handkerchief that I swore belonged to Mr. Allen. He folded the handkerchief making sure to hide the large embroidered A on the corner and placed it in his hip pocket. He wouldn't look at me. He was too hurt. I could tell even at this early time in his life that Richard had a lot of rage in him. At the time I thought that our dad had spanked him so much that he was very resentful of any type of physical punishment. He didn't want anyone touching him. And even though he had not confided in me I knew that as soon as he was old enough that he would run away. I also guessed, and rightly so, that he was planning on killing our father and that that was why he had been so interested in learning about cars from Mr. Allen. Sylvia's death, which he blamed on Dad, had been the last straw. But things were not that simple. There were other sources for his rage as I would find out later.

My Mom was right. It wasn't good manners to be laughing at the way people talked but you had to agree that the lady was funny. All she seemed to be able to talk about was cooking. She was leaning across the aisle on one elbow toward my mother shouting to be heard above the noise of the bus.

"She was saying the other day that if you add just one teaspoon of vinegar to your boilin' water your poached eggs come out perfect all the time. Now isn't that somethin'?"

Her husband suddenly realized she had stopped talking and automatically he replied, "Sure is," like he was really thinking about it. "You just never know," he said some more.

My mother was acting like she was going to use all of this.

"When it calls for three tablespoons," the lady yelled, "add one more. Make it four. You'll see the difference. I bake the best biscuits in Hobbs," she said, real proud of herself. "Best pie-crust, too. Melts in your mouth."

"For sure," her husband agreed.

He was looking out the window, having wiped the condensation off and concentrating on the conversation at the same time.

"Put up twenty-four quarts of tomatoes last year," she informed my mother out of the blue.

"Good God," my mother said. She was trying to act surprised and impressed. "That's a lot isn't it?"

"For sure," the husband replied.

"It sure is," the lady screamed. "Cousin Connie put up twenty-four but her jars were littler than mine. Mine are the old kind of jars. The ones from the ole' timey days when a quart was a quart."

There was just something very funny about the lady. She looked like a little fat hen, like one of Mr. Allen's hens, Gertrude, the one that cackled all the time to tell the whole world that she had just laid an egg. Her legs were short and only the tips of her shoes touched the floor. She kept trying to cross her legs but she couldn't. Every time she tried, her short thigh would slide off the top of the bottom one.

Richard finally looked at me. He was feeling better. We were laughing on the inside. We didn't want my mother to hear us.

"All you have to do," she was saying, in a voice hoarse from screaming, "is not grease the cookie sheet. That way it'll stick to the bottom and not run off." God only knew what she was talking about now. "You're going to eat it off the pan anyway." Whatever it was she was referring to she seemed to think that she had been the first to think of the idea.

I caught a glimpse of the road sign through the sleet as we went past it. It said Seminole—20 miles, Odessa—85 miles.

The weather had not changed. The only advantage we had was that we were now traveling south and the wind was coming more from the rear. The driver was not having as much problems seeing the road.

Listening to the lady did make the trip a lot shorter and she kept our minds off the cold. She talked to Mom about cooking until we got to Seminole. At Seminole about half the people got off including the four men that had been drinking and playing cards. Most of these passengers were making a connection with the big bus south to Odessa. We would continue to Hobbs on the same bus. Mom got off for a short while, just to get a rest from the lady, I suppose. We could see her inside the little bus station talking to the ticket lady and the bus driver. She drank some water from the faucet and then looked at the post-cards on the rack. The bus driver said something to her and she followed him to the bus.

"Next stop, Hobbs, New Mexico," he shouted. "Anyone goin' to Odessa should be off this bus. Do you all understand? This bus is going to Hobbs. This bus is not goin' to Odessa...not goin' to Odessa. Any Mexicans here that don't comprende?"

The lady thought that the bus driver was funny and she giggled at Mom. She was being quiet for once.

At Seminole we turned west once again and into the full force of the norther. The driver was having trouble seeing the road again.

"I'm so glad you all are going to Hobbs," the lady said. "For a minute there I thought you were getting off at Seminole. But then I says to Harry, 'Why didn't the children get off?' And Harry says, 'What makes you so sure that they're her children?' 'Why she hit 'em,' I says. They are your children, aren't they?"

"Yes," Mom gave the tired answer.

"Your husband is in Hobbs?"

"No, he's in Artesia."

"It's pretty in Artesia," she informed us as she crossed her arms under her bust. She looked at us and said, "You'll like it in Artesia. But Hobbs is prettier."

You could tell just by watching her eyes that she had run out of things to say about Hobbs and she was desperately trying to get back to her cooking. "You know," she said, her voice almost gone, "the secret to a good stew?"

Mom shook her weary head.

At Hobbs we had a rest stop to eat and the couple got off. She was glad that the monthly visit to their daughter and her husband and grandchildren in Brownfield was completed. "I wish they would move back to Hobbs," she told Mom. "There's nothin' in Brownfield. But like I told her, your life is with your husband." Mom let them get off first and she continued to tell Mom her life story even as she walked off the bus. They waited for the bus driver to get their suitcase out from the under-side of the bus and when theirs came out the husband took it and they walked away, in silence, exhausted, her voice gone.

The bus station in Hobbs was a restaurant and we sat at the counter to eat. We had hamburgers and milk but no french fries. My brother Richard and me were hungry. While we were waiting for the hamburgers Mom started to get after us again. She said we had been disrespectful to the lady. She blamed Richard but Richard blamed me. He said that I had started it all when I told him the lady reminded me of "Gertrude the hen." My mother didn't appreciate this at all and she knocked Richard and me on the head with her knuckle in front of all those people.

The hamburger was good. I could hear Richard chewing in between sobs sitting on my mother's other side. Worse still I could see him in the mirror across the counter and he saw me and I'll never forget his face, his mouth full of hamburger and milk and crying.

When we got back on the bus my mom sat us down and told us to behave. The other passengers were staring at us wondering what it was we had done. My brother Richard had quit crying and after everyone was back on the bus and the driver got us going I could see that sticking out of Richard's jacket pocket was a spoon and a fork he had stolen. God help us, I thought to myself, if my mother gets wind of this.

We were headed north, more into the blizzard than ever before. It took us longer to get to Lovington than it had to get from Seminole to Hobbs. We could no longer see outside. At Lovington several passengers got off and no one got on. We would stop only to load and unload in Maljamar and Loco

Hills. The bus driver didn't want anyone getting off the bus unless they really had to.

My brother Richard and me were scared and cold. The old bus made strange crying noises as it crushed the ice on the road. We got close together and Richard put his arm around me and held me close to keep me warm. I was thinking that maybe one of us could grow up to be a bus driver. What I liked was when the bus driver got to a place and he opened the bus door and stepped out like he owned the world and he stood by the door and held out his hand to all the women stepping down. The young men he ignored. He was always looking somewhere else when I got off the bus, talking to somebody, like I wasn't even there when I stepped down. That's really what I wanted to do when I grew up, be able to ignore someone like me.

CHAPTER 22

We arrived in Artesia in the dark. The hum of the bus had put a lot of the passengers to sleep. I could see their heads dozing off. I could see the lights from the town as I kept cleaning my window. It looked like a large town, a lot bigger than Tahoka anyway. Richard was asleep next to me and I woke him up to show him the town from the top of the hill. He leaned over me and looked through the window. "What is it?" he asked, rubbing his eyes.

"Artesia," I said.

"We're there already?"

"Yep. You've been asleep for hours."

Mom was looking out the window in the quiet of the bus and she said, "Have you boys seen Artesia, how pretty it looks at night? Look at all the little lights. It looks like a Christmas tree."

The bus entered through the east side, crossed a river and went on directly to the heart of town. The people in the bus, the ones sitting ahead of us that could see through the front started to talk, restless, relieved to be there, eager to get out. Some were reaching over their heads to the bins pulling down packages and small suitcases wrapped with twine. They were starting to ignore each other again like they had at the bus station at Tahoka. They were no longer friendly as they had been when we were having trouble with the storm. The word that we were coming into the bus station was not being passed back. It was everyone for himself.

The bus went past the station and turned right and went half a block and turned right again into an alley that led into the garage at the rear. Five or six buses were there loading and unloading their passengers, the ice and mud melting off them in puddles in the warmth of the garage. The buses looked warm together.

By the time we got off the bus our suitcases were out and we took them and carried them inside the waiting room. Mom was looking for our father. She would not find him. Aunt Betty had come to pick us up. "Jim is with Robert workin'. They left today and won't come back till Friday. Look at Richard and Jim," she said, trying to gloss over the feeling of rejection that we felt because our father had not waited for us. She turned us around and admired us. "My, Christie, but they've grown. Look at 'em?" She was asking Junior and Dolly to look at us.

"Yes," Mom said, having waited her turn, "but look at Junior and Dolly. They've even grown more." Junior looked like a small Clarence, beefy headed and heavy browed, dumb, with short fingers. Dolly was something else. She was beautiful and although she was covered up I could see she had long legs and a very nice face. She wasn't delicate in her features. Her nose was not small. Her mouth was full-lipped like Aunt Betty but I could see some of Uncle Robert's features in her. Her eyes were a lot like Uncle Robert's but not exactly like them. You could see the resemblance to both Aunt Betty and Uncle Robert in her that you couldn't see in Junior. In Dolly the best of both parents had come out and she had turned out to be a very good-looking girl, a lot prettier than Mitzi. "Look at little Jimmy look at Dolly," I heard Aunt Betty say.

"They always liked to play together, remember? Do you all remember when you played together for days on end?"

Finally it was Mom's and Aunt Betty's turn. They embraced and cried as the people walking by in the waiting room ignored them. "Christie...Christie..." Aunt Betty cried. "You don't know how I feel for you. I feel so bad. I feel like I let you down when you needed me most."

They were holding hands now, looking at each other. Mom said, "Don't feel bad. You and I go a long way to be bothered by stuff like that. You know how it is. It's partly my fault too. I knew Mr. Allen didn't tell you everythin' right. I should have gotten on the phone but I couldn't think straight. Believe me, I was going through hell and no one to really talk to."

"I still feel bad about the whole thing but you're right, Christie. Mr. Allen didn't say much. He acted like the funeral was over already."

"Well, that's the way he was. He was hard to figure out. I had a hard time living there. I was grateful but if I hadn't had the boys to think of I would've left right away. But I'm sure you feel bad and I don't want you to."

"Come," Aunt Betty said, putting her hand around Mom's waist, "let's get out of here and go home. You all need a good meal."

I could see from the outside that Aunt Betty's house was bigger than the Allen's. They didn't own it, though, and once inside I could see that they didn't have the furniture or the nice things the Allens had. The house looked almost empty. We were standing in a fairly large room that was like a living room, dining room and kitchen all in one. There was only a sofa and a chair and a chiffonier in the living room, a table with five chairs in the eating area and behind that the kitchen. Half-way, on either side of this room was a hall. Each hall had two bedrooms and ended at a bathroom. Aunt Betty had figured that the adults would stay on one side of the house and the children would stay across on the other side. Junior would share his bedroom with us and across the hall from us would be Dolly. Richard and me took our suitcases into Junior's room and he showed us the dresser drawers and the closet space we could use. We unpacked and hid the suitcases under the bed.

After supper Aunt Betty and Mom washed dishes and sat down to talk. Aunt Betty had lit a cigarette and had placed an ash tray and a pack of cigarettes next to her cup of coffee. She crossed her leg and began to talk. We knew that that was a sign that she was going to talk for a long time.

Dolly, Junior, Richard and me had gone to Junior's room where he was showing us everything he had received for Christmas. He had gotten a lot of toys. Dolly had climbed up on Junior's bed and was watching us as we sat on the floor between the two beds. She was not interested in playing with toys. I couldn't help but look at her once in a while when she wasn't looking. She was sitting cross-legged like an Indian, covering her legs with her skirt. She was looking at Richard, like she was studying him.

"You're cute," she told Richard, interrupting what Junior was saying. "You've grown a lot since I saw you last and you've grown cute."

Richard blushed and we all giggled. He wouldn't look at Dolly. She was smiling.

"Knock it off," Junior said to her as he took out a deck of cards.

"What if I don't want to?" she pouted.

"You're cute, too," she said. I looked up to her when she said "too." I knew she meant me. I thought I could keep from blushing, but I couldn't. I couldn't remember if Mitzi had ever said that to me. I didn't think so. Mitzi was not that forward. I wasn't used to being called "cute." Most girls would say how

short I was for my age. I didn't think I was cute. Once my mother covered
my mouth and said I would look very handsome if it wasn't for my mouth.
She did this showing me off to a neighbor.

"Aw, Dolly," Junior said. "Why don't you leave 'em alone? Let 'em be.
They're too young for you."

She took her skirt in both hands and lifted it slightly and fanned her thighs
with it. I was kneeling right across from her, in front of her, and so was my
brother Richard. Junior was giving her his back. She knew he couldn't see
what she was doing.

"It's hot in here," she said.

I had seen the inside of her thighs. I looked at my brother Richard to see
what he was doing. He acted like he had not seen anything. Then she did it
again. This time I thought I did see something else. This time I knew Richard
had seen something. But it was so dark once you got past the thighs. Junior
was looking at us like we were crazy. Our eyes were glued on Dolly. "What's
the matter with you guys?" he asked. His head was bent down as he shuffled
the cards. "Do you or don't you want to play? Let's get with it, you guys.
Quit payin' attention to her. She's goofy."

"I am not!" Dolly shouted.

"You children behave in front of company," we could hear Aunt Betty yell
from the kitchen.

"You are too," Junior said.

"I am not," Dolly replied.

"Yes you are."

"No I'm not."

"Yes you are."

"No I'm not."

They kept this up for a long time, growing quieter as they went so that
Aunt Betty would not hear them. Finally Dolly changed the subject. She said
to Junior, "You're a queer."

And he replied: "No I'm not."

"Yes you are."

"No I'm not."

This went on for a while, too. Richard and me just sat there listening. Then
Junior got fed up and he shouted, "Goddamit, shut up or I'll break your
fuckin' face!" something that he had learned from Uncle Robert.

Dolly jumped off the bed. She opened the door and pushed her butt up like she was going to fart at us and at the same time she stuck out her tongue at Junior and she left, leaving the door open.

Her room was right across the hall from ours and she ran into it and slammed the door. Junior was too concerned with his card game to pay any attention to her.

"What's goin' on?" came Aunt Betty's voice from the table.

When no one answered her, she yelled, "You boys get out of that room and come here right away."

When he heard Aunt Betty, Junior got angry and threw the cards on the floor and walked out and not being sure ourselves what to do we followed right behind him.

My mother and Aunt Betty were talking about my sister Sylvia, how bad it had been.

"She got sick so all of a sudden," my mother was saying when we got to the table, wiping the tears from her eyes. "We were on our way to come be with you all. We had loaded the truck and started off. We were in what I thought was good health. No one had even coughed for a while. I was so happy that we were all feelin' good. We hadn't been travelin' any at all when Sylvia started to feel bad. It kept gettin' worse. Then the truck broke down. Everythin' that could go wrong went wrong from then on. Jim gets all nervous and angry like he does and takes off, takes off on a night like that when I needed 'im the most. And me with Sylvia dying in my arms, the boys there in the truck with us tryin' to keep warm. It was awful, just awful." Aunt Betty smiled at us and beckoned to us to sit. She placed her finger up to her mouth to tell us to be quiet while Mom was talking. She had smoked about ten cigarettes by then. Mom hardly noticed we were there. She kept on. "At first the doctors were sayin' it was just diarrhea and then dehydration from the diarrhea. But after a couple of days they were real concerned. It seemed to me that they were confused. First they'd do one thing, then they'd do another. Finally," my mother said, wiping some more tears from her eyes, "they sent off some stool from her to Lubbock and the test came back positive for polio. Polio! Can you imagine it? Where did the poor child get polio? No one knew. You should have been there. One doctor wanted to give her enemas. But she had diarrhea, the nurse told 'im. There were only two doctors and they were arguing about what to do. Finally, Dr. Morgan, the one who seemed to know what was goin' on ordered an iron lung from Midland. It never arrived. Then a friend of mine, a deputy, said that they should have ordered one from Lubbock. My poor baby died in my arms."

"But she may have died anyway," Aunt Betty said.

"I know that," Mom cried, "but it still makes it hard to take. Don't get me wrong. I thought they tried everythin' that they knew how. They did their best. It was a real small hospital."

Aunt Betty tapped the ash off the end of the cigarette. She was looking very serious. "I'm glad you're not angry. A lot of times I see people get angry over somethin' like this and they live with this anger for so long that it affects their lives. I'm glad you're not feelin' that way."

"No. I feel we did all we could. You should have seen the people. They were all so nice to us. They really helped us all. The boys 'specially. They gave 'em clothes, everythin' you could imagine. Every stitch of clothes they own except for the new jackets and the flannel shirts was given to them. No, I have no bitterness with anyone. I do ask God why he did it and I can't get an answer. The Jehovah's Witnesses say that when you die it's good. You'll be resurrected on Judgement Day. We will all be together then."

"Well," Aunt Betty said, "I still feel bad about us not goin' to the funeral. No matter what you say and how much you forgive me I don't think I'll ever forgive myself. The day of the funeral I knew I had screwed up. I should have just not paid any attention to Bob and I should have taken the bus. I promise, Christie, that I'll never do that to you again."

"I hope you don't have to."

"Yeah, you're right," responded Aunt Betty, exhaling smoke. "I hope there ain't another time. Not for the children anyway. We older codgers can die and no one'll mind."

She looked at the cigarette in her hand and she smiled. She took a sip of coffee and Mom did too. Softly, like it pained her to change the conversation, Aunt Betty said, "Bob and Jim are doing great."

Mom looked at her cup and did not reply.

Aunt Betty looked at Mom and held Mom's arm. "How do you feel 'bout Jim?" she asked. "I mean, he deserted you and the kids when you needed 'im the most. He gets here in the old truck all by himself tellin' us all these lies."

"What did he say?"

"You really want to hear?"

Mom nodded and said, "I might as well."

"Well, he said that you'd run 'im off. Had stayed with Jack."

"Jack?"

"That's what he said."

"I haven't seen Jack since Jim was in prison and that's a fact."

"Well, he's got it in his mind that you love Jack and that you wanted to stay with Jack. That Jack had followed you to Tahoka. That it was all planned. He never said anythin' about Sylvia bein' sick or Sylvia bein' in the hospital. We didn't know about Sylvia bein' sick until you called."

"I don't know where he could have gotten that idea. You know he can lie better than anyone in this world. He's sick, you know that."

"Hell, yes," Aunt Betty laughed, "I know he's sick. I bet you he won't mention anythin' about Jack to you. But what you goin' to do?"

"What can I do?" Mom said. "I'm already here. There ain't much for me to do. He's my husband. He needs me."

"I'm kind of relieved to hear you say that," Aunt Betty sighed, "because I thought we were fixin' to have us the biggest fight of our lives when they come home on Friday."

"I only wish that what he lied about was true. Then Sylvia would be alive...Jack? Did he really say that about me and Jack?"

"He really did. I didn't believe 'im and neither did Bob. Bob told me later on that there was somethin' wrong about the whole story. But promise me one thing and that is that you won't mention a word about what I said. Don't mention Jack's name. I don't want that on my conscience. No sirree."

"That's okay with me but if you want to know the truth, he escaped from the sheriff in Tahoka. The deputy left 'im handcuffed to the truck while he took us with Sylvia to the hospital. When he went back for Jim, Jim was gone. He'd started the truck somehow and he took off. It's a good thing he wasn't in jail for something serious, if not they'd have tracked 'im down. They were really glad to get 'im out of town."

"What'd he do?"

"When he left us that night he went to a beer-joint and got drunk and got into a fight like he always does and he got beat up and arrested for disturbin' the peace. They still have a warrant for his arrest."

"That's why he couldn't go back to the funeral."

Mom looked at Aunt Betty like she was relieved that Aunt Betty had finally found out what had happened. "Sure," Mom said, "if he'd gone back they'd have arrested 'im."

Aunt Betty lit another cigarette. She studied the tip and rolled it around inside the ashtray. She shook her head and started to laugh. "Forgive me for laughin'," she said, "but Jim said that you didn't want 'im in Tahoka."

'The sheriff wanted 'im in Tahoka," Mom said and they both laughed.

We did too but it felt strange to be laughing about our own father. Outside we could hear the wind beat against the house.

"Well, he got here..." Aunt Betty couldn't remember the exact date. She was thinking. "It must have been a day late because he said he had to lay over somewhere to fix the truck. Can you believe that the truck hasn't broken down one single time since he got here? Well, anyway, he got in and on that same day he went out and sold all his tools and all that junk he had in back of the truck. Don't ask me where he sold it. He came back cleaned out and with money in his pocket and a couple of bottles of whiskey. Bob and him drank all that day and Bob told 'im what they ought to do and, by golly, they've been doin' it ever since. I do remember that they got stinkin' drunk they were so happy to see each other, bein' the only two left in the family and all."

"Knowing them," my mother said to Aunt Betty, "I'm sure they're up to somethin'. And it usually ends up that we're in trouble."

'Yeah, you're right..." Aunt Betty answered. She seemed to me to stop in the middle of the sentence, worried at what she knew the two men were doing.

There was a crashing sound against the wall on the north side of the house. Everyone at the table stopped to listen, startled. "It's just the ice breakin' off the roof," Aunt Betty said and everyone was quiet once more. Aunt Betty lit another cigarette and inhaled the smoke deeply. She exhaled it slowly. We were still recovering from the loud noise the ice had made as it fell against the wall. "It's been a long day for you all," she said to Mom. "When did you all leave?"

"It sure has been," Mom said as she raised the cup of coffee and blew on it and then drank from it. Her eyes never left the window. She was looking outside through the kitchen window at the snow and the drifts as they stacked up against the houses across the street. "We left at close to eleven," she said. "Which reminds me, I need to use the phone to call the Allens to tell 'em we made it."

"Help yourself," Aunt Betty said.

"I"m goin' to keep track of all the calls I make," Mom informed her, "so I can pay you back at the end of the month."

"Don't worry about it, Christie. You ain't goin' to be makin' that many calls. Bob says I can stay on the telephone longer than anybody he's ever seen. Take your time."

Mom went over to the telephone on the kitchen counter and dialed the operator and gave her the Allen's number. Aunt Betty got up and poured some more coffee.

We all waited for the phone to ring. Mom took a deep breath. "Hello? Hello, Mrs. Allen?" she spoke. "Yes, that's right. It's Christie.....Yes.....Yes, we got here all right.........I know. We were in it all the way over. It took us eight hours to get here.........Well, it was a big storm. It's still goin' on right now. How is it there?................Yes, I can imagine.................Did some of them die?..........Well, tell 'im we feel sorry for 'im...............It's about that cold here. Very cold. They say it's the coldest that it's been since nineteen thirty.....Thirty-two? Well I knew it was somewhere around then.....They're fine. They did fine on the trip. I was afraid for 'em but they didn't seem to be scared. I was more scared than them..........Well, that's right. They don't have that much sense at that age.....That's true too. Well, I won't keep you any longer. I just called to let you all know that we got here all right.......Well, that's okay. I still have enough from what Mrs. Able paid me....No. I hadn't included that in the total. I hadn't cashed the check, that's why. So I got more than I thought. It's sweet of you anyway, but I'm just keepin' track of all the phone calls and I'll pay Betty at the end of the month.....She's doin' well...I'll tell her........ Thanks anyway.........Say hello to Mr. Allen and Wilma and Arlan and everyone. Be sure and tell 'em we're doin' fine and already settled down.........I'll call again. Goodnight......God bless you too."

"They sound like good people," said Aunt Betty, who had been listening intently.

"They sure are," replied Mom, "they treated us like family, better maybe."

"Speakin' of family, last Wednesday was Robert's birthday," Aunt Betty said. "The twenty-fifth of February."

"That's right," Mom remembered, "I'd almost forgotten. How old is he now?"

"He turned thirty-seven. He was born in 1916. Time flies."

"It sure does," my mother agreed.

"What'd you all do?"

"I didn't do anythin'. Bob and Jim were out with the Indians and they said they had a hell of a celebration." Aunt Betty then turned to us sitting around the table and she realized we were not with the conversation. "You boys can go play in your room, Junior," Aunt Betty told him. "Maybe now you all can learn to behave and quit shoutin'."

We would have preferred to have seen our father that same night. That way we could have gotten over all the pain and hurt right away. As it was, now we had to wait for one week before we would confront him. We lived all that week in desperation trying to imagine over and over again what it was going to be like. Richard and me could see the worry in Mother's face. It was not a good week at all.

CHAPTER 23

On Friday night we all bathed and waited for Uncle Robert and my dad to come home. Mom had dressed up and fixed her hair and made up her face, but Aunt Betty had had her hair teased into a beehive at the beauty shop. When she and Mom got back from the beauty shop Aunt Betty got off the car with her hair wrapped in toilet paper. She was not to touch her hair for the next week, wrapping it every night when she went to bed. Earlier that night Mom had made up Aunt Betty's face as we watched. "You have nice eyes," she told Aunt Betty, "you ought to accent 'em." But she said it without thinking like she was very nervous about something else and she was trying to say something to clear her mind. We got to eat supper early so that we would not be in the way. After we ate, we were sent to our rooms to wait. Aunt Betty and Mom sat down and drank coffee and talked. Every car that came by, every noise disturbed and worried us. I could hear Mom getting up and sitting down and Aunt Betty nervously telling her to keep calm, that everything would be all right. Richard was in bed trying to read a comic book. Junior was playing with an airplane. I was sitting on the bed looking out the foggy window, worried at what might happen when Uncle Robert and my dad arrived. They were violent men. Dolly was in her room playing her scratched records.

I saw a beam of light across the vacant lot in back of the house. It was coming on Main Street parallel to the house. I followed the lights as the vehicle kept on and on, never turning. When it got to Twenty-Second Street the vehicle turned. At the intersection of Pinon Street instead of turning it continued straight and into the driveway. They had arrived. My heart missed a beat and I felt light-headed. Richard put down the comic book and stared at the ceiling. His color changed. I knew exactly how he felt. We would have given anything to be back in Tahoka. Junior kept on playing with his airplane.

We heard the truck engine stop and the two men get out. It took them a very short time to get up on the porch. We could hear the laughter and the men stomping their boots on the porch cleaning the mud and the ice off. Another great crashing sound came from our side of the house. A large chunk of ice had fallen off the roof overhang. Richard shot up from the bed with the noise. I had almost fallen out of bed. Junior laughed at us. "You guys gotta get used to that," he giggled.

Mom and Aunt Betty had grown silent. The large wooden door opened and the men came in. Aunt Betty screamed like she was so glad to see Uncle Robert. We knew she wasn't. She was asking how everything had gone and the next thing we heard was her footsteps running to our room and Dolly's room. "They're here," she shouted, opening our door and sticking her beehive covered head and painted face into the room like a jack-in-the-box. I could sense the insincerity in her voice; I could see it in her eyes. "Children, the men are here. Come on out and say hello to your fathers."

She brought us out and stood us in line to wait to be greeted. Dolly was first and next to her was Junior and then Richard and then me. My dad had not yet greeted anybody. He stared at Richard and me and then at Mom and I could feel him colder than the ice-covered roof on the house. He looked thinner. He had taken his jacket off and the clothes he was wearing were too big for him. He still insisted on buying clothes that were too big for him, never admitting to himself how small he was. He had grown a large moustache that covered his mouth and made his eyes look smaller and closer together, like some small fierce animal backed up in his cave. He had gone directly to the kitchen and found a bottle of whiskey in a cabinet by the sink and was drinking from it. Uncle Robert had grown fatter. He was hugging Aunt Betty and rubbing her large rear. She was laughing, holding her cigarette away from him to keep from accidentally burning him, standing on one foot and then the other as she leaned against him. He turned loose of Aunt Betty and looked at Mom. He walked over and hugged Mom at the shoulders. Then he hugged Dolly and shook Junior's hand. When he came to us he said, "Well, well, well, look at this. Ain't these boys grown since I last saw 'em. When was the last time I saw 'em?"

Aunt Betty was prepared for the question. She and Mom had been talking about it for the whole week. "We saw 'em in Corpus five years ago."

"That's right," Uncle Robert said, holding on to my cold hand. "That was the night of the big fight when Jim got drunk and wanted to beat up your mom. Remember that son?"

"Yes sir," I said, thinking what a way it was to remember.

"And Richard. How you doin' big man?

"Oh, all right," Richard said.

"They're all in school already. Christie and me enrolled 'em on Monday and they started that same day. They really like it here."

"I'm glad," Uncle Robert said. "I'm glad for the both of you. Glad you're glad and glad you're in school. Don't be no dummy like your dad and me. Go to school. Shit, this ain't no life having to work so hard. Yet, Christie, we're doin' good. Right Jim?"

Aunt Betty said, "Jim, why don't you and Christie say hello to each other? There ain't no sense just standin' there like you both don't exist. Come on, hug each other. Let by-gones be by-gones."

"Fuck, Jim, don't be an ass-hole...say somethin'," Uncle Robert told him.

My father and Mom walked toward each other and Mom put out her hand and he shook it.

Suddenly and out of nowhere Uncle Robert shouted at the top of his voice, "All right, all the goddam children to their rooms. We grown-ups have got to get drunk and it's not goin' to be a pretty sight. Git! Everybody git!"

As we lay in bed we could hear them talking. Mom and Dad were arguing about that night in Tahoka and Sylvia. Mom called him a sonofabitch. I thought they were going to come to blows. I could hear the chairs being thrown aside. I had never heard my mother be so brave. At one point she said that if she had a gun she would kill him. My dad said that he did have a gun in the truck and he would kill Mom. Uncle Robert stopped it right there. He was large enough and this was his house. Aunt Betty remained silent, afraid that if she spoke and got Uncle Robert angry he would start on her. The conversation changed to their jobs. They did not want to tell Mother what it was they were doing. Aunt Betty was trying to protect her from knowing. She kept telling Mom that that was the men's area. She never interfered with Uncle Robert. Mom kept insisting. She wanted to know so that she could be prepared for whatever came. She said that she might want to be prepared to leave on a moments notice, which now seems prophetic. In his drunken state Uncle Robert decided to speak up. "You really want to know, Christi?" he slobbered.

"Yes I do."

"This is not what we plan to do all the time. You understand that? This is just a sideline to keep us going for the winter. You see, there ain't much goin' on in the winter around here. All of New Mexico shuts down. It's too cold to work outside. So we work inside."

"Doin' what? If I know you and Jim it's somethin' that's not supposed to be done. It's got to be illegal."

"Sweetheart, you hit the nail on the head. Your dumb husband and me are selling whiskey to the fuckin' Indians and they're lapping it up."

Again we were startled almost out of our beds by the crashing sound of large pieces of ice falling against the wall of the house right by the window. The wall shook and seemed to move toward us. The feeling of doom that I felt then matched the feeling of doom that was in my brother Richard's and my heart. We had heard what they were doing and it did not sound right.

The school wasn't much. Of all the schools we had been in, this one was the worst. About one-third the class was people like us, poor whites, the other third were Mexicans and the other third were Mescalero-Apache Indians bused in from the reservation. Not one group could get along with the other. Richard and me learned very fast to be very careful. We tried to be friendly with everyone. Junior had told us that that was the best way and even if he hadn't that's still the way Richard and me were going to do it. We didn't want any trouble from anybody. We figured our father was going to be in enough trouble by himself without us adding to it. And besides this town was not like Tahoka. It wasn't real friendly. We never made friends like Clarence or Jim or Phil. Another problem we had was that everything we did we had to do with Junior and there wasn't anyone that liked him. He was too clumsy and dumb.

During recess every group went off and played by themselves. The Indian boys had a game where they all stood in a circle and kicked a little leather ball around trying to keep it from hitting the ground. Whoever dropped the ball had to go into the center of the circle and the other Indians took turns trying to hit him with the little ball. The Indian girls just ran around in a circle holding hands and laughing. We mostly played soft ball and our girls played volleyball. The Mexican guys liked to wrestle and the girls played volleyball off by themselves.

Whenever the three groups were together it usually ended in a fight involving this Indian boy that everyone called Cochise. We were all afraid of him. He was old and big and he pulled the few hairs of his moustache out during class. Sometimes he would be off in a corner getting drunk during recess. He was the one that usually started the fights. You could make him go into a war dance just by calling him Cochise. He didn't like to be called Cochise, so Richard and me never called him that. He didn't seem to have any sense. He had a wild stare to him, like he was going to do something mean and you couldn't figure out what it was going to be, but you could bet it was going to be something out of the ordinary. One time he climbed the flag pole and tied his feet together and dangled by his feet upside down until the volunteer fire department came over with a ladder and undid him.

Junior said that Cochise was full of shit—not to him, to us. Junior was as scared of him as we were. There were times when I felt sorry for him.

Cochise had a human tooth that he carried in his pocket. It was long and shiny with a long root that was darker brown than the rest of the tooth and you could see that the edge had worn off and was smooth and blunt. He had bored a hole through the root and had passed a little wool string through it so he could find it quickly in his dirty jacket. He could reach in his pocket and bring out his hand faster than you could see. And when he would open his hand he would pick out the lint and throw it on the ground and finally there in the middle of his palm would be the tooth with the brightly colored wool string. He would point the tooth at the sky and say something in Apache that made him hyperactive, wanting to do strange things like fight or hang by his heels. Once in his rage it would take ten or more boys to calm him down. Once he was restrained he would start to giggle and usually, as a sign of self defense, he would then urinate a smelly, oily type urine in his pants. He said that the tooth belonged to his great, great, great grandfather, Geronimo.

It was usually this one boy that gave everyone trouble. But Mrs. Trevino, our teacher, handled him well. She kept sending him to the Principal's office and back and forth he'd go all day long. The other Indian boys were regular guys but you never got to really know them. They were bused in in the morning and after school the bus would be waiting for them to take them back to the reservation.

We didn't hang around with the Mexican guys. They were too rough for us and besides they lived in a different part of town. They all had knives and were always cutting each other.

Mrs. Trevino was nice. I don't see how she put up with the class. You had to feel sorry for her with everybody fighting and not many of us really wanting to be there. She did as good a job as was possible. She could speak English, Spanish, and Mescalero -Apache. So you really couldn't say anything about her without her understanding you. She was half Mescalero-Apache and half Mexican, short with droopy eyes and straight hair and fat with a flat face and small teeth. All Indians had little teeth. She had the class separated into three sections and she would say one thing in English and then she would ask if everyone understood. Always there would be someone who had not understood so she would have to explain what it was she meant in Spanish and Mescalero, and in English too.

Dolly was in Junior High so she didn't go to school with us.

By the end of school in the last part of May we hadn't learned much but we were happy. School was out and we were just thinking of all the things we could do for the summer. Mom seemed happy as long as our father was not around.

Artesia had two rivers. The Pemosco River ran through the south side of town, west to east, and its waters were clear and cold as they flowed from the melted snow of the Guadalupe and the higher Sacramento mountains. All farm land to the south of the city was irrigated from this river. To the east about two miles from town was the Pecos River, the same one that curves through West Texas and meets the Rio Grande north of Del Rio. All irrigation of farm lands to the north and west of Artesia and from there south on either side came from this river. Most of our recreation during that summer took place at the Pemosco River or on its clay banks where one could find many caves that had been excavated by children, like us, through the years.

Mainly what Junior, Richard and me wanted to do for the summer was stay out of the house and play either out in the yard or in the street or on the river. We knew that the more time we spent around the house the worse it was going to be, so we tried to get out to the river as much as we could. We were all happy. We had all passed to another grade. Junior was going to go to the seventh grade, junior high. Richard had been demoted during the year so we were going to be in the fifth grade together, if we stayed in Artesia, as Junior reminded us. He was right too. We were not to stay.

We were having as little as possible to do with Uncle Robert and Dad. They were gone from Monday through Friday every week. That left Aunt Betty and Mom around the house and they were usually in a good mood, joking and laughing as long as the men were not around.

Uncle Robert and Dad seemed to be doing all right. They didn't say much about what they were doing. We all knew that they were selling whiskey to the Indians. What I couldn't figure out was how much home repair they were doing. They must have been doing some work just to look honest. We could see that in back of the truck they had carpenter's tools and pieces of lumber and shingles. I'm sure that they were putting up a good front. If I knew them, though, I was sure that they were selling whiskey a lot more than they were working.

"Didn't I tell you, little brother," my uncle Robert would say, poking my dad in the ribs with his finger, "that this was the best job you'd ever have. Yessiree. We've got the best of both worlds."

"It's like havin' a license to steal," my dad would say.

"Well, you fix a fuckin' roof, right?"

"Yep."

"Who's to know if you did a good job or not? Shit, it don't rain in New Mexico."

"Damn right," my father would say as he took another drink. They were both drunk by now.

"The Indians don't care. That's what I like about 'em. They don't give a shit. Hell, they're gettin' their whiskey on schedule. Bam. Bam. Bam," he said as he chopped the table with his hand, "like clock-work."

"They love that whiskey."

"Fucking A they do."

"It's like a license to steal."

"Better."

And it must have been true because we had more money and ate well and dressed better than we had for a long time.

CHAPTER 24

Summers in Artesia were hot. There was no spring. We went from cold icy winds to deep heat in no time. The sun was like a fire-ball held so close to your body that you could just barely stand it. If it had been any closer it would have burned the skin. That was why we loved to play in the cool river waters or inside the caves on the clay river banks where it was moist and cool.

Even before school was out we had found a cave that was big enough for Junior, Richard and me and we had staked it out, put our names out in front so that no one else could use it. We didn't think of making room for Dolly although once in a while she would come over with us. Sometimes she would bring her friend, Liz, with her. At first I thought Junior liked Liz but he never said anything about her and as far as Richard and me knew he never made a move toward her. Junior was the type, though, not to want to be around Dolly and her friends. He thought they were a nuisance, that they talked too much and giggled too much. Liz, her best friend, was a thin tall girl with a real narrow face and close set eyes, but she was cute. She wore her hair real short and neat. I didn't think she liked either Richard or me, not as boyfriends anyway. I don't think she liked anyone that we knew.

Most of the time Dolly stayed in her room by herself or with Liz, posing in front of a mirror and changing clothes every few hours. She wanted to be a model she said to my Mom and Mom said, "Well, if that's what you want to be that's what you'll be." Aunt Betty didn't want her thinking about being a model. "Don't be putting silly ideas into her head," she told Mom. Dolly believed Mom and she would prance in front of the mirror and she would keep a magazine on the bed and look at the models then she would pose just like they did. Sometimes she wanted to be a movie star, especially when she'd come back from a movie and she'd talk to the mirror or to Liz, if Liz was there, saying something like, "Well, I declare, Mr. Jones, I never thought you'd ask me to dance. Oh! I'm sorry sir, but my dance card is all filled up. Oh well, maybe I'll scratch Michael off. I'm sure he won't mind." Then she would twirl and look at her skirt to make sure it had twirled just like she had wanted it to. "Lawdy, Mrs. Clete," she would say in a heavy southern accent, "I do declare the child looks just like a Humphrey. Well, he's got the Humphrey eyes, the Humphrey nose, the Humphrey mouth."

We had been listening to all this across the hall and Junior stuck his head out from his room and yelled, "And the Humphrey ass, like yours."

Dolly threw a shoe into our room and slammed her door. "Queer!" she yelled. Junior picked up the shoe and threw it back. We could still hear her behind the door going through the movie dialogue she had just heard that day. Today it just happened to be a southern drawl.

She was still a flirt when it came to Richard and me. She still loved to push her dress up on her thighs like she didn't know what she was doing. I know she enjoyed seeing our wide-eyed reaction to what she was doing.

Most of the days we were going to the cave to play. The cave had been there many years and you could see where a lot of guys had played there. The entrance was narrow and not very high but once inside the room was big. You couldn't stand up in it but you could sit without stooping. We used to keep candles in a hole in the wall and we would light them and sit on the cool dirt and talk.

This day Richard had cigarettes and we were smoking and enjoying ourselves when we heard the girls outside the cave. Dolly crawled in ahead of Liz, showing us, through the top of her dress, her hard little boobs dangling like pears, moving from side to side as she crawled in. Right behind her was Liz, thin Liz with her little hips and thin face and small round boobs.

"Hey guys," Dolly said as they crawled in, "whatcha doin'?"

"What does it look like we're doin'?" Junior answered.

"Smokin'?" she asked.

"Yeah, smokin'," Junior said. "We're too green to burn. Why don't you all get out and leave us alone."

"Don't you want us to stay?" Liz asked, innocently.

"I don't," Junior said, looking at us to make sure we were backing him up.

"Well, I declare," Dolly said in her southern accent, "Junior Pie is upset 'cause some girls come into his cave."

Junior threw the lighted cigarette against the wall sending sparks out in all directions. He said, "Shithead," to Dolly as he crawled out and left. "You guys can stay here if you want to," he told us, "but I'm leavin'." We could all see his big rear-end move like a bear as he crawled out. The girls were laughing, holding their noses as he crawled past them acting like his rear-end smelled. He left and we could hear him running on the ground above us.

We offered Dolly and Liz a cigarette but they refused and instead they took our cigarettes away from us and they blew smoke in our faces and Dolly said to us, "What's all this secret stuff with you guys? We didn't mean to get you all upset. What are you doin' that we can't find out about?"

They put out our cigarettes on the floor.

"We aren't doin' anythin'," I said and I looked at Richard.

The candles were flickering, shining their light on the girls. I could see plainly and I could see, like Richard could see, that Dolly was sitting down in front of us with her dress pulled up over her thighs again. Then we noticed Liz was inching her dress up too. They were looking at each other and giggling as Dolly said, "You two go outside and then we'll call you in."

"What for?" dumb Richard asked. I could have hit him right there.

"We're playing a game," Dolly said and she giggled some more. Her skirt was getting higher.

"But what kind of game is it?" insisted Richard.

"You just keep quiet and I'll show you," Dolly whispered. "Just go out and stay right by the entrance, then we'll call you in. Don't go away. Promise you'll stay?"

We promised and I managed to push Richard out of the cave in front of me but just as we got out here came Junior running by the river toward us like someone was chasing him. He wanted us all to go home, he said. He was tired of playing in the caves. He asked about the girls.

"They're inside," Richard told him. Junior poked his head through the entrance and yelled for the girls to come out. They were lucky Junior had not seen them and what they were doing. They quickly blew out the candles but it took them a while to come out. I could imagine what they were planning for us: What Pete had promised us and never could deliver.

Later on that summer Dolly was to put me through the experience that would enslave me to her for a long time. It was June and very hot. Dolly had come with us to the river to see us swim and Liz had come along too. Junior and Richard were swimming and I was drying myself in the sun. I noticed that Dolly and Liz had disappeared. Then Liz came walking from the woods towards me and whispered that Dolly knew I was in love with her since that day in the cave and she thought she was in love with me and she wanted to see me. Liz told me that she would take me to where Dolly was hiding. She took me by the hand and up the river bank past the cave and led me into the woods. And there I could see Dolly hiding behind a tree, facing away from me. All I could see was part of her back. Liz pointed me in Dolly's direction and shoved me. Off to one side I could hear Richard and Junior splashing in the river. I walked slowly toward Dolly crushing the leaves under my feet. I could tell she knew I was coming. I could see her move her arms. I looked back and Liz was standing where I had left her. Slowly I kept walking toward Dolly, taking a step at a time, careful not to do anything wrong. I was next to her and she turned to me and asked me to get in front of her at arms length. She drew me toward her and she kissed me lightly on the mouth. My knees buckled slightly. Then she asked me to kneel down. She was in a trance. I knelt down in front of her. She was looking at the sky, the clouds passing by over the tree tops. Then she slowly picked up her dress, gathering it up with both hands into a roll around her waist until I could see her panties. She reached with her right hand inside her panties at the waist and eased them down slowly and I saw it for the first time and I swear to God I didn't know what to do. I felt the rush of blood to my head and I thought I would faint. She pushed her panties down to her thighs and left them there. She took her right hand again and using her fingers she slowly opened it up so that I could see the inside. I never knew it had so many things. She let go of her dress as she drew me closer to her and the dress fell over my head, covering me up. She grabbed the top of my head under the dress and pulled it to her and made me kiss it. I felt her jump. She held me there for the longest time until Liz cleared her throat.

Liz came to get me, helped me get on my feet and she took me back to the river. "She really loves you, you know," she said. "She wouldn't do that for anyone else."

I wasn't about to tell my brother Richard or anyone, for that matter, about what had happened.

She was to do that to me several more times, once again in the clump of trees by the river, one time in her room and another time while she was taking a bath at the house when no one else was around except her and me.

That last time in the bathroom I had tried to touch it but she slapped my hand and said I was a naughty boy and didn't truly love her. She was driving me nuts, and I guess I don't have to tell you that I was playing less and less with Junior and Richard and more and more with Dolly.

CHAPTER 25

Dolly was using me by holding out the great expectation of things that were yet to come—like sex. She was doing just enough to keep me interested. I guess she thought that if she allowed me too many liberties that I would tire of her. How wrong she was. I wasn't dissatisfied. As a matter of fact, what I was getting from her now was more than I had dreamed of. For the first time I felt physically superior to Clarence and everyone like him, even Pete. For a while, while it lasted, I even noticed that I walked like I knew what I was doing.

It had been my luck up to that time that the two girls I loved had shown their affection in a funny way. Mitzi had liked me, but as a friend and harmonica player to keep her entertained. She had not put me in the role of a lover. Dolly was treating me the same way. I was worried that I was always going to be like the little dog that watches all the other dogs make love to the female. I even thought about giving up the harmonica. I would then be loved for myself and not my talent, little as it was. There were some very obvious differences between the two girls. Dolly was more straight forward, smarter, conniving, an expert at getting what she wanted. She was more sexy than Mitzi. Mitzi had a dark, moody, foot-dragging side to her, like she had been abused early in life and would never recover. Mitzi acted like she was doomed. Dolly was happy, mostly, except when she wasn't getting her way and then she was hateful, but in a sexy kind of way. I always thought that she would get pregnant many times before she got married. And besides that, whoever married her was going to have to be a man with a capital M.

Junior and my brother Richard weren't suspecting anything. If Junior had found out he would have told Aunt Betty and Mom and we would have been in a lot trouble. I also think that Junior would have killed me, if Uncle Robert hadn't, or Dad, or Mom, or Aunt Betty—everybody.

As it turned out everyone thought I was sissified to want to be with Dolly most of the time. They must have been amazed at how much abuse I took from her and how much I catered to her whims, how much like a servant I was to her.

The summer had been a quiet one. But then my father and Uncle Robert came in drunk one Saturday night and caused a very serious argument. It was past midnight and they must have been drinking all the way from Mescalero. They had made their whiskey run last all week and now it was time for them to have some fun. Our window was up. The night was hot and the moisture from the river made the night air very humid. We heard the truck come into the driveway right by our window and we could hear it mash the gravel under its grinding wheels.

The truck doors slammed one right after the other and we heard the men curse and go up the steps and then they stamped their boots on the porch. A dog barked in the distance trying to protect itself from whatever noise the two men were making. Uncle Robert barked back at the dog and my father laughed. They opened the door and came in stamping their feet trying to see who they could wake up.

We could hear Aunt Betty and mother get up. They were sleeping together. We could hear the men talking and laughing. The women were quiet. I was hoping, and I'm sure Richard and Junior were too, that they would leave us alone. I remembered I didn't have any underwear. Mom had forgotten to wash. I had been sleeping alone in the small bed by the window. Richard and Junior were asleep together. Dolly had gone to bed early that night.

I heard the footsteps in the hall. Junior and Richard had thrown the sheet over their heads. The footsteps came closer and closer and the drunken voice was that of my father. Suddenly the door flew open and he turned on the lights. He tore the sheet off me and he saw that I was naked but he didn't care.

"Get your harmonica," he growled at me, "we need to hear a song."

I was looking as fast as I could, in a panic, for my pants. My heart was pounding. I knew my rear-end was out in the open and I knew my father was staring at me. "Don't you wear no underwear, shithead?" he said. I didn't answer. I had found my pants and was putting them on. I reached for the harmonica in the top drawer of the dresser.

"Leave the child alone," I could hear my mother say.

"He needs to play us a tune," my father yelled to her from inside the room. He was close enough that I could smell the whiskey on his breath. My brother Richard and Junior weren't moving under the sheet.

"He needs to sleep more than he needs to play," my mother yelled back.

"Goddam it, woman," my father yelled back to the kitchen, "leave me alone. Bob and I want to hear the kid play. Now put on some clothes real fast and come and play for your uncle and me."

I finished putting on my pants and he pulled me out of the room and pushed me down the hall.

"Now play us somethin'," Uncle Robert demanded. "Anythin'."

Uncle Robert and Aunt Betty and Mom were sitting at the table. I could smell bacon cooking in the skillet. Uncle Robert had two bottles of whiskey and he was pouring some for himself, Dad and Aunt Betty. Mom was drinking coffee and looked like she was in pain. I looked at her and she looked down at her coffee. There wasn't much she could do to help me. I was on my own.

I started to play but Uncle Robert stopped me. "This ain't fair," he said and he got up and went back into our room and after much pushing and shoving he brought Junior and Richard with him. Richard was wearing Mr. Allen's pajamas holding them up with his hands. "Now, that's fairer," he said. "Now you all serenade us. Sing goddamit," he said and banged the whiskey bottle on the table.

"Squeal like a pig," my father said real slow to Richard. "Let me show you all how this little boy can squeal like a pig. Squeal," my father repeated. "Come on, shithead, you've done it before. Quit acting like a little tough guy." Richard was not doing anything and Dad was getting angry.

"Let 'im be," my mother said, finally. "Let Richard be. He's suffered enough."

"I won't let 'im be," my father said, and I could feel the anger in his voice. "If I want the little bastard to squeal I'll make him squeal."

He jumped out of his chair at Richard and he grabbed my brother Richard by the ears and started to twist them to make Richard squeal. But Richard didn't make a sound. I had quit playing. Everyone was looking at my father and what he was doing to Richard. "Squeal! Squeal! Squeal, you little bastard!" he screamed. Richard was turning blue.

"Leave 'im alone!" my mother screamed. She was trying to get up to help

Richard but my Aunt Betty was trying to hold her down on her chair. "Leave 'em alone," my Aunt Betty was yelling to my mother. "You'll get hurt."

"I won't leave 'em alone! He's hurting Richard. Leave Richard alone!" she yelled.

My uncle Robert was laughing at the whole thing. "Don't squeal, son!" he yelled at Richard. "Show the motherfucker you got guts."

Richard was crying, not loud, but tears were rolling down his cheeks as my father twisted harder and harder and harder.

"Okay," my uncle Robert said, now that the situation had gotten out of hand. "Jim, that's enough. Leave the boy be."

My father was like an animal that wouldn't turn loose. Richard had let go of his pajamas and they had fallen to the floor and he was standing naked in front of us, crying, and he slowly twisted with the pain as he fell to the floor. But he never squealed.

I would have hit my father if I had been big enough. I would have taken him on.

My Uncle Robert screamed, "That's enough! Let go, you motherfucker!" and my father let go as Richard collapsed.

"That little bastard never squealed," my father yelled.

"Leave 'im alone," my mother told him in a real quiet voice. She was ready to fight.

"Let's have a drink," Aunt Betty said, trying to get everything and everyone back to normal.

"And you?" Uncle Robert asked Junior, "what the hell you doing here?"

"Nothin', sir," Junior answered, trembling in his pajamas.

"Well all of you get the shit out of here before I whip everyone's ass," he said and we all took off. Richard managed to pick up his pajamas and he ran naked behind us.

Dolly opened her door as we ran into the room and she said, "What's goin' on? What's all that noise?"

Aunt Betty heard her and yelled, "Shut up, you slut, and go to bed."

All night, it seemed, we could hear them talking, arguing. We could hear my father still angry, threatening my mother, and we could hear my mother. She wasn't backing down. We could hear Uncle Robert threatening my dad. We could hear Aunt Betty trying to be nice to everyone. There was a scary silence and then we heard the sound of chairs being pushed around. Uncle

Robert and Dad were fighting. We heard the sounds, the crashing of furniture, the heavy noises made when a body falls on a wooden floor, the cries of the women as they try with all their might to separate their men without waking the children, the pushing and shoving, the grunts, as two men fight each other. "Get up, you sonofabitch!" Uncle Robert screamed. "Get up so I can beat the shit out of you." We could hear all the voices in the silence of our room and I guess my father was trying to get up because we could hear Mom and Aunt Betty shouting at him. "Stay down, Jim!" Aunt Betty screamed and begged. "For God's sake stay down. He's goin' to kill you if you get up."

"Come on motherfucker, get up!" Uncle Robert said, teasing my father. "I need to hit you one more fuckin' time."

My father must have gotten up. We could hear running footsteps toward the door. "He's gettin' away!" Mom screamed.

"Let 'im go!" Aunt Betty yelled.

The door slammed shut and Dad ran down the stairs. We could hear him right by our window. He vomited and then got in the truck and spun the wheels as he drove off.

Finally we fell asleep and in the morning I could see Richard from the back as he lay in bed asleep. I could see his protruding ear, swollen and black and blue. He was breathing hard. Both his ears would be like that for several weeks.

And from that time, after he healed, his ears were mangled and scarred. In prison they would call him Jug because of his ears, a name I understand stuck with him for the rest of his short life.

No one knew where my father went or when he would return.

CHAPTER 26

Our lives never seemed to be the same again. My brother didn't talk much for a long time. He would eat with us and then go off by himself and hide during the day. Junior didn't want to be around him. It seemed to me that it took forever for his ears to heal. Aunt Betty wanted to take him to the doctor but Mom was afraid that the doctor would ask how it happened and Dad would get in trouble. If Dad got in trouble, Mom told Aunt Betty, then we all would be in trouble. "They may even take Richard away from us," she had said.

"We don't have to tell the doctor the truth," Aunt Betty explained.

"They have ways of findin' out," Mom said. "Maybe they'll keep Richard in a room by himself and ask 'im all these questions. Maybe they'll call the police and have the police themselves ask 'im questions." She thought about it for a while and she was more convinced than ever that she was doing the right thing. "No, no. We can't take the chance," she said, shaking her head.

So they kept it quiet.

Dolly was going crazy with her modeling. She had me sorting her clothes, putting all of them, the few that she had, on the bed every morning. I was helping her dress. Liz would come in and laugh at me. Being a girl herself, she found it funny for me to be paying such a high price for what I was getting. I didn't like her sense of humor. Dolly didn't notice Liz's snickering, being so engrossed in her make-believe career.

I was feeling bad about Richard being alone so much. After all, we were always close and we had always told each other what we felt. The idea that he didn't want me around bothered me. So one day, when I saw Richard going towards the river, I told Dolly that I wasn't feeling well and I couldn't work for her. "That's fine," she said, like an old movie star talking to her maid, "take the rest of the day off or more until you feel better. Liz is coming in and she'll help me."

I ran out of the house and followed Richard and he stopped and looked back at me and he motioned for me to come along, which surprised me.

"What are you doin'?" I asked him when I got close.

I had expected for him to be angry but he wasn't. I should have known that Richard could never be angry with me. We were so close. I could not look at his ears without feeling the pain. They were back to their normal color but were crooked and bent. I didn't know then that the scars were going to contract and the ears were going to look worse.

"Goin' to the river," he told me. "Want to come along?"

"Yeah," I said. I was glad he invited me. I felt like old times.

"Where's Dolly?" he asked me.

"Oh, I don't know," I said to him, lying. I didn't know why I lied except that maybe I felt ashamed of what I had been doing. I knew exactly where she was. She was in her room, naked, trying on clothes. "You goin' to the river?" I added quickly.

"Yeah," Richard said.

When we got to the river Richard went to the river's edge and took some cool water and massaged his ears with it. When he finished we went inside the cave and we found our candles and matches and lit them and we sat and smoked. We were quiet for a while, not knowing what to say.

"How're you feelin'?" I asked him.

I could tell he still was sore around the ears just by the way he moved his head.

"I'm okay," he answered and then he said, "I'm lyin' to you, Jimmy. I'm not feelin' okay." He threw a twig he had been playing with at the wall and he started to cry. He sniffled and wiped the tears on his shirt. He grabbed a small rock and threw it against the wall.

"I'm sorry about what happened the other night," I told him. "I just wish I could have done somethin' about it."

"Like what?"

"Well, like kick him in the balls."

"That's not goin' to do any good. Then you'd really be in trouble. Then he'd take you and beat you up worse than he did me."

"I wish I could have done somethin'."

"Well, you couldn't. I didn't expect you to get in trouble over me."

"I just wish I could have done somethin'. Anythin'. You don't know how bad I felt when I saw what was happenin' to you."

"That's okay," he said, wiping some more tears from his face. "I'll get even some day."

"Someone is goin' to kill 'im before you get old enough to hurt 'im."

"No they won't," Richard said. "I ain't waitin' that long."

"What do you mean?"

"I've been plannin'," he said and he crawled over to the corner and removed dirt that was covering a wooden board. Underneath the board was a hole that he had dug out. He reached into the hole and brought out an automobile repair manual and a pair of what looked to me to be pliers, but they weren't. "These are wire cutters," he said, "and this book tells you all about pick-up trucks like ours. It tells you about brake lines."

He wiped the snot off his nose on his sleeve as he thumbed through the pages. He had almost worn out the part about the brakes.

"I'm doin' the sonofabitch in," Richard said about our father and I could see he meant it. He took a last drag from his cigarette and then threw it at the wall. "I'm goin' to kill 'im. I got it figured out. I've been thinkin' of this for a long time, even before what happened the other night. All I do is cut part way through the brake lines and then when he's on his way to Mescalero to sell whiskey to the poor Indians he's got to step on the brakes over and over, 'specially on the mountain road. He's got to!" he said, clenching his teeth and hitting the manual with his hand. "He's got to step on that brake hard enough one time where the line breaks and he's gone. He's gone," Richard said, as though it were true, like it had already happened. "He'll lose control of that damn ol' truck and he'll get killed. He'll run off the road and go over the edge of the mountain and that's it. I can see it happenin' in my mind. If and when they find the sonofabitch no one'll be able to tell what happened. The Indians know he wasn't any damn good. Everyone'll figure he was drunk. Maybe all that whiskey will catch on fire and burn him up. Everyone'll figure he had it comin' to 'im. After the accident when the police come over to the house to tell us that he's dead I'll be laughin' to myself. The sonofabitch finally got what he deserved."

"What about Uncle Robert? What if Uncle Robert is with 'im?"

"Uncle Robert has got to take his chances just like he's takin' his chances hangin' 'round 'im and the Indians. But, if we can get 'im not to go that's fine. But if we don't, then it's too bad. I ain't goin' to try too hard. Nobody gives a shit about 'em anyway. I think Aunt Betty'll be glad if he dies."

"What about Mom?" I asked him.

"I don't figure she cares one way or another," he said, "not after what happened to Sylvia."

I looked at my brother Richard by the light of the candles and I felt like I was looking at someone I didn't know. I could see his mangled ears by the candle-light and they made shadows across his face that I had never seen before. He was going to kill our father even if it meant killing Uncle Robert. I couldn't convince him that it wasn't right.

I wished now that he hadn't told me his secret. Why had I said I wanted to come with him? I had been so happy and innocent with Dolly.

CHAPTER 27

I thought Uncle Robert was doing all right without my father. On Sunday he worked diligently getting his supplies ready for the week and on Monday morning very early he left for Mescalero driving the old rusty maroon car, the car riding so low on the ground that it almost bumped the ground with its rear-end. He came back on Friday for what we thought was another load of whiskey. He looked worried and he asked for Dad. As far as we knew no one had heard from him. He asked Mom if Dad had left any money with her and she said no. He left the house right after he got in. He had to find Dad or the money, one of the two. They were both in real trouble. I could hear him talking to Aunt Betty and Mom. He could not tell them the trouble they were in until he found Dad. He did not find him Friday night. Saturday morning he went again and he came back empty-handed late that afternoon. He was more worried than I had ever seen him. He couldn't even talk but sat at the table drinking whiskey with tea and reminiscing with Aunt Betty and Mom as though the coming days would be his last on earth.

That Saturday night, after he had been gone one week, my father returned. He drove up the driveway fast and he got out of the heated truck, staggering drunk. We were in our room and Junior, Richard and me saw him through the window. He looked ragged and thin like a stray tom-cat that had been fighting and breeding during the week. Still he looked cocky, like he belonged there and had never left, like he had just gone for an errand and everyone would be glad to have him back. Uncle Robert and Aunt Betty and Mom were in the kitchen. We didn't know if they could hear him or not.

We heard the front door slam, then Uncle Robert's deep voice. My father answered him and I heard the running footsteps, hard pounding steps from a heavy person. The whole house seemed to shake. I remember exactly that I heard my mother scream as though she was seeing someone being killed.

Junior bounced up from his bed where he was sitting and ran to the door, although I knew he was scared to listen, afraid of what he might hear. My brother Richard was unusually calm and I could see from his eyes that he was thinking beyond what was happening. We could hear Aunt Betty's squealing screams and my mother was begging Uncle Robert to leave my father alone. I couldn't take it any longer. I leaped from the bed on top of Junior and shoved him out of the way. I opened the door and ran out into the hallway. I could see that my Uncle Robert had my father down on his chest on the floor, holding him down with his left hand around his neck, hitting him with his right fist. My mother and Aunt Betty were grabbing at him, trying to get him to stop, but each time that his fist pounded downward like a human piston they could not stop it. He was much too strong for them. When I saw all this I felt a deep pain in my heart like I was going to die young. I thought I couldn't take too much of this anymore.

Just then, I heard the roar of a car by the side of the house. I looked through our door and out through the bedroom window and I saw by the light from our room that an old beat up brown car had rolled into the driveway. Next, I saw two large men with flat brim hats get out. Uncle Robert had heard the car and had stopped hitting my father. At first his clenched fist stayed suspended above his head as he remained undecided whether to hit him one last time or not. Finally, he let go and they both looked at each other like they were wondering if the trouble they were in had just now arrived. Slowly, without making a noise, I crept down the hall to where I could see the front door. The strange men came up the steps slowly and into the porch light. Their clothes looked old, stained and dirty, like old mule skins with wrinkles that could never be removed. They were Mescaleros with their flat noses and small eyes. They wore the traditional flat brimmed black hats with a small cluster of brightly colored feathers on the band. Both had braided hair indicating a high position in the tribe. The older one knocked on the door with a heavy hand and the whole house shook. The heat of the night made his face shine like wax under the light. I couldn't tell why they bothered to knock. Everyone could see them through the screen.

Uncle Robert and my father got up and Aunt Betty and my mother ran to the kitchen. Uncle Robert and Dad saw the men and without saying a word they went outside to talk, like they knew the Indians.

Slowly I crawled backward into the room. Junior was in bed in the shape of a ball all covered with his sheets. I looked for Richard but could not find him. Junior whispered from inside his cocoon of sheets that Richard had jumped through the window when he heard the fight. He was hiding out somewhere outside the house. Had he run off because he was afraid of getting beat up again? I asked Junior if Richard had said anything? Had he run for the cave? Was he planning on spending the night in the cave? Junior threw up his hands inside the sheets and said that Richard just opened the screen and jumped out without a word. Was there a chance that Richard had come back in without Junior knowing? After all, Junior had been under the covers all this time. When we couldn't find him we turned off the lights and Junior went under the covers again. He was very afraid of the Indians. I was too, but I stood by the door. I could hear Aunt Betty and my mother talking in low painful voices. Then I went over to the window and felt the hot breeze come into the room. I was sweating more than I had any other night.

I guess what was really scaring all of us was that the older Indians usually didn't get out of the Reservation unless it was something real serious.

I could see outside from the dark room the figures of the four men talking in the driveway. Uncle Robert was explaining something to the Indians and they were listening with interest. I could see their hats move up and down as they nodded their heads. My father was talking now that Uncle Robert had stopped. It looked like he was begging them about something. He was waving his hands as if saying that he felt shame in his heart. The Indians seemed disgusted and they turned around to leave but Uncle Robert grabbed them by their sleeves and it looked like he was begging them not to leave. They stopped when my Uncle Robert grabbed them but they jerked their sleeves away from him. The older Indian, the "Communicator," was talking and moving his hand up and down, pointing his finger with the other hand at my father. When he was through Uncle Robert said something but it seemed they didn't want to hear anymore. Instead, the older Indian spit on the ground and covered the spittle with a kick of dust from his foot, a sign in Indian language that the conversation had ended in disgust. My father was trying to stop them but they kept side-stepping him. As far as I could tell, the younger Indian had not said a word.

They got in their car and slowly backed out. As they did, they shined the lights on the driveway and to my great surprise, I could see my brother Richard under Dad's truck. My heart stopped. I thought for sure the Indians had seen him. They kept backing up slowly and then turned the old brown car into the street and left.

Neither Uncle Robert nor my father could see under the pick-up. They were too close, almost leaning against the truck. Richard was right by them, at their feet. He was as motionless as if he were dead. The horrible thought came to me that if Uncle Robert and Dad decided to leave in the truck that they would discover Richard and Richard would be in a lot of trouble.

My father started yelling at Uncle Robert and Uncle Robert shoved him against the car, which was parked in front of the truck. My father acted like he was going to hit Uncle Robert but before he could do anything my Uncle Robert hit him in the stomach with a blow that would have felled a cow and my father screamed in pain and doubled over and started to puke dark stuff. He staggered to the far side of the car and I couldn't see him anymore but I could hear him puking.

My uncle Robert came inside and I ran over to the door and cracked it so that I could listen. Junior was still curled in a ball covered up in a sheet breathing very heavily. He asked what happened, not wanting to see, and I told him about the Indians and how they had spat on the ground. I didn't tell him about his father hitting my father.

Uncle Robert was inside by now. He was talking to Aunt Betty and Mom and then I heard my father come in.

"I'll tell you what this sonofabitch has done," Uncle Robert yelled, talking about my father. "He's gone and got our ass in a crack. That's what he's done. And if we ever get out of this mother-fucker alive I'm goin' to kill the sonofabitch...brother or no brother."

There was a moment of silence. I could just see them in my mind's eye even though I wasn't there. My mother would be looking down at the table, shaking her head in her hands. Aunt Betty would be sitting with her legs crossed, shaking her leg, looking at her shoe, smoking her cigarette. My father would be looking at his brother, Uncle Robert, with a mean stare.

"What'd you do?" my mother asked my father. "What've you done now?"

My father didn't answer.

"Ain't you goin' to tell 'er?" my uncle Robert shouted. "Tell 'er, you no good sonofabitch."

"No," my father replied, "I ain't sayin' nothin'."

"Well, goddamit, I'll tell 'em. You see, Ol' Jim here, he thinks he's hot shit. Everywhere he goes he fucks up 'cause he thinks he's hot shit. He's been like that ever since he was born. Hell, he was born fucked up. Nobody had to fuck 'im up. He was born fucked up. Shit-head..." my Uncle Robert said and I could feel him getting angrier and angrier like he would start the fight again. "He's so fucked-up he thinks he's cute, like a little boy. He always was a little fucked-up boy. That's why he takes advantage of the little children. He knows he can beat 'em."

"Well," I could hear Aunt Betty say, "from the way you talk it really must be bad. Are you going to tell us what happened?"

"He's all fucked up!" Uncle Robert screamed.

"We know he's not the man you are," my mother said, "never has been. But don't you think you've got some blame coming for that?"

"What do you mean?" Uncle Robert said.

"You've always treated 'im like a kid. And he's not a kid."

"Now don't no one pull this big brother shit on me," Uncle Robert answered. "I'm tired of protectin' this little fucked up shit. I ain't doin' it no more. Now I'm gettin' blamed for 'im being the way he is. Shit! If I'd a known what was comin' I'd a left the little shit-head to die in Oklahoma. Killed a man! Shiiiiit! He thinks he's a big man 'cause he killed a man. Goes 'round braggin' about it to everyone. Sure he killed a man but it wasn't fair and square. He didn't kill no man fair and square. Sonofabitch never tells anyone how he ambushed the poor old man over a piece of ass so old and ugly no other man woulda given two cents for. Just his pride. Little man got his pride hurt. If it hadn't been for me they'd've killed 'im in Oklahoma."

My father had not said a word. Everyone was silent again.

"Wellllll, shiiiut," I heard Uncle Robert drawl. A chair moved across the floor. "I'm gettin' up and gettin' me a beer. Anyone else want one? Mom? Christie? Jim?" I couldn't believe he was offering my father a beer after everything he had said about him.

I could hear him open the refrigerator. After he brought beer for my father and Aunt Betty and himself, he sat down. "Well," he kept on, calmer, "we're in a fuckin' mess. First of all, this shit-head here bugs out on me all last week. You should've seen me tryin' to save my own ass. He takes the Indian's money and he don't show up for the week. The Indians, they don't give a fuck about anythin' or anybody. They want their whiskey and they want it now. They've given us their money. Fuck-up here has it and he's spendin' it on liquor and women at the whore-houses. All this time I'm making excuses to the Indians about their money. I promised them on my father's grave that we'd have the money or the whiskey by the end of the week. The Indians, they don't give a rat's ass about excuses. They've been fucked around for hundreds of years. They don't take kindly to that shit. A man takes their money on his word or on his handshake and that's good enough for 'em. But you've got to produce. If you don't produce you might as well kiss your ass goodbye. Well, shit-head here spends the Indian's money. I don't know about it but I suspect that he's out somewhere spendin' it on himself. I'm hopin' and prayin' that he's not but I know the sonofabitch too well. In the meantime the Indians don't believe me for shit. They say I can't come home until shit-head here gets back to the reservation with their money or their whiskey. They don't care which one, but they would prefer the whiskey. I couldn't get away. They were watchin' me. Well, I figured that shit-head would at least show up by Friday with some thing—money, whiskey, excuses, anything so that we could get back on their good graces. I kept holdin' 'em back, holdin' 'em back, talkin' to 'em all week long, makin' excuses, buyin' time. But when shit-head here didn't show up on Friday, the Indians go wild. I've got my ass in a crack. I think they're goin' to kill me. They say they might kill me just to teach shit-head here a lesson. Mother-fuck! I lose my ass to teach shit-head here a lesson? Lesson? What a goddam thing to happen to me! I was thinkin' that the worst thing ever happen to me was bein' in the same family with this sonofabitch.

"Well, anyway, I've been pretty good to the Indians. Many a time I've given more'n they pay for, a little bottle here and there and they really appreciate it. They know I'm honest. And compared to shit-head here, I can be trusted. Friday at sun-up they had me all tied up and ready for an Indian beatin' when the Chief steps in. The Chief says I can come home on one condition. And that condition," he said, slowing down a bit for emphasis, "was to promise to take shit-head back with me on Monday mornin'. So bright and early Monday I'm taking shit-head here to the reservation and he better be takin' some money or some whiskey or his ass is gone. Yes sir, them mother-fuckers are goin' to slice up your ass in tiny little-bitty pieces and they may just eat it."

"And the Indians that were here a while ago?" Aunt Betty asked him, excited and nervous.

"Well, the Chief, he's no dummy," my Uncle Robert explained. "He's sent 'em over for insurance. Just in case we try to get away. You see, he trusts me but he don't trust me that much. Blood is thicker than whiskey, the Indians say. Those were the same two Indians that were watchin' me at the reservation. They know damn well that I might just change my mind once I get over here. It was a hell of a deal gettin' out of the reservation. I knew that they were followin' me. I wasn't born yesterday, you know. Let's face it. The Mescalero Apache don't trust too many people. They don't even trust themselves. How do you think they out-lived every goddam Indian tribe in the Southwest? Hell, you all don't know what it's like to do business with these people. Hell, they're the meanest people in the world. You think I'm shittin' you? You know what the Apache used to do with his horses? They'd ride a horse until it broke down then they'd sit down and eat 'im. That's the goddam truth. They stole everythin' they ever had. Shit, that's why they didn't kill the Navajo. They'd wait for the Navajo to plant his corn and raise his horse and then they'd attack the poor Navajo and take most of it away from them. They'd leave just enough to keep the dumb-ass Navajo workin'. Shit, they didn't want the Navajo to die. The Navajo was their meal ticket. And mister...you know what we're up against. Ol' little man here, shit-head to be exact, is between shit and shinola. He thought he was Mr. Big Man and know it all. Well, you fucked up good this time, shit-head."

"I wish you'd stop callin' 'im shit-head," Aunt Betty said, gently, trying to get the two brothers to make peace.

"Well, he's got shit for brains is what he's got."

"We've been in bad trouble before," I heard my mother say.

"Oh Christie, please don't bring that up," Aunt Betty replied in a nervous, chilly voice, like it scared her to even think about it.

"She's right," my father said, finally speaking up. "She's damn right. We got things we done together that no one, no one, knows 'bout 'cept us four. It'd be a shame if someone ever finds out."

"Like whose goin' to tell 'em?" Uncle Robert asked. "Not you I hope."

"No," my father said, "I just meant that no one ought to know."

"I thought there for a while you were threatenin' me," Uncle Robert said. "'Cause if you were I was fixin' to beat the shit out of you again."

I didn't hear my father answer.

"He didn't mean anythin'," my mother said. "Did you, Jim?"

"No, I didn't. I just was talkin' out my ass, that's all."

"Like you do all the time, you mean," Uncle Robert reminded him.

"But we do have that between us," my mother said, bringing back the conversation. "We've been through hard times before."

"I just don't like that kind of talk," Aunt Betty said. "I just don't like to dig up the past. What's done is done and that's it as far as I'm concerned. To me it's like it didn't happen at all. It's been such a long time ago. I've forgotten all about it and so has Bob. Now if you two want to start diggin' up ghosts then it's your business but I don't want any part of that. If you want to do it you'd better leave this house cause I ain't bringin' ghosts back alive into his house."

"It ain't like we're diggin' up ghosts," my mother said. "I just said we'd been through some tough times together before. Maybe we can overcome this like we did the other time. That's all," my mother said, "and I won't mention it again."

"You know how much I love you both and the children," I heard Aunt Betty say to Mom. I knew that she felt sorry for what she had just said. I could tell she was crying. "But you know me. I don't want to hear about that again as long as I live."

"Sorry," my mother apologized.

"What the fuck we doin' talkin' about that," Uncle Robert said. He was starting to talk slurred. "I need to change to whiskey now," he said.

My father, I was sure, was sitting there quietly having one drink after another.

I could hear the gurgling sound as Uncle Robert poured whiskey into his glass. "What shit-head here needs to do is gather himself up by the balls and tell us what he's going to do. Well, shit-head, what are you going to do? You ain't got much choice as far as I can tell."

"What do you mean?" my father asked.

"Well, you ain't got much choices. If you don't show up with me on Monday morning they'll track you down and kill you."

"How 'bout you?"

"If I show up without you they'll probably kill me and then track you down and kill you. Either way if you don't show up with me I get killed. In other words, you're goin' whether you want to or not."

"What happens to me then?"

"Well, I'd have to talk to the Chief. Hell, I don't know. They'd want their money back or they'd want their whiskey...or you."

"I ain't got the money," my father said.

"Well," Uncle Robert said, slowly, "I figured you didn't. That would be askin' too much of you. Now why did I know you'd spent all the money? Isn't that just like this mother-fucker to pull shit like that?"

"So you don't have the money, right?"

"That's it," my father answered.

"I ought to turn you over to them Indians right now. Let 'em take you and kill your miserable ass so that you wouldn't be a bother to anyone ever again. Shit, I wish to God I'd a drowned you when you was a baby."

"Too late now," my father said.

"Says who?" Uncle Robert said, and I heard him get up from his chair.

"This ain't goin' to do us any good," Aunt Betty said. She sounded like she had composed herself. "None of this talk is goin' to get Jim off the hook."

"I'm afraid Jim can't get off the hook," Uncle Robert said.

"Let me ask you somethin', big brother," my father spoke. "What would you do if you were in my shoes? Now think it over real careful. Don't just jump out and answer. Think about it. What would you do?

"Me?"

"Yeah, you."

"I'll tell you what, shit-for-brains, I'd be prayin' right now, gettin' ready to kiss my ass goodbye."

"What if I don't show up on Monday?"

"The Indians'll kill you and if they don't then I'll kill you," Uncle Robert said.

"Now, now," Aunt Betty interrupted, "let's talk sensible. No one's goin' to kill no one. Let's be practical about this."

"What do you mean?" my mother asked.

"Well, let's think about it for a while."

"Well," Uncle Robert said and I heard him slam the table, "we'd better come up with somethin' real quick 'cause we only got one day. Shit man, I'm gettin' another drink."

"Don't drink too much, honey," Aunt Betty said.

"Shut up," Uncle Robert shouted at Aunt Betty. "And don't... don't tell me how much to drink. I know exactly how much is enough."

"I hate to see you drink too much," Aunt Betty said, "because tomorrow will be a rough day on all of us. God only knows what we need to do to get out of this mess."

"Whatever," mother said, "we've got to face it together. Don't you all think? I feel like beggin' you all for help. If it does any good...I'll beg. I'm beggin' for our sake...the children, me, Jim."

"No need to beg," Aunt Betty replied. "All of us are in this together. You know that it don't matter what Bob says...we're goin' to help you all out all we can. The trouble is we need to think of what needs to be done. First of all what we need is money. Isn't that right?"

"You're fuckin' A right," Uncle Robert said.

"Don't no one have any money?" she asked.

No answer. It seemed everyone was thinking and broke.

I could hear Aunt Betty flicking the lid on the cigarette lighter, lighting a cigarette. "Well," she volunteered, "it's very simple. We got to think of sellin' somethin' that'll get us enough money to get us out of this trouble."

I knew what big trouble we were in. Stealing anything from an Indian is a serious crime. It's taken as a highly personal thing. The Indian that is robbed loses face until he gets revenge. I didn't much care if they took my father and punished him. I know I'd feel bad about it but it wouldn't be life and death to me. What really was worrying me was my mother, Richard, Uncle Robert, Aunt Betty, Junior and Dolly and me. What were they going to do to us? I didn't know what Indian law said about that when it came to us. I had learned from my Indian classmates that when things go wrong, Indian to Indian, the whole family is involved. And here we were, my father had stolen money from a whole tribe.

My brother Richard poked his sweaty dusty head above the window sill and looked inside the room, his eyes as big as black walnuts. He was trying to see if it was safe to climb back in. He looked scared and tired, the sweat pouring down his face. He pulled himself half-way up the window and then he pulled one leg over the sill and he rolled in. He was shushing me with his finger to get me to keep quiet as he stayed down on the floor. He was very quiet himself, trying not to let Junior know what he was up to.

Junior was still under the sheet, breathing slowly and in rhythm so I was sure he had finally gotten tired with the events of the night and had fallen asleep. He never knew what Richard was doing. As far as he was concerned Richard had run away to keep from getting beaten up again.

Richard got up and was dusting himself off. Across the hall I saw that Dolly had awakened, had cracked the door, and was listening to the conversation. I could only see a slit of her face through the crack in the door. She stuck out her hand and waved at us and said something in a whisper but I couldn't hear. I tried to lean out into the hall to hear her, hoping that she was inviting me over to her room but without saying anything else she giggled and closed the door slowly and quietly.

"You kids go to sleep," Aunt Betty shouted from the kitchen. She had that sense of radar like most mothers do. She couldn't have heard us.

"I wonder how much they heard?" Mom asked.

We heard chairs being pushed back and then Aunt Betty's and mother's footsteps coming down the hall. Aunt Betty opened the door to our room but we had already jumped in bed, fully clothed.

"You boys go to sleep, you hear?" she said.

My mother was there too. "You two go to sleep right away," she said, meaning Richard and me.

Aunt Betty poked Junior with a finger. He didn't move. He was asleep. "He's dead to the world. Ain't that a great way to be?" my Aunt Betty said about Junior and then she and Mom went across the hall to Dolly's room and we could hear her telling Dolly to go to bed and get some sleep so that she would grow.

My brother Richard was in bed next to me, chewing his finger nails and popping his knuckles. "I did it," he whispered. "I didn't cut through the lines all the way. All I did was run the wire cutters all the way around and around and around until I could feel the groove in the copper. There's only a very thin part of copper holdin' the lines together."

"They're made of copper?" I asked. I didn't know.

"Yeah," he answered quietly and I could see his profile by the light coming through the window. I could see his eyes blink once in a while. He was thinking.

I was thinking too. What was going to happen when the brakes failed? There was going to be a big accident. I was hoping that if anyone was hurt it would only be my father and nobody else—like Uncle Robert, or an innocent Indian, or us.

"Richard?" I whispered, and he turned around. "Richard, we're in a lot of trouble with the Indians."

"I know," he answered. "I heard 'em talkin' when I was under the truck. I know exactly why they're in trouble."

"You heard it all, I guess," I said.

"Yep, I heard it all. They're lyin' to you all. There's more to it than they're tellin'. They're only tellin' us half the story. I knew shit-head wouldn't be able to keep from screwin' up," he said. "How many times has he screwed it up for us?" He didn't let me answer. "Jillions," he answered himself. "Jillions and jillions. He ain't no good and that's all." Then he whispered to make sure Junior wasn't listening. "I told you I'd kill 'im. He'll be dead Monday. I hope to beat the Indians to 'im."

A dog that was still up that late at night made a lonely crying sound, crying about being so alone and in so much trouble, that came through the window and sounded like he were right beside us. Chills went up my back.

Richard was going to kill our father. The wheels had been set in motion. There was no going back now. I guess you could say I was an accomplice.

CHAPTER 28

Bright and early on Sunday Aunt Betty and Mom woke us up and fed us a big breakfast. I felt that this could be our last meal together. Uncle Robert and Dad came in from working on the truck and they looked worried. They ate fast without looking up. They were wearing the same clothes that they had on last night, not having gone to bed. Aunt Betty had already eaten standing up at the kitchen counter and had gotten through right away, gulping her food, which meant that Mom had to eat in the kitchen also. She and Aunt Betty were washing dishes even before we were finished.

Richard was sitting next to me, his fingernails greasy even though he had scrubbed his hands over and over with plenty of soap. We had had a hard time going to sleep after we had gone to bed. We had talked most of the night in whispers so that Junior would not awaken and hear what we were saying. Richard said he was glad he had done it. I couldn't get him to admit that his plan might kill someone else. He kept saying that he was right and I was wrong. He believed that he had to kill our father for the things that our father had done. "He's got to pay," he whispered. Deep down, though, I suspected that Richard felt bad. He just was not going to admit that what he had done was wrong. He had convinced himself that he was right and he would not listen to me. There was no turning back for him. And then again I don't know what we could have done to change things now. My best bet was to go along with Richard and try to protect him as much as I could.

Aunt Betty walked over to the table wiping the soapy dish-water from her hands. She said, "You children hurry up and eat and go outside and play. Go away. Get out of our sights. I don't want anybody comin' back to eat until tonight. That's why there's all you can eat this mornin'. Get your fill right now...Junior?"

"Yes, ma'am?"

"Did you hear me?"

"Yes, ma'am."

"And you, Dolly? Did you hear what I said?"

"Yeah."

"Don't yeah your Mom," Uncle Robert said, giving her an ugly stare. He finally looked up from his plate. My father looked up also and I quickly looked down at my plate so that he would not see that I had been looking at them.

"Yes, ma'am," Dolly replied.

"You boys heard your Aunt Betty," mother said to Richard and me. "Go out and play and don't be botherin'."

"Can we just play outside in the yard or can we go to the cave?" Junior asked his mother.

"Whatever you all want. Just don't be buggin' us."

We decided to stick close to home for a while so we played in the yard after breakfast. Junior wanted to play cowboys so that Dolly wouldn't play. Dolly didn't want for us to play cowboys. Junior said that cowboys was what we were going to play and that Dolly could just sit and watch us. Dolly ran inside and cried to Aunt Betty about Junior. An angry Aunt Betty ran out swinging a large white belt with holes in it and whacked Junior on the back of the knees as she held him by the arm and Junior kept running in a circle, twirling Aunt Betty around with him. She kept on whipping him as he screamed like the monkey on a rope Richard and me had seen at the zoo. "Don't! You! Bother! Me! Again! To-! Day! Do! You! Under-! Stand?" And every word she spoke was a whipping across the back of the naked leg. When she got tired of hitting Junior she let him go and Junior fell to the ground exhausted. Saliva was drooling from his open mouth to the ground as he cried silently for a long time. He was not breathing. Aunt Betty nudged him lightly on the ribs with her foot. Suddenly he inhaled a great gulp of air and let out a scream that lasted forever. "Be quiet," Aunt Betty said, leaning over him, "the neighbors are goin' to think I'm killin' you." Aunt Betty was inside by the time Junior sat up. It took him a few minutes to get his bearings and then an anger overtook him and he jumped up and ran to Dolly like he was going to hit her. Dolly acted like she was going to scream and Junior stopped in his tracks. He knew better than to hit Dolly. "Bitch!" he said to her as he ran on by. He rubbed his legs and limped slowly to the car and sat in its shade on the ground. Richard went over and sat with him as he inspected the red welts that the white belt with the holes had made.

Dolly ran inside in a huff. Junior and Richard were sitting by the car doing nothing except breaking off little pieces of a twig and throwing the pieces on the ground, a habit that Clarence had passed on to Richard and Richard had passed on to Junior. Junior was not talking, as though he couldn't believe that his mother had whipped him. This was sort of new for him. I had never seen Aunt Betty or Uncle Robert hit him. He must have felt used and dirty and not loved. One of the things Junior always said to other guys was that our family always acted like animals, always fighting and our dad beating us up, that they were better than us. It looked now like they were no better than us and sad to say I was glad to see Junior being whipped around just as he had seen us.

I really didn't want to be with Junior and Richard. They weren't much fun when they were together. And besides, I was more interested in what Uncle Robert and Dad and Aunt Betty and Mom were talking about. I went back inside the house and when everyone turned to see me I lied. I told them that I needed to go to the bathroom. Mom shook her head. I excused myself and went into our bathroom. I locked the door, put my pants down and sat on the toilet.

"The car. The car." Uncle Robert was crying. "I hate to let go of the car. But what can we do?"

"What else we got?" Aunt Betty said after him. "That's the only thing of value besides this ratty furniture. How much you think we'd get for this? Don't answer. Let me tell you it ain't much. That's why I figure the only thing of value is the car."

"What about the truck?" my mother asked.

"Don't be silly," Aunt Betty answered.

"She's right, you know," Uncle Robert said. "That fuckin' truck wouldn't bring fifty dollars. It's a pile of shit."

"I worked hard on that truck," Dad whined. "It ought to bring more'n that."

"Yeah, but even if it did," Uncle Robert told him, "we still need a lot more."

"Tell me again," Aunt Betty spoke, "how much do you all need?"

"We'll need about a hundred dollars," Uncle Robert said. "I figure that we owe 'em that much, maybe less. I'm over-shootin' the mark, but I'd rather have more'n not enough."

"Well, that settles it," Aunt Betty said. "You all go out and see what you can do."

"I just hope he takes the car as collateral," said Uncle Robert. "If he doesn't we're still in trouble. If he does we got it made. Now shit-head, let me tell you what we're goin' to do so you won't screw up the deal. I'm going to ask three hundred and fifty and he can keep the car as collateral. He'll probably come back with a counter offer of two-seventy-five. I'll compromise. Make it three hundred. That's a good price for that car. With the three hundred we'll use one hundred of that to buy the whiskey that we already owe the fuckin' Indians. That's the money you stole. You'll owe me that. We'll buy another extra one hundred dollars of whiskey. I figure the Indians are goin' to really celebrate when they see us. And somethin' we've forgotten. July the Fourth is a holiday for 'em and that's tomorrow. They're really goin' to celebrate."

"Hell, that's my birthday!" Dad said. "I almost plumb forgot."

"Well," Aunt Betty said, "with the things that went on last week who was goin' to remember?"

I could hear Mom say, "I thought about it but I didn't figure anyone wanted to celebrate your birthday."

"It's too late to be thinkin' of shit-head's birthday," Uncle Robert scolded them. "Anyway, we'll have one hundred dollars left. We'll use a little of that as hush money. The rest we need just in case the Indians don't want their whiskey and just want their money back. You see, they may have already found 'em another supplier. They ain't stupid, you know. We ought to make some money any way you look at it. We've just got to keep our cool, that's all. The way I'm thinkin', right now we ought to come back with three hundred dollars or at the worst, two hundred dollars and one hundred dollars worth of whiskey. That'll be enough to get the car back."

Aunt Betty asked, "What'll we do after that?"

"Well," Uncle Robert replied, "we'll be broke. But at least we'll be alive. But remember, little brother, whatever it costs I'm keepin' track. And you're goin' to pay me back. This time there'll be no fuckin' excuses."

"Are we or aren't we agreein' to this thing?" Dad asked. "I mean, if we're goin' to be agreein' then let's get goin'. If not, let's quit the bull shittin' and let me sneak off right now. That way I'll maybe get a runnin' start on the Indians."

"No one said anythin' of the kind," Aunt Betty said. "It's just that Bob feels kind of betrayed by you. And who can blame 'im? You left 'im all alone out there all last week. He went through hell. He did. He really did."

"What I want to know is why did he go back?" Dad asked.

"Because, shit-head," Uncle Robert explained, "I thought that you were there. Do I need to say more in front of the women? If I had known you were goin' to bug out on me I'd a never gone back. I'd a let 'em come into town after you like they wanted to do all fuckin' week long. They knew all along that I wouldn't steal from 'em. It's really you they want."

"You two go on," Aunt Betty told them. "This has gone far enough. You ain't goin' to get much done blamin' each other. We've hashed this over all night long and it ain't done us any good. You all need to go and get somethin' done."

It really amazed me to hear Aunt Betty talk. She seemed to have control of the situation. It amazed me that Uncle Robert was letting her talk for him. Now I knew who the smart one in the family was.

I flushed the toilet as hard as I could and walked out through the front room and everyone watched me in silence. Uncle Robert and Dad were up from their chairs and were getting ready to leave. I heard their footsteps close behind me as I walked out.

My father got in the truck and tried to start it several times. He had to jump out, raise the hood, and readjust some thing. Once inside he tried it one time and it started. He backed the truck out of the driveway and into the street. Uncle Robert's car, the rusty maroon one with the low rear end, started with a roar of black smoke and a heavy idle. He backed the car out and he took off toward town. My father followed him in the truck close behind.

I had noticed that Richard and Junior were not around. They had gone to the cave. I wished that Richard had been there to see our father take off in the truck. As it was it fell on me to be the one with his heart in his throat.

I could hear the phone ringing inside. My Aunt Betty answered and yelled for my mother who was in the bathroom. Mom came out running. It was grandmother calling from Corpus. She wanted to know how we were. "We're doin' fine, Mom," mother said. "We're doin' just fine. Jim is doin' great...Yes...Yes...No... Yes...Yes, we're doin' fine. I hadn't written in a long time I know...Yes...Yes...Well, there hadn't been any news to speak of...They're both fine. Growing like weeds...Richard is fine. He had a little accident with his ears. You won't believe this but you know how dumb

Richard is. He got his head caught in a car door...Yes, a car door....Jim....Yes, Jim was slammin' the door real hard and Richard was gettin' out at the same time and got his head caught by the door...Jim was careful. It was just an accident....No, he didn't need a doctor he's all fine now. It just looks a little messy...Yes...Yes...Well you'll see what I mean when you see 'im. No...No, mother. Don't go into that. I miss her very much. You know she was my favorite. Not that I don't love the boys but she and I were different. I miss her every day. I still cry for her everyday....Yes....No....Yes... Yes, I cry for her every day. I remember her every day....I'm sorry. But...Yes...Yes...Yes...Yes....No...I didn't mean it that way. It was just too far to come. I understand....Yes...Well, sure we're doin' fine....No...I wouldn't lie to you. Jim and Bob have a good job. They're still workin' with the Indians... Yes....Yes....the government. No...Not that...they're still fixin' houses on the reservation. Doing well...Little Jimmy? Oh, he's fine. No trouble at all. All the teachers say he's very smart. You know how quiet he is around people...Yes...Takes after his grandpa....That's right. He and Richard give me a hard time sometimes but little Jim is fine, growin' like a weed but not as fast as Richard....No....Yes...Yes, Richard....No.... Yes, I know...Well grandpa wasn't big either...Five, nine? I thought he was shorter than that. Well, little Jim's goin' to be about that tall or maybe shorter. He ain't growin'...No...No, he's not smoking. Not that I know of....Well, I'll ask 'im but I don't expect 'im to tell me. He plays his harmonica and hangs around mostly with Dolly, the little girl....Well, Junior and Richard are older and they kinda leave 'im behind...Yes...Well, she's fourteen...I know that's not a little girl. She's a good girl...Well, they're outside playin.' I can see little Jim. He's sittin' by the door listenin'....Well, that's okay. I'm sure you won't hurt his feelin's...Yes...Okay...Maybe soon. I don't know yet. Jim was saying that maybe we'll be by soon. I don't know yet. Jim was saying the government money is running out pretty soon...Oh, mother. You know there ain't much work in Corpus....No...No...No...No, he doesn't want to work at Corn Products...Celanese? No, that's in Bishop. He hates drivin' to Bishop everyday...Well...Well...Well you know there ain't much more...No, he don't want to work off-shore...Well, you know he's always been particular where he works...Okay...Okay...Oh, they're okay. We hear from the Allens pretty often, maybe once a month she writes just to keep me up to date...We'll see you soon....I love you...We'll see you soon....I love you too." And she hung up.

I was thinking about my grandmother and her phone call when Uncle Robert drove up. He jumped out of the car, slammed the door hard and didn't say a word. Usually he'd say something but he looked preoccupied.

"Goddamit, mother-fuck," he shouted, once he got inside the house.

"What's the matter now?" Aunt Betty asked him, nervously. "How come you're back so soon? Where's Jim?"

"Wait a fuckin' minute," he yelled. "Wait a fuckin' minute! I need the title to the car. Where's the title?"

"I don't know," Aunt Betty replied. "I always leave those things to you."

"Can't you for once, goddamit, remember somethin'?"

He was running inside the house like a crazy man opening and closing drawers, throwing things all over the floor. "Goddamit," he kept saying when he didn't find the title in a drawer.

"Maybe it's in the bedroom," I heard Aunt Betty say. She sounded nervous.

My mother was worried. "What happens if you can't find it?" she asked.

"Your husband's ass is mud, that's what," Uncle Robert said and he kicked shut the drawer on the chiffonier in the living room. "Goddam house, you can never find a fuckin' thing when you need it around here."

"What happened to Jim?" my mother asked.

"He's with the whiskey man trying to soften 'im up. We got us a deal. Hell, this ain't no use," he said in desperation and he hurried into his bedroom to search.

We could hear him cursing, emptying and throwing drawers against the wall. He came out empty-handed. "Where is the envelope that I keep the car papers at?"

"I don't know, Bob," Aunt Betty cried. "I keep tellin' you I don't keep track of that stuff."

He cursed some more and ran back into his room and at the same time he yelled for Dolly. Dolly came out of her room, unhurried, wondering what the fuss was all about. Uncle Robert came out of the bedroom looking for her. Dolly was wearing a black wool-dress she had been trying on. "What in the shit are you doin'?" Uncle Robert screamed. "What are you wearin'? Don't you realize it's July the third...summer? It's one hundred and ten in the shade and you're wearing that dress?"

Dolly was not paying him much attention. She had her nose up in the air as if she wasn't going to be made to feel bad. "Is that what you called me for?" she said, sarcastically, "to talk about my clothes?"

"Oh, shut up and help me find somethin'," Uncle Robert said, ignoring her back-talk. Some other time he would have laid into her. At the present he needed help desperately.

"What are you lookin' for?"

"I'm lookin' for the fuckin' car title, that's what I'm lookin' for. Do you remember the envelope with the car papers?"

"Yes, I do," Dolly replied. "It's in the box in the closet in our bathroom behind the towels."

Uncle Robert ran into the bathroom and we could hear him tearing up the closet. There was silence for a while and then he came out looking real angry and he said, "What a fuckin' place this is when the only one that knows what the fuck is goin' on is a little girl." I could see through the screen door that he looked straight at Aunt Betty and Mom when he said it. He had the envelope in his hand.

He ran out and took off in the car, leaving his customary cloud of black smoke behind. As he sped away I saw one Indian in the old beat up rusty car take off and follow him. I imagined that the other Indian had stayed to keep a close watch on my father. I went inside and it was unbelievable the mess he had made. He had come in so fast and had left so quickly that it felt like he hadn't been there, but there was the mess to prove it.

Aunt Betty and my mother would be busy for a couple of hours picking up and straightening drawers. I went toward my room. I could see Dolly's door open and I peeped in. She called me in.

"Now don't be undressing in front of little Jimmy," my Aunt Betty yelled at her. She must have seen me go into the room.

"No, I won't," Dolly said as I walked in. She closed the door and locked it. "What do you think I am, crazy?" she said and no one could hear her except me.

I sat on the floor in front of the mirror as she took off her wool dress, pulling it up over her head and messing up her blond hair. She had on a bra and panties. She stood in front of the mirror and posed and then she'd change her pose, moving one hip up and then the other. Then she'd throw her head backwards and give out a laugh like a photographer was taking her picture. She kept her arms folded over her breasts, like she was being real careful that I wouldn't see them.

She didn't know it but I had seen her breasts several times (two) already. The first time was when she and Liz crawled into the cave. The second time was purely accidental. As I was walking from the bathroom back to my room very early one morning I noticed her door slightly opened and I decided I would peek in and when I did I saw that she was asleep on her back. She had kicked the sheet off her chest and it lay gently across her hips. I had never seen this part of her body before. I saw her small breasts standing firmly on their own. Her slow, steady breathing made her breasts move slightly outward and then back toward her body. I was in a trance. Every breath she took attracted me closer to her breasts. Before I knew it I was inside the room, standing by her bed. What a beautiful sight she was. Mitzi may have been pretty and I had seen her breasts but Dolly was beautiful. Her skin was like polished marble with soft transparent blond hair that shone like gold in the sun that filtered through the window. I didn't dare touch her. I didn't want her to awaken. I could have stayed like that forever but I heard a noise coming in the direction of our parent's rooms and I had to close the door. I had trapped myself inside Dolly's room. She woke up slowly and when she realized she was bare and cold she covered herself. She didn't see me. She turned to her side and dozed off again. When I was sure that I could get out I left and went back to sleep.

"What do you think of this pose?" she asked me, waking me up from my day-dream.

I was still trying to gather my thoughts. "I don't know," I said.

"What do you mean you don't know?"

"I just don't know."

"Do you want to do it to me again?"

The question caught me by surprise and I blushed.

"It looks like you don't."

"I do though," I said.

"Well? Do you like this pose?"

She sprang over by the bed and lowered her panties to the floor, exposing her darker pubic hair. I felt my heart ready to explode. She sat down at the edge of the bed and widely opened her stretched legs. I couldn't believe that she would be up to this with all the problems we were having. The Indians might be going to kill us all and here she was wanting me to do it to her again. "Come over here," she ordered and I obeyed her like a zombie. She made me kneel down and she grabbed the hair on the top of my head with both hands and pulled my mouth between her legs as she spread them wider apart. She shook like she always did and closed her eyes. In a way she was right. I forgot all about our worries during those moments.

"Dolly?" Aunt Betty yelled as she and mother cleaned the mess. "Don't be showing off to little Jimmy, you hear?"

"I ain't," she yelled back.

She jumped up from the bed, knocking me down, and put her panties on. Quickly she put on a white skirt with a yellow sweater.

"What do you think of this?"

"I don't know."

"You don't know nothin'," she said, like she was getting angry with me. She undressed again.

"Well, maybe I do know," I said. "That last pose was good. Not great, but good."

"Well, how about this one," she asked, and she twirled around in her panties and bra.

"That was great!" I exclaimed. "Just great."

She was driving me crazy, very crazy.

Aunt Betty tried the locked door. Then she knocked and Dolly let her in. "Dolly," she said, "you ought to be careful how you dress around little Jimmy. He's too young to be seein' the likes of you. Put on your clothes and get out here in the kitchen and help us out. Little Jimmy," she said to me, "go outside and play. You're too young to be seein' Dolly dressed like that."

"Your Aunt Betty's right," Mother said, as I walked out. "You're much too young to be seein' Dolly dressed like that."

Outside, my brother Richard and Junior had come back from the cave and were throwing a ball at each other, playing catch. Junior was trying to act like he knew how to pitch, like the pitchers we saw in the movies raising his leg high to throw the ball. You could still see the raised purple belt marks on the back of his legs where Aunt Betty had hit him with the white belt with the hole in it. Richard was squatting like a catcher.

"Come on, cauliflower ears," Junior yelled at Richard, "see if you can catch this!"

He reared back and threw the ball as fast as he could and Richard caught the rubber ball bare-handed. Richard turned to me and asked if I wanted to play. I said no. I didn't feel like doing anything. I was trying to get over what had just happened. Those were things that needed to be thought about for a while.

Richard threw the ball way over Junior's head and Junior cursed him. Richard came over to me and sat down on the steps while Junior was off chasing the ball.

"How do you feel?" I asked him.

"Okay, I guess," he answered and he wiped the sweat and dust on his sleeve.

"What if you kill 'im?"

"That's what I want," he said.

"What about us?"

"What about us?" he asked back.

"What happens if we're in the truck when the brakes give out?"

"That's the trouble with you, fart-face," he said to me, "you're always thinkin' of yourself." And he got up and went around the corner, like he didn't want me talking to him anymore.

As he walked away we could hear the familiar sound of my Dad's truck coming up the road. He and my Uncle Robert were in the truck. They drove up fast and excited. My Dad slammed on the brakes and they held. The wheels locked. The truck stopped and so almost did my heart.

They had driven right by where Richard was standing.

"Hello, shit-heads!" Uncle Robert greeted us as he and Dad jumped out of the truck.

We said "Hi" to Uncle Robert. Dad waved his hand without raising his arm, like everything was under control. There was a smile on their faces and I could tell they had been drinking.

The truck bed was full and covered with tarps. I imagined that it was full of whiskey.

Uncle Robert's car now belonged to the whiskey man, whoever that was, until they got the money to buy it back.

"And with the way things are goin'," Uncle Robert said, "we ought to have the money by the end of the week when we sell all the whiskey."

"That'll be so nice," Aunt Betty sighed, as she puffed on her cigarette and had a shot of whiskey that night, "we'll be back to normal then."

CHAPTER 29

On the morning of July the Fourth, early, about three or four, I woke up and could hear my father, Uncle Robert, Aunt Betty, and Mom in the kitchen. I could see the light from the dining room shining under the door. They were speaking in hushed voices, not wanting to wake us up. They must not have slept very much. They had been awake celebrating when we went to sleep at ten.

Shortly I could smell the coffee brewing and the bacon frying and then the noises of people eating: the scraping of the forks against the plate, the slurping of the coffee, the noise of the knife as it sawed against the plate.

They were getting ready to leave for the Indian reservation. I could only hear the sounds of voices, like droning bees. I was praying that everything would go all right and that Uncle Robert and Dad would come back safely. I was praying that the brakes would not go out on the high mountain passes where the narrow dirt roads twisted and turned dangerously. I cringed to think about them dying. What a burden for my brother Richard to have to bear. I tried to imagine what type of prayer the Allens would have for something like this. But I'm sure they had never gone through an experience like this.

Richard was asleep next to me. Ever since he had tampered with the brakes he had taken to sleeping with me instead of Junior. He needed to talk about it. Last night he had cried when I scolded him about what he had done but he still wouldn't admit to being wrong. The problem Richard had was that he couldn't undo what he had done. To do it he would have to confess about what he did and he knew that he might not survive that. At the least he would have to leave home. So he found it hard to admit that he had made a mistake. The brakes on that truck were going to go. The only question was when?

I wanted to open the door so that I could hear. I got up and opened it and went to the bathroom. On the way back Mom got after me and told me to go back to sleep. I turned around wiping my eyes and went back in the room. But I left the door open. By this time Richard was awake too and I could tell Junior was faking being asleep. He was moving his foot from side to side.

"Goddam it's a pretty morning," was the first thing we heard Uncle Robert say and we almost started to laugh. It was still night-time and you couldn't see anything outside. It was hot though. The air pushing through the windows was like the air at the bakery. We couldn't imagine what Uncle Robert would be looking at to call it a pretty morning.

We could hear them sipping their coffee.

"You got everythin'?" Uncle Robert asked Dad.

"Yep. I got everythin." It's all loaded up," he said.

"Well," Aunt Betty said, "Christie and I'll be prayin' for you all. Hopin' everythin' is goin' all right. We'll be nervous like a whore in church so you all get done and come on over...Do you think you ought to call us, Bob? Just to let us know how you all made out? Christie and me'll be goin' crazy by the end of the day."

"We'll call if we have the time. But don't you bet on it. We'll probably be too busy to get to a phone. It's a long way to a phone out there."

Mom asked, "Do you all think you can straighten out this mess and be back today, like we talked 'bout last night?"

"I don't know, Christie," Uncle Robert answered. "It all depends. We may just have to stay the whole week. Depends on what the Indians have to say about us. We may fix a roof or two. Who knows? Hell, they may kill us when they see us."

Aunt Betty pleaded. "Don't talk like that. That ain't goin' to happen. Please Bob, if you all are stayin' the whole week, call us. Will you...please? If not it's goin' to drive us crazy. We may just be worried enough to call the law to go over and check on you."

"Okay, shut up. We'll call," Uncle Robert said. Then he spoke to my father. "Just remember, shit-head, when we get there we go straight to the chief and we get someone to unload the whiskey and you count it. You understand?"

"Yep."

"Don't do like that time when you didn't count it and we got short-changed. We can't afford to be givin' anythin' away."

"I won't."

"Count the mother-fucker two or three times and let the Indian know you're countin' it and write it down and let the god damn Indian or the guy we call the wampum-man count it too and let 'im sign it."

"I know! That's enough. What do you take me for?" my dad said. I could hear him sipping his hot coffee.

"And don't short-count us. We've lost some money on these orders before."

"Not much," Dad informed him.

"I know not much," Uncle Robert said, "but shit, you add a little here and a little there and it makes for some money after while. Ol' man Wrigley gets a few pennies for his gum but he sells it by the shitfull and he's a millionaire. Owns the baseball field and the baseball team. All on fuckin' pennies. That's what I mean," he said and we heard him rap the table. "These pennies all add up."

"I wisht I knew ol' man Wrigley," my father said. "I bet he's somethin' else."

"Fuckin' right he's somethin' else. Smart. He made it the easy way, in pennies."

"We ought to think of somethin' like that," my father said.

"Well, Jim, ol' shit-head, this is no time to be thinkin' of that. We had us a bird nest on the ground. We had us a license to steal and you screwed it up."

"You could make a lot of money doin' somethin' like that. I mean, sellin' somethin' everybody wants for a few pennies. Maybe we can go into candy. Remember the candy Mom used to make?"

"Why do you want to go into that this mornin'? Forget about all that. All you'd do would be to mess it up anyway. Look at what you did. You fucked this one up and we were doing good."

"It ain't over yet," my father reasoned.

"I hope you're right," Uncle Robert answered. He thought about it for a little while and then he continued. "You're right, Jim. It ain't over yet. If we can get the Indians to trust us again we'll be in good shape."

"They trust you, Bob. Didn't you say they trusted you?" Aunt Betty added to the conversation.

"Sure they trust me. I've never double crossed an Indian in my life. I know better. I like a good head of hair on my head all the time. And that's somethin' you've got to learn, Jim. You can't fuck around with the Indians and you sure can't be fuckin' around with their women."

My father was quiet. I could see him in my mind playing slowly with the coffee cup, tilting it one way and then another on the table.

"So after you count the whiskey I want you to go to the council, whoever is there, and I want you to say you're sorry. I'll've talked to 'em by then. I'm not goin' to tell 'em anythin' except how sorry you feel...unless you want to make up a story on the way over so we both know what you're goin' to say. Make up a good lie. Tell 'em your kid was sick, real sick. You needed the money badly. The Apaches love children. Throw in somethin' about the kids, how sick they are, how much they love you. Any shit like that. Hell, maybe you could even tell 'em about little Sylvia and how she died and you needed the money for the coffin. Maybe they'll understand. Just be careful. Don't over-do the goddam thing to where no one believes you. If the council says you're okay then we're in. But like we agreed last night, if it looks bad and things turn out for the worse we'll get in the truck nice 'n easy and we'll get out of there slow but as fast as we can. No need to attract attention. We need to stay pretty close together so's we can leave right away if we have to."

Dad spoke. "What do you think about the money? I think I ought to get it right away. Maybe even before we unload. What do you think?"

"When it comes to that, Jim, if we can get it before we unload it'll be fine. You just try to get the sonofabitch," Uncle Robert said. "I don't have to tell you that. I'll just trust your judgement. Remember that they've already paid for some of that whiskey. That's why I'm bitchin' at you. The count's got to be perfect to keep everythin' honest. Hell, they may not want the extra whiskey. They may just want their money. They'll be watchin' like hawks to be sure we don't screw 'em 'round. Get the money the best way you can...if we have any comin'. If everythin' is okay we'll stay and have a good time. Remember that this is their July Fourth celebration. It has nothing to do with our July Fourth or your birthday. The Indians don't give a shit about the United States or you. They're just celebrating."

"I'm ready," I heard Dad say.

Uncle Robert said, "Do you want us to get our story straight before we get there?"

"We'd better," Dad said. "We've got plenty of time to talk it over on the way."

I heard the chairs being pushed back and my Uncle Robert said, "We'd better get goin' if we want to get there by eight."

We heard the two men walking around the house and then the front door opened and closed and they were outside. One of them, probably my father, started the truck after several tries and we heard the gears crunch in place. The over-loaded truck moved out slowly, its small engine crying in a whine, its headlights shining into our room as they backed up into the street. I felt like jumping out through the window and running to the truck to tell Dad and Uncle Robert to stop, to warn them of the danger they were in. But I couldn't. How could I explain what I knew? How could I warn them without killing my brother Richard?

I dozed off with another worry on my mind: What if the brakes fail and they are not killed or injured but they are picked up by the police for smuggling whiskey into the reservation? That, I was sure, would be a prison sentence.

Later in the morning we woke up again to the sounds of Aunt Betty and mother talking. We could smell the bacon and the eggs and the coffee and the bread. It felt like we had been through two nights.

"Come on children," Aunt Betty cried out, opening the door to our room and Dolly's room. "Come on, come on," she said, "today may be a long day. We got lots to do. A lot could happen today. You're Dad and Uncle Jim've left early this mornin'. "

"Oh Mom," Junior cried, "can I stay just one more hour?"

"No, you can't. You want me to get the belt to you again?"

Junior got out of bed with the sheet around his waist, dragging it on the floor. Dolly came into our room sleepy eyed and yawning. She was wearing a short translucent night-gown. "What's all the racket about?" she wanted to know. "Can't you people let anyone sleep? What was that all about? I couldn't sleep with all the noise last night."

We were staring at Dolly. We could see the outline of her boobs against the sunlight.

"Get out of here, you hussy," Aunt Betty said. "Don't you see these men around you? Aren't you ashamed of yourself?"

"Mother," she corrected Aunt Betty, "these are boys, not men. You keep callin' 'em men."

"Well, they are men and you should be a little bit more decent about your body."

Junior gave out a cackling laugh as he walked around dragging the sheet looking for his clothes. Dolly got angry. She turned on one foot and stuck out her tongue at us and raised her butt to us as she left. Aunt Betty couldn't control her. She walked out of the room talking to herself. "That girl is the biggest flirt I've ever seen," Aunt Betty said.

"Time to eat!" my mother yelled from the kitchen.

We dressed in a hurry. Aunt Betty said that we had to eat fast, again.

"You all sure act sleepy and tired," Aunt Betty said when we were eating, she and Mom watching us eat. They were leaning against the kitchen counter trying to act normal but I could tell they were worried about Uncle Robert and Dad. They kept whispering at each other while looking at us.

"Look at Richard," my mother said, "and little Jimmy. You two look like you've been up all night long."

Dolly was eating slowly, trying to get Aunt Betty mad. She said, "They probably were up all night with all the racket you all were makin'. I know I was."

"Shut up, Dolly," Aunt Betty yelled. "One more word out of you and I'll take your Dad's white belt to you like I did Richard yesterday. I'm in a powerful mood today. Your father and Uncle Jim are in a hell of a mess and we don't know what's to become of us. Today is the day that might determine what we're goin' to be doin' for a long time. I ain't in no mood to take any of this shit from anyone. You ain't too old to whip, you know. I'm tired of this back-talk and this bitchin'. You ain't the woman of this house, goddammit. I am!"

"You boys heard what Aunt Betty said," Mom warned us. "That goes for me too. You all go out and play. We don't need to be worryin' about you all. We got enough worries as it is."

That morning we dragged around the yard, tired, and finally in the afternoon we decided to take a lazy walk to the cave. I decided to go with Richard and Junior. I didn't see much going on with Dolly today. She didn't look to be in a very good mood. In the cave we started talking and smoking. Junior was worried that Uncle Robert would get hurt by the Indians. What would he do without a father, he asked? Self-centered as he was, we didn't pay too much attention to his concerns. We were glad that he had something to worry about, for a change. So we let him smoke and talk and the more he talked the sleepier we got. I don't remember what happened next but we fell asleep for several hours.

We woke up to the sounds of screams! Dolly was on her hands and knees at the entrance to the cave crying and at the same time screaming for us to go home quickly. She was very excited, her mouth dry, her tongue glued to the roof of her mouth so that we could hardly understand her. Her whole body was shaking. There was an emergency but that's all she could get out, she was so upset. We got enough out of her to know something had happened to Uncle Robert and Dad and that we had to get back home right away. We all ran back home in the twilight and we left Dolly far behind and we could hear her screaming about what had happened. She was screaming something about a nose but I was sure I was hearing wrong. She wasn't making any sense. I could see Junior in front of all of us. He was crying, wiping his nose on his shirt, running as fast as he could. Richard was right in front of me and I guess he must have thought he killed Uncle Robert and Dad cause his legs were quivering as he ran and he was starting to stumble. I do know he was as white as a ghost.

CHAPTER 30

I could see that Junior's long legs were tiring. They were beginning to quiver with every stride he took. Crying as he was, it was hard for him to catch his breath. Richard had caught up to him and was passing him slowly, even though Richard's legs were looking shaky. Even I was catching up to Junior. I looked behind me and Dolly had fallen down, exhausted. She had had to run to the cave and now she was having to run back. I debated whether I should run back to help her. I cursed myself for looking back, for being so concerned with Dolly. I should have stopped and gone to help her but I didn't. I looked behind me once more and saw that she had gotten up and had started to run again, this time at a very painfully slow pace. She was holding her side and crying. I passed Junior and he was crying like a baby, his mouth open. His nose was draining and snot and tears were rolling into his mouth. He grunted in pain with every stride he took.

Richard got there first. The fear that he had killed Dad and Uncle Robert had made him run faster than anyone of us. As I reached the small hill that separated the houses from the river bed I felt good to see that the truck had made it back. It was parked in the driveway. Richard was in the front yard when I got there, looking nervously around the truck. In a way he seemed relieved. His color had come back. We could hear my mother and Aunt Betty screaming from inside the house. When I got close to the truck I noticed that it had been pelted with rocks. My father had a wild scared look in his eyes as he ran out with a bucket of water and he opened the hood and poured water into the radiator. He was trying to pour so fast that he was spilling a lot of water on the hot engine, making the cold water sizzle and steam. He had not said a word to us. Junior finally made it. He staggered into the yard. He wasn't sobbing anymore. He managed to climb the steps and stumble into the house.

Dolly was not far behind, almost falling with each step, and she almost had to crawl inside.

I heard Aunt Betty scream when she saw Junior for the first time. "It's your father!" she cried out to him. "It's your father! We don't know where he is. We don't know if he's alive or dead!"

Richard and me ran inside when we heard the screams. My mother was standing by Aunt Betty as Aunt Betty sat at the table covering her face in her hands. "Where is he?" she kept screaming through her fingers as she cried. My mother was trying to keep Aunt Betty calm but it wasn't possible. Mom was crying too. Aunt Betty began screaming at my father. "What did you do? What happened? Where's Bob? What did you do with 'im?" Dolly was crying and so was Junior. They were sitting on either side of Aunt Betty, holding onto her closely.

"Oh, Betty," Mom cried as she kept hugging and squeezing Aunt Betty, "if only we hadn't come. We've been a curse to you all."

Like a squirrel, my father ran inside and he was going through our stuff in the drawers of the chiffonier. He was throwing all of it into the center of the living room floor. "You need to help me load up the fuckin' truck," he yelled at Mom. "We need to get the fuck out of here!"

We were standing by the door not knowing what to do. He looked at us and he yelled for us to load the truck. "Throw everythin' you can in the back," he yelled. "We've got to get out of here and fast." To Mom he said in a mean way, "Are you goin' with me or not?" as he ran toward the bedroom. He came out with a bundle full of clothes wrapped in a sheet and threw it with the other pile in the middle of the room. Mom tried to wipe the tears from Aunt Betty's face but she couldn't keep up with her crying.

Richard and me ran into our room and quickly took our clothes and put them in a sheet and tied the sheet together and then dragged the bundle out and threw it on the truck. We ran back as fast as we could and got the other bundles in the middle of the room and dragged those to the truck too.

Aunt Betty had quieted down a little and my mother was barely crying. Dolly, holding back her sobs and not knowing what to do for her mother, was brushing Aunt Betty's hair back to get it away from her face. Junior was sitting on the floor with his mouth open watching everything like he couldn't understand what was happening.

My father had come back alone. That much we knew. God only knew where Uncle Robert was and my father looked like he didn't have time to tell us. After she was sure Aunt Betty was all right, mother got up and started helping us get our other things together. Richard and me were in the back yard trying to get the old barrel we'd brought from Texas rolled out to the truck and when my father saw us he called us shit-heads and told us to quit, to leave it behind. We didn't have time.

When we went back in, Aunt Betty was having crying fits again, letting out a yell when she was about to cry herself out and then hitting her chest with her fist, scaring Dolly and Junior.

"It's not that bad!" my father shouted out to her once we had thrown everything in the truck. "Betty, I told you before. Bob's all right. It's just that I couldn't find 'im and I had to leave in an awful hurry. I swear to you on our mother's grave that Bob's all right. I tell you that the Indians love Bob."

"But how can we be sure, you no-good sonofabitch?" Aunt Betty growled at him like she wanted to kill him. "How can you know how he's doin'? You can't even take care of yourself, you dirty lyin' bastard!"

My father tried to hold her hand but Aunt Betty shook her hand away from him. "Betty, you can call me anythin' you want. You can act like you don't want to touch me. It don't make any difference. You ain't goin' to get me pissed off. I ain't got time. Shit, it's my life that's on the line. Don't you all understand? Don't you worry about Bob. He knows how to take care of himself."

Mom grabbed Dad and I thought she was going to hit him. "Jimmy, you can go by yourself!" she screamed. "I ain't leaving until we straighten this thing out. Jimmy, it ain't fair to Betty not to know all that's happened. Tell us again. And this time tell us everythin'. What happened?"

"I told you I had a fight, goddammit," my father cried out in a hurry to get out. "It wasn't even my fault. You know how the damn Indians are. They've got to fight. I didn't do nothin'. No matter what anybody says, I didn't do nothin'. It wasn't my fault. They were gangin' up on me. I was losin' bad. They had me down but the guy I was supposed to be fightin' made the mistake of puttin' his face next to mine. Goddam, I don't know why I did it but I reached over with my mouth and bit his nose off. I was like a mad dog once I tasted that blood. I just couldn't let go until I had bit right through it. The Indian jumped up from the fight screamin' and yellin' and holding his bloody face. I spit out his nose and it rolled on the dirt and when the other

Indians saw the nose on the ground covered with dirt and blood it drove 'em crazy. They were runnin' after me. They had their knives out! They were goin' to kill me like it was part of their game. I ran and I ran and when I got to the truck I got in and took off."

My dad went over to the sink and got a glass of water. He rinsed his dirty mouth out a few times and spat the water into the sink. He refilled the glass and gulped it down and then waited a few seconds for the water to clear his throat. He kept on with his story as he leaned his back on the counter, still holding the glass, looking at the floor.

"Robert ..," he started, almost choking with emotion, "had said...that we should stay together...just in case...We knew how bad the Indians can get over nothin' once they start drinking... but he wasn't around when I got to the truck. I couldn't wait for 'im. Betty, you understand that, don't you? I...just... couldn't wait for 'im. Betty, he wouldn't've waited for me. The Indians were gettin' closer and closer." Dad wiped the perspiration and dust from his face with his sleeve. As scared as I was, I wished that I had been around to see all of this. "Shit, I'm sure they're after me now," he said quietly, putting the glass on the counter. "That's it, Betty. That's all the story... Christie, we don't have much time. Bob's okay. The Indians like 'im. He's like one of 'em. They don't like me. It's only me they don't like. He's okay I tell you. He'll be back, probably in a day or two. He was kind of feelin' good the last I saw 'im. Goddamit, we had it made too. The Indians swallowed the story. We had it made. But you know that nothin' ever goes right with me." He shook his head and said, "Shit...They ain't goin' to kill 'im, Betty. So quit your crying. They love the guy. Bob knows their ways. Now if I'd be there I'd be dead by now. Christie," he said, heading toward the door, "it's time to leave." My mother had already gathered what few things in the kitchen she owned and she threw that on the back of the truck and we all piled into the truck—my father and mother up front, my brother Richard and me in the back sitting against the cab, our legs under the same old dirty tarp that our Dad had stolen from the oilfields in Tahoka, sitting on a cushion of tied sheets filled with clothing, bedding, a few pots and pans and my mother's favorite pillow and her favorite quilt that her mother had let her take when she got married, the quilt wrapped around my sister Sylvia's teddy bear.

Aunt Betty and Dolly and Junior had come out to see us pack and go. They were not crying anymore, relieved, I guess, that they had finally gotten rid of us.

Richard looked scared getting in the truck. I don't think he ever figured that we were going to have to ride in the truck. I knew that he was thinking that he just might be going to kill all of us. I was scared to get on the truck but what could I do? If I refused to leave everyone would have thought I was crazy. I could not just come out and tell the truth. That would have put Richard in a lot of trouble. Dad would have killed him right there like a dog. And yet we were all likely to get killed. The brakes had not failed through all that driving and I was sure that they were about ready to go at any time now. But I had to be loyal to Richard. I had to take my chances. I would do like the Allens—pray. I would pray for us.

"I want you two farts to listen and listen good," my father spoke to us before he got in the truck. "It's more'n likely the Indians are after me to kill me. So you two be on the look out. No sleepin'! Keep your eye out for 'em. Just bang on the cab if you see 'em. I'll take care of the rest."

I looked over to Dolly as I sat on top of the bundles in back of the truck and I couldn't face her. I felt so embarrassed. I did not feel worthy of being her slave. At the same time I could tell that in spite of what had happened to her father that she felt sorry for us. Junior appeared stunned with all that had happened. He was trying to smile and wave good-bye. Aunt Betty was on the running board, half her body inside through the window as she hugged and kissed Mom. "Remember, Christie dear, that I love you," we could hear her say, over the noisy motor.

"I love you too," Mom cried out. "I'm only sorry to be of such bother. It never seems to end with Jimmy."

"Oh, Christie," Aunt Betty said to her as she let go and jumped off the running board, "some day it will all change. He'll grow up."

And our mother let out a laugh that stopped us cold. "Are you kidding?" she asked. "Jimmy'll never grow up. Bob has to die before he changes."

"Don't even say that, Christie!" Aunt Betty yelled above the noise of the truck.

Dad gunned the motor several times and cleaned out the soot and vapor from the muffler. He jumped out of the cab one last time with the truck running and checked us and the tail-gate and he had difficulty rehooking the chain on the tail-gate with what he held in his hands. He had his small rusty gun. Richard and me were scared. There was going to be a shooting.

He jumped in the truck and my mother looked at us through the rear window and we could see from her look that she was very worried, just like us. She did try to smile, to ask us, I guess, to forgive her.

Aunt Betty was crying and so was Dolly. Both were holding on to each other trying to get away from the soot of the muffler. Junior was letting the tears run down his big cheeks, trying to smile and wave at the same time. He looked like he had urinated in his cover-alls.

Aunt Betty yelled as we reached the road. My brother Richard and me could hear her saying that we had forgotten the clothes in the washing machine. Mom didn't hear her and we just waved at them. There was no way we were going to stop for some thing like that.

We sped out of Artesia and we were trying to look for Indians in every direction at once. Several times Richard and me were so excited that we were sure a car full of Indians was following us and we were about ready to knock on the cab when they turned off to another street.

We didn't have to wait long for them though.

We were driving in Indian territory about a mile outside of town when we saw the familiar old beat-up Indian car. The two Indians had parked on a dirt road off the highway and were patiently waiting for us, drinking Uncle Robert's whiskey. We all recognized the car as soon as we passed it. There was no doubt. Richard looked at me and me at Richard at exactly the same time. As soon as we passed them they took off behind us. Richard and me started pounding on the cab as hard as we could. Dad was weaving over the road trying to get his gun out of his belt, yelling scared that he had already seen them. Mom was leaning out through the window on her side screaming at us. "Your Dad says to get down low! Get down as low as you can get! They're goin' to shoot!"

Richard and me got down completely under the tarp and dug our way, like ground-hogs, under the bundles. We could feel the truck swaying more and more from one side of the road to the other. We could hear and then feel the whacking noise all around us as the bullets hit the truck. We could hear the engine noise of the car getting closer and closer. The Indians were closing in on us. They were going to kill us all. Dad was firing back blindly right over our heads, not able to look back and keep the truck on the road at the same time. Mom was yelling, "You boys stay down! Stay down! They're shootin' at us!"

Dad had run out of bullets and we could hear him yelling and cursing for another clip for the gun. The Indians were so close that gun fire was exploding over our heads. Dad emptied the new clip at the Indians in a matter of seconds and was yelling for more. Mom was trying nervously, her hands shaking badly, to fill the old clip. One Indian bullet hit our rear window and we heard it shatter and our Mom scream when the glass hit her on top of the head. I guess Mom was able to load the clip with her trembling hands and with the glass all over her because by the time the Indians were right next to us our Dad was able to fire straight into the car and then there was a silence that my brother Richard and me thought was the silence that came before death.

We kept our eyes closed for the longest time and the truck went on a straighter course and started to slow down. We thought we were going to die but we could no longer hear the Indians firing at us. Richard and me couldn't take it anymore. We stuck our heads out and we could see the Indian car far in the distance. Steam was roaring out of the engine. Dad had hit the radiator and they had had to stop. Mom stuck her head out and yelled into the wind. "You all can come out now! It's over! Be ready to duck again if we need to! We're still in Indian country."

Richard and me were trembling. We couldn't control our fright. We could see the large holes in the cab where the Indians had shot at us. I couldn't see how they had missed Mom or Dad but thank God they had.

We didn't stop for anything or anyone. It was night time by then and Richard and me were very tired. We were having a hard time staying awake. Each passing of a car or truck brought us to our senses. A truck load of Indians followed us for about five miles before we got to Carlsbad and that kept all of us on edge. We didn't doze off then. We poked our heads into the cab and we saw that Dad had his gun ready although he figured they weren't after us. These Indians were probably from the southern part of the reservation and they hadn't heard about the fight. We were in luck, for once. Just as we entered town, the truck with the Indians turned off. We could hear the Indians singing. They must have been drinking. They were celebrating their Fourth of July.

We stopped and filled up and checked the truck for the first time at Carlsbad. In the light, the attendant didn't know what to make of the truck.

He kept looking suspiciously at the fresh bullet holes on the cab and the dents made where the Indians pelted it with rocks this morning. My Dad kept telling him to hurry up but he kept looking at us like he was trying to remember what we looked like just in case the sheriff showed up looking for us. I wanted more than anything to ask if we could check the brakes but I controlled myself. I was going to have to wait for just the right time and when that time would be I couldn't tell. As it happened, later on I didn't have to ask.

From Carlsbad we drove on to Loving without seeing a single car. Mom yelled back to us as we crossed Loving. She wanted us to know that we could go ahead now and go to sleep. Richard and me hugged each other and we dozed off.

At around midnight we woke up to a clear sky when the steady reliable whine of the old pick-up truck started to slow down. We had just crossed the New Mexico-Texas border and my father was stopping the truck by the huge state of Texas concrete map and we all got out and my father started laughing. He took the gun from his belt and shot into the air and I was surprised at what a little popping sound the gun made. It had sounded like a canon when it was going off over our heads.

We drove a little farther and that night we parked the truck on the sandy banks of Red Bluff Lake. Richard and me slept in fits, still scared that the Indians would be after us. Dad slept with the gun in his hands. I slept in fits. When I would wake up I would wake Richard up and we would look around in the stillness and silence of the night, the frogs sometimes making their sounds, the crickets rubbing their legs and I remembered and Richard did too the night when our sister Sylvia got sick in Tahoka.

In the early morning we were awakened by some fishermen launching their boat. They eyed us suspiciously, like the attendant had done at Carlsbad, but they acted like they had not seen us. If the sheriff had asked them about us they would have told him that they had not seen anyone.

We got up and washed in the lake and took off. But not before Dad walked around to the bluff where the lake must have been the deepest and he took out the gun from his belt and threw it into the water.

We stopped at the first country store we came to and we bought baloney and bread and milk and the old man there looked so much like the man in the grocery store in Tahoka that I felt like asking him if they were related but I didn't because we were in a great hurry and besides I didn't want to create an impression on the man, just in case the Law was after us. We ate our breakfast, plus the candy that Richard had stolen, in the truck on the way.

Luckily, the brakes had held up all this time but at Fort Stockton right after we gassed up, as my father was pulling out to cross the highway that went to El Paso, the brakes gave out and we slowly rolled to a stop in the ditch, the truck stopping at an angle that almost had us tilting over.

We stayed at Fort Stockton for two days having the brake lines fixed. The mechanic couldn't believe that we had not gotten killed. He kept telling my Dad that the brake lines had been cut through just enough to weaken them. He had never seen anything like it. All four lines had been worked on but only one gave out.

"You were lucky, Buddy," he said, chewing his tobacco. "I hate to be the one to tell you but there's somebody out there that wants you dead in the worse way."

Dad shook his head as Richard and me looked away.

"Buddy, someone really wanted you dead," the mechanic said as he shined a light behind each wheel, the truck high up on the rack. He whistled his surprise. "Let me show you, Buddy. See here? Someone who knew what he was doin'. This one is almost gone. If all four had gone out not one of you would have lived."

"Goddam Indians," Dad spat.

"I don't know an Indian that knows anythin' 'bout cars," the mechanic informed him. He looked at our father and asked, "What you been up to anyway?"

Dad laughed and said, "Nothin'. Really."

The mechanic spat tobacco and said, "Hell, the truck's all shot up and dented. The brake lines have been cut. Shit, if you don't know you're in trouble you ain't got much sense."

"I'm doin' okay," Dad told him.

The mechanic studied our dad for a while and spat out an old wad of tobacco that had turned white. He chewed off a fresh plug and put his tobacco pouch in his back pocket. "Okay, hell," he said getting under the car, "you look like you've been shot at and missed and shit on and hit."

The mechanic had promised that the truck would be ready Thursday afternoon so Thursday afternoon we all went to pick it up. When we got there the mechanic was washing his hands under a tree by a water faucet that came out of the ground. He spat and said, "It's ready. You can take it."

Our dad turned around so that no one could see his money roll and peeled off the money. "Here you go, pardner," he said to the mechanic.

The mechanic counted out his money and satisfied that it was correct placed the money in his pocket. "Don't go messin' around with any more Injuns," he said, grinning.

"You got that right, pardner," Dad said, laughing.

We didn't leave Fort Stockton that night. Instead we went back to the motel. Mom wanted to get an early start in the morning.

That night Mom called Aunt Betty to see how they were doing. Aunt Betty was happy. Uncle Robert had called and was doing all right. The Indians loved him and they wanted to keep on buying whiskey from him. She did mention what Richard and me already suspected, that Dad had kept the extra one-hundred dollars and they couldn't get the car out of hock. Uncle Robert had no way back unless he found a ride this weekend with one of the Indians. She was happy again but a little bitter that Dad had kept the money. But they would get the car back somehow. Uncle Robert understood. He knew Dad had to leave or be killed. He only wished Dad would have left some of the money behind with Aunt Betty. They had taken the Indian to the doctor to sew the nose back on but the doctor had laughed in their faces and had thrown the nose away. She invited us over whenever we wanted. (Fat chance.)

We left Fort Stockton Friday morning, early, still on Highway 285, the same road that brought us out of Artesia. We traveled south through Sanderson and Dryden and Comstock, all little towns with nothing to remember them by.

At Sanderson, Highway 285 ends all of a sudden, for no reason. When I grew up I looked at a map and thought it was funny to see that a highway that begins at Denver and travels downward through the Rocky Mountains, through some of the most beautiful places in the world and then on through New Mexico, through Santa Fe, would end like this, in Sanderson. We stopped at Del Rio to buy something to eat: baloney and bread and this time mustard. And something to drink. Dad let Richard and me drink a soft drink for the first time in a long time because we knew he felt guilty about stealing the money from Uncle Robert.

We stayed on Highway 90 all the way to Eagle Pass. At Eagle Pass we slept at a roadside park at the southern edge of town and no one disturbed us except for some old dogs that had smelled the baloney in the truck. After the dogs left, my brother Richard and me were comfortable sleeping in the truck bed.

Early in the morning we took off for Corpus Christi. We went through little towns like Encinal and Freer and San Diego and Alice. And when we got to Robstown we were so excited that Richard and me started to laugh. We were almost at our grandmother's home.

The early evening fog, loaded with the smell of salt water and stale fish and shrimp, led us into Corpus Christi, our father cursing because he couldn't see the streets. Finally, after Richard and me thought that we would be lost forever, we turned into the familiar crushed-shell driveway and the truck stopped, giving out the smell of burning oil and rubber. The soot from the muffler came up over the tail-gate and tried to get us but Richard and me jumped out from under the tarp and ran to the house.

Our grandmother was waiting for us.

"My, but the boys have grown," she said, barely rubbing our heads and thinking of Sylvia.

We were home at last.

My mother was to stay in Corpus Christi for the rest of her life. I was to stay until I graduated from a two year college. Dad and Richard were another story.

Dad kept on being violent, coming home drunk just about every night. More and more he wanted to beat Richard like Richard was the cause of all his problems. Many times we called the police and he was put in jail.

Mom and Dad argued more and more about Sylvia, like they couldn't forget her and were trying to blame each other for what had happened to her. It was a relief for everyone when one day he came in, beat up but sober and talking as if he owned the world, like he had another one of his schemes, and decided to pack what little clothes he owned and he left in his old truck.

Richard was not to live with us for long either.

I warned him over and over again, but he started stealing more and more and for no reason, stealing everything that he could get his hands on—money, food, jewelry, clothes, trinkets, knives, anything. Finally, an old bicycle that he brought home one day was traced to him and found to have been stolen. He swore that he had bought the bicycle from a stranger for the five dollars.

He had no defense and we had no money to defend him. Mom had to go before the Judge and stood up and said that she couldn't take care of him.

The Judge placed him in a juvenile home in Gatesville, Texas. He was supposed to have gone to Gatesville for three months but he couldn't take to being caged up and he kept trying to escape. So more time was added on for bad behavior and he wound up serving two years for stealing the old five-dollar bicycle.

We found out from his probation officer in 1964 that he had been let go, but he didn't come home. I did not see him or know where he lived for some ten years, until he was twenty-four. At that time, when I found out about him, I drove to see him at the Texas Prison System in Sugarland, west of Houston. This time he had stolen a car.

His ears had never healed normally and they called him Jug.

BOOK TWO

CHAPTER 31

I had an unnatural premonition of death lingering over me during the day. It occupied most of my wakeful thoughts like a stifling acid scent about me making it very hard to concentrate. In the only class of the day, I had the students write for almost the fifty minutes. Write. Write anything that you want to write about, I said, wiping the scent from my eyes. It was a joy to be able to see just the top of their little freshman heads as they wrote. No one would interrupt my thoughts. Once in while some one would look up—at me, the ceiling, looking for a word, just the right word. Immediately I would look the other way for fear that the little rascal would get up to ask me a question. I didn't want to be bothered.

That night as I lay in bed I was awakened by the shrill sound of the telephone ringing, the premonition having come, finally. It surprised me enough that when I awakened I thought the sound was the alarm clock and I was reaching for it when Anne grabbed my hand and told me it was the telephone.

I awoke in a progression of disoriented steps that seemed to take me forever. When I realized who I was I knew it was the telephone. My confused mind was starting to reach consciousness. The next step was a vague feeling that I didn't know where I was. The room seemed queerly strange to me, like I hadn't lived there at all. I wondered how I had gotten there. At the same time my soggy brain decided to relive, mingled with these other thoughts, the memory of an early morning in a strange California motel where I had awakened with the urge to pee and had gotten up and had walked directly into the wall. But the next feeling that came over me was a reversal of the seemingly natural progression that had started my orderly return to consciousness: I had known who I was an instant before and now I didn't. Then my mind began in earnest to sort out the events that had led me here. In a speck of time, the protracted instant that it takes one to fully awaken, I recognized that I was in the apartment on Mulberry and I realized who I was. I thought to myself that I had better stop moving so much.

The phone was still ringing.

"Answer that, will you please," Anne said. She sounded miffed.

"Hello," I said.

"Hello?" asked someone through the receiver. I wanted to guess that it was my mother but I had made that mistake before.

"Jim?"

"Yes."

"Jim?"

"Yes."

"Is that you, Jim?"

"Yes, it's me," I said.

"Who is it?" Anne asked. She was sitting up in bed, unconcerned that her small breasts were exposed, lighting a cigarette.

"My mother," I answered. I knew Anne didn't know my mother from anyone else but she had asked.

"Jim? Are you there?"

"Yes, Mom, I'm here."

"You don't know how hard it's been to get a hold of you. I've been callin' all over Austin for you. Finally, one of the men who had a catalog found your name and he called a friend who had a friend who knew you from the college and he begged for the phone number and really Jim you shouldn't ought to have an unlisted number. And if you change to an unlisted number at least you ought to send it to your own mother. We had a hard time and 'specially today when I really needed you."

I didn't answer. What could I say? I had forgotten to send my new number to my mother.

I had just gotten a divorce. That was the reason for the unlisted number. My wife and I had parted on friendly terms but you never know. Some people have adverse delayed reactions to emotional experiences or so my psychology friends tell me. So I wasn't about to take any chances. I moved, by choice, for about the tenth time in the last two years and I was now living in a small apartment. I teach Freshman English at the University of Texas at Austin and have been doing that for a long time, long for me anyways, longer than I thought when I took the job. And with the daily evidence of the inordinate longevity of English profs staring me in the face, I don't believe I'll ever do any thing else. It's like we're super-glued to the job.

Anne, the lady sleeping next to me, is Anne Whatever, Anne Magee really, one of those ladies with large thighs and small tits that abound in college towns, walking the streets at night, always coming from the library, browsing at the book-store, taking one night course a semester just to piss off the faculty. Anne is what we classify as a professional. She is not nor has she ever been my student. I never take advantage of my students. Actually, the ones that want to go to bed with me are not very bright and the bright ones already have someone, usually a very bright guy with old clothes that's into the dirty look—weekly baths and teeth cleaning, ear wax already darkening at the opening of the ear canal—who delight in waiting at the teacher's office, stinking up the place, just to shoot the shit, as equals, as if you didn't have anything better to do. Anne Anyway, is in her thirties like me. I am now thirty-five, thank you, and I survived. I knew I would. I survived my parents.

I had been unhappily married for six or seven years depending on who you believe, the Justice of the Peace or the Catholic Church. My wife insisted that the civil ceremony was good for fornication but not good for social intercourse. She wanted undeserved respectability. I, on the other hand, wanted to teach senior classes, courses in the four-hundreds. She never understood why I wanted to move on. She loved Austin. She would never leave the hill country. I wanted to go where I could fit into my profession, not into the landscape. Besides, once you've seen one hill you've seen them all.

So we divorced. And, as life would have it, I stayed in Austin and she left.

In the early years she came in one day telling me that she had been out checking real estate and had found a duplex that was ideal for us. We could live in one-half and rent the other half and use the rent to pay...Well, you've heard the spiel. That was how original she was. How could I have married her?

I met her at Taco Bueno on 9th street where I had gone one night for Mexican food. She was sitting alone, looking desperate, and I asked her if I could join her. That's how desperate I was. She seemed so intelligent at the time. She said she was a university student having to drop out one semester, get money laid up, go another semester, that sort of thing. And you know me.

I was raised to be a sucker for a good story. We lived together for two years before marrying and still she had not enrolled in school. She kept offering feeble excuses and I believed her. I became suspicious. Then one day while at the Registrar's getting transcripts mailed out for job applications, I decided I would ask to see her records. I was playing a hunch. I knew I couldn't see anyone's records but my own but, to my surprise, I was told that even if they could let me see the records there were none to see. She had no transcripts. She had never enrolled.

Well, anyway, that was all in the past now. And I felt good about it. There was nothing to divide among us for a settlement. When I found out that she had lied to me I purposely never accumulated anything for her to share. I was extra careful that she not get pregnant. One dumb-ass in the family was enough. I made sure she took a double dose of birth control pills.

Then Anne came along. Anne was smart, educated, conniving, ruthless, and, all in all, a good psychologist. She wrote horribly. But she said that in her profession it was what you wrote not how you wrote it that counted and she charged one hundred and twenty-five dollars an hour to prove it, which made me inclined to believe her.

You remember that I never had much so I didn't care about things like money. All I wanted was for my teacher's retirement to keep me in food, clothing and shelter in my later years—comfortable, as my Jewish friends say. That's all, comfortable.

I knew that Anne was leaving soon. I just didn't make enough money to compete with her. She was afraid that the hopeless difference in our salary would be our downfall. She could afford the better things. I could afford things, but not better; there is a difference. Money, she said to me one day, speaking psychologically, can make you feel a hell of a lot better about your self. "Why do you think the Mexicans and the Blacks are always killing each other?" It sounded reasonable to me. But at what point, at what jingle in your pocket, would you stop killing each other? "Oh, then," she replied, "you start killing someone else." Perfectly logical to me. I always thought that people killed each other in Texas because they didn't have air-conditioning.

Anyway, Anne said she was leaving and would start going out with other men. I could see her if I wanted to and if she wanted to but I had to call first and make a date, no more of this dropping in. It made her feel used. What can I say? Her salary was larger than mine.

How I wish Anne didn't smoke. I could feel Aunt Betty around me every time she lit up. That's the only thing that truly bothered me about her. Her salary, her body, all those things I could live with. But I didn't badger her about it because, to save face, it could have been the only thing I could use as an excuse for saying I left her. I had just hoped that if I did use it that she didn't hear about it. I didn't want her to hear that something so flimsy would tear us apart. Regardless, I could feel that very soon I wouldn't have to concern myself with the problem of cigarette smoke. And then I read where second-hand smoke, the one coming out of the smokers lungs was worse than the original smoke, the one inhaled into the smoker's lungs. It's hard to believe. What will we learn next?

"Your father's dead," my mother said on the telephone. I could hardly hear her. I thought for a second I had heard wrong.

"What did you say?" I had to ask.

"Your father, Jim. He died this afternoon."

"How?"

"He died from clot in the lungs."

"Who called you?"

"His friend in Fort Worth."

"Where are you?"

"Corpus," she said, short for Corpus Christi.

"Are you going to Fort Worth?"

"I thought I'd wait, 'specially with this cold weather," she said. "I really don't know what to do yet. Heck, he might've wanted to be buried here in Corpus. But right now I don't know."

"When will you know?"

"What happened?" Anne wanted to know. She was taking a drag on her cigarette, a long one, the type that makes ex-smokers salivate. She let out smoke from everywhere it seemed: her mouth, her nose and I swear even her eyes. Her face was lost in a cloud.

My mother was talking on the other side and I covered the mouthpiece and said, "It's my father. He's dead. Died this afternoon."

"Where?"

"Fort Worth," I whispered, "clot in the lungs....So then you don't know when the funeral is, do you?"

"No," my mother replied. "But I'll call back and let you know the

particulars. I need to call your Uncle Robert and your aunt Betty to let 'em
know. He'd been in the hospital."

"You should have called me then."

"Well, I didn't find out until today that he was. And even if I had known
I have a hard time figurin' out when to call you about 'im. You and Richard
hate 'im so much that I just don't want to tell you all anythin' about 'im. I
didn't even know if you wanted to know that he passed on. I just figured I'd
tell both of you and you all do what your conscience tells you to do. I know
how you all feel about 'im."

"That's got nothing to do with the way we feel. Sure I want to go to the
funeral. And Richard?" I asked. I could feel the discharge of adrenaline as I
waited for her to answer. Why hadn't she said anything about Richard in the
first place? Had he done something wrong again? Where was he? In prison?
"Have you called him?"

"No, but I'm fixin' to," she said, without telling me where he was.

Finally, I had to ask, "Where is he?"

"Oh, he's here in Corpus," she said so matter-of-factly that I knew he
wasn't in trouble. It was a relief for me. "On parole, as usual. Can't get 'imself
out of trouble ever. He's workin' at a body shop at Flour Bluff. Doin' okay,
I guess. You know him. He hardly ever comes by and when he does he doesn't
say much. Always wantin' money. He ain't like you, Jimmy. I need to get
hold of 'im but he doesn't have a phone. The only way to get 'im is durin'
the day at the shop. I sent a little Mexican boy that lives down the street to
go tell 'im at the place where he lives but he came back and said Richard
wasn't home. He's out drinkin' I bet. He's been told not to drink on parole
but he does anyway. How're you goin' to tell Richard anythin' anyway?"

I ignored her criticism of Richard. "How long was Dad in the hospital?"
I asked. Now that I knew that Richard was all right I was trying to get her
back to the conversation.

"Oh, they said about a week, somethin' like that. You see, he broke a leg
dancin' in Fort Worth at a honky-tonk. Then he'd been operated on on his
leg right away and they put a pin in it. Then he was doin' fine, or that's what
they thought."

"Who called you about him?"

"Curly. He's one of your father's friends in Fort Worth. You all never did
meet 'im. He'd been stayin' with Curly and his family for months, livin' in

the wash-room. Curly said that everythin' was goin' fine. No one thought there'd be any problems. This morning he had breakfast and was feelin' pretty good and he got up to go to the bathroom and he keeled over on the commode and he died in the afternoon, they said."

I didn't know what to say. What do you say without sounding uncaring when someone like my father dies? I answered, "Well, Mom, call back when you know about the funeral." I knew that hadn't sounded right.

"Do you really want to go?" she asked me.

"Yeah, why not?"

"Well, do you think Richard will go?"

I didn't know. I hadn't talked to Richard since my grandmother's funeral, that was several years ago, a long time. I didn't know how he felt about our father now. I only knew that at that time in 1964 when I visited him in prison he was very bitter. He kept telling me that he was sorry he hadn't killed our father. But today? I didn't know. He may have mellowed.

"You're the one that's going to have to find out, Mom. He's right there in town and it shouldn't be hard to reach him and tell him what happened. It's up to him if he wants to go to the funeral. I wouldn't push him, if I were you. If he wants to go, fine. If he doesn't want to go, fine. Don't push him. Don't make him feel guilty."

"I won't," my mother said. And then after an embarrassing silence she said, "Well, I just called to let you know. I just don't know when to call up about your father. It seems it's always wrong," and she hung up.

So it had finally come. The dreaded event in every man's life—the death of his father, his creator. I had heard friends talk about that unforgettable moment in their lives. Grown men cried like children. Some felt that a part of their lives had been lost forever. Beautiful childhood memories rushed through them—fishing with Dad, hunting with Dad, playing ball with Dad, all normal everyday joys that some take for granted.

As soon as I hung up I lay in bed oblivious of Anne and I sincerely made the effort to cry. Anne, in her innocence, tried to comfort me and she brought me a glass of water. She thought I was breaking down. But what I was doing was almost choking as I tried to bring a tear to my eye and I couldn't do it.

So what did I do? I started coughing and laughing. It was supposed to be one of the most important events in a man's life and I couldn't cry over the bastard's death.

"Surely you have some feelings of warmth for your father," a Yaley friend and fellow student named T. Ashley Brooker had said long ago when I used to try to be what I was not. "Even the slightest hint of love. Oh, surely you're not the type that hates his father for being so successful. Or maybe if you examine it closely you're the type that feels a hatred for your father for what he does to your mother. You know what I mean. Oedipus, that sort of thing?" Everyone had laughed, even the Chairman at Stanford.

I had felt like getting up and leaving before I told them the truth. I had felt like saying, "Oedipus? That's a bunch of shit. There is no Oedipus complex in poor families. That shit is for people that can afford it. No, you sons of bitches, I hate my father for being the mother-fucker that he was, for being the fucking coward and fucking drunkard that he was, for being the fucking cheat and liar and woman-hater that he was. I hated him for what he did to me and I hated him for what he did to my brother Richard. I hated him because when Sylvia died he couldn't get to the funeral because he was a wanted man. And I suspect that even if he hadn't been a wanted man he would not have made it to the funeral. I hated him for leaving us stranded in West Texas to live on hand-outs, for selling whiskey to poor Indians, for screwing Indian women and biting noses off Indian men. I hated him because he treated his family like shit and tried to make everyone else feel good."

"Do you need the car?" Anne asked.

"I don't know," I replied. "Will you please turn off the light."

"You're welcome to have the car for as long as you need it."

"Thanks," I said.

"You know your car's not running good."

"I know," I said. I couldn't even keep a goddam car running good. That's the legacy he had left behind. I was not worthy of a good car.

I wandered off to that same night at the graduate student's party at Stanford and I remembered that I got up and left and then I cried when I was alone because I couldn't tell anyone what I felt without exposing and embarrassing myself.

I got up and turned the light off that Anne had forgotten and went back to bed.

"I'm sorry," she said. "I forgot the lights. Do you want me to hold you close?" she asked.

"No," I replied, thinking of Richard, how we slept together, "I'm okay. I don't need pity. I don't need anybody. I never have and never will."

"That's too bad," she said, turning. "It wasn't pity. It was love. I feel for you."

CHAPTER 32

The phone rang in the morning, in the cold room, at seven o'clock just as I was sitting alone at the small card table eating cold cereal and milk for breakfast. I was sure it was my mother so I picked up the phone and said, "Hello, Mom." But it was Anne.

"I left real early," she said, but I knew that. She had not been there when I awoke. "It hurt that you didn't need me."

"I'm sorry," I said. "But Anne, that's the way I am. That's the way I've been raised. I just can't rely on anyone. I can't let lose, in other words. My emotions are a very private thing with me. You know that."

"Well, I don't," she said. "You ought to let yourself go one of these days. It's bad for you not to release your emotions."

"I suppose the next thing you're going to tell me is that I'm going to explode?"

"Yes, something like that, but emotionally."

"Is this professional advice?"

"Yes and no," she said. "It's more of an observation from a friend that loves you."

"Thanks for the advice," I said. "Hey, I've got a class at eight."

"Do you need my car?"

"No."

"Truly. I'm not saying it just to feel a part of your grief, just to feel important."

"I know," I answered. "It's just that I think my car can make it anywhere."

"Call me if you need help," she said and I could tell she felt sorry for me and I didn't want that.

I really didn't want that much care and attention being paid to my father. He was dead and that should be it. Why should a Ph.D. in Psychology be worried about his goddam funeral? Why should she be worried about my attending?

"Call me, you hear?" she said and hung up.

I was late for class. I had to run into the bedroom and put on a clean shirt and a tie. I picked up my jacket and overcoat on the way out. As I closed the door the phone rang again. I rushed back in and answered it. This time it was my mother. I tried to tell her I was in a hurry but she had to start at the beginning. Did I understand what had happened? I sounded awfully sleepy. I had to hang up.

I ran to class into the cold wind of the morning. It had drizzled during the night and icicles had formed on the north shingles of every apartment house. The sidewalks were slippery with ice. I crossed the street next to the University on a red-light and I heard a warning whistle but I kept running.

I was out of breath but I got to class as the buzzer sounded. I took off my overcoat, an old shapeless cashmere Emily had bought me because she thought I would look more like an Ivy Leaguer and less like a South Texan. I placed the coat on a chair by the radiator at the corner. The smell of moth-balls from the coat lingered on my shirt. I was careful to move the chair away from the radiator for fear that the heat would activate the billions of camphorated molecular particles imbedded in its wool. I made a mental scan of the room and everyone seemed to be there for class. As I started to talk the secretary knocked lightly on the door-jam and she came in. She whispered that my mother was on the telephone. It was an emergency. I whispered back that I knew already and that she was to tell my mother that I would call after class. She left in a hurry, a puzzled look on her face, wondering what this was all about.

I wasn't in any mood to talk to freshman about writing and how bad they were. Oh, I had a few that were passable but most of them were horrible. I had had the misfortune of having bad classes this fall. Or maybe it was me. I confess that for the past several years I had begun to feel as though I had reached a dead-end. My career was going nowhere and I'm sure it affected my teaching. Also, I had come to realize just how much teachers suffered, which was exactly the opposite of what I had thought growing up. What a disappointment that was. Going in, I had felt as though they had had full control of their lives. In my young world they were, like the bus driver, to be envied—giving out grades, opinions, in effect saying who was successful and who was not.

I awoke from my mental wandering with the students looking at me, anticipating when I was to begin the class. I was thinking that I would make them write for the fifty minutes as I had done the class the day before. But what were they to write about today? They were waiting for me to speak. Everyone had a pencil in their hand and their clean sheet of spiral paper was ready to accept anything I said. I could sense the palpable anxiety in them, how truly and genuinely anxious they were to please and to please me, of all people. I was so important to them. I felt sorry for them. They had the wrong hero.

"Class," I said, "I have a confession to make." I was going to tell them what a sham this education business was. Somewhere we had all lost the zeal to teach and we were now mostly concerned with showing our students how dumb they were, that we were in the business of insulting students, not teaching them. I was going to tell them that I wasn't any smarter than anyone there. It just so happened that I was the teacher and I could only teach what I knew. That made me smart in their eyes. But that was, unfortunately, an artificial smartness. I was going to tell them to pursue knowledge and not put their hopes in teachers and in classrooms, that I should be treated with the same respect that they gave their father, if he was a wise man, that I was not to be idolized, that I had much too many problems to be an idol, that I suffered from the worst of maladies—bad breeding. Of course I didn't say all these things. No one would believe me. Instead, in a burst of compassion for my fellow man, I said: "You are the best class I've ever had."

They breathed a sigh and laughed and enjoyed the compliment. I'm sure they believed it.

I knew what they were to write about today.

"Take some paper, and I don't care how much, one sheet, two, five, whatever, and write about your father's death. If he hasn't died try to imagine what it will be like. Do that for me this hour, please. And when you're through, please place your paper on top of my desk and you are excused."

And with that I hurried to my coat and walked out of class and went straight to the office. The secretary had a number for me to call. It was my mother's number.

"Is anything wrong, Jim?" the strong voice behind me asked. It was my boss, Dr. Widenhoffer.

"I'm afraid so, sir," I said. "It's my father. He died yesterday."

He took a step backward. He grabbed his heart and said, "What a shock, Jim," he gathered his composure. "I'm really sorry to hear that, Jim," he said, shaking his head. He took out his pipe from his coat pocket and fiddled for his tobacco pouch and found it in his rear pocket. He began to stuff tobacco into his pipe mashing, it into the bowl with his thumb. "You'll probably need some time off then."

"Yes sir," I said.

I still felt nervous around the man and yet I'd worked for him since I had received my Ph.D in 1969. He was the type that never let you know where you stood, more like a parent than a mentor. I often wondered if after eight laboring years I may have been wasting my time there. That's why I had wanted to leave but Emily refused—the hill country and that sort of thing if you remember. I was an Associate Professor but where would I go from here? I had received my Ph.D. in English from Stanford, but I didn't have anything to show for it.

"You've just chosen a field that's hard to break into," he said to me when I first started teaching. He had great expectations of me, he said. But there had been others who had been there longer than I who were equally or better qualified, "more experienced," he had explained.

Now as we looked at each other eight years later, I wondered what he thought of me. Had I been a failure? Had the din of great expectations turned into nothing more than a muffled disappointment so common in academia? Was I dead weight now? How did he see me? I was afraid to ask. So we never spoke about my career, my future. We spoke instead of little things which didn't matter, as though my career were a mutual embarrassment and it should not be mentioned. Of course, he appreciated not being backed into a corner, not having to make a decision.

"When is the funeral?" he asked.

He had lit his pipe and was trying to keep it going. He was using the butane lighter the faculty had given him for Christmas. He smoked a mixture of two popular blends, one a rough cut with stub-like pieces of stems and twigs and a smooth cut, a fluffy type like the hair on the tail of a squirrel and together both burned short and nauseatingly sweet, like burning maple and licorice mixed with cat shit.

"I don't know, sir," I replied and I kept hating myself for calling him "sir." Why couldn't I call him by his first name? Or no name at all?

"There's nothing definite then?" he asked, looking askance.

"Well, we, or my mother I should say, is arranging the funeral. She just called but I missed her. She should be calling again."

"Nonsense, Jim," he said picking up the receiver and handing it to me, "No sense waiting. Go ahead, you call her. Charge it to the department. The state of Texas can afford for you to make just one call."

"Well, if you say so."

Why did I talk like that when he was around? I sounded so inadequate. "If you say so." What an ass-hole. I didn't know what got into me. I just couldn't be myself. Not only did I talk clumsy, I became clumsy. I would place my hand on my chin and then I'd remove it suddenly as if I had done something wrong. I'd lean on my elbow and then I'd move out of that position into another and then another until he would be looking at me in a curious way as though I was about to lose my senses.

I was being clumsy again thinking about how clumsy I was. I tried to pick up the telephone from the secretary's desk to place it on the rail in front of her so that I could dial but the telephone wouldn't move. I didn't know what the problem was. In those eight years I had never used the secretary's telephone. I had been told by the older teachers that it was not considered proper. I tried harder to dislodge the phone thinking that perhaps it was resting on suction cups. The harder I tried the more the boss stared incomprehensibly at me. I was sure that he was thinking that by now, after eight years, I would know that the secretary's telephone was bolted to the desk.

The secretary finally asked me to please come around through the swinging gate to get to her desk. I had lost the piece of paper with the phone number that the secretary had given me. I looked through all the pockets in my jacket, turning them inside out. Like a fool, I found the paper in my shirt pocket. My cashmere coat was giving me problems. It was hard to dial with it around my arm. The boss said he'd take it but I didn't want to give it to him. That would be too much. So I banged the receiver on the desk and quickly went to the corner where I saw a chair and I placed my coat on it.

Dr. Widenhoffer looked at me with an understanding smile. "Take it easy, Jim," he said, lighting his pipe again for the fifteenth or twentieth time. "You're nervous, I can tell."

I just knew that when raises and promotions came along this was going to be the moment he would think of first.

I dialed and the line was busy. Mom was calling Uncle Robert.

"Well, wait a few minutes and try again," the boss said. "In the meantime, Jim, let's see who can take your classes for you. Let's see. You're teaching.....?" He hesitated to let me tell him.

My God! The sonofabitch didn't even know what I was teaching! Fuck the raises! Fuck the promotions! I was lucky to have a job!

"Freshman English," I said, meekly, mumbling appreciatively.

"Freshman English," he said, repeating my words exactly and he seemed not to be bothered or surprised at all. Earlier in my career I would have expected him to say, "Well, Jim, what's a talent like you doing wasting your time teaching freshmen?" But he didn't seem to be concerned. Little did I realize it at the time but his job was on the line also and his concern for my career was the last thing on his mind. His job was simply to put one body in front of each class and he didn't care how he did it as long as it was done. If he matched the talent with the class, well, good, but if he didn't he was past worrying about it. He thought a while, drawing on his pipe with his soft feminine mouth. "Freshman English. Freshman English," he kept repeating. "Well, we'll see. We'll take care of it for you, Jim. You go on home and let us know how things are going, the funeral and such. We would like to send flowers, you know. The Department, I mean. It would be appropriate under the circumstances."

I felt I was being a nuisance. I didn't want to bother any one, especially not Dr. Widenhoffer. I apologized for any inconvenience I may have caused his secretary. I said that I was hoping that the funeral would be on a Saturday so that I could drive over Friday night and come back Saturday night or Sunday morning, that way no one would have to take my classes.

"Nonsense, Jim," the boss said. "Take your time. I'm sure you're terribly depressed over the whole thing. From the looks of you, I don't think it's hit you yet." He shook his head for my benefit and stared blankly at the floor. "What a shock it must have been," he whispered.

"Yes, it was," I replied, lying through my breath.

"Of what did he die?" he asked firmly, trying not to end a sentence with a preposition.

I had given up trying to call from the office so I had gone and retrieved my coat. I wanted out. I didn't want to call in front of the boss. I didn't want him to listen to what my mother would say.

"He died of a clot in his lungs," I said, checking the coat to make sure it was turned inside out.

"Poor fellow," the boss said. "Must have been a terrible thing."

"Yes, it was," I lied, again.

"What was his field, Jim?" he asked. He was firming the cold ashes down into the pipe bowl one more time before re-lighting. It was a ritual that I estimated occupied most of his waking hours.

"I guess you could say he was into several things."

"Diversified, I imagine. Good for him."

"Yes, diversified," I said.

CHAPTER 33

I wanted to get out of the office before Dr. Widenhoffer could pursue the conversation, no telling where it would lead us. He had heard enough about my father as far as I was concerned. I took off in such a hurry that I left him dumbfounded, his unlit pipe dangling from his mouth. He recovered enough to be able to speak to me before I crossed the door. I stopped when he called my name. "Jim," he said, pointing at me with his cold pipe, "don't forget to let us know if you need anything. We're here to help. We're family and all that, you know."

I replied, "Yes sir, thank you," although I knew that he didn't mean it. Nonetheless, I was not about to be an imposition on a boss that didn't know or cared what my job was.

I went by my office and checked the mail, lingering for some time as I slowly opened envelopes. I had received an answer from Harvard. Harvard thanked me for the query but they did not accept cold applications. If they had need for my services they knew where to find me. I threw the letter and envelope into the trash. I sighed heavily to see if that would make me feel worse about my father's death. I was trying to kill time. I didn't feel like talking to my mother. I had cleared all the correspondence on my desk. I returned to the classroom and only a few students, the conscientious, the ones who make life easy, were still there wrestling with their thoughts. The buzzer rang and the few that were left finished hurriedly and threw their papers on my desk and walked out. I gathered the papers, took them to the office and sat down and skimmed over them. I was in no mood to go to the apartment just yet. I wasn't feeling right. Could it be that I felt something for the man? Or could it be that Dr. Widenhoffer's child-like innocence about my father had made me feel guilty for never having told anyone the complete truth about myself? But how could I tell them without demeaning myself?

Every student had written something good about their father, reminiscences of days long gone by—childhood memories of their fathers as they laughed and played together, gentle feelings. That was it. I couldn't get over the gentle feelings that these young people were writing about. Several students had written that their fathers had indeed been dead for several years and that they wrote from first hand experience of the profound grief they felt, not only at the exact time of death but ever since then. It fascinated me to read that of this group all of them remembered exactly what they were doing when death had come. Several of the girls and one young man had cried while writing. I could see the tear stains on the paper. The most poignant reading was from a young man who had lost his father recently. He wrote of how painful his father's death had been, of how much he missed his companionship. I sat there holding the paper and I thought of how lucky he had been. I would be sure to tell him after I returned.

As much as I dreaded it, it was time to go home and talk to my mother about the funeral. I unlocked the drawer in my desk and took out some money that I had hidden there in an envelope, cushion money just in case Emily had put me in a hole. I counted two hundred new dollars. I gathered my coat into a bundle, locked the office and took the two flights of stairs at my end of the building instead of the elevator. I left the building by the side door. I was trying to evade my colleagues, who I was sure had gotten wind of what had happened from Dr. Widenhoffer. I did not feel like discussing my father's death with them. I did not want to have to affect any feelings whatsoever. I was tired of feeling guilty about lying for the sonofabitch.

I did not feel the cold at first. I walked back, my hands in my pockets, my coat draped over my left arm. Slowly I started getting very cold. It had started to sleet. I unfurled the coat and put it on, turning the collar up, my face hidden behind the wide collar. A former student whose name I couldn't remember had tried to walk next to me but after a short while he had sensed that I didn't want company. I felt sorry for him, that I didn't feel like talking. I remembered that in my youth I had hated professors who looked down their noses at the students. At the cold and shadowed intersection he turned right, excusing himself and saying, feeling badly about himself, that he'd see me later. Instantly, I felt like running to him and telling him that some other day I would be better company, that I would treat him civilly. I felt sad for him as I saw his lonely figure, like my brother Richard, fading from my sight.

Just then, as he melded into the sleet, another student came running out of a building and joined him, shaking his gloved hand. I felt relief that he had friends to tide him over life's little bruises.

"The reason you feel so disturbed about what your students wrote," Anne said, making coffee, "is that basically you feel you were cheated out of a normal childhood."

"How do you know?"

"Oh, I'm paid to figure out things like that."

"And you can figure it out without my telling you?"

"Pretty much so. There are little things I can't guess at, but the larger things, the basic orientation that you have is easy to deduce. All I have to do is work my way backwards."

"Like from where backwards?"

"Oh, I can take your basic attitudes, your feelings that come out in your conversations and more or less tell you with a high degree of accuracy what has caused those feelings. I've known, for example, that you didn't love your father. (She didn't realize she was putting it mildly.) Your mother I'm not so sure about. I do know that you don't love her very much. You resent her. Well, maybe you're ashamed of her."

"That wasn't so hard to figure out, was it?"

"Well, yes and no. You could have been faking it. Some men do, you know. They feel that they should not feel emotions... love, tenderness, that sort of thing. So they hide it. But you," she said, blowing gently on her coffee, "you did not love your father. And last night proved it." She could tell she had made me feel uncomfortable. "I'm sorry," she said, holding my hand.

"What else?" I asked.

"Do you really want to know?"

"I don't know. Do you think it does me any good to bring it out?"

"Only if you feel that it would help. If not, let it be. You've been severely traumatized as a child. I know that. You have all the classic symptoms."

She had made me blush. My guilt was showing. I took some coffee, hoping that she would ignore my vulnerable condition.

"Well?" she persisted.

"Well what?"

"Aren't you going to ask me what I see in you that makes me know that you were severely abused as a child?"

"No," I answered, not wanting to rehash the trauma again. I already knew.

"You're intelligent enough to have outgrown those years or at least I hope so. Let me just tell you one thing. Just remember that it wasn't your fault. You're not the guilty party. You didn't deserve to be treated like that. You just got a bad deal in life."

"Thanks," I replied, "thanks a lot. What should I do now, curl up in a ball and die?"

"No. You need to compete as if nothing had ever happened to you. Let's face it, you've been running with a different crowd for a long time. You've been educated." She poured some more coffee for me. "This will warm you up," she said. She was sitting across from me at the small card table gently turning the cup in her hands. "You've come up through the maze that is Anglo-American lower class. Red-necks. And to top it off you made it as an abused child and it's been tough. It's tough when you have to deny your childhood. That's a very important part of your life, maybe the most important. It's tough when you have to deny your parents. It's tough when you find out that all this time, when you were being abused, that all your colleagues were growing up happy and secure. I can imagine that right now you wish you had never gone to college. You feel that you would have been happier as a laborer. Ignorant, with a set of ignorant friends. Just think, you would be king of the hill then. No competition." She took a swallow of coffee and looked at me over the lip of the cup. "You know Jim, every person that has done what you did has paid for it psychologically. You've got to develop a hide thicker than an elephant and yet you've got to let people care for you. You're lovable, you know. That's the hardest part, believing that and letting people get close to you without resenting them."

If there were any newly emerging feelings on my part, it was that I felt slightly dazed that she was able, given my coldness, to accurately categorize my life and in such a simple manner, as if she were picking pieces of me from a menu. Suddenly I sat up straight as I became fearful of what was coming next: Richard. She knew about Richard in a cursory way. I had chosen not to discuss Richard in detail with her. She knew that I had an older brother and that was all. I was beginning to feel that maybe I shouldn't have mentioned Richard, that I should have kept him to myself. I felt that what Richard had done was between us and no one else needed to know. Besides, he was the only viable link I had to my past and I did not want Anne to dissect him, to destroy him and destroy me in the process. I wanted desperately to change the conversation. I knew she was leading me in a panic toward Richard. "Why are we talking of all this shit?" I demanded to know. "What brought it up anyway? Let's not get so serious. Hey, why aren't you at work?"

"I had some time off this morning. I knew you'd need someone to talk to. And truthfully, I felt that this was a great opportunity for you to come to grips with your youth."

"What's got into you? You can't seem to leave me alone this morning." I was blowing in my coffee. "Has my mother called?" I had finally warmed up. As a matter of fact I was becoming irritably hot. I felt like ripping off my jacket.

"No, not since I've been here."

"And tell me again, what are you doing here?" I got up and removed my jacket and threw it on the plastic chair in the bedroom and came back to sit down. I yanked at my tie and loosened my collar. "Why aren't you working this morning? And why are you so interested in my childhood problems all of a sudden?"

"Do I detect a slight irritation in your voice?"

"Shouldn't I be irritated with all this prying into my life?"

"I'm interested because you're going through some trauma right now. Maybe you don't even realize it. I just thought that if you spoke about it you would be able to handle it better. I wasn't very busy this morning, anyway. I didn't have any scheduled appointments. Oh, there might be a drop-in or two, but you know, the privilege of the doctor is that I can always say I have an emergency. It's a great way to get out of things."

"What about some poor fool who needs you desperately? What is he doing? Slowly going insane all by himself?"

"He can wait," she laughed mildly. "Anyway, insanity is like good wine; it takes years and years to produce." She brushed her short manly hair back with her left hand and with the right she took out a pack of cigarettes and lit one. She blew the first smoke down between her legs so as not to offend me. "You're ashamed of your family?" she asked in an undeniable way, almost like telling me the truth. I felt the boiling rush of blood go through me. I had been ashamed for such a long time. 'What field is he in, or more accurately, in what field is he?' Diversity! I was glad he had come up with the answer. The boss was glad my father was safely diversified. Yes, he was into whores, pimps, shit-heads, rednecks, cowboys, beer, whiskey, wine, moonshine, dancing, stealing, fraud, gambling and all around pussy-hunting. Squirrel shooting, he called it when I was growing up. How degrading it must be to the women to have your most intimate part called a squirrel. What about the squirrel?

"I know, Anne, that I am ashamed of my family. Okay?"

"You're ashamed of Richard?"

"Yes and no. I respect Richard in many ways."

"Tell me. Tell me more about Richard. Why don't you?"

This was exactly what I was afraid of, that she would catch me at a vulnerable moment and I would tell all about Richard. She was partially successful. Without knowing why, I told her that Richard was a thief as a child. I felt afterwards that I had told her this much to see if that would satisfy her, hoping that she would leave Richard alone, giving her a tender diversionary piece of the flesh so that she would not go in for the kill. She persisted. She asked, "Why do you respect Richard?"

"Well, at least he has rebelled."

"And you don't respect yourself because you didn't? Is that it?"

"I think I respect myself. It's just that Richard was wilder. Less afraid. I wish I had been more like that."

"And what else?" she asked.

"Richard, you mean?"

"Yes, Richard. Why do you think he had a compulsion to steal?"

A compulsion? I had never thought of it as a compulsion. As a child I thought of it as Richard's irresistible pastime, something to do. I knew it was wrong, but not that wrong. But a compulsion was something else, like a pervert that had to do it. Loving him as I did, I never thought of him as perverted.

"I don't know," I replied. "I didn't think of it as a compulsion."

"Well, suppose I told you that psychotherapists believe that someone like Richard is actually very angry with his life. Suppose I tell you that your brother feels that somehow he had been deprived of something in his life and he needed to replace it by taking something, anything he considers of value, to replace this feeling. It makes him feel good to steal. It satisfies him."

"What about when he stole for someone else?"

"Like for you?"

"Yes."

"Very basic," she replied, "he thought you needed to fulfill these feelings also. He was just helping you out. He felt that you felt the same way but you weren't about to steal. Really, if he stole for you, he must have loved you very much. Look at the risk he was taking for you."

"I know he loves me very much. I love him very much. That's why I think of him so often and what he did for me, aside from the stealing. As young as he was, he was like a father to me. I came first. He protected me. I guess because of me he never had a chance to be a kid. That's why I'll never turn my back on him."

"No one said you had to," she said.

"Well, I'm not. I just wanted to go on record."

"You're afraid of feelings for your family?"

"I agree to that," I replied. I was ready to concede any thing. I wanted to be left alone. I was thinking of Richard more and more and he was worrying me. My mother still hadn't called. What was the delay?

"You've found out that a lot of your friends had it better than you. Your Ivy League crowd has given you the guilts. You feel inferior."

I was hoping she would stop. We had been through this already. No need to slap me with it again. "Really, Anne," I said, "I don't give a shit about Freud and Jung and all this psychology crap. The only reason I feigned an interest in Jung was to get in your pants. I only know what I feel. That's what's important to me. And right now I don't feel very good. You're making me sick. You're making me angry."

"Guilt?"

"Call it guilt if you want to. But I call it anger."

"You're angry your father died without ever fulfilling your dreams of what a father should be. Don't you realize..."

I had to interrupt her. "Listen, Anne, sweetheart, please don't tell me what I'm angry about. How can you sit there and tell me what I'm angry about? How do you know?"

"It's my job," she replied.

"Don't talk to me like that!" I shouted. "I'm not one of your goddam patients. I won't have you talk to me like that."

"Like what?" she screamed.

"Like you're better than me. Like you know more than me. Like I depend on you."

She looked at me as though she had gotten the upper hand, as if she had won some kind of psychological battle. "Let's drop it, okay?" she said. Then she took her last desperate swipe at me. "You're in no condition to talk."

"Anne," I pleaded, "I'm in perfect condition to talk. Don't you understand. Jesus Christ, do all your patients have this hard a time getting you to listen?"

She jumped up from her chair and she was furious. "You, you ingrate!" she yelled, throwing the lighted cigarette into my coffee.

"But Anne," I begged, as she angrily put on her long coat, threw her scarf around her neck, adjusted her gloves and started toward the door. "Anne, please," I said, walking in front of her to keep her from opening the door and leaving, "can I tell you why I'm angry? Please?"

"No," she said as I let her shove me out of the way. "I really don't give a fuck about you."

After she left I started laughing. I was angry, I was trying to tell her, because after all these lonely years in the shadows, the man I admired at one time, my boss, and the man who had admired me at one time, my boss, didn't even know what courses I was teaching. After all the time and effort I had put into my beloved career, I was pre-destined to be the old Associate Professor who stagnates at one course and who becomes the preferred target for office and student jokes and who eventually starts to dress badly (You see, I had already started.) and who starts to drink to forget who he is (I had already started some of that too). I was going to carry Anne one step deeper into the irremediable degradation of this man: He starts to lose everything, but mainly respect, his self and the respect of others. He gets cancer of the stomach (or is it the pancreas or the liver?) and the only thing he can eat without vomiting is cold watermelon or chocolate covered ants and he dies in the shadows one lonely night in an old rusty screened-in porch in back of an unpainted old rented house under a solitary naked yellow light-bulb as he wears a green celluloid visor while playing an interminable game of checkers against himself. (There is the small soft thud as the head bows over and hits the wooden checker-board displacing all his hard earned kings. His dying left hand gropes hurriedly into his pockets for an object as though he cannot die without it and then having found it, his lifeless grip relaxes and a Phi Beta Kappa key falls gently from his palm and through the slatted floor to the ground below where tomorrow a mouse, thinking that it is something to eat will take it and taste it and then unceremoniously shit on it so that no other animal could mistake it for food. And since he has told everyone not to bother him ever, ever, ever, no one comes around to see him and he is dead five or six days covered with fire-ants before the frugal landlady finds him. He has the pattern of an Acme checker eternally and deeply embossed into the purple skin of his forehead. At his funeral, only the chairman and the faculty representative are there. His brother could not make it, being sicker than the deceased. Cryptically, he sends a spray of flowers for the coffin. His condolences read: "Cancer, cancer everywhere and not a spot to treat." He was the comedian in the family.)

The phone startled me. It was my mother.

"How are you feeling?" she asked me without saying who she was.

Everyone was concerned about how I was feeling. I wanted to scream that I felt great, absolutely great, like I'd never felt before. My father had died and I felt great about it. The only negative feeling I had was the inconvenience his death was causing. I wanted him buried and out of sight as soon as possible.

"All right," I replied. What could I say? "And you?" After all, he was her husband.

"I'm holding up," she said and I could sense the hypocrisy in her voice. They hadn't seen each other in many years. Like me, she was trying to make herself feel bad.

"When's the funeral?"

"Saturday," she said, "tomorrow."

"Where?"

"Corpus."

"Corpus?"

"Yes, they're bringing the body over and we'll have the funeral Saturday. The body'll be here this afternoon."

"Saturday?" I asked.

"Yes, Saturday, Jim. Now that's tomorrow. Do you understand?"

She was right. Today was Friday. I was in luck. I would only miss this afternoon's class. "Yes. It's tomorrow. I'll be there late this afternoon or early tonight," I said. "I'm taking off in a little while. I need to call the office and get someone to take my class this afternoon. After I do that, I'm clear."

"I'll be expectin' you," she said and this time she sounded like she needed help, pity. She was crying.

"Who else is coming?"

"Well," she replied, "Richard'll be here, for sure. I spoke to 'im last night. Your Uncle Robert'll be here and so's your Aunt Betty. They took off early this morning."

"From New Mexico?"

"Oh, no. They live in Abilene. They've moved to Abilene. Now I'm not sure, but they said they'd come by San Antonio and pick up Dolly. Dolly's in San Antonio. She's divorced, you know. Got two kids, a boy and a girl, I think. Anyway, they was goin' to see if they could come by San Antonio and pick Dolly up." The line was silent for awhile. She was thinking of who else. "Junior's comin' too, I suppose. He's livin' in Abilene too. And I guess some of your Daddy's friends'll be here. But God only knows. It was so sudden. It's hard to get the word out fast. Preachers don't want to bury anyone on Sundays no more so I couldn't wait till Monday. That's a long time, don't you think? He died on Thursday. That'd make it four days if we buried 'im on Monday. That's too long, don't you think?"

I had already lost her in the conversation. I was thinking that I had to call the office, get my clothes packed, get to the service station, get gas, check the tires, water, oil, get a new wiper blade for my side at least, maybe get a new battery. (It would be embarrassing for me not to be able to start the car in Corpus.) I needed a tie, a new tie. I almost forgot I had to go by the bank and cash a check. I would need more money than the two hundred dollars from the drawer. Just in case Richard might need money. I really had to get going.

My mother was waiting for my answer. I said "Yes," on a gamble.

"I thought so too," she said, content that I had agreed.

"Mom, I've got to go," I pleaded. "Don't feel that I'm pushing you. It's that I have a lot to do. I'll see you early tonight or late this afternoon. Okay?"

"Okay," she sniffled. I heard the voice crack. She was crying. "I just can't help but think that we'll be together again for another funeral," she sobbed.

CHAPTER 34

I resented my mother's hypocrisy, her new found concern for my father, and her veiled reference to my sister Sylvia, using the long forgotten memory of her death as though freshening the wound would get me in the mood for the funeral. I hated to tell her that it would have taken a lot more than that.

I was able to reach Imelda, the secretary, on my first try. She'd be glad to tell Dr. Widenhoffer that I would be gone in the afternoon. She would get someone to take my afternoon class. She seemed unduly concerned for my welfare. I told her I was doing fine and I thanked her and told her not to worry unnecessarily about me. Her message to me was that Dr. Widenhoffer had said for me to take at least one extra day off to recuperate from such an irreparable loss. He had tried to tell Imelda of the indescribable pain he had felt the day his father died. "He was almost crying," Imelda whispered into the telephone. "If it hadn't been that he had his pipe in his mouth I'm afraid he would have. He understood perfectly well what you were going through."

What I was going through was trying to get out of town. I packed in a hurry. I was getting lucky. While packing I had found a brand new tie hanging in the closet. It had been hidden between two shirts.

I threw the suit-case in the rear seat along with my cashmere overcoat. It had quit sleeting and I thought I could sense that the sun was trying to shine through the overcast skies.

The first stop was the bank and that took almost no time at all. Once again, though, I had to stop short an unwanted conversation. This time I did it with a little more tact. The teller recognized me as one of her son's former professors and was going on about him as she slowly counted my money. He had graduated in the summer and was into computers and had received a job offer from a high-tech company in town—very heavy stuff with good pay. She was thrilled. I escaped by telling her I had an emergency and would talk some other time. I ran out of the bank leaving her disturbed as she asked me what the emergency was. As nice as I had been to her son, could she be of any help? I was gone before I could answer.

The service station had a battery but did not have the wiper blade. All they had was the whole wiper arm and blade and it was going to cost me six dollars. I only needed the blade. I knew there was an auto parts store four blocks down the road so I took off and when I got there I had to take a number from under a flashing red bulb to make sure I would get waited on. When my number was called I tried to explain to the thin coon-faced little man across the counter what I wanted. He removed his cap and scratched his bald head, went to a catalog and started looking. He went back into the storeroom.

I was left at the counter to read all the special warnings and advices tacked on to the wall. "In God we Trust," one red and white placard said, "Others pay cash." "No Personal Checks Cashed Without Proper Identification and a Texas Driver's License." "We do not lend tools! Please do not even ask!" "Please do not open carton unless you are prepared to buy it." A picture of a hobo standing on a mound overlooking the rail yard quoted as saying, "When I was in business I used to give a discount to all my clients." "Ten per-cent re-packaging charge." "All custom-made hose sales are final." "Refund only with receipt." "Ten dollar charge on return checks, no exceptions." "If you must spit on the floor, I must kick you in the ass. P.S. Your ass is easier to find than the floor." Somebody was selling an engine: "For Sale, 1973 Chevy V8, 295 HP, Stinson Valves, Never raced. Call Jerry." And it gave a phone number. "If God had intended for Texans to ski, he would have made bullshit white."

The short man with the pointed ears and closely set eyes returned with a set of wiper blades. He totaled up the sale, rang it up and I paid him. As I was leaving he shouted a number so that he could wait on someone else.

The blades plus the installation came to roughly six dollars anyway. But I figured I had two good wipers instead of one. The battery was no problem except for the cost. The old battery had a thirty-six month guarantee. It had eight more months to go but by the time the young man amortized the original cost and how much refund I should get, it still cost me around thirty-five dollars.

I drove out of Austin on U.S. 81 to San Marcos. The roads were in good shape except at the bridges where the freezing road crews were spreading sand to break up the ice. (That was the type of job Anne had said I would have preferred—spreading sand on the icy highway. I thought about it and I felt a lot better in my warm car. I could take a lot of disappointment in my own field before I got the urge to spread sand on an icy bridge.) I decided that I was not going to make good time so I slowed down and relaxed. For what I had waiting, I wasn't in any hurry.

At San Marcos I took the time to drive around the campus at Southwest Texas State University to see if I liked it. It was a small campus and I figured it wouldn't take much time. I had recently thought of applying there for a job. As close as it was to Austin I had never been on the campus. The setting was beautiful, the rolling hills and the crystalline river but finally, after about ten minutes, I realized the gross futility of moving once more and I left.

I took Texas highway 123 to Seguin and from there to Karnes City, Kenedy, and Pettus. At Beeville it began to get very cold. The warming sun had set and almost immediately the night rolled in along with occasional layers of thinly veiled fog. I was getting closer to the Gulf. I stopped for a cup of coffee in Beeville and I listened for a while to the men at the Cafe talk about how really cold it was. I was back in the car and warming up again in fifteen minutes. Next came Mathis, and then Sinton. At Sinton I remembered a friend who had been a student with me who had died in Austin at a very early age of a cerebral hemorrhage. As I left Sinton the fog began to get thicker and more persistent. I could hardly see the road. I should have realized that the small amount of haziness I was picking up outside of Beeville was going to get worse the closer I got to Corpus. I had slowed down to make sure I could stop in case there was accident in front of me. I could not stop for fear of getting hit. Several times I thought I was going to crash into someone stopped in the middle of the road. I would scream until I realized that it was only an eerie ghost-like illusion caused by the reflection of my own headlights. I was scared and by the time I got to Corpus I could have used a drink, several as a matter of fact. Suprisingly, once inside the city the fog had cleared. I could breathe easier now. I could see. I was overcome with the joy of being alive. I accelerated. I could feel the wind gusts from the Gulf push the car to one side. Thank God I had fixed the windshield wipers. My premonition had been right—again. I crossed downtown and traveled south to the old neighborhood.

The front lights were on in Grandmother's old stucco house. I parked on the oyster-shell driveway. There were no other cars there. I took my suit case from the rear seat and my cashmere coat and as I got out I felt the blast of cold air from the Gulf and it blew the door shut catching my legs between the door and the frame. I felt both my shins crushed between the heavy metal and I cursed the wind out loud. I was in pain. I fought the door and the wind and ran to the house and went in without knocking. I was not going to wait for someone to answer the door.

I hadn't seen my mother or Richard since Grandmother's funeral. They were sitting in the living room as I came in. Both peered at me suspiciously, startled as I pushed through the door, not able to recognize immediately who I was. I had come in so suddenly. Surely they had heard the car but then I realized the wind was gusting so strongly that they could not have heard.

Richard looked very thin and yellowish by the shadows of the table lamp, as if he had been sick. I was hoping that maybe it was the dim light in the room that gave him that color. He had grown a small belly that was exaggerated that much more by his thinness. He was drinking straight whiskey. Mother was the same as always, thin and young-looking for her age. She was wearing a black dress, black stockings and black shoes. As opposed to Richard, her skin looked fine and pink.

I was trying to remember when Grandmother's funeral had been as we three embraced and mother held onto me and cried. "My two little boys," she sobbed. "My two little boys." I could feel Richard's thinness, the open frailness of his bones, as I embraced him. He smelled of liquor and tobacco and old clothes that have been stored in a trunk for a long time. I wondered who had given him what he was wearing tonight. He had on an old blue summer suit with baggy pants and a coat with lapels so wide that the wings extended almost to the tips of the shoulders. He was wearing a wide, painted tie with his yellowish-white shirt. His ears had gotten smaller and more wrinkled like a newborn animal. He had been working in the sun and his face was deeply lined, much more than the last time I had seen him. He was holding my hand, weeping at the happy sight of me, and I could tell from the roughness of his own hand that he had been working hard. He kept looking at me as if he admired something that I had done, like a proud parent with a prodigy, until he made me feel unworthy. I let go of his hand. He smiled gently, his eyes red from drink and crying and I could see what I was going to have to ignore, that he had lost most of his front teeth.

We sat down, Mother on the sofa, Richard on a wooden chair next to the sofa and I sat across from them in what was once the favorite chair in the house. I knew that they had planned that I was to get the honored seat.

"You remember how you all used to fight over that chair?" my mother asked me and then she turned to Richard. She was trying to talk of things other than our father's death. She would never change. It was her way of sneaking past the tortures of reality. I could sense how everyone was feeling. We didn't know what to say.

"Yes," I finally replied. And that felt like the wrong thing to say since no one agreed.

"Well, he's gone," she admitted. She looked down at her hands on her lap and thought. Then she gave a deep sigh.

"I was beginnin' to feel like the sumbitch was goin' to out-live us all," Richard said and I laughed.

My mother didn't know what to say. She started to scold Richard but she started laughing with us.

"Your Uncle Robert and your Aunt Betty and Junior and Dolly made it in late this afternoon," she said. "They're at the funeral home right now but they ought to be back in a little while. There's nothin' goin' on over there anyways. I think the undertaker said they'd only been one visitor this afternoon and that's about all."

"Well, Dad didn't have too many friends," I said. "When did the body arrive?"

"Early this afternoon. Around two."

"Where's the body?"

"At Fisherman's," Richard said. "You know where Five Points at? Well, it's a few blocks off Five Points on Alameda. It ain't far. Right, Mom?" He took out a cigarette and lit it. His hand was shaking.

"No, it's about a five, ten-minute drive." She got up and said, "You must be cold. Let me get you a drink."

She got up, went to the kitchen and came back with a bourbon and handed it to me. "Are you drinkin' a lot?" she asked. She caught me by surprise.

"No," I responded. "Oh, I drink every day, but not much. A drink here and there." I was lying. I was drinking more than I should. I felt better about myself when I drank.

She sat down on the sofa again and Richard got up and he went to the kitchen and came back with a half-full glass of whiskey. I noticed that Mom had not offered him a drink. But that was the problem of living close to home where you get taken for granted.

It was interesting to me that this was the first time in several years that we had been together and we had nothing that we wanted to talk about. I was still trying to remember when in the shit Grandmother had died. In time, everything that came to my mind was too desperately painful to mention and I was sure mother and Richard felt the same way. I did know that I was not feeling anything toward my mother. For some reason I had found it repugnant to embrace her. In a way she had been partly responsible for all of our problems. She was looking at me, crying, and I felt that she knew what I was thinking. Above all else, she did not want a confrontation with our past.

This was what all this small talk was about, a diversion to keep Richard and me from making her feel guilty, a guilt, incidently, that I knew she felt very deeply. I don't know at what age it had dawned on her that she had been to blame for the way we had been treated. But since then she had needed for Richard to stay in trouble. This was her way of placing the blame for our father's unpardonable behavior on Richard and not on herself. Simply put, Richard deserved what he got because of the way Richard was. She was just the innocent mother trying to keep her family together, trying to keep her son out of jail. Just imagine her devastation if Richard had gone straight, if Richard had proved her wrong and left her to shoulder the blame. But, as I was to find out tonight, there was more to it than that.

We heard stomping foot-steps on the porch and the sounds of voices that reminded me of other years in Artesia. The door opened and along with a rush of cold air in came Uncle Robert and Aunt Betty and behind them a woman of such great beauty that I immediately recognized as Dolly. Behind her came a man as big as the door he was closing who I supposed was Junior. And I saw him and Aunt Betty running around in a circle as Aunt Betty whipped him with the white belt with the holes.

My aunt Betty, as always, was the first to embrace me. She was crying and talking at the same time and she was not making any sense. She still smelled as I remembered her at the bus station in Artesia, of rising yeast and tobacco. Uncle Robert came over and shook hands without making too much out of it, showing me that he still was the big man in the family and that I didn't count. He went directly from me to the kitchen to get a drink without inviting me.

I shook hands with Junior. Dolly came over and gave me a kiss on my cheek.

Oh, what a rush of memories she brought to mind when I smelled her sweet breath! I saw her lying in bed on her stomach in the early morning hours, asleep, naked from the waist down, her short nightgown having worked its way up in the restlessness of her erotic dreams. I could see her beautifully smoothed and rounded buttocks with blond body hair so fine and pure and glistening in the sunlight. She rolled over in her continued restlessness and her blond pubic hair sprang up with a life of its own as a deliciously tangled mass straight across the top of her spongy crotch and then disappeared between her legs. She barely opened her legs, moaning in her stupor, and I couldn't see. I couldn't see. I felt like screaming.

She stood in front of me without moving or speaking and smiled. She was incredibly beautiful. My mind took me back once more for a very short while, a second or two perhaps, while I remembered Liz, her friend, taking me by the hand to where Dolly was hiding in the clump of trees by the river where she was preparing herself behind a tree so that when I stepped in front of her she could raise her dress and pull her panties down and she would show me her cunt and make me kiss it over and over again. Since I was already there, I remembered the two times in her room while she was changing clothes and I was her servant and again on the edge of the bathtub as I dried her after I had bathed her when we had been alone one afternoon.

As she stood in front of me I wondered if she remembered the other years. Was she thinking of the same thing that I was? Was she feeling the same as I was feeling? Was she blushing? I thought she was. I felt I was getting an erection and I had to suppress it by thinking of the funeral.

"What do you think of Dolly?" Aunt Betty said ripping me away from my thoughts.

What could I say. She was a beautiful woman. I wished that I had had Mitzi there to compare the two. How had Mitzi grown?

"She's as beautiful as ever," I said, and Dolly blushed for sure this time.

"And Junior? Isn't he big?" my mother said, excitedly, as if being big gave him an advantage in life.

Yes, he was big and he was fat. He had taken a seat by the door and he was holding on to the knob. He had grown huge glove-like hands that seemed boneless. He wore a sheepskin coat and a western shirt and jeans and boots. He had not taken off his coat yet and he looked massive, like a large animal with its hide turned inside out.

"He weights two-eighty," Uncle Robert said. He was proud of it too. He had returned from the kitchen with a glass of bourbon and he was sitting by Aunt Betty on the sofa. "Down from two ninety-five. Right, Junior?"

"Yup, I've lost a little," Junior replied as if they had never had this conversation before and yet it sounded rehearsed.

"He quit drinkin' all that goddam beer," his father said.

"That'll do it," Junior said.

Dolly so far had not said a word. She had gone to sit next to my mother. She looked uncomfortable, sinking into the sofa, her long legs in the way. She kept looking at me as if I were going to tell something about her.

So far the conversation was what I had expected. I took a sip of the bourbon. I had grown up with this type of mentality but I had out-grown it, I thought so anyway. I was wishing Dr. Widenhoffer had been with us to hear this, to hear us talk about how much Junior weighed. Was it two-eighty, or was it three hundred? When was it two-ninety-five, ninety-four? Well, that was one month later after he quit drinking all that goddam beer. Now he was drinking whiskey. Not as fattening, Uncle Robert said. But it packs a wallop, Aunt Betty said, laughing, puffing on her eternal cigarette. She was beginning to drop ashes on herself. Then Junior started laughing about something and Uncle Robert asked him what was so funny and Junior said he just remembered last year going deer-hunting at this time and what had happened to his hunting partner and Uncle Robert and Aunt Betty laughed. Richard, my mother, Dolly and I listened to them laugh.

I was hoping they would not tell us the story but they did. My mother was getting tired. She was yawning more and more. She had not slept well, I presumed. Richard was looking at the floor, the cigarette in his hand burning to a long ash. He was deep in thought about something.

I wished I had known what he was thinking about. He was always such a private and lonely person. I needed to be alone with him.

Junior was still talking, laughing, and Uncle Robert was helping him along with the story.

"But," Aunt Betty yelled, "it ain't good to be hogging the conversation." And she woke us up.

"Well, Jim," Uncle Robert said to me, "do you want to go see your Dad? I'll take you over if you want to go."

I didn't want to go but Richard said that I ought to get it over with and my mother agreed with him. "At first I thought that maybe you shouldn't go in this weather but Richard is right," Mom said. "The funeral is tomorrow and you ain't goin' to see too much of 'im then."

Dolly still had not said anything so I asked her if I should go.

She looked at me very seriously for a moment and then she said I ought to go. I agreed. She had looked at me so intently that I had felt a chill on my scalp.

"Oh, ho," Aunt Betty said, "look at 'im. He only does what Dolly says for 'im to do. I knew there was always some closeness between the two of 'em."

My mother was distraught enough that she didn't pay much attention to what was being said. She too, like Richard, was caught in reverie.

What were they thinking, these two? I kept looking at Dolly every chance I had. I caught myself staring several times. I was hoping I wasn't obvious. I found I couldn't help myself. She was still as blonde and as sensuous as she had been at fourteen. I could still feel her erotic magnetism, drawn to her like an iron filing, as she sat across from me. She had grown only a few inches. It was hard to believe that she was thirty-nine and had children. Where had all my time gone? She looked twenty-nine. She was as long-legged as ever and she was wearing a very well-fitted black skirt and a mouton coat over her grey wool sweater. She wore a small diamond pendant on a thin gold chain. If it had been possible for me to marry her, I would have somehow managed to cover her in gold. She apparently had a good job.

Uncle Robert got up and yawned and stretched and said it was time to go if we were leaving. Mother said she was going to bed to see if she could sleep now that she had her family together. She looked old as she walked slowly, almost stumbling in the dark hallway.

"You boys sleep however you can," she said as she faded into the dark. "Bob and Betty are in the small room, and Dolly and me are sleeping together. Junior, you sleep on the sofa and Richard, you and Jim can sleep on the chairs, or whatever."

Richard said that I would sleep with him at his place. He had plenty of room. I noticed he didn't invite Junior.

"Suit yourself...but I don't think a man in Jim's position should sleep there. If you know what I mean," my mother said to Richard as she went into the bedroom and gently closed the door.

Dolly said goodnight and smiled at me. She went down the hall and went into my mother's bedroom. Aunt Betty yawned and got up and said she was tired from the trip and she had better go to bed. She went into the small bedroom.

We put on our coats, except Junior who had never removed his, and we went out into the cold night air and we got into Uncle Robert's car, an old four door Chevrolet sedan, and we were on our way to the funeral home.

It was past eleven.

"Are you sure we can get in?" I asked Uncle Robert. It was cold in the car and we were all shivering.

"Oh, yeah," he answered. "The Mexican that takes care of the place lives in back. Don't he Junior?"

"Yup," Junior said. He was sitting up front with his dad. So far tonight he had not spoken directly to Richard and me.

Then abruptly, Uncle Robert said, "Fuck it, Junior, get the fuckin' bottles out. Let's have us a drink on ol' Jim."

We found out why Junior had not taken his coat off inside the house. He had two bottles of whiskey in his belt. He pulled them out and he took a large swallow and groaned, as if he had been poisoned and he wiped the top with his hand and he passed the bottle around. We each took a swallow, Richard taking the biggest one.

"Goddam, Richard," Junior said to him, finally speaking to one of us, "I didn't know you loved the stuff so much."

"Well," Richard answered wiping his lips, "once you've been away from it for a long time like I was in prison you get to appreciate the stuff. Makes me feel good. Feelin' good, that's what it's all about." He lit a cigarette, blew on the match and threw it on the floor board.

Uncle Robert spoke. "Shit man, I wish your daddy was alive right now. What fun we'd have." He was talking and holding on to the bottle. He took a drink and passed it to Junior. "Some shit-head he was. Biggest shit-head I ever knew and I can say it 'cause he was my brother." He shook his head like he couldn't believe what he was thinking. "Damn!" he said and hit the steering wheel with his open hand. "I'll never forget the sonofabitch left me behind at the reservation that time. You all remember that? Good thing the Indians knew me good. Shit. If they'd a hadn't I'd been dead long ago. Shit, it's been that long since I've seen you boys. We've been over and seed your Mom though, haven't we Junior?"

"Yup," Junior said. He took a swallow and passed the bottle to the rear where Richard and me were sitting.

"Hell, we came over several times when your paw and your maw were still livin' together. What a hell of a time we'd have. We'd fuck 'round here in Corpus or go over to Alice or the whore houses in San Diego. One time we went to Laredo. Took the whole family, didn't we Junior?"

"Yup."

The bottle had made the round and was back in Uncle Robert's hands. He was resting it against the steering wheel.

"Sumbitch!" Uncle Robert cried and he swung at the steering wheel again, almost knocking the bottle down. "What a shit-head he was." He took his swallow and passed the bottle again to Junior. "You boys never knew what happened, did you?"

"I knew," Richard said.

"How in the shit would you know?" Uncle Robert said to Richard.

"You'd be surprised," Richard said. "I know a lot of things."

"Well, you better keep your mouth shut."

"Don't worry, I intend to."

"You're interfering with my story, goddamit. Well, the sumbitch had gotten this little Indian girl pregnant. That was what all that shit was about. You boys remember we kept sayin' we had problems with the whiskey? Fuck, it weren't true. Your dad had knocked up this good lookin' Indian girl and her family was out to get his balls. You know them Apaches'll cut off your balls if you fuck around with their women. What a shit-head he was. Your dad was a shit-head and you all can't deny it."

I looked at Richard. He had been looking at me. This was the conversation Richard had heard when he was under the truck that night. He had never told me. I was hearing it for the first time. Uncle Robert slowly turned onto Alameda at Five Points. He was still talking. We were still drinking.

"He almost got killed, you know. But he was like a snake. He had to fight the girl's brother to get out alive. And you know what that sonofabitch did? When he and the Indian were rolling on the ground fightin' he bit the Indian's nose off! Hell, by that time even the girl wanted to kill 'im. I'll never figure how he got out alive."

He stopped talking and then he realized that we weren't going to say anything. I didn't care anymore. I would rather not hear the inane conversation. I had had enough disappointments in my life. The whiskey was beginning to get to me. He couldn't stand the silence. "Well," he said, "all that about havin' trouble with the whiskey was a pile of shit. We did need whiskey though, 'cause the Indians wanted that in payment for what your dad had done to the pretty Indian girl. And let's face it, boys, ol' Jim loved that Indian girl more than anything in the world. Hated to leave her in the worse way. He was thinking of ditching all of you and becoming an Indian. Loved 'er 'til he died. Laughin' Eyes they called her. Beautiful Indian girl. You ain't fucked 'til you've fucked an Indian. An Indian girl'll tighten up her pussy like nothin' you've ever known before. It's like a death grip and she'll keep you there inside of 'er for as long as she wants. You can't move! I mean, you can't push it in and you can't get it out. It's the damnedest thing you'll ever feel. You get tied up like a dog. Now boys...that's good pussy."

I was beginning to feel like I should have stayed at home. The conversation was making me feel anger. The car was getting too hot. I took my coat off. I could feel the congestion of blood in my head. I felt warm and red. I was conscious of how much I was blinking. It was the whiskey. We had finished a quart of whiskey in that short time and Richard was asking for more.

"I've got more," Junior said, pulling the other bottle out. "Don't you all panic."

"Shit, he loved 'er more'n he loved your Mom, that's for sure. Sonofabitch wanted to stay with the Apaches but they wouldn't take 'im. They thought ol' Jim was a coward. He weren't no coward. Hell, he was ignorant. That's what he was. Yeah." He was agreeing with himself. "And he was a crook and a shit-head, pure and simple."

I was hoping that he would stop. He was making me ill. The last hard swallow of whiskey was taken in anger and it had been more than I had intended. As soon as I swallowed it, I knew I would have trouble. I should have spit it out but that would have been unmanly. It was that last drink, the one that changes a person from feeling good to feeling nauseous. I looked ahead and for an instant I saw two of everything. Then I shook my head and I could see normally.

Uncle Robert turned off Alameda onto a large parking lot and went around to the rear of a metal building and parked under a covered drive-way. We got out and immediately I felt the cold wind. It was a disorienting shock coming out of the hot car into the freezing temperature. I reached into the car and, fumbling, got my coat and put it on. The weight of the coat somehow brought a fleeting memory of Emily, my drunken brain setting up a comparison of her and Dolly. And then I thought of Anne and what had happened this morning, how so much had been said and yet how much had gone unresolved. I should have let her have her say. I wished I had trusted her enough to have brought her with me. If she had been with me tonight she would have understood. Now I knew I had lost her. Then I thought of Dolly, her nakedness as a young girl and nothing, no other woman mattered. Richard was by me and I saw him as a ghost of his former self, young and care free, his face as smooth and caring as always, his ears erect and unscarred and I saw in the shadows of his presence the ghosts of other years—Clarence and Jim and Phil and the beloved Allens, being nurtured by Nurse Wilma, eating from the hand of the old man at the grocery store and Clarence's mother dead with the wounds made by the screwdriver that Clarence had used to tightened the blade in Richard's knife.

"What's the problem with shit-head?" Uncle Robert was inquiring about me. He was talking to Junior and Richard. I was standing by the car, holding onto the antenna, numb from the cold and the whiskey. I couldn't move.

"Smart or not, he's a shit-head just like his Pa," I heard Uncle Robert say, his voice off in a drunken distance.

CHAPTER 35

"Is he drunk?" I could hear Uncle Robert ask.

"Yeah," Richard said. "He ain't used to drinkin' like that."

"You ain't showin' much respect," Uncle Robert said and I thought he was talking to Junior but he was referring to Richard.

"To who? To you?" Richard answered.

"To anyone. No one. Who the fuck do you think you are?"

"What's the matter with you?"

"You piss me off. That's what. The way you answer me. Yeah. Yeah. Yeah, shit! Have some respect, goddammit. I'm your uncle."

"I don't give a fuck if you're my uncle," Richard told him.

"Don't pay no attention to jug ears, Dad," Junior said. "He'll just piss you off. Make you have a heart attack. He ain't worth it."

Uncle Robert said angrily, "Junior, leave me the fuck alone. Go back there and get the Mexican guy to open up the fuckin' place for us."

I could hear the crunching of his large weighted boots on the macadam as he walked away in search of the night watchman. The excessive noise made by him distracted me and I looked up and saw him with his large sheep-skin coat, his hands in his pockets, his walk almost effeminate. I was trying to keep my balance. I decided that maybe I should lean against the car and let go of the antenna. I did, but in stages, for fear that I would fall and make an ass of myself. Consciously and with great concentration, I first placed the outside foot forward and felt the cold ground with it. I leaned slightly forward, releasing the weight on the hind foot. Next, I slowly twisted my body to the right, clockwise, and I was more or less facing the car. I then moved, slowly again, the foot that had been at the back toward the car and followed with the other foot. This had me face to face flush against the car. At the same time I could still hear Uncle Robert and Richard arguing.

"Hell, I fed you, you sumbitch when no one wanted to have anythin' to do with and your fuckin' brother over there. And that's the respect I get from you, you fuckin' jail-bird."

"You better shut your fuckin' mouth," Richard said, quietly. "I'm a tough customer and you had too much to drink. Just you watch what you're sayin'. You said enough already, you loud- mouthed sonofabitch. Jim never knew nothin' about Dad and the Indian woman. But you had to tell 'im. You been itchin' to tell 'im all these years. You just couldn't keep your goddam mouth shut!"

"It's about time he knew. Who the shit does he think he is? He ain't better'n us. You always made him out better'n us. Always tellin' us how smart your little brother was. He's always acted like he was better. He ain't worth shit. Just like you. And if I want to tell 'im 'bout Jack too by golly I'll tell 'im. He ought to know your Mom ain't the little dainty woman she claims to be. You know goddam well she fucked Jack. You know goddam well—you saw her when I saw her. If your Pa had been with us he would've killed 'em both. And you and me too, probably, for havin' seen 'em. You saw her fuckin' just like I saw her fuckin'. And that's the truth! You ain't goin' to deny that, now are you? Too bad shitbrains over there's drunk. I'd like to tell the little sumbitch off to his face so's he knows what a pile of shit he came from. Maybe then he wouldn't be so high and mighty."

"If you weren't my uncle I'd jump your fat ass and beat the shit out of you. Now you better keep your mouth shut and not say that again."

"You ain't the man to do it. You're a pile of shit! Your pa was right. You ain't worth fuck."

Richard threw the cigarette toward Uncle Robert and when it hit the macadam in front of him it exploded with the cold air into hundreds of fiery cinders.

"Sumbitch...You tryin' to burn me up or what?"

"I ain't tryin' to do a goddam thing except shut you up."

I was still facing the car, leaning against the fender. I didn't know whether I was going to vomit or not. I was sure that the argument was helping to make me ill. I couldn't believe what I was hearing. Was it the truth? Was that my mother they were talking about? If it was, then I had been right when I told Anne that Richard was the only vestige of family life that I had remaining. Or was I dreaming?

What were they going to do? Were they going to fight? Regardless, I was in no condition to keep them from fighting if they wanted to.

I felt an irreparable sadness as the inordinate weight of all those heavy ghosts that Uncle Robert had talked about and that had been around me for such a long time settled in my heart. I had not been prepared for such a heavy burden. I vomited a small amount of bourbon and stomach contents on the hood of the car. I looked around when I finished and no one had noticed and I felt better.

Uncle Robert was banging on the door. "Goddamit, open the fuckin' door. Can't you all see I'm freezin' my ass off? Where the fuck is Junior? What the shit is keeping 'im? Dumb fart's probably knocking on the wrong goddam door. What a shit-head he turned out to be. All he's got is a big ass. Lot's of blubber. Dumbest sumbitch in the family. Walks around with his big ass like a jailhouse cook." Then to Richard, "You ought to know what I'm talkin' about, you bein' in jail all the time."

He was trying to force open the locked door. He had his foot on the door jam and was trying to leverage his weight against the door handle. Richard had gone over and was looking in through a section of glass next to the door. "Here he comes," Richard said and we could see the shadows against the wall as Junior and the night attendant came up the hall way.

"What the fuck took you so long?" Uncle Robert shouted through the door. Luckily the attendant didn't hear him or if he did, he paid no attention to him.

He and Richard were together at the door, as if they had never had an argument. I stopped to think, confused, the taste of bile and stomach fluids and cheap bourbon in my mouth. Had they been talking or had I imagined it?

The attendant unlocked the door. He was a Mexican-American with a large moustache and small eyes and thick lashes. He was short but he weighed a lot, causing his arms to stick out like a rag doll. He was dressed in khakis and was wearing house shoes. He let Uncle Robert and Richard in and I slowly followed behind them. Vomiting had made me feel better. At least I was not in a constant panic, indecisive about whether I was or was not going to vomit. My stomach felt more settled. The attendant looked at me and shook his head. He could tell I was drunk. He was holding the door open. "You've been drinking a little bit too much? You're the son that came from Austin tonight?" he asked. I nodded, afraid to speak, my throat raw from the vomitus.

"You want to see your dad?" Again I nodded. "Come in," he said. "Come in. Let me lock the door. I don't want anyone else coming in. We're supposed to be closed."

The center double doors in the vestibule led into the main chapel. The doors were open and I could see the large room with its pews, the lights subdued. We followed the attendant down a hallway to the left side of the vestibule. There were small rooms off the hallway, each with a group of chairs set in front of the casket for private mourning. The attendant was leading the way and Uncle Robert and Junior were together behind him. Richard was behind them and I was staggering behind Richard. We went past four private rooms before we came to the last room, the one with my father's body. By the time I got there the other men had gone into the room. I stayed outside for a while with the attendant and I read the announcement on the bulletin board that had been prepared for him. It read: James (Little Jimmy) Jones, died December 1, 1977. Born: July 4, 1917. Funeral: Saturday, December 3, 11:00 AM.

The attendant left and I went in, and Uncle Robert, Junior and Richard were gathered at the head of the casket. I walked hesitantly toward them not knowing what to expect. I had last seen my father when Grandmother died. I thought that it would have to be four or five years but you couldn't tell. If you measured time by funerals we would always be off. It might have been five years ago for all I knew. I had not seen him since then. He had come to the funeral, and he and Richard had gotten into an irrational argument at the house and they had almost come to blows. I had taken Richard away from the house and we had stayed at a motel. After the funeral they seemed to get along better and Richard and I took him to the bus station and left him there. I remembered that he had been coughing a lot then and he appeared thinner than ever, like Richard. On the way to the bus station he had told us what his plans were for his future. He was going to go into the house-trailer business. He might even go into it with Uncle Robert. He gave out a little pathetic laugh and looked strangely at us to see if we believed him. We all knew he was lying. He didn't have the money to buy a house-trailer much less go into the business. I double-parked in front of the station and told him to get out. I had not meant to be rude, but the words came out wrong and the situation was such that I couldn't apologize. He grabbed his small cardboard suitcase and got out and didn't even look back. He had not even said "Thank you." And yet I felt bad.

As I walked toward him, the first I saw of my father was his nose projecting over the edge of the casket. He looked very clean, like someone had scrubbed him with a stiff brush until he turned pink. I didn't remember him ever being so clean. His face was thin, as always. His mouth was so tightly shut that he could still have the nose of the Indian inside it, the lips colored red and very, very thin, thinner than he normally had them. The hairs of his narrow eyebrows were short as if he had been trying to groom them before he died, trying to look younger than what he was. His hair was thin but long the way he preferred it although it made him look cheap. It was combed very neatly back. He was dressed in a black suit, a white shirt and a solid black tie. His once fearful hands were crossed at his heart and they looked very small and delicate, like a woman's. They had cleaned his fingernails. The cuffs of the shirt were large and they made his wrists look very thin and fragile. I had never noticed before but like me he had almost no hair on his hands. He had been embalmed without an expression.

Uncle Robert was leaning over the body and he was crying. "Goddammit, every time I see 'im I cry. I just can't help it. I raised this boy, you know. I raised 'im when no one gave a good goddam about 'im. Look at 'im. He looks like he's ready to talk. Sumbitch! I wish he would get up and talk. Tell us where the hell he's been and what it's like. Wouldn't that be somethin'? Shit. If anybody could get away with it ol' Jimmy could. What'd I give to have 'im sittin' down havin' a beer or a drink. Sumbitch could drink. He weren't no pussy." He looked at me. I was already looking at him. I knew he was referring to me.

All in all my father made a good-looking corpse. At last I had seen something that he had done that looked right. Richard and Junior had taken seats in the front row of chairs, tired at having had to stare at the body since this afternoon. I was standing at the end to the casket next to Uncle Robert. Uncle Robert kept shaking his head. "No one loved 'im like I did. He never did anythin' that I didn't forgive 'im for. That's the kind of brothers we were. He weren't a bad person." He looked at me, tears in his eyes, and said, "I know you all hate his guts but I don't. He led a tough life. Did you know that? Did you and your shit-head brother take that into consideration? Hell, he thought he was doin' all right by you all. That's all he knew." He wiped the tears with his coat and went and sat down with Richard and Junior. He bent over and hid his face in his hands.

I was looking over the top of my father's head and he looked like a different person. I was searching for something in him that I could love, but all I could see was where someone had made a tiny incision at the back of his head behind the part of the hair. I was trying to sympathize with Uncle Robert, to feel something for the man. But I was lost in the unforgivable memory of that night in Artesia and I kept looking at his effeminate hands and it surprised me that they could have done so much damage to Richard's ears.

Junior had taken out his bottle and was passing it around. He offered some to me and I turned him down. I was through for the night.

The attendant came through the door. "What's goin' on?" he asked. He had heard Uncle Robert crying. "You guys had enough?" He had seen the bottle.

"I think you're right," I said. "We'd better be leaving."

The attendant scratched his head as he looked at Uncle Robert. He said, "It's gettin' late, boss. I need for all of you to leave before I get in trouble."

He took us back through the hall. I was feeling so much better. I could talk. I could think. I could stand and walk.

He unlocked the door and Uncle Robert and Junior were out first. I followed them and said to the attendant, "Thank you. You were very kind."

"No problem," he said. "Glad you could see your dad. I know how it is."

"See you tomorrow," I said and I buttoned my coat and went into the cold gulf wind.

"Not me," he answered. "I only work nights."

"Thanks again," I shouted as I walked to the car.

When I got there I asked for Richard. He was not in the car. "He's probably taking a leak," Junior said. We waited a while and then Uncle Robert started the car to get it warm. We saw Richard run out of the funeral home. The attendant had almost locked him in. The attendant let him out and Richard was standing at the door on the outside talking loudly to him. Richard waited for the man to walk away from the door then he ran to the car. When he got in Uncle Robert took off in a hurry.

"Where the fuck you been?" Uncle Robert asked Richard.

"Nowhere. Talkin' to the gentleman," Richard said.

"You ain't got no sense, you know that?" Uncle Robert shouted.

"What do you mean?"

"Shit, we're all here freezin' our balls off and you're talkin' to the goddam Mexican. Don't you have any sense?"

"Let's just drop it," Richard said and he took out another cigarette and lit it. He threw the match on the floor.

Uncle Robert was watching him through the rearview mirror.

"Listen, moron, don't throw the fuckin' matches on the floor. Don't they learn you nothin' in prison?"

Richard picked up the match and put it in his coat pocket. "No," he said, puffing on the cigarette. "They don't learn us a fuckin' thing, except keepin' your goddam mouth shut."

Junior took out the bottle again and took a large swallow and passed it on to Uncle Robert. He took some and passed it back to us. Richard tipped the bottle and made it gurgle. I faked taking a drink, pushing my tongue into the opening to prevent the whiskey from going inside my mouth.

"Goddam it," Uncle Robert cried, "it's the shits when a man dies and his sons don't give a fuck! Sonofabitch!" He hit the steering wheel with the palm of his hand. "Little Laughin' Feet'd be cryin' if he knew his dad was dead. But the Indians, they know how to respect the dead. Shit, a fuckin' dead Indian dog gets more respect than Little Jimmy does from his own family."

This was Uncle Robert's way of telling us that the Indian child my Dad had fathered was named Laughing Feet. In a way it was beginning to get comical. There had been too many surprises for one night and Laughing Feet had been the end, too much. I just couldn't cope anymore.

If my academician friends could have seen me now. If I went back and told them everything that had happened to me tonight and everything that I had learned about my family they wouldn't have believed me. And thank God for that. I was glad I had not invited Anne after all. My family was depressingly worse than I had thought. And the night was young. Hard to believe, but it would get worse. As a matter of fact, I could see Richard in the shadows of the car preparing to unleash more ghosts than he or I could handle.

How could I explain all this shit to anyone? Laughing Eyes, almost my stepmother had it not been for a fight in which my father bit the nose off an Indian. Laughing Feet? My half- brother? Blood brother? Indian brother? I had a half-brother that was a Mescalero Apache Indian? Jack? Whoever he was. Maybe my father? Was I a bastard? Illegitimate? Was Richard my brother or my half-brother? Was Junior my cousin? Maybe Uncle Robert was not really our uncle? Then Dolly was no relation of mine. I started to laugh. I couldn't do anything else. Uncle Robert was looking through the rearview mirror. "What's the matter back there? Are you crying?"

Richard was trying to figure out what I was doing. Like Uncle Robert, he couldn't tell whether I was crying or not.

"No," I said, barely able to get the words out, "I'm laughing." I had the giggles.

Uncle Robert pounded the steering wheel again and said, "Well, if that don't beat shit! I've seen fuckin' dead Indian dogs get more respect than that. Poor ol' Jimmy. In a way I'm glad he's gone, gone away from these ungrateful sumbitches." He took a shot of whiskey. "Tell you what, Junior," he said.

"What's that?"

"I'm so pissed off that come tomorrow after the funeral we're gettin' the shit out of here. I ain't stayin' here longer than I have to with these ungrateful sumbitches."

I couldn't help it. The whole affair had become a caricature. I couldn't stop laughing.

CHAPTER 36

Uncle Robert drove on in silent anger, taking a drink now and then from the bottle and passing it on to Junior without offering any to us. At the house Richard and I got out of the car first and we moved my car out of the driveway so that Uncle Robert could park on the oyster shell. I parked the car in the street and I ran into the house to get my suitcase. Inside, the house was deathly quiet. The women had gone to sleep. Mother had left the dim table lamp on in the living room. She had made the sofa into a bed for someone to sleep. I took my suitcase and got out and ran to the car. Uncle Robert and Junior were at the stairs drinking the last of the bottle as I ran past them.

The wind was dying down by the time we arrived at Richard's place, a little metal building not far from the funeral home behind the body-shop where Richard worked. As we arrived I did not see how I was going to be able to stay with Richard. It did not look, from the outside at least, that we had enough room. Quickly I went over in my mind that I could have a drink and then beg off and get back in the car and drive to Mother's and sleep on the chair. Junior's big ass would be on the sofa. I left the suitcase in the car; I was that sure. The watchdog barked at us as we got out and when he recognized Richard he jumped out of an abandoned car and came over, trotting, to be petted. "Hi, Spot," Richard said to the dog. "How's it goin'? Nothin's happenin' tonight, huh?" The dog wagged his long tail vigorously, trying to show Richard how much he loved him. "Best friend I have," Richard said as he turned loose of the dog and we walked to the door. The dog followed tentatively, knowing he had not been invited. At the door he begged unashamedly to be let in, licking Richard and rolling on his back. Richard looked down at him. "Go away Spot," he said. "You know you can't sleep with me. We'll get in trouble. You've got to watch out to make sure no one steals anythin'." Spot understood for the thousandth time and went back inside his car. No harm in trying, he thought. It was cold. Richard said, "That dog will do that to me every time. He'll wear me down once in a while and I'll let 'im in when it's real cold. Tonight isn't that cold. He can take it. No one's stealin' when it's real cold anyway so I figure he don't need to watch over the place then." He looked back again to make sure the dog had disappeared inside the old car. "He's persistent though."

Richard opened the thin metal door and we went in to the dark room. He asked me to wait at the door while he turned on the light. "It's kind of dangerous in here in the dark," he said. And when the light came on it began to swing from its long cord and I was stunned to see that he was living in one room that was also used as storage for used car parts. And there hanging on the walls and piled on the floor were the fenders, wind-shields, engines, mufflers, bumpers, doors, trunks, hoods and quarter-panels standing upright against the wall. From the ceiling hung tires and tubes and used bicycles and long lines of cable among the exhaust pipes, each item casting its own swinging shadow throughout the room so that Richard looked like an apparition eerily swarming with ghosts. At the far end was a counter, a bare wood counter-top on two-by-fours with a shelf underneath. Built into the counter was a sink with a single cold water pipe and on top was an electric hot-plate. Behind the hot-plate, neatly in a row, were a group of coffee cans. I was sure, with out asking, that only one of them had coffee. The others were being used by Richard for storage to protect the food from the wharf-rats and the mice and the fire ants.

Off to the left side against the wall was a low car seat neatly made into a bed. In the middle under the light was a table with two chairs. To the right, against the wall, was another low bed made from a car seat. It too was neatly made up. It was where Richard intended for me to sleep. He had been expecting me. Besides the made beds, I could tell he had cleaned the place.

"You got anythin' to unpack?" Richard asked. He had kept on walking toward the counter.

It was cold inside the room. I couldn't see where he had a heater.

"Yeah, I've got some stuff," I replied, appalled at where he was living.

"You didn't bring your suitcase in? Go get it and I'll plug in the hot-plate," he said, rubbing his hands to warm up.

I did not want him to know that when I first saw where he lived that I had not wanted to stay. Now having seen how he was living, I felt pity for him.

I would have to stay. He had prepared a bed for me. It would be an insult if I left.

I went out into the chilly night once more and the turbulent gulf wind had calmed down for the night. The fog, the same one that had given me so much trouble on the road, was beginning to back up toward the Gulf. I could see the moisture in the air illuminated like giant halos surrounding the street lights. As I stood by the car I felt a chill and a loneliness that made me shiver. It appeared that he was destitute. I felt bad that I had complained about myself now that I had seen the way he was living. I felt hopeless. Then I thought about how bad he must have felt.

The dog had come slowly toward me from inside the abandoned car. He stretched and yawned and shook his skin and met me at my car. He checked the car out by going around slowly smelling of it. I'm sure he had already done this and had urinated on every wheel at his own leisure but he was showing off for me, sort of earning his keep.

He smelled my suitcase as I got it out of the back seat and as I swung the suitcase around to close the door, he imagined I was going to hit him with it so he gave out a protective yelp and sprang away from me. When he realized I meant him no harm he came to me slowly as if nothing had happened, as if he had never been scared. I knew then what kind of dog he was.

Richard had plugged in the hot-plate and was going to steam some water to warm up the room. It felt warm already. I took my coat off and placed my suit case on the floor by the bed on the right wall. That's where Richard had pointed to when I asked him where I was to sleep. Of course, it didn't make any difference to him what bed I took. I could take them both. He could sleep standing up. But that bed was the best one, he said.

Finally, after I had taken my coat off and we sat down at the table I knew it was time for Richard to talk. He had taken a new bottle of whiskey and two glasses and a pitcher of water and placed them between us on the table. He poured whiskey into the two glasses and added water. I felt like asking him why he didn't live with Mom, but then I realized that Richard was smart enough to figure that out. He just couldn't live with our mother, just as sure as I couldn't have lived with her. He was right; I would have preferred living in a shack.

I wanted to start the conversation because I wanted to clear the air about what had happened tonight between Uncle Robert and Richard. "What was that all about with Uncle Robert?" I asked.

"Mother-fucker. He don't have any smarts."

"Forget about Dad and the Indian girl. What about Jack?"

"You don't want to know. What the shit you want to know for?"

"Because the truth is important to me."

"Shit. The truth hurts. Forget about this Jack shit. You're doin' all right as it is. It's not important. You're important."

"Richard," I said, "it's important to me. I would like to know."

He peered at me across the table. "Do you really want to know?"

I answered, "Yes, and if you don't tell me, I'm leaving. I'll get it out of Uncle Robert somehow."

He lit a cigarette with the butt of the one he was smoking and he added whiskey to his drink. He looked at me seriously. "Do you remember that time when Uncle Robert and Aunt Betty and them came over to Corpus to visit a long time ago? Remember the time when Dad and Mom got into a fight and Dad almost broke Mom's arm?"

I remembered.

"I was eight years old then. Remember everybody ganged up on Dad and he took off? Exactly like he did in New Mexico? Remember the next day Uncle Robert wanted us to forget the whole thing and Dad gone and all, so Uncle Robert wanted to take us to North Beach? Mom didn't go because she had a sore arm. Remember? Remember I got sick to my stomach and Uncle Robert had to leave you all there with Aunt Betty while he brought me home? Well," he continued as he took a drink and a drag from his cigarette, "when we got home we went in and we could hear voices. Uncle Robert whispered to me to be quiet. We tip-toed down the hallway and when we got to Mom's and Dad's room he crashed through the door expectin' to find burglars. You know how strong the sonofabitch is. I stayed in the hallway where no one could see me. But I could see what Uncle Robert was seein'. Mom was in bed fuckin' with Jack. He had 'er with her legs over his shoulders up in the air and he was fuckin' 'er hard, Jim. Mom screamed when she saw us. Jack came off 'er and ran and got his clothes and ran right past me. He stopped at the door and dressed real fast and he ran out. He didn't even look at me. I was trembling and crying in the hallway. I had never seen anything like that in my life. Uncle Robert took me into the kitchen and told me that if I ever said anything to anyone about what I had just seen that Dad would kill me and Mom. Mom never said anythin' to me. She acted like it never happened. She came out of the room like it hadn't happened. That's all," he said. "You wanted to know, you dumb shit. So now you know. What good is it goin' to do you?" He took a drag from his cigarette and blew the smoke down between his legs. He looked up and his eyes met mine and I didn't know what to say. He had painted a disgusting picture in my mind of my mother in bed with a man and I felt devastated, unclean. He was crying but trying to smile to ease my pain, the deep lines in his face grown harsher by the revealing light.

"That's what Uncle Robert was talkin' about tonight. He says that Mom kept on seein' 'im. Dad thought so too but he could never prove it. I don't know. I never saw 'im again during those other years. I do know that she sees 'im now. She don't make no bones about it. You're the only one she hides it from. But that ain't hard on her. You don't show up but once every five years. He stays at the house pretty often. Sometimes I think he spends the night."

He took a long drink, waiting, I imagined, for some response. I had come prepared to condemn my father for what he had done to us, but now I had to add my mother's condemnation. "I'm sorry I made you tell me," I said. "I don't want for us to ever talk about it again. Do you agree?" He nodded slowly. "Listen, Richard," I said, "I've got some extra money. Can I give you some?"

He had quit crying. He looked at me suspiciously, sensing that I didn't approve of the way he was living, which was what I was trying to avoid. "Naw," he said, "I don't really need anythin'. Most people have too much as it is. All I need is a little to eat and a lot to drink. This is my food," he said and he took a long swallow from his drink.

"You ought to move with me to Austin," I said.

"Thanks," he said, grinning with the gap left by the missing front teeth. "I can't, though. I'm on probation. I can't leave the fuckin' town. I got to report to the probation officer. They wouldn't let me leave." He raised his glass to me as a toast. "But thanks anyway. I know you mean it."

"Sure, I mean it. It would be nice."

"Yep. It would. I was in Austin lots of times."

"You were? Why didn't you call me?"

"I was just bummin' 'round. I had some people with me you wouldn't't've liked to meet. Not very good people. Bums. You know what I mean."

"Regardless, you should have called me. I mean it. It upsets me that you were in Austin and didn't even look me up."

"Believe me, you wouldn't have liked it, Jim. These guys were bad news."

"It doesn't make any difference. You should have looked me up. Promise me you'll look me up next time."

"If there's a next time."

"How would you feel if I came to Corpus and didn't look you up?"

"I'd be hurt."

"Damn right you'd be hurt."

"Jim, I'm sorry. What else can I say? I was bummin'. Let's forget it, okay?"

"All right, but don't you ever do that to your only brother again."

"I won't," he said, turning the glass slowly on the table.

"Well, I haven't seen you in a long time. What's up?"

"Not much. I did do short time since I saw you last. Hell, I did time for somethin' I didn't even do. But it's all the same everywhere I go. Once you've been in prison, Jim, no one forgets. There's never been a place I've been that it hasn't caught up with me. Just when I'm settlin' down it comes back to me. I can't seem to get away from it. I can't get married, can't have a family. I'm just goin' to die just like you see me here." He pointed with his glass at the room. Then he took a large swallow. "The last time we were together I almost beat the shit out of the old man. Remember? Now the sonofabitch is dead." He was staring at his drink.

I was starting to drink again. I didn't particularly want to talk about the argument he had had with our father. I was still recovering from the story about Mom. "That fight didn't do us any good," I said. "We never got to talk about what happened after Sugarland."

He took out one cigarette from his shirt pocket. He had learned in prison never to take out the whole pack. You'd never see it again if you did. He lit the cigarette and blew out the match.

"After Sugarland I went on to Houston to see if I could find work. I was on probation you know, just like I am now. But I'm on probation now for somethin' else. Anyway, I was on probation in Houston. Tried to work. Couldn't find anythin' to make a decent livin'. So I started hangin' around the dope-heads and pretty soon I was into the stuff. Tried suicide two or three times. Cut my wrists. Here, let me show you what it looks like." He turned up his hands for me to see. "Went to St. Joseph's several times. Dried out. Then I got strung out again. Got into a hell of a lot of trouble on dope." He took a drag from his cigarette. "There's a lot of money behind this dope thing." He stopped to pick a small piece of tobacco from his tongue. "That was in sixty-seven, sixty-eight, seventy, around that time. But I bet it's worse now. Lots of money behind it."

He took a drink and emptied the glass. He refilled it half and half with bourbon and water.

"Who's in this dope thing?"

"Lots of people. Everyone I know. Here in South Texas, most people that have a lot of money and don't work. Just look at how it works, Jim. The guy with the money gives it to a junkie. The junkie goes and buys the stuff in Mexico, brings it back, goes to Houston, San Antonio, Dallas, Fort Worth, Corpus. All of it is arranged up front. You know where you're goin' to get it, how much you're goin' to pay for it and where you're goin' to take it. I'd take it to a pusher and he gives me the money. The junkie, that's me, comes back with ten times the money you gave 'im. Ten times. You give 'im one thousand and he shows up in a week with ten thousand. Now that's a pretty good profit. The junkie takes all the risks. Like me. That's what I was doin' in Houston. Somebody gave me money and I'd drive to Laredo, Piedras Negras, Matamoros. Then I'd get the stuff—marijuana, coke, heroin, you name it—and bring it back and sell it. They'd give me the money and I'd take the money back to the first guy. He'd give me my cut. Two, three hundred. That's more than a week's pay. Not bad. And you get a good car along with it. You get to travel. See the country-side. That ain't bad."

"No, it isn't," I agreed. It really wasn't, except that it was illegal.

"But then you get caught. You always get caught and you keep your mouth shut. If you don't they'll kill you. What's funny is that even if you do talk nobody'll believe you. It's your word against theirs. And who's goin' to believe an ex-con? The lawyers'll make you wish you'd've kept your mouth shut. Hell, one of the lawyers that sent me to prison had given me money to make a buyin' trip to Mexico. The sonofabitch prosecuted me with a straight face. The judge that sentenced me to Joliet told me he'd go easy on me if I told 'im who'd given me money. Shit, the guy was crazy. I told 'im, 'Judge, if I told you that, I'd be a dead man in twenty-four hours.' He laughed. He said he understood. Even the fuckin' lawyer laughed."

"So you've been to Joliet too?" This I hadn't been told.

"Yeah. Joliet. Good place. That's where I've been since I last saw you. I was in Joliet. Better'n Sugarland or Sealey or Huntsville. None of them places are fit for a human bein'."

He had emptied his drink and he poured another one. I had slowed down. I was still on my first drink. I realized that I needed to feel good in the morning.

He finished his cigarette and took a drink. He said, "I'm goin' to tell you somethin' I've never told anyone before. You're my brother, right?"

"I'm your brother," I said.

"You promise not to tell anyone about what I'm goin' to tell you?"

I agreed. He looked at me and he started to cry and shake his head. He was feeling for a cigarette in his shirt pocket. "All because of that dead sonofabitch," he muttered. He found the cigarette and lit it. He took a long drag and took a drink. "In Sugarland we were in there like animals. You remember the place, don't you? You went to visit me there, didn't you? You could hear the screams at night. Young men gettin' raped. Jim...men fuckin' men. Do you understand that? What kind of people these are? Do you know, Jim, what it is to get raped? Raped, Jim. I'm talkin' about somebody stickin' it to you up your ass. A big black nigger with a dong like a donkey that tears your insides out, that makes you bleed so much that I had to have a transfusion and an operation to close up all the tears he made? I'll never forget the sonofabitches! I screamed and screamed but no one came to help me. I screamed for you, Jim. Where were you? You never came to help me."

He stared at me defiantly for a few seconds. He finished his drink and poured another one. He had gone through half the bottle by himself. He puffed on his cigarette. His hands were shaking violently. He lit a match and then realized that his cigarette was already lit. He threw the lighted match on the table towards me. I couldn't answer him. How could I have helped him? He was crying and appeared to have lost control of his senses.

"Do you know how it feels, Jim? I got raped in Sugarland at the ripe age of twenty-four! Just when I was feelin' like a man, somebody comes over with his buddies and tells me he's goin' to fuck me 'cause I looked good to 'im. I tried to kill myself then too but it wasn't any use."

He took a swallow and looked at me. His eyes were red and sunken from crying. His face was beginning to turn an ashen color. He tried to grin and I saw the gap between his teeth. I could see his gnarled ears move as he tightened his jaw. "Hey," he said, seeming to come back to reality, "who started this up, anyway?"

"I did, Richard," I replied, relieved, "and I'm sorry."

He looked at me with a drunken blank stare. "You're sorry," he said, faintly. He shook his head. "How do you think I felt? How do you think I felt when Dad beat the shit out of me? Let me tell you somethin' else you never knew about me. Now that the sonofabitch is dead I can tell you. Do you know that one time he beat me so much that I crapped in my pants? I ran and hid so you wouldn't see me and I took my shorts off and cleaned myself with 'em and threw 'em away. Why, Jim? Why did he have to beat me? What was there about me that he hated?"

"I don't know," I said, bothered. "Maybe he saw himself in you when he was young. But why are you telling me all this?"

"I need to be heard," he said, "that's why. Now that he's dead, I need for you to tell me what the shit was goin' on. He can't hurt you anymore. You can tell me, Jim, if you know." Slowly, he repeated, "I need to be heard, goddamit." He spilled some of his drink as he exaggerated each word by tapping his glass on the table. He put out his cigarette. "From reform school I went on my own," he said, his words becoming more and more slurred. "I enjoyed my freedom. Went where I wanted. Did what I wanted. Bummed around. Hoboed a little. Winoed a little. Got to know people. Dumb shit! I thought I was havin' a great time. Never bothered with time. That's what was the best. No time. No Sundays or Mondays or Fridays. Doing what you want. You Jim, you were in school doin' what you wanted to do. I was in a different school, Jim. It's called fuckin' 'round. But as always, I got caught. Little things. Stealin'. Burglary. Nothin' big. Little shit. One time when I was inside this house on a burglary, I thought about you, Jim. I thought what you would say if you saw me do what I was doin'. I vomited on the floor. I was that ashamed...I started servin' time. One year, jail time. Two years, jail time. Once I got five and went to Gatesville. Back to reform school. I weren't of age to go to prison yet. I stayed clean five or six years. I say I stayed clean but what I mean is they never could catch me. I got smart. Then one day I fucked up and got caught. I was twenty-three and goin' no place in life except to the Wall. Huntsville. Well, the Wall ain't nothin'. Good place. Good food. Work the shit out of a man. Then I get a transfer to Sugarland. They needed more men out there in the fields. Like a dumb sonofabitch, I volunteered. By that time everybody's callin' me Jug because of my ears and I hate all them bastards for callin' me that. My ears never healed right, Jim. You remember, Jim?"

I did.

"Do you know that one time after I got out of prison I followed Dad around to see if I could kill 'im? I shadowed 'im for about a week. I was goin' to kill 'im and make it look like an accident. Sonofabitch never gave me a chance so I gave up. You remember that night that sonofabitch almost twisted my ears off cause I wouldn't squeal like a pig?" He threw the match box at the ash tray and knocked it off the table. "We couldn't do anythin', could we, Jim?"

"No, we couldn't."

"We didn't have anyone to stand up for us, did we?"

"No, we didn't."

"You couldn't help me, could you?"

"I couldn't. What could I have done?"

"You were always lookin' after your own ass, weren't you? You and Sylvia. You never raised a hand to help, did you? How many times did you see 'im hit me? Did you ever help me, Jim?"

Tears were forming in his eyes, and even I was weeping because the shameful memories of those other years had caught up with me tonight as I saw Richard in front of me slowly being transformed into the animal that we had all made him, and all the ghosts that had been swinging in the room stopped and their shadows were beginning to engulf both of us with their pain.

"It's those times that stick in my mind, Jim. I can't get 'em out! Can't work my way through 'em. I see those times just when I'm about to be the happiest. Then it kinda destroys me. I go hay-wire. I'm not the same person...If you hear anythin' bad about me, Jim, it ain't cause I'm a bad person. I just can't help it. My mind's all screwed up and I go hay-wire...I'll be sorry for it after. I know I will and I'll run to some other place and someone'll find me and turn me in for somethin' I've done wrong a long time ago and...so it goes. Jailbird, like Uncle Robert says. That's what they call people like me. I'm a jug-head, a jailbird and you can't get much lower'.n that...Can't keep a job. Look at where I have to live. Who would live in a place like this? Anytime anythin's stolen or missin' everybody thinks it's me. Everythin' that can go wrong is my fault, just because of my reputation. Isn't that the shits?"

He poured himself some more bourbon and he lit yet another cigarette after I found the matches for him on the floor. The room was beginning to feel hot. "That's all that I am! A hay-wired, crazy sumbitch. Jailbird...Jug Head. I just can't be happy, Jim. I'm goin' crazy! I just can't be happy," he cried. "All those bad things keep comin' back to me. I can't... take...too...much of this...anymore!" he screamed.

He grabbed the glass and threw it against the wall. He threw the cigarette at me hitting me in the chest. I quickly brushed it off my coat. He stood, as well as he could, holding on to the table to keep from falling and he teetered round and round and looked at me as if he didn't know who I was. I shuddered as I saw the profound hate in his eyes. He looked insane. He bared his gapped teeth and growled like a vicious dog. He grabbed his gnarled ears and started pulling and pulling and pulling on them and he started squealing like a dying pig. He ran to his bed and he slowly took his coat and put it on. He was completely disoriented, lost in his own tortured mind, now turned diabolical. I had never seen him like this. This is what he meant when he said that he lost control. Waves of trembling passed through me and I could feel the hair on my neck stand on end. What a horrible experience. What a horrible sight I was witnessing, a man transformed into a raging animal possessed by all the hatred of all his years. My own brother. I was deathly afraid he would attack. I had to walk slowly toward the counter to give him room to escape through the door.

"You won't stop me, you sonofabitch!" he screamed at me. "You'll never be able to stop me!"

He slowly backed over toward the door, still watching me, as if I were someone to fear, someone to prevent his escape. He reached behind him for the knob and slowly turned it, opened the door just enough for his escape and he fled, slamming the door behind him.

I had never been scared of Richard, but I was scared of him then. I quickly turned off the hot plate, put on my coat, got my bag, found my keys, turned off the lights and ran to the car. I could hear dogs barking from everywhere as they followed Richard's insane progress through the neighborhood. I imagined him running madly through the streets. I shuddered again.

He was a man gone mad.

I ran to the car and locked myself in. Suddenly, I heard a violent noise on my window. Someone was trying desperately to get in. I completely froze. My hair was standing on end; I was sure this was the way that I would die, at my brother's hands. My body was numb. I turned quickly toward the window. I had to see if it was Richard trying to get to me. I saw a blurred face grinning through the glass. A most unusual face. In the fog I couldn't make out who it was. I started the car as the creature scratched at the window, still trying to get in. I backed the car out as fast as I could. I was not able to see through the fog. Finally as I backed up into the street I could see that it had been Spot, the dog, looking in through the window, trying to get approval. I lowered the window slightly and I could hear more dogs barking. They were following Richard's trail.

I drove back to Mother's house. The door was not locked and I settled in and slept on the chair, the favorite one, the one we used to fight over. My heart was still pounding but after a while the small flickering flame from the gas heater mesmerized me to sleep. I slept in my clothes.

CHAPTER 37

It was nine-thirty in the morning, and my mother had been bothering me about Richard since seven when she had awakened me to eat breakfast. She wanted to know about Richard. I was not about to tell anyone what had happened last night. I felt it was better if I blamed a misunderstanding between us to explain why Richard wasn't with us.

"Did you have an argument?" my mother demanded to know.

"Yes...and no," I replied. I wasn't sure how to plead.

"If you had an argument, it was his fault. I know Richard. There's somethin' wrong about 'im, always has been and I guess always will. He can get in trouble just standin' still. I don't know what I did to deserve a son like Richard. God knows I tried with 'im. But he was just never any good. Always stealin'. Now Sylvia, she was good...and you, Jim. Although Sylvia didn't live long..." Her voice faded out as she thought about Sylvia. She was addressing herself more to Aunt Betty than to me.

Aunt Betty was nodding her elaborately coiffed head, a swirling African termite mound of hair, ill at ease with my mother's talk about Richard.

We were all sitting in the living room waiting for him as I read the newspaper. My father's name was in the obituaries. It surprised me that they had followed my mother's wishes and used his nickname, "Little Jimmy." It gave the column an undignified quality and I was ashamed that my name was listed as a surviving son. But my mother probably didn't think it was tasteless. She asked me to save the page after I was through so that she could cut out the article.

Uncle Robert was sitting in the chair I had slept in. He had been the last to bathe this morning and his thin wet hair was slicked back much like my father's in the casket. He was dressed in an embarrassingly tight lime-green double-knit western leisure suit with a string tie adorned with a large polished brown agate at his throat. He was wearing a pair of almost new square-toed gray boots with dancing heels. He seemed proud of the way he looked, proud that he had gone out and intentionally chosen and bought the outfit. He was barely able to cross his legs. He was cutting his nails with a pocket knife. He had not spoken to me this morning, nor had Junior.

Dolly looked beautiful. She was wearing a brown tweed jacket with a beige blouse and a dark brown wool skirt and a pair of very delicate dark brown shoes. She had a folded trenchcoat on her lap. She had been up early working on her hair. The smell of hot curlers and the sound of the hair drier had been the first things I had noticed when I was awakened by my mother. She was sitting next to Aunt Betty on the sofa, leaning forward, listening to the conversation, her hands clasped around her knees.

Junior was dressed in a strong-colored blue double-knit western leisure suit with a herringbone pattern. He had invested a little more on his boots, a pair of brown alligator-print riding boots with dancing heels. For some reason his suit also fit very tight. His coat had a patch of suede on the right shoulder as if he had expected to shoot birds at a moment's notice. He wore no tie and his large goutish neck sprang in and out as he breathed, much like a frog. He looked ready to explode. He was cutting his nails just like his Dad. He was standing at the door, impatiently waiting to leave.

Aunt Betty was wearing a brown, double-knit pant suit that fit extremely tight also. She was having to sit straight like a mannequin. She was wearing old loafers and black socks. She had been smoking since we had arisen. Around her neck was a very thin gold-plated necklace with an irregular small diamond that didn't shine. On her left breast she had an Apache Indian broach done in silver and shaped like a musical note.

Mother was wearing a plain black dress, very old in style and faded that seemed to have been saved for my father's death. It had a small white patch of embroidery up front at the neck. She was sitting next to Aunt Betty on the sofa, after all these years still fanning away Aunt Betty's tobacco smoke. She had decided to wear make-up that Dolly had loaned her, but she used it very hesitantly, underpainting her lips, and she looked odd as she talked, as if the voice was out of synch with her mouth.

I was wearing my best suit, heavy 100% black wool. What else do you think Emily would have bought for me? Tailor made in Hong Kong. Another surprise Christmas present. I had never realized that wool, unlike cashmere, itched and wrinkled so much.

"Maybe I ought to go see if he's asleep," I said.

"You'd better run over there," Mom said, worried. "No tellin' what's happened."

I left them talking about their usual things. Mother had exhausted her indelicate condemnation of Richard and when I left they were talking about children in general. Why someone is good and why someone turns out bad. I was glad to leave when Aunt Betty had started to compare Richard to me. "What a wonderful son Jim has turned out to be," she said. "Just like my Uncle Joe's son. He's a sergeant in the marines..."

I was glad to get out. It was going to be a nice day for the funeral, cold with some wind but dry.

I drove to Richard's. The body-shop was open and I could see men working. They stopped work to look at me as I drove into the driveway. I stopped in front of the little metal shack and got out. It looked smaller now in the day times. The dog was stretched out by the front door. I knocked as the dog got out of my way. No one answered. I remembered that I hadn't had the time nor a key to lock the door so I turned the knob and gave the door a gentle nudge and it opened. Inside, things were as we had left them the night before. The whiskey bottle and the water container had been knocked on their side and had spilled over the table. I did not remember when that had happened. My glass was on the table. Richard's glass was on the floor, shattered. The room smelled of whiskey. It seemed colder inside the room than out. I looked toward his bed and no one was there. Then I looked to the other bed and no one was there either. He had not returned.

Outside, the sun was so bright I had difficulty adjusting my eyes to the light. I returned to the car shielding my eyes with my hand. The dog stuck his head out of the window of one of the abandoned cars and barked like he didn't know me. A short heavy-set man had come out of the rear door of the body-shop and was walking toward me. I stopped at the car door and waited for him. He lowered his eyes as he approached me and spoke. "Can I help you?" he asked.

"Yes sir," I replied. "I'm looking for Richard. I can't find him."

He laughed and said, "Hell, we can't find 'im either. He's supposed to be at work today and he ain't showed. I was just fixin' to call the probation officer. Are you a probation officer?"

"No, I'm his brother."

"I didn't think you were a probation officer. I never seen you here talkin' to Jug before...So you're Jug's brother? Never knew he had a brother."

"I don't get over here very often."

"Where you from?"

"Austin."

"Pretty town. I like Austin but there ain't too much goin' in the line of work. You work up there?"

"Yes."

"You're not jail meat like Jug, are you? You don't look like it."

"No. I'm not jail meat."

"Then you turned out better'n Richard."

"Who's to say."

"You know I got to call the probation officer. It's the law. I hired Jug through the state and they give me some help with his salary. If I don't report 'im I'm an accomplice or somethin' like that. I could get in a lot of trouble. You understand I gotta do it."

"Yes," I replied, "you've got to do it."

"A man's gotta do what he's gotta do. And Jug didn't show for work."

"He's supposed to be at a funeral."

"Funeral? The shit you say. He didn't say nothin' about no funeral. Who died?"

"His father. Our dad."

"Jug never said nothin' to me. Goddamit. Jug never said anythin'. I thought he'd run off. Now why do you think Jug wouldn't say nothin'? But it's just like 'im. He never says nothin' to nobody. I say to 'im, 'Jug, get to know someone. Open up a little. Be friendlier so's people can be friendly with you.' You gotta take that first step I always say. But he just goes on his way."

"It's getting late," I said. "The funeral is at eleven."

"Well, Jug may be at the funeral home already waitin' on you. That's probably where he's at. Tell 'im I ain't callin' the probation officer but you tell 'im he's got to be back Monday morning bright and early ready to sand some cars. We got lot's of work to do. Tell 'im I'm sorry about his dad."

I drove back hoping that the man was right and that Richard was sitting at the funeral home waiting for us. I should have gone by the funeral home but I felt I didn't have that much time to waste.

"Well," Uncle Robert informed us all, "what'd you expect? Did you really think he'd stay sober long enough to make it to his father's funeral?"

"Did he go to bed last night?" mother asked me.

"No, he didn't. As a matter of fact he sort of lost control of his senses. He left the house, running down the street."

"Gone crazy," my mother said. "That's just like 'im. Well, what'll we do?" she asked and she reflected on what was happening and she sighed.

"We'd better get going," I told her. "If Richard makes it, fine. If he doesn't, I'm not going to blame him."

"Well, I am," Uncle Robert interrupted.

"It's none of your business," Dolly said to him. "It's not really any of your business. Why don't you leave Richard alone. I know I haven't said anything about 'im, but I feel like you all are raking 'im over the coals over somethin' that he has no control over."

"She's right," I said. "There's nothing that we can do about it. Richard is Richard, just like Uncle Robert is Uncle Robert."

"Don't you compare me with Richard," Uncle Robert shouted back angrily. "Don't you ever do that." He had finally spoken to me.

"I'm not comparing. I'm saying all of us are different."

"You can say that again," Junior murmured, under his breath.

"And you, Dolly, what gives you the right to say anythin'?" Uncle Robert complained.

"I've got a right just like everyone else," she replied. "I feel sorry for Richard."

"Well, I don't," Uncle Robert said.

"Me neither," Junior agreed.

"We need to go," I said and I winked at Dolly and she smiled that disarming smile like I had seen so, so, many times in New Mexico, and I thought of her again but this time my mother nudged me and said, "Let's go, quit actin' the fool with Dolly."

"They always loved each other so," Aunt Betty said, laughing. "Too bad they're first cousins." She had managed to stand up with Uncle Robert's help and she was straightening her pant-suit.

"Who knows for sure?" I said and they all looked at me as if I was crazy.

"Who knows what for sure?" Uncle Robert wanted to know.

"If Dolly and I are really first cousins," I said.

"I declare," Mother said, putting on her coat, "you're talkin' now like your crazy brother Richard."

Standing in the driveway we decided that all of us wouldn't fit in one car. It was agreed on that Dolly and I would go in my car and the rest would go with Uncle Robert. I suggested that Dolly and I go by Richard's once again just to be sure he hadn't returned. Everyone agreed, for once.

In the car I could feel in her an erotic presence like no other woman I had ever been with before. What a shame she was my cousin, like Aunt Betty said. She was staring at me unashamedly as I drove, showing no signs of remorse for what we had both done as children.

"I haven't seen you in a long time," I said, keeping my eyes on the street. And then I blushed; I realized I had unintentionally made a pun.

"Well, it hasn't been because I didn't want you to see me," she said.

"What do you mean?"

"I've lived in San Antonio for over a year now. It's only a couple hours drive. I'm there all the time." She emphasized the all in a very seductive way. "As a matter of fact I've been waiting for you to come over. Maybe go over old times with me."

"I didn't know you were in San Antonio. Why didn't you call to let me know?"

She gave a throaty laugh. "I make it a point never to be the first to call a man. Later, yes."

She was sitting sideways, facing me, with her legs slightly apart.

"Getting together would be nice," I said and I knew it wasn't a great reply or even a good one. I tried to salvage the damage. "It would be great to go out and talk about old times, wouldn't it?"

"That's what I said," she replied.

"I know," I admitted. I sounded meek, weak, babyish, like the shithead that Uncle Robert called me.

"Don't let me forget to give you my address before you leave."

"I won't," I said. "You can bet on it."

Goddamit, I couldn't talk! I was like a college freshman. My mouth was dry.

"Are you going back today?" she asked.

"Yeah. I think so. Right after the funeral. How about you?"

I was putting my words together a little better.

"I wanted to leave today," she explained, "but the family wants to stay until tomorrow."

I did not want to tell her that Uncle Robert was angry and wanted to leave immediately after the funeral. Or maybe Uncle Robert had changed his mind this morning. Maybe he wanted to stay. Hell, I was leaving. They could stay. I was the one that wanted to get out of town. And I wanted Dolly to ride back with me. What harm would it do? I enjoyed her company so much. It was, after all, an innocent flirtation and a stimulating fantasy. "Well," I told her, "you can ride with me. I'll be glad to go by San Antone. (Goddammit, why did I say San Antone, like a West Texas red-neck?) I'll be glad to drive you over."

"Hey," she cooed, "that'd be great. Terrific. We could talk about old times then. And I'll tell you what..."

"What?" I asked in anticipation.

"You can stay over with me. I've got the place all to myself this week. The children are with their father. We can go dining, dancing. You can sleep over."

I could not produce saliva. I could still smell her, as always, and the highly charged visions that swept past me made my heart race and my palms sweat. I drove without seeing the road, entranced, blinded by her words even though I knew that she was making a fool of me, that there would be no dining and dancing and no sleeping over. She giggled as she noticed my helpless condition.

I turned into the driveway at the body-shop and parked at Richard's shack. I got out, excusing myself to Dolly so that she would not get out and see how Richard was living. I ran to the door and opened it and nothing had been disturbed. Richard was not there and there were no signs that he had returned. I quickly got back in the car and drove off. As I drove by the body-shop, I saw Spot, my brother Richard's only friend, asleep, taking in the sun by the door of the building. He opened one eye and saw that it was me and he went back to his nap. He figured I wasn't worth barking at anymore.

Dolly said, "What was that all about?"

"That's where Richard lives," I replied.

"In that shack?"

"Yes," I admitted, "but it's roomy inside. Richard has it fixed nice. Hell," I lied, "it looks better than my place."

"Well," she laughed, forgetting about Richard, "if that's the case I need to go to Austin and help you decorate it. And at the same time," she added, "you can introduce me to some of your rich friends. I'm single, you know."

At the funeral home the somber hearse was parked under the covered driveway ready to take into its dark curtained interior the coffin and the deceased body of one James Jones, Little Jimmy to you, pardnuh, and to transport the shithead to a small cemetery on the outskirts of Flour Bluff, Texas, among the buffel grass and the grazing cattle, to be buried, laid to rest, for all eternity. Amen. We would finally be rid of the sonofabitch.

Uncle Robert's empty car was already there parked behind the hearse. I parked behind him. The cold wind was being blown from the gulf into the city. I had my overcoat on. Dolly had put on her coat at the house and had not removed it in the car.

We got out and ran inside, Dolly holding onto her hair. As I ran by Uncle Robert's car I saw that the spot of vomit had stained the hood. He or Junior had tried to wipe it off. We walked to the left at the entrance as I had done last night and then down the hall. I could see my mother, Uncle Robert, Aunt Betty and Junior standing outside the private room. They were talking. Richard was not with them.

As we approached my mother said, "Did you find 'im?"

"No. He wasn't at his place. He's gone."

Mother let out a gasp and then she said, "Maybe it's just as well."

"What's going on?" I asked. "How come you aren't inside with the body?"

Mom said, "Jim, the room is locked. I don't understand it."

"We may be a little early," I said. "They've got four other funerals."

The funeral director was walking toward us.

"Here comes the main man," Uncle Robert said, faking a low voice. He was hard to take even at a funeral.

"You ought to show more respect for the man," Aunt Betty scolded him.

"Hell, he is the main man here. Ain't he?"

He looked at Junior and Junior said, "Seems like it to me."

The funeral director was a large man, heavy set. He did not look like a funeral director. He could have been a wrestler, a wholesaler, a job that took him away from people. That seemed more appropriate for him. He had a worried, preoccupied and sad look on his face. He shook hands all around. He had met every one but me. He was glad to meet me. He had heard about me, a university professor in English at Austin. Someone had told him. Mother had told him, he remembered. Who else? He had small hands for such a large man. His face was wrinkled from being out so much, funereally speaking, in the Texas sun. He wore his hair in a slicked-back style like Uncle Robert and my Dad's cadaver. He was dressed exactly as I was, in black, except for the white shirt. He had some yellow hairs sticking out of his right ear. He looked at all of us with bulbous eyes, like a salamander.

"Who is the immediate family?" he asked.

"We all are," Uncle Robert told him.

"By immediate family I mean wife and children."

"Just my mother and I," I said.

"Will your other brother be coming soon?"

"No," I said, looking at the group, "he's very sick this morning. He's taking it very hard."

The funeral director shook his head as if to show us that he understood. "Will you two be so kind as to step into my office. I need to talk to you about procedure, what to expect, what to do...financial arrangements. That sort of thing. The rest of you, if you would be so kind as to go out in the lobby and wait."

"Can't we be with the body?" Aunt Betty cried.

"I'm afraid not at this time," he said. "The body is being arranged and prepared for the funeral. You'll get to see him in a short while, I'm sure."

He waited for Uncle Robert and Aunt Betty and Junior and Dolly to walk off toward the lobby.

He gestured with his hand for us to follow him down the hall to where his office was. He opened the door and let us in. We sat in front of his desk. The director closed the door and locked it. He walked past us and went around and sat down. He opened the drawer and took out a pack of cigarettes and offered them. He lit his cigarette with a shaking hand and inhaled the smoke as he leaned forward, nervously looking at Mom and me. He started playing with the ash tray.

"I'm sorry for any inconvenience this may cause you. And I apologize before-hand for lying to your friends. I just had to get the two of you in here by yourselves. I don't know how close you all are to the people waiting outside so I decided that I would speak to you in private...You see, we've had an unfortunate thing happen," he began.

"What do you mean?" I asked.

"Well, let me explain," he said, nervously. "We have very, very good security in our funeral home. Excellent security. As a matter of fact, we have a double tier of security. We have one man that sleeps here at night, an attendant, and we have a patrol night-watchman. We pay for that service. It's part of our complete security package. Of course, we have the city police also, but we don't rely on them."

He stopped to suck on the cigarette. His hands were trembling so much that he could hardly raise the cigarette to his mouth. Perspiration beads were beginning to form on his forehead.

"The patrol comes by every two, three hours and checks the outside, makes sure everything is in order."

I became impatient. I asked, "I don't understand what that has to do with my father."

Mom looked at me, confused.

"Well, like I was saying," he continued, raising his shaking hand in my direction and ignoring my question. "We have perfect security. But early this morning the patrolman, while checking the front door, noticed someone had jimmied the lock and the patrolman came in and checked around but found nothing. He checked on the attendant and as he explained it to me, the attendant woke up and they checked around the building both inside and outside and they both swear they found nothing or nothing unusual I should say."

Mother and I were completely engrossed in what the man was telling us. But where was he leading us to? He put out his cigarette and offered us some again. He lit another cigarette. He apologized for smoking so much. He had tried to quit several times and he hadn't smoked in a week. He swallowed hard.

"They both have testified to the police," he said.

"The police?" I asked, astounded at what I was hearing.

"Yes...the police. If you will only allow me to finish. They both have testified to the police that they saw nothing or anyone inside or outside this building. The patrolman requested that the attendant call me to notify me of the facts of the matter. The patrolman called on his radio and reported the entry or the attempted entry. At that time they were not sure if any one had entered the building or merely tried."

He puffed on his cigarette and swallowed again.

"Are you sure you don't want some coffee?" We declined. "I immediately called the police just to be sure. I didn't know whether something had been stolen or not. We do have some vandalism once in a while. Young kids out at night having a good time. The police were here before I was and they checked everywhere, saw everything starting from the inside to the outside premises and everything was in order. Our petty cash box was not touched. Nothing in back, in the embalming room was touched so the police took our testimony, logged the call, checked in to headquarters and they left. The patrolman also excused himself and departed. The attendant went to his room, gathered his stuff and left. It was seven o'clock by now. It was time for him to leave. He said goodbye and left."

The director looked around the room with his large desperate eyes. He lit another cigarette off the stub of the second one. He was shaking so much that he had a hard time touching the two ends of the cigarette. I knew by the way he looked at us that we were about to find out what had happened. My heart was beating furiously. Mom appeared dumbfounded, dulled in her senses.

"I...I...I...I began my daily check as is always my custom," he continued. "I...I re-checked this office first and everything was in order. Then I went to the front of the building and began to check our private rooms. First I checked Mr. Arredondo and everything was in order. The coffin, etcetera, the flowers. Mrs. Jackson, next down the hall was in order. Everything was fine. Next, Mr. Wilson's body seemed a little off center but that could have happened in the moving of the coffin. They get moved in order for us to clean the room behind the coffin. I adjusted Mr. Wilson and that was all. In the next room Mr. Garza was perfect, just as we had laid him out. Well...your father and your husband," he said, nodding to me and to Mom, "was next. I checked him and everything seemed in order. I rechecked the candles to make sure he didn't need any more. Like I say... everything was in order."

He took a long puff from the cigarette and he let out the smoke slowly, as if he would rather not continue.

"Well, suddenly, things didn't look right to me. I looked at the deceased over and over again. I didn't have my glasses on. I didn't think anything of it. It wasn't my fault. It wasn't anyone's fault. Remember I told you how sometimes these bodies shift around when we move the coffins. Well, I thought maybe something like that had happened. And besides I knew from the attendant that you (He pointed at me.) and some men had been over last night to view the body. And I'm not saying anything about that. It's perfectly all right with me that you all came over. It's all right with me that the attendant let you in although we try not to make it a practice. I thought to myself, well, these men were here last night and maybe that was the problem. Maybe someone had moved the body. I also noticed that there were some wet areas around the collar and on his clothes. Maybe someone had cried a lot over the body?"

"I couldn't say," I replied. "I was not present all the time. Uncle Robert was crying over the body. Maybe he grabbed him and hugged him. It's possible. If that's the case I'm sure we can get him to apologize to you."

"Well, I was thinking along those lines anyway," he said, ignoring me. "Someone had moved the corpse and had gotten it wet. When? I didn't know. But...But when I looked down real close, face to face, I could tell that he was laid up wrong. His head was too far down in the pillow. That was it. His head was too far down and his face was too covered up..." His voice trailed off. He lost his composure. He recovered and said, "I put my glasses on to be able to see up close. Then...then I put my hands on his head to raise it up on the pillow and as I raised the head and brought it up I saw...Well, I saw the most gruesome sight I have ever seen in my life. Someone ... We don't know who, mind you. But someone had cut the ears off the deceased! And then, with my glasses on, I realized that the wet spots were actually very sharp and fine puncture wounds on his chest. That was where the wetness was coming from."

My mother was motionless for a few seconds. Her face grew more and more distorted as she came to understand what had happened. You could see her mind working. Her mouth opened wider and wider and she screamed. She screamed so loud that the funeral director jumped back from his chair and he ran around to her and tried to cover her mouth with his handkerchief. I was jolted out of my chair by the last words the man had spoken. I found myself standing against the door. Mother and I knew who had done it.

The funeral director was kneeling by my mother. She was weeping unconsolingly. He was trying to keep on talking. "I immediately opened the rest of the coffin to see if I could locate the ears...What a horrible mess this is. What a horrible thing to have happened."

My mother let out another scream as the funeral director spoke his words.

"I know Madam how hard this is for you. You must, though, realize it's very hard for us. We've been working on the body since early this morning and everything is back to normal. We found fifty two wounds on the chest. Unfortunately, we never found the ears. We have covered that up real well. Well enough that you cannot tell the difference. He looks normal, as you can see for yourself. I suggest you go on with the funeral as planned. The police were called and they have interviewed every one involved. They have reassured me that the corpse is released for burial. They will, of course, be calling on you for any information you may be able to give them."

He had regained the composure he had lost. Apparently he was over the worst of it. His voice calmed down. He looked for his cigarette and not being able to find it he lit another one. He sucked on it nervously a few times.

"Who could have done such a thing? Did your father have enemies? The mafia? I've heard that the mafia is capable of doing things like this."

"My father had a lot of enemies," I replied. "Very many. The list of people that could have done this would fill a page."

"It is beyond human comprehension." He puffed on his cigarette and gazed at us. I had returned to my chair. I was calming down. Mother was bent over crying softly. "The police have said that they can, if we so desire, dust for prints. You and I know that this is a messy procedure and it will delay the funeral. Besides, the police cannot guarantee any results. Especially when you consider that a lot of people were here last night, touching the coffin, maybe even the body."

"We wouldn't want a search for fingerprints," I said. I put my hand on Mom's shoulder. "Mom? We don't want any fingerprinting, do we?"

"No," she sobbed quietly.

"Very well, whatever you say," he said. "They said for us to call if we wanted anything done. I'm sure they'll be relieved."

"We would like to get this over as fast as possible," I informed him. "My mother and I are very upset over this and the less time it takes the better it is for us. And one more thing. We would appreciate it if what was said in this room stays in this room. The people that are with us may not understand. Not that it's any of their business, but I just don't want them to know."

"I can understand that," he replied. "I do want you to know that I've been in the funeral business for forty years and I've never had this experience before."

"I would appreciate it very much if you follow our request," I said to him. "They must not know what happened. We are not going to press charges on anyone, whoever it is. We're just anxious to get it over with."

"Very well," he said, standing up. "I'm glad you look at it that way. I myself have been a nervous wreck since early this morning," and he lit another cigarette, making it two that he had lit at the same time. He left one burning cigarette in the ash tray and walked to the door and unlocked it. He spoke before he opened the door. "By the way, the company appreciates your attitude. The publicity would have damaged our reputation beyond repair. I have been ordered to tell you that there will be no charge for the funeral. It's on the house, as the saying goes. The funeral, then, is at eleven thirty. You're welcomed to stay here if you wish. I'll send for your friends to come join you. By the way," he said, thinking of something, and he came back to his desk and opened a side drawer, "this is purely for medicinal purposes," and he brought out a half-gallon bottle of whiskey and a stack of paper cups. "See you in thirty minutes." He opened the door and he remembered something else. "I understand there will be no services here, only at grave-side. Is that right?"

"Yes, that's right," my mother said, sobbing. She had not quit crying.

I caught him before he left. I had suddenly remembered how intimate Uncle Robert got with the body. "We have a problem." I said.

He looked at me wondering what else could go wrong.

"It's Uncle Robert, the older heavy set man that came with us. He's my father's brother and he's been hugging the body. What happens if he hugs the body and notices that the ears have been severed?

He thought a minute. He said, "I'll think of something. Don't worry. We'll do our best."

The director closed the door slowly behind him and I imagined the relief he felt to have gotten this mess out of the way.

One of the assistants opened the door and Dolly and Junior and Aunt Betty and Uncle Robert came in. Uncle Robert and Junior immediately saw the bottle and Uncle Robert said, "Goddam, so that's what you all been doin'? Drinkin' up a storm and not sharin' with your uncle and your cousin. Let me have a drink. You want one, Junior?"

He poured two cups full even before Junior answered. "What the shit is goin' on? Why aren't they lettin' us in the room? Why can't we see Little Jimmy? Shit. What's going on?"

I had to make up something. I could not trust the funeral director. He seemed so unimaginative. "They're having to clean up Dad," I said. "They think one of the damaged veins in his lung ruptured during the night and a lot of embalming fluid had spilled over his face and hair."

Everyone was making a face. It was repugnant. "How gross," Dolly said.

"It makes me want to vomit," Aunt Betty said.

Uncle Robert was serious, looking at his boots, his drink in his hand. He said, "Shit, what else can go wrong with poor ol' Jimmy?"

I had to make sure he behaved once we got in the room with Dad's body. I said, more to him than to anyone else, "They requested that no one touch the body. Any small amount of pressure might just cause the fluid to start coming out again. There is also a danger that other vessels might rupture."

"Goddam," Uncle Robert said, "it's that bad?"

"That's what they say," I replied, and I poured myself a cup of whiskey. I sat in the funeral director's chair, quietly thinking, as was everyone else. I was thinking that Richard had finally done what he set out to do so many years ago. He had, at least, symbolically killed his father and avenged the deforming of his ears.

There was a knock on the door. The funeral director wanted to talk to me in private. I left the room and followed him. "I just want you to see what we've done. We hope it meets with your approval," he whispered. He unlocked the door and led me to the coffin. He pressed a lever under the lip of the lid and the lid popped open. Dad looked normal, just like he had last night. I could not tell anything had been done to him. The funeral director lowered the pillow on either side of Dad's head and I could see what Richard had done. He had not only cut the ears off, but he had cut quite a large piece of skin both in front and behind the ear, exposing the formalin blanched flesh underneath along with its thin layer of fat. I was beginning to feel nauseated. He fluffed the pillow around the ears, hiding them. "How does he look?" he asked, proud of the work. "It looks fine to me," I said. I didn't want to see anymore. "And by the way, I don't think Uncle Robert will touch the body."

"That's a relief," he said. "Now I'll go get everyone and we can start."

He had us all in the room with the body and he said a short memorized prayer as he lowered the lid. Uncle Robert stroked Dad's forehead once and that was all. He let out a muffled cry as the lid snapped shut. The funeral director and two assistants helped us wheel the coffin out through the side door and into the hearse.

We got in our cars and followed the hearse through town and on to Flour Bluff. Dolly was quiet except when she sighed once and said, "He was mean to you all, wasn't he?"

At grave-side we unloaded the coffin and placed it on the heavy straps that would lower it into the ground. A preacher spoke briefly. Not having known my father, he remarked, it would be presumptuous of him to either praise or criticize him. He was there to see that the man received a proper burial. All men were entitled to that, regardless.

As the cold wind howled at my ears, standing next to my mother and across from the preacher, I was engulfed, as Richard had been, by the shadows of the punishing ghosts of other years, making me think of another cold day in December when I stood at the small grave-side at my sister Sylvia's funeral. How well I could feel the presence of their shadows: Mrs. Smith, my teacher, and her husband; Mrs. Abercrombie, Richard's teacher, with her husband; and Nurse Wilma, Dr. Morgan, Arlan, the deputy, and Mrs. Peters, our Elementary Principal; the beloved Allens; and the Preacher who was so eloquent. I could feel the unwanted rain of that day and the numbness of the cold. I looked over my shoulder and I could see the deputy leaning against the car. I could see Richard standing at mother's other side, weeping for his sister as I was. I could see the staining rain drops as they fell on the coffin. I remembered feeling like yelling for the rain to stop, to stop punishing my sister's little coffin.

Suddenly I realized that what Richard had done had not been as horrible as I had first thought. This was not his way of getting even, the last desperate act of revenge. It was a cry to all of us to remind us for all eternity of what our father had been. I realized that all our lives he had been the brave one, the one who did not hide behind words as I did. And how strong he must have been to withstand living in the outer shadows of our family and having been solely and irreparably burdened by all its ghosts. Finally, I realized the ultimate truth of what Richard had done. He had, like a true father, sacrificed his life for me. What a beautiful and noble thing for him to do. And that was when I started to weep, resting my brow on my arm. I realized I had not deserved him, just as we had not deserved our father.

In 1982, God only knows why, but on the day I received word that I was being promoted to full professor, on a day that I should have celebrated, my mother called me to tell me that Richard's old probation officer had called. Richard had been found dead in a room in a little hotel in Chicago. Would I please go and claim the body? It was the least I could do.

I flew to Chicago and identified the small yellowing body that was my brother, that had once given me a stolen harmonica for Christmas. I flew him back and I buried him along with the indeterminable weight of the massive ghosts that had been his companions for all his life. I buried him next to my father because I had come to realize that they were one and the same, and I felt that these were not the other years but the other times, the times for forgiveness.

After the funeral, as we sat at the darkened house alone by the dim light of the table lamp, Mom asked me for one last favor. "Before I die," she said, "I want to go see your sister Sylvia's grave. I won't die in peace until I see that she is bein' taken care of. I need to make arrangements for that. We can go this summer if you'll agree to take me."

I told her that I would take her. That was the least that I could do.